3 1951 00097 6152

P9-DEX-771

FIC
Kra   Kraft, Eric
            Herb 'n' Lorna

DEMCO

HERB
'n'
LORNA

Also by Eric Kraft

THE PERSONAL HISTORY, ADVENTURES,
EXPERIENCES AND OBSERVATIONS
OF PETER LEROY

HERB 'n' LORNA

A LOVE STORY

by Eric Kraft

Crown Publishers, Inc.

New York

West Lafayette Public Library
West Lafayette, Indiana

FIC
Krq

While I was at work on this book, I was assisted by a fellowship from the National Endowment for the Arts. I am grateful to the endowment for the encouragement and assistance provided by that fellowship.

Excerpt from *The Analytical Engine,* by Jeremy Bernstein, courtesy of William Morrow and Company, Inc.
Excerpt from "Within a Budding Grove," from *Remembrance of Things Past,* Vol. One, by Marcel Proust, translated by C. K. Scott Moncrieff, courtesy of Random House, Inc.
Excerpt from "Can You Identify These Charms?" courtesy of LIFE Picture Service, Life magazine, © 1938 Time, Inc. Reprinted with permission.
Excerpt from *One Hundred Years of Solitude,* by Gabriel García Márquez, courtesy of Harper & Row, Publishers, Inc.

Illustration Credits: 1. From *The Illustrated London News,* May 17, 1845. Courtesy of Wenham Historical Society.   2. Photographer unknown.   3. From National Archives, 86-G-2J-6.   4. Photographer unknown.   5. Photographer unknown.
6. Reprinted from *The Studebaker Century,* copyright © 1983 by Dragonwick Publishing Co., Inc. All rights reserved. Used by permission of Asa E. Hall and Richard M. Langworth. Photo from the collection of Asa E. Hall.   7. Reprinted from *The Studebaker Century,* copyright © 1983 by Dragonwick Publishing Co., Inc. All rights reserved. Used by permission of Asa E. Hall and Richard M. Langworth. Photo from the collection of Asa E. Hall.   8. Courtesy of Herb and Lorna Piper.   9. Photo by Martinus Anderson; courtesy of LIFE Picture Service.   10. Photograph number 514826, copyright © 1987 by Studebaker National Museum. All rights reserved. Used by permission of Studebaker National Museum.   11. Courtesy of Mark T. Canning.

Publisher's Note: This is a work of fiction. The characters, incidents, and dialogues are products of the author's imagination and are not to be construed as real. Any resemblance to actual events or persons, living or dead, is entirely coincidental.

5/88 B+T 10.77

Copyright © 1988 by Eric Kraft
All rights reserved. No part of this book may be reproduced or transmitted in any form or by any means, electronic or mechanical, including photocopying, recording, or by any information storage and retrieval system, without permission in writing from the publisher.

Published by Crown Publishers, Inc., 225 Park Avenue South, New York, New York 10003 and represented in Canada by the Canadian MANDA Group.
CROWN is a trademark of Crown Publishers, Inc.
Manufactured in the United States of America

Library of Congress Cataloging-in-Publication Data

Kraft, Eric.
  Herb 'n' Lorna.
  I. Title.
PS3561.R22H47   1988   813'.54   87-22163
ISBN 0-517-55941-2
Book design by Dana Sloan
10 9 8 7 6 5 4 3 2 1
First Edition

For Bill 'n' Edna

. . . the idea that one has long held of a person is apt to stop one's eyes and ears; my mother, for three whole years, had no more noticed the salve with which one of her nieces used to paint her lips than if it had wholly and invisibly dissolved in some clear liquid; until one day a streak too much, or possibly something else, brought about the phenomenon known as supersaturation; all the paint that hitherto passed unperceived was now crystallized, and my mother, in the face of this sudden riot of colour, declared, in the best Combray manner, that it was a perfect scandal . . .

—Marcel Proust
Remembrance of Things Past:
"Within a Budding Grove"
(translated by C. K. Scott Moncrieff)

One never knows, do one?

—Fats Waller

HERB
'n'
LORNA

Preface

For years, I tried to avoid writing this book. If the choice had been mine alone, I would never have written it. Recently, however, events beyond my control forced me into writing it and forced me, in the writing of it, to confront a moment that ranks high among the unsettling moments of my life, the moment that, I think, marked the end of my overextended egocentric period and so, perhaps, the end of my youth: the moment when I learned that my maternal grandparents were involved in—virtually the creators of—the animated erotic jewelry industry.

The discovery came—actually it was forced upon me by two informants—on the day of my grandmother's funeral, three years after my grandfather had died. That morning, May Castle, my grandparents' friend of longest standing, gave me a box, inscribed to me in my grandmother's hand. Inside the box were twenty-two pieces of erotic jewelry and erotic sculpture. With them was an account, just a few words, written by my grandmother, of my grandparents' involvement with erotic arts and crafts. I read it quickly, breathlessly, but I had many things to attend to that morning, and I didn't have much time to think about what it meant before I left for the Episcopal church, where the funeral service was to be held.

Sitting in a pew at the church, half attending to the service, I began to consider my new knowledge. You can imagine how it affected me. It shook me. Not only had I never known anything about this interest of my grandparents', but the whole notion was so far removed from my idea of them—their personalities, their interests, their talents as I supposed I understood them—that I couldn't even imagine where it might fit. Eroticism, I realized with some embarrassment, had never played an important part in my mind's eye's version of my grandparents' lives. How I had misjudged them! I had belittled them, diminished their lives in a way that I wouldn't have wanted mine diminished. Eroticism certainly played an important part in *my* life; how could I have been so thick-headed and arrogant as to ignore the likelihood that it was as important—or, to judge from the evidence they had supplied me, even more important—in theirs? I was ashamed of myself. I was also flabbergasted. I was struck, with a suddenness and force that felt like a physical blow, by the realization that even now I was wrong in my understanding of them. I had, in the course of an hour or so, come to think that eroticism had "played an important part in my grandparents' lives." That couldn't be anywhere near the truth. If what my grandmother had suggested in her note was true—and the carvings she had included testified that it was—my grandparents had played a leading role in the development of the erotic imagination of their times! It was much too much to handle all at once, at such a time. It was as if my grandmother had in her posthumous letter introduced me to two people I had never met before, people who had been hiding inside my grandparents, people with genitalia. Who were these people? Why did my grandmother want me to meet them?

When I was a child, I called my grandparents "Gumma" and "Guppa." Originally, the names were just mispronunciations of "Grandma" and "Grandpa," of course, but as time passed they became terms of endearment, and I continued to use them long after I was able to say "Grandma" and "Grandpa" clearly. I shifted, uncomfortably, to something like "Gram" and "Gramp" for a brief time during adolescence, when childhood leftovers embarrassed me, but I soon returned to "Gumma" and "Guppa," and once back never strayed again. I think that underlying my persistent use of my childhood names for them was an assertion that my grandparents were, and would always remain, the Gumma and Guppa I had known when I was a child. My Gumma was large and soft, generous, enduringly pretty, pleasant, devoted to the domestic arts, the provider of huge beige-and-white meals—biscuits, boiled onions, chicken, cream sauces, and potatoes prepared in a thousand ways, the best of them a German potato salad that filled the house with the pungency of vinegar and bacon—an amateur logician and mathematician, occasionally a repairer of jewelry, a reader of best-selling novels, mostly historical ones. My Guppa was small and quick, apparently always either amused or puzzled, a talented and hard-working salesman, a tireless home handyman, an amateur inventor, a happy tinkerer. Now, after so

[2]

many years, and after it was too late, Gumma was, it seemed to me, asking me to get to know them as someone else entirely, as what other people called them: Herb and Lorna.

Someone nudged me. My mother. I looked at her. She nodded ever so slightly. What did that mean? Had she discovered, from my expression, what I had been thinking? Did she know about the jewelry Gumma had left me? Had she, perhaps— She nodded again, in the direction of the pulpit, and gave me a little nudge. The eulogy. Of course. The eulogy.

I got up. I mounted the pulpit in a fog. I looked around at the congregation of mourners. Who among these friends, relatives, and acquaintances knew the truth? Was I the only one? Or was I the last to know? I took my remarks from my pocket. I read them. I had written a little catalog of my grandmother's kindnesses, as I knew them. When I had written it, I had worried that it would be too much for me to read without breaking down. Now I found that I couldn't concentrate on it. I read, but I wasn't paying attention to what I was reading. My eyes were on the paper, but my mind was on the animated copulation of tiny ivory men and women.

Worse, I was getting excited—sexually. I was standing in the pulpit at my grandmother's funeral, reading her eulogy, and (out of sight of the mourners, thank God) clenching and relaxing my thighs, rotating my pelvis, twisting and squirming, trying to shift my erection, which was thrust painfully up against the elastic band of my briefs, into a more comfortable position. Still reading, I reached into the side pocket of my pants, reached through the leg hole of my briefs, and pushed the tip of my penis out from under the elastic. That was better, but I was immediately seized by the fear that everyone had noticed, that they had been able to tell from some shift of my shoulders exactly what I had been doing. I scanned the congregation. They were sniffling and blubbering and dabbing their eyes and blowing their noses. I wondered whether my grandmother had imagined this moment and presented me with the problem of her eroticism as she might have presented me with one of the logical puzzles she enjoyed so much. She always wanted to make me think. She always warned me against taking things for granted, against the blindness of assumptions. Was she doing me another kindness, inviting me to solve her puzzle instead of mourning her? I wasn't sure whether to smile, or blush, or cry.

In the afternoon, after my grandmother had been buried, there was a buffet dinner at my parents' house. The afternoon passed. The crowd dwindled. My grandparents' closest friends and admirers remained through the afternoon and on into the evening, drinking and telling stories. As the evening wore on, no one became more sentimental than my old high-school friend Mark Dorset, who, after a while, as if he'd been quite deliberately working up to a level of intoxication that would allow him to say what he had to say, took me aside and said that he had something to give me, a memento of my grandparents that he had had in his possession since my grandfather had died three years before.

From his pocket he took what seemed to be a pocket watch. He pressed the stem, and the lid popped open. Inside were three tiny ivory figures, two women and a man, sexually entangled on a miniature bed. "Just look at that workmanship!" said Mark.

I did. Immediately, I could see that this was even better than any of the pieces my grandmother had given me. (I know now that the little trio was the best work they ever did.) In the carving of the figures, I was certain, I could recognize the work of my grandmother's hand, her fine eye, her loving touch, her sense of detail. In the smooth mechanical animation, I was certain, I could recognize my grandfather's ingenuity, his fascination for the complex and puzzling, his love of impractical gadgets. I stared at the trio and their performance. My throat was tight. My eyes were wet. I was dumfounded. I was grief-stricken. I was proud.

But I was also envious. Mark's initiation into my grandparents' secret had preceded mine. By three years. Why? Mark had a story, of course. I listened to him tell it, and while I listened I tried to wear the amused look of one who knows it all already, who has heard it all before. In truth, though, it was news to me, and it hurt to hear it from someone other than my grandparents. Why had they never told me? Why had they told Mark before me? My fear of the answers to those questions was one of the things that for so long kept me from writing this book.

Over the years, my grandparents' story has come out little by little. Some of their former neighbors in Punta Cachazuda, Florida, where Gumma and Guppa retired and taught clandestine classes in erotic sculpture, began exhibiting the work they had done under Gumma and Guppa's tutelage. Newspapers picked up the story, and soon people all over America began "discovering" pieces of erotic jewelry in their closets. The work that Gumma and Guppa and others did in this line has been hailed as some of the most important American folk art of the twentieth century, but it has also been condemned as perverse and worse. I tried, until recently, to ignore it. I confess that my reason was selfish: I wanted to hold on to my child's-eye view of my grandparents. I wanted to hang on to Gumma and Guppa. I still clung to the comfortable and familiar notion of Gumma and Guppa that I had developed as a boy. From time to time I received requests from collectors of erotic jewelry for information about those two strangers, Herb and Lorna Piper, pleas for any little anecdote about their work in "coarse goods"—that is, erotic jewelry. I turned down all such requests with the explanation that I couldn't say anything abut their work because I never saw them at it, and I never knew that they had engaged in it until after they were dead. I never bothered trying to explain that I felt I didn't even know Herb and Lorna Piper.

When, just a little more than a year ago, I received an invitation to attend the opening of the exhibit of American Erotic Jewelry at the Smithsonian Institution, I at first thought that I would decline that, too. However, when I read, in the *New York Times,* that the exhibit had become the target of angry protests before it had even opened, my feelings changed. Accompanying the article in the *Times* was a photograph of a crowd picketing at the Smithsonian. One man stood in an aggressive posture, with his fists clenched and his chest puffed out, glaring at the camera. He wore a T-shirt with the fig-leaf emblem of the "Prude Pride" movement. Printed across it was the slogan

I'M PROUD TO SAY
I'M ASHAMED OF MY BODY!

In the article, a spokeswoman for Mothers Against Sex was quoted as saying, toward the end of a disquisition on the pernicious effects of erotic jewelry, "A lot of people don't realize that there's an entire community in Florida where senior citizens turn out this perverted stuff. Can you imagine that? I ask you, America, is that how you want your grandmothers to end up—posing naked for some old perverts?

It's sick. I mean, just think of those wrinkled old people—I tell you it's just sick. You can't tell me that this has anything to do with artistic expression or freedom of speech. This has to do with only one thing, s-e-x."

That did it. "Oh, no," I said to myself. "That isn't all there is to it. There is much, much more to it than that."

I determined then that if my grandparents' story was to be told, I wasn't going to leave it to the tabloids. I was going to tell it myself, and I was going to tell it as completely as I could. In that attempt, I have drawn on my grandmother's account, my memories of my grandparents, interviews with friends and relatives, historical documents, supposition, and imagination. Most of what they thought, felt, and experienced went unrecorded. Most of the documents they might have left were destroyed, burned in the Hapgood Brothers' warehouse fire. I have tried, therefore, to tell the story as it *probably* happened. The facts may be wrong, but I think the spirit is right.

I am indebted to many people, institutions, and other sources for their help in preparing this biography, including, in no particular order, the Historical Society of Chacallit, New York; the Boston Athenæum; the *Punta Cachazuda Bugle*; the erotica and esoterica department at the Smithsonian Institution; the Studebaker National Museum; Asa Hall and Richard Langworth's *The Studebaker Century*; *Life* magazine; and my parents, Bert and Ella Leroy. The book could never have been written without the reminiscences of Herb and Lorna provided by May Castle, whole chunks of which I have included unedited, just as they were transcribed from the tape recordings of our conversations. Thank you, May, for your help. I wish you had lived to read the result. I hope you would have liked it.

Peter Leroy
Small's Island
June 2, 1987

1
In Which Lorna Is Born into the Huber Family, of Chacallit, New York

My grandmother, Lorna Huber, was born in Chacallit, New York, fifty miles or so northwest of Albany, in the valley of the Whatsit River, a tributary of the Mohawk. The name of the town has a curious etymology. The first English settlers arrived around 1680, some fifty years after William Oughtred developed the first calculating instrument that could be called a slide rule. These settlers knew the Mohawk name for the place, which meant, loosely, "place where many fur-bearing animals can be taken but the land is really too steeply sloped to allow one to make a proper camp." However, since the settlers couldn't pronounce the Mohawk name correctly and were, in the English manner, disinclined to learn to do so, when they were asked where they hailed from they made a bit of comic business out of struggling to pronounce the name, delivering three or four mispronunciations, and then shrugging and saying, "Oh, What-y'-may-call-it."

The term *What-you-may-call-it* was, by the middle of the seventeenth century, already well established in English as a humorous substitute for anything the name of which a speaker had forgotten, couldn't pronounce, had never known, or didn't consider worth learning. The *Oxford English Dictionary,* in the entry for *What-d'ye-call-'em,* lists *what-you-may-call-it* as a variant, and cited there we find Chapman writing, as early as 1598, "Why hees a what you calt." In 1600 we find Shakespeare himself writing, in *As You Like It,* "Good euen good Mr what ye cal't."

Apparently human nature and the techniques of comedy were little different in those days from what they are now, because the citizen of "What-y'-may-call-it," having raised a laugh by lampooning the name of the town, added what is known to stand-up comics as the "topper." After a suitable pause, the citizen would add, "It's on the bank of the What's-it River," and, presumably, have his listener in stitches.

In time, the town became widely known as What-y'-may-call-it, and then, through clipping and elision, What-y'-ma-call-it, What-chamacallit, Whatchacallit, and, finally, Chacallit. Similarly, the river came to be called the Whatsit.

The first Hubers in America, Kurt Huber and his sixteen-year-old bride Inge, arrived in the Whatsit Valley from Germany in 1730, at just about the time when the first members of the Studebaker family were settling in Pennsylvania. In Germany, the Hubers had been farmers. History does not record what reasons Kurt Huber had for choosing Chacallit, but, to judge from the poor soil and steep slopes, he certainly can't have intended to farm there. At the time, fur trapping was really the only industry, but Kurt seems to have worked as a road builder. A history of Chacallit published in 1866 says of Kurt, "It is to him that the town is indebted for some of its handsomest streets." That history also says, "He was a bold, fearless man who refused to remove to the fort, where the other settlers fled on account of the Indians." Inge was known for her caustic wit and dark beauty. An admiring but wary diarist of the time marveled, in a sketch of Inge, that "so sharp a tongue should lurk behind such plump, alluring lips." Kurt Huber died just two months before the signing of the Declaration of Independence. Following his death, many objects of value that had been presumed stolen by Indians during raids were discovered among his road-building tools and supplies, and as a result Inge and her eleven children lived under a cloud for the rest of their days.

Throughout the nineteenth century, the manufacture of gentlemen's furnishings, which had begun in Chacallit on a very small scale, as little more than a cottage industry, a way for families to supplement their incomes when fur trapping was off, grew steadily in economic importance, and thanks to it, the town grew and prospered. For generations, the Hubers of Chacallit strove to efface the memory of their infamous ancestor Kurt by establishing themselves as a family of unremarkable drudges wholly devoted to the stolid, uncomplaining performance of dull work. The gentlemen's furnishings industry offered numerous opportunities for work of that type, and as the industry expanded the Hubers filled more and more of the positions in the undistinguished middle of its work force. Now and then Inge's genes produced an impish, quick-witted beauty or Kurt's produced a rogue, but most of these were, for the greater good of the family, suppressed or sent away, and the Hubers trudged along at the soft center of Chacallit's success.

Chacallit's rise in the haberdashery industry was purchased at the expense of some self-esteem. The men's furnishings business took itself quite seriously in those days, and the name of the town, because it did not suggest high seriousness, top-notch standards, and vaulting aspiration, might have stood in the way of further growth. When the Excelsior Celluloid Collar Company became interested in building a mill in Chacallit, Excelsior officials made clear their feeling that the company would find it an embarrassment to be known as the Excelsior Celluloid Collar Company of Chacallit because of the humorous connotations of the name of the town. "We fear," the board of directors said in a letter to the mayor of Chacallit, "that in a short time we would be known, not openly, but behind our collective back, in a snickering, mocking way, as the Whatchamacallit Collar Company."

Stormy meetings followed, but soon the citizens of Chacallit made an offer that satisfied the company: they offered to rename the town Excelsior. (According to diaries and letters from the period, there was some interest in changing the name of the river to Celluloid at the same time, but nothing came of it.) A precedent was established, and throughout the rest of the nineteenth century, whenever a larger and richer men's furnishings company hesitated about building a new mill there, in a town named for one of its rivals, the citizens would vote to change the name of the town. As a result, the place was known at various times as Acme (for Acme Fancy Buttons), Premier (for Pre-

[9]

mier Furnishings), Hermes (for Hermes Brand Gentlemen's Necessities), and Atlas (for Atlas Glovers & Hatters).

Late in the nineteenth century, however, the attitude of Chacallitans changed. Ralph Waldo Emerson never visited Chacallit (the difficulty of winter travel in the Whatsit Valley in those days kept him from venturing into Chacallit on his winter lecture tours), but there was an Emersonian flavor to the decision reached by the citizens of Chacallit in 1833 (just shortly after Emerson's death) to revert to the "rightful name of this place, Chacallit, now and forevermore, and be no more the pliant whore of industry."

Some have argued that the people of Chacallit (or, more accurately, of Dr. Scott's, as the place was then known—for Dr. Scott's Links and Studs) sensed that they had made themselves far more ridiculous in the eyes of the rest of the world by attempting to escape their past and to please each new suitor than they would ever have been made by the name Chacallit and were, therefore, returning to the earlier name in the simple spirit of "enough is enough." However, I think the Chacallitans may have been moved by nobler sentiments than that. In "Self-Reliance," Emerson had written:

> Traveling is a fool's paradise. . . . At home I dream that at Naples, at Rome, I can be intoxicated with beauty, and lose my sadness. I pack my trunk, embrace my friends, embark on the sea, and at last wake up in Naples, and there beside me is the stern fact, the sad self, unrelenting, identical, that I fled from. . . . My giant goes with me wherever I go.

Chacallit's own transcendentalist, Wilhelm Huber, my great-great-grandfather, a sharp-witted descendant of Inge who refused to be silenced, expressed his abhorrence of Chacallit's name-changing in remarkably similar terms:

> This business of changing the name of our town is a foolish practice. . . . We imagine that if we call ourselves Naples, or Rome, we will become intoxicatingly beautiful, and the Naples Collar-Pin Company will come a-courting, or the Roman Sleeve Garter firm will affiance us, and we will then, at last, be laughing-stocks no longer. We

tear down our old signs, erect our new signs, and embark next morning on a new life as Naples, but in our mirrors we still see the stern fact, the said self, unrelenting, identical, that we meant to flee from: our giant, ourselves.

By the turn of the century, Chacallit was again Chacallit, and the town was supplying suspenders, cuff links, collar stays, belt buckles, tie tacks, and the like worldwide.

With the arrival of the twentieth century came a slow decline in interest in men's furnishings, and that, of course, meant economic decline for Chacallit. For decades this was a gradual slipping, but then in the period following the Second World War the bottom really fell out of the domestic men's furnishings market. There were many reasons. Primary among them was the belief among younger men that everything had been changed by the war, that nothing was the same, that nothing prewar had much of a role in the postwar world, that the world had broken forever with its past, had left its sad old self behind. Interest in suspenders, detachable collars, shirt studs, and cuff links disappeared among younger men as if overnight. Though some interest in such haberdashery persisted among the older, more conservative, and wealthier, those men were increasingly attracted to the products of the rebuilding Europe, especially those of England and Germany, which were thought to be of a quality that the domestic products couldn't match. (How ironic that the people around Chacallit who lost so much to that competition should be mostly of English and German ancestry themselves, and proud of it. Many people in Chacallit still distribute gifts on Boxing Day, and there's still an annual wurst, kraut, and potato salad festival every summer.)

For nearly three decades following World War II, Chacallit slept. It was awakened at last by a local boy, Deke Schumacher, who, riding the crest of a wave of success as vice president for Computer Furniture at IBM, walked away from it all in a huff one day and returned home, to the steep hills of Chacallit, beside the rushing waters of the Whatsit, to start his own computer furniture company. Sales of the ChacalliTech Computer Scooter, a platform—actually a whole line of platforms of various sizes—that can be installed under computer components, allowing one to move them around at will, exceeded even the sunniest predictions of Deke himself. What the ChacalliTech ads say about the Scooter (borrowing, probably unconsciously, from a nineteenth-century advertisement for Studebaker wagons) is true: "The Brightest Star in the Computer Furniture Firmament Is the ChacalliTech Computer Scooter™."

Chacallit today is, in outward appearance, remarkably like the town in which Lorna grew up, and that similarity is the result of a pattern of economic decline and renewal that first isolated Chacallit from architectural modernization and then rescued it from physical decay. Had the town prospered throughout this century, modernization and overdevelopment would certainly have obliterated its past. Instead, Chacallit dozed until the ChacalliTech prosperity brought new hope for the future and an urge to restore and preserve the past, with the result that, when I visited, I found that I could easily imagine life in Chacallit as it must have been in the early part of this century, when Lorna was a girl.

When Lorna was born, the century had just turned, and the mills hummed, turning out suspenders, collars, collar stays, cuff links, money clips, and the like. Money seemed to flow into the town as swiftly as the swollen waters of the Whatsit in a January thaw. Today, the gentlemen's furnishings that one finds in the bright shops along River Road are likely to come from Japan, but prosperity has returned. The old brick mills along the Whatsit have been painstakingly restored, and some of the stern, handsome buildings now house the humming facilities of ChacalliTech.

All along River Road a visitor will find, in other resurrected mills and warehouses, charming shops—among them the Tie-Tack Tack Shop and Hotcha-Chatchkes (a treasure trove of a place that specializes in gewgaws of the 1920s)—and intriguing *boites* and restaurants, including Chez Mom (a homey eatery where one can get *tarte aux pommes* and *façon de Mom,* and the day's special is always listed as *Les Restes*), Eau Boy (an all-water bar with more than a hundred domestic and imported waters), 24-Karat Studs (a gay bar), and the Sleeve Garter Pub (where a Huber tends bar).

The Whatsit Valley is a pretty but forbidding area. The winters here are long and cold, as they were then; the autumn woods blaze with color, as they did then; the spring earth is fecund and odorous, as it was then; the summers are damp and languorous, as they were then; and all the year round the night wind howls in the valley as if it held a grudge, just as it did then.

The houses in Chacallit are plain and staunch. Only stubborn people could have built their houses here, notched the hillside for foundations, cut and fit the stone, created a level foothold for each house, for themselves, always working against the slope, always working against gravity. It is as if the difficulty of building here was part of the attraction that Chacallit held for its early settlers. Here was a place where they could test themselves, their resolve, and their aspirations against the slope, against the unrelenting downward tug. The builders bequeathed to the generations that followed them a test no less difficult, for they, too, have always to battle the tug of gravity. The young and well-to-do employees of ChacalliTech who now pay high prices for the staunch hillside houses, who paint them, furnish them sparely and brightly, and landscape their yards with plants that never grew in the valley before, find that the rain washes the grass seed down the slope, the garden cart wants to roll across the lawn into the drainage ditch that runs beside the road, and croquet is a nightmare.

The house where Lorna was born is tall and narrow, perched on the steep northern slope of the Whatsit Valley. A narrow, highly crowned road runs along the uphill side of the house, turns sharply in front of it, and drops steeply, running past the downhill side of the house and on downward, past more houses, set in tiers on the hillside, winding down toward the river below. From the front porch of the Huber house, one can see the river here and there through the trees and, strung out along both banks, the mills and, alongside the mills, back from the river, climbing the hills on either side, the other houses of Chacallit.

In that narrow house, on Lorna's christening day, after the christening itself, my great-grandparents, Richard and Lena Huber, invited their friends and neighbors to meet their third daughter more informally, in the parlor of their home. Richard Huber was a "production anticipator" for the American Garter Company. It was his job to monitor the sales of the company's products, record them, chart them, note seasonal and regional trends, and predict future production levels and materials needs. His was the sort of job that would today be done by a computer. Lena was the daughter of a production anticipator for Gryphon Grip-Tight Patented Fasteners. Their marriage represented a precisely horizontal alliance in the Chacallit social scheme.

Richard served his guests beer, wine, and root beer in the parlor and urged them into the dining room, where the table was covered with food: hams, sausages of six kinds, breads and rolls, honey and preserves, smoked mackerel and eels, sprats, cheeses, a smoked goose and a smoked turkey, and, at either end of the table, two enormous bowls of potato salad. However, the guests showed no strong inclination to eat. They remained in the living room, content to drink and look at Lorna and remark on the odd beauty they saw in her.

In the dining room, Lorna's sister Bertha stood in front of one of the bowls of potato salad, mechanically and purposefully filling a plate with it, piling the potatoes in a mound, as if she were daring gravity to make the uppermost chunks fall. One did, and Bertha stooped to pick it up from the floor, mashing it a bit as she did, perhaps from clumsiness alone. Another fell. She was making a fine mess.

Clara, now the middle of the three Huber daughters, moved to her sister's side and whispered to her without looking at her.

"Bertha," she said, "you're taking too much. You'll get a smack if you get caught."

Bertha didn't even pause when Clara spoke. She pressed another spoonful of potato salad onto the mound, and under her breath she said to Clara, "Nobody's looking at me. They're all looking at her. You just be quiet, and no one will even notice."

Clara half turned toward the adults, who were clustered around the wicker cradle where Lorna was displayed. Clara could see only backs, for all the adults were turned toward Lorna, and they were so tightly crowded together that she couldn't see either her mother or the little cynosure. She saw her father standing outside the crowd, with his hands behind his back, rocking on his heels. Clara didn't have to see his face to know that he was beaming, that he was proud of his new daughter. Uncle Luther stood beside him, his right arm flung across his brother's shoulders. Clara saw that what Bertha said was true; no one in the living room would notice what they did in the dining room. She turned toward the table, took a plate, and began piling slices of turkey as purposefully and mechanically as Bertha had filled her plate with potato salad.

When Bertha's plate was as full as she could make it, she began making her way toward the door to the porch, scuttling sideways, so that her illicit heap of potato salad was hidden. She pushed the door open with her hip and slipped outside, onto the porch. When she was safely outside, she let the door slide off her hip, and it swung against Clara's elbow, jostling her so that a slice of turkey fell onto the floor.

Bertha sat on the porch railing, and, just as methodically as she had filled her plate, she ate all the potato salad she had taken. Clara watched, amazed and terrified. She tried to emulate Bertha's methodical determination, but she couldn't come near to finishing all the turkey she had taken. Quietly, she slipped back into the dining room and replaced most of it. When she came back outside, Bertha was under the porch, vomiting.

The problem was Lorna's elusive beauty. Clara and Bertha were envious of it from the moment they saw her, although they never quite realized that that was what they envied. In fact, they hardly considered Lorna attractive. Most of the time Lorna's appearance seemed to them just on the pretty side of plain. Her beauty really did seem to live in the mind, or the heart, of her beholder. Bertha and Clara never saw it, but Lorna possessed, throughout her life, an elusive loveliness that showed from certain angles at certain moments, for certain people, a beauty that could enchant a person in the blink of an eye and then would disappear if she turned her head or touched her hair. That fleeting beauty might return a moment or an hour later, all the more tantalizing and desirable for having been away, for being so hard to see clearly, for being so like a twinkling star on a hazy summer night. Bertha saw and understood the effect of this scintillating beauty, even if she couldn't see the beauty itself, and it seemed to her bewitching and unfair, an advantage given to Lorna over her, for she was a homely, large-boned, gangling girl.

That intriguing beauty never left Lorna, not even in the last years of her life, not even when she was ill, when she looked older than she was, when she was pale and weak, and her skin hung in loose folds. Her beauty in age was not of the type that is a lingering reminder, the lingering remainder, of youthful beauty, the type that makes people say, "She must have been a beauty in her day." It was an unchanged, undiminished quality; perhaps it was really a manifestation of inner beauty, and only its representation, never its essence, changed as Lorna aged, so that it was always appropriate to her age and condition.

According to May Castle, Lorna's friend and confidante for more than forty years, Lorna never forgot Bertha and Clara's teasing.

> She told me that at an early age, and I mean quite an early age, while Lorna was still sleeping in her parents' room, Clara and Bertha began to call her Cinderella. Well, Cinderella! Isn't that rather a stupid thing for two sisters to do, call their younger sister Cinderella? If Lorna was Cinderella, Clara and Bertha would have to be the ugly stepsisters, wouldn't they? Well. I met those sisters on a couple of occasions, when they were grown women, and I would say that they might have been passably good-looking girls once, perhaps when they were very young, but they had become—well—dowdy and positively homely. I really think they brought it on themselves. Do you think that can't be done? Believe me, it can. And those husbands of theirs! At any rate, Clara and Bertha began calling her Cinderella, out of envy you see, and anger, and because Lorna had this absolutely haunting beauty. Well, my dear! It was haunting, you would have to call it haunting. It would positively light her up at unpredictable times, and the sisters must have been—well!—just depressed as hell by the sense that everything would work out for Lorna the way everything worked out for Cinderella, in a way that things would never work out for them, because of this odd beauty she had, you see. Well, they kept it up as she grew, and then when the sisters began to have suitors, the fellows loved to bounce Lorna on their knee, and so on. And when Lorna began going to dances, the sisters were still unmarried and they were still going to the dancehall themselves, hunting. Well, their men friends would bring little Lorna punch and ask to be put on her card, and they began calling her Cinderella, too. But when they said it, these young men, there was moonlight in it, you see. Well, only then did it dawn on Clara and Bertha that they might be creating a sort of Frankenstein's Cinderella. Don't you just love the idea? Well, they decided that perhaps they had better knock it off. But it was too late, you see, because Lorna had been hurt, terribly hurt, by her sisters' taunting, so hurt that she had no love, no affection of any sort, left for them, and because she was determined now that this name

she had endured, this Cinderella that she'd heard so often as a taunt would become a—badge—or a—title that she could take to show that she had won in the end. When she sent birthday or Christmas cards to her sisters she signed them Cinderella, and when she had a daughter of her own she named her Ella.

2

In Which Lorna's Uncle Luther Becomes the Father of the Coarse-Goods Trade

The croquet ground rules that have been kept by the Hubers fill a small book generations old, maintained and expanded by successive occupants of the narrow house and passed along with the house itself. It makes an interesting historical document. Of the following samples from this book, the entry made in 1910 is of particular interest, because it was added to the rules by Lorna, in her hand, when she was nine.

> No player may drive the ball of another player in a downhill direction. [1856—just three years before Lieutenant Amédée Mannheim, of the French artillery, developed the form of slide rule that endured until the development of the electronic calculator]
>
> No player may drive the ball of another player on a course so close to the contour of Ackerman Hill that the net effect will be the same as if the ball had been driven on a downward course. [1888]
>
> No player may drive the ball of another player into the new

drainage ditch along the upward border of the front lawn, since a ball so driven is certain to roll through the new culvert and continue on an accelerating downward path. [1901]

Driving the ball of a player who is injured or who does not have the full use of his fingers is not fair play. [1910]

Any player who causes any ball to roll downward and be lost, whether by direct or indirect means or by accident, must pay for it or replace it. [1930]

When the ball of another player is driven, it must be driven uphill only, and if an uphill ball starts rolling downhill, it MUST be caught before it rolls off the property. [1952]

It would be more fun for everybody if no player drove the ball of another player in any direction whatsoever, because it's really the pleasure of the game that we ought to be interested in and not the whole competitive thing. [1969]

All croquet balls and mallets used on this court shall be made exclusively of wood. The use of mallets made of carbon-fibre compounds or of aluminum alloys is expressly forbidden. In fact, those damned aluminum baseball bats that make a sound like "pwong" are not to be used within earshot of this court either. [1983]

Lorna had a specific person in mind when she protested against driving the ball of a player "who does not have the full use of his fingers." It was her uncle Luther. Uncle Luther was tall and quiet and dark. He had a pointed chin and deep-set eyes; those would have been his most prominent features if his right hand had not been so terrifying a curiosity. The forefinger was normal, but the other three fingers ended at the first knuckle. They had been sliced off by the machine that cut the clamps for suspenders from thin sheets of brass, while Luther was demonstrating the speed at which he wanted the machine run. "As neat an amputation as any surgeon could have done," Luther enjoyed saying.

The chain of events that led to Luther's losing his fingers began in 1902, when Luther bought a Studebaker Brothers Gentleman's Road

West Lafayette Public Library
West Lafayette, Indiana

Cart. In fact, he bought two. In the spring he bought a standard cart, and he enjoyed driving it so much that in the fall he bought another and had it fitted with runners as a sleigh, for the winter. The Gentleman's Road Cart was a lean, handsome, jaunty, bachelor-uncle's sort of vehicle. Both of Luther's were beautifully painted in red Chinese lacquer, with gold pinstriping. He kept them polished and gleaming. "I would never drive a dirty cart or sleigh," said Luther, in the way that bachelor uncles make pronouncements about the principles that underlie the life they make for themselves. Bachelor uncles tend to accumulate such words to live by and, as time goes by, tend increasingly to live by them. I suppose that this happens to all of us, but there is something about bachelor uncles, perhaps the fear that if they fall there will be no one to catch them, that makes them behave like umpires over their own behavior, interpreters of an ever-lengthening rule book, like the Hubers' rule book for croquet.

The rules in Luther's book became increasingly bizarre after he bought the cart and sleigh. His rules about cleanliness became stricter and stricter: his mustache was always clipped, the lacquer on his cart and sleigh always gleamed, his shoes were always shined, and so on. At the same time, however, his rules governing and defining acceptable behavior for a man of his age and station became laxer and laxer, especially those governing his conduct with young girls. Before he bought the Gentleman's Road Carts, Luther's work at Cole & Lord's Gent's Accessories had been marked by a simple Huber conscientiousness and lack of imagination that had earned him a series of small promotions and an office that overlooked the rushing Whatsit.

He drove, at that time, a sensible and unremarkable carriage, and he drove it in a brisk but sensible fashion. He smiled at the young girls of Chacallit but kept his distance.

The Gentleman's Road Carts did something to him. He drove the sleigh along outlying roads and through fields like a madman in the winter, and he was nearly as wild when he drove the cart through the streets. His daredevil driving earned him the spoken condemnation and unspoken admiration of most of the other men in Chacallit, and it earned him the attention of young girls. Increasingly often, he took one of the mill girls riding with him, and increasingly often he brought the girls—flushed, giggling, exhilarated—home with him after their rides.

He brought to his work the reckless daring that he had discovered in his driving. The new daring led to the accident in which he lost his fingers, but it also led him, for the first time, to give his talent its head. He produced some striking designs for cuff links and shirt studs, and eventually he created the profitable industry that lurked in the shadows and dark recesses of the gentlemen's jewelry business, the branch that came to be known as "the coarse-goods trade," not for the quality of materials and workmanship that went into the goods, for they far surpassed that found in most other jewelry produced in Chacallit, but for their erotic content.

Luther created the coarse-goods trade almost by accident. He was sitting at his desk one morning, daydreaming about one of the girls in the workroom, a new one, who was working in sight of his office. While he thought about the new girl, he sketched her, on a sheet of the drawing paper that he kept handy on his desk, at his right hand, for recording ideas for new jewelry whenever they came to him. He recorded the girl not as he saw her in the workroom, but as he hoped soon to see her, in his bedroom. When he studied the sketches he had made, he discovered a curious thing: his sketches of her aroused him, whetted his appetite for her, better than observing the girl had. In the sketches, he had given her a mix of coyness, shyness, fear, and lasciviousness that he sought in all the girls he pursued but that none ever quite provided. There was a knock on the glass of his office door. Luther looked up, waved his "typewriter" in, and slipped the page of sketches into the drawer in which he habitually put the sketches he made for new jewelry ideas. You can guess the rest. That page went, in a stack of other pages of sketches, to the man who conducted "outlet studies" for Cole & Lord's, work that today would be called market research. He was, it happened, another Huber, one so devoted to the family policy of unblinking dullness that he prepared a straightforward report on the marketing potential of jewelry based on Luther's sexual fantasies and submitted it with his reports on all the other sketches Luther had sent him. "I presume that these would be made into cuff links and shirt studs," he wrote. "They would be a specialty item and not likely ever to sell well to the broad middle. They are, however, likely to sell well among men of a certain degree of sophistication, in larger cities and abroad. I predict few buyers in the towns, and none at all in the rural areas. The likely buyer may consider these goods works of art and be, therefore, willing to pay considerably more for them than for similar goods that depict, to give the first example that comes to mind, dogs. It might be best to buttress this perception of the goods by offering them only in the most expensive materials. Finding outlets will be difficult. None of the stores that currently sell our links and studs, to extrapolate from the inquiries I have made, will carry them. This need not be an insuperable difficulty, however. Might not drummers sell them directly to the customer?"

Luther was no fool. He had unwittingly created a new product with great potential, and he had been handed an innovative marketing strategy. In Albany, he found an organization that could put that strategy into effect: "Professor" Alonzo Clapp's bookselling business. Clapp already had an army of door-to-door salesmen selling books. Luther reasoned that there was likely to be a good overlap between the audience for books and the audience for erotic jewelry. He struck a deal with Clapp, enlisted a few of the very best artisans at Cole & Lord's, and the coarse-goods industry was launched.

Whenever Uncle Luther came to visit, Lorna couldn't stop herself from looking at his damaged hand; it was terribly fascinating. Clara thought the hand was horrible, and she prayed, after her other prayers, silently, when she was in bed, with her hands together in the dark, that Uncle Luther's hand would be made normal or that he would wear a glove always. She felt her stomach fill with cold when she looked at the hand, just as it filled with cold when she sat behind Bertha on their toboggan at the top of Ackerman Hill, and she too couldn't keep herself from looking, just *couldn't* keep herself from looking, no matter how many times she told herself to look only at Uncle Luther's eyes or only at his chin. Bertha, who was eight years older than Lorna, felt that Uncle Luther's hand was one of the things that made him better than other people. She made a point of taking his hand whenever he arrived for a visit, and making a little curtsy while she held it, because she wanted him to know, wanted everyone to know, that his hand didn't frighten her, that she didn't mind the way it was.

It was Luther who occasioned the first manifestation of Lorna's interest in, and talent for, sculpture. For Lorna's fourth birthday, Luther made her a papier-mâché duck. He painted the duck in lurid colors,

colors that have never been seen on a real duck, colors that Luther supposed would please a four-year-old girl. It was a large duck, large for Lorna, who had to use both her chubby hands to hold it. After dinner, while Lorna's parents and her uncle Luther were still sitting at the dinner table, Lorna sat in the parlor, on the davenport, holding the duck.

"That's an ugly duck," said Bertha. She had come into the parlor silently, and she stood in front of Lorna, looking down at her and her duck. Bertha had in the past year or so begun to think of the affections of Uncle Luther as hers, rightfully hers, only hers, in part because Luther had begun to call her "Little Lady" or "My Little Lady," but also because she had determined, secretly, that she would marry Luther when she grew up. Now he had given Lorna a papier-mâché duck that he had made himself. Bertha snatched the duck from Lorna to look at it more closely.

"This is an *extremely* ugly duck," she said. She looked at Lorna to see what effect she was having on her, and Lorna, who had been looking into her lap, lifted her head and looked up at Bertha, and it was one of those moments when Lorna's elusive beauty shone. Bertha wanted to hurt her then, wanted to hurt Lorna immediately; the urge to hurt was so pressing that she couldn't allow herself the time to design an injury, could only strike with the crudest sort of blow.

"Uncle Luther," she said slowly, leaning closer and closer as she spoke, "wouldn't give you an ugly duck like this if he liked you. He made this duck for you so you'd know that he doesn't like you."

Lorna watched Bertha turn the duck over in her hands. Lorna still thought the duck was beautiful. What Bertha had said hadn't changed that. But what Bertha had said, and the way she had leaned toward Lorna when she said it, had changed the way Lorna thought about Bertha. It had shown Lorna that Bertha hated her.

"It's mine!" Lorna cried. She reached out and tore the duck from Bertha's hands. It seemed to hang in the air for a moment, that heartbreaking moment when we realize we've made a terrible error and imagine that if we act quickly enough we can reverse it, and then fell to the floor. A crack opened along the neck, and the feathers in the tail were bent upward crazily.

"And you're welcome to it," said Bertha. She turned on her heel and walked out of the parlor, up the stairs, and into her room.

Crying, Lorna carried the duck into the dining room and asked

Luther to fix it for her. She told him, when he asked, that she had dropped it. She never told him how it had happened. She watched while Luther made some papier-mâché and patched the broken parts. When he had finished, Lorna asked him to teach her how to make a duck like it, and Luther agreed. Over the next several weeks, he showed her how to make papier-mâché and how to work with it. She made a series of ducks in imitation of the one that Luther had made for her, and her ability to work in the medium improved with each. Luther was surprised and pleased. She had a talent for imitation, and she had a good eye. He provided more complex models, and he helped her refine her technique. She continued to progress.

Bertha watched with a jealous eye. She felt that Lorna was taking from her something that was hers, the affections of her uncle Luther, which she valued far more than the affections of her parents, whom she considered hopelessly enthralled by the magic beauty of the little interloper anyway.

Luther also provided the occasion for Lorna's introduction to the acrobatics of sex. It happened a few years later, one winter, on the day of Luther's first sleigh ride of the season.

The first sleigh ride of the winter was an event that Luther began to anticipate in the fall. He needed the infusion of daring that he got from that first ride of the winter, and his need increased throughout the fall. He lived in two rooms, down in the valley, near the mills, but he kept his sleigh in his brother's barn, behind his brother's house, beside his brother's boxy farm wagon, where it stood idle until the winter. In the winter of the year in which Bertha turned sixteen, after the first good snowfall, when Uncle Luther arrived to take the sleigh out for the first run of the season, he found Bertha sitting in the sleigh, waiting for him, shivering. She begged him to take her with him on the first ride, though she knew that he always made the first run alone.

"You know that I always make the first run alone, Bertha," said Luther.

"I know you do," said Bertha. "But this year I want you to take me with you."

"I'm inclined to drive like a madman on the first run, Bertha. I don't want to put you in danger. You'll have to wait until tomorrow."

"I want to feel the danger," said Bertha. "I want you to take me with you, Uncle Luther."

He insisted that she get out. She insisted that he take her with him. He tried to lift her from the seat. She threw her arms around his neck, and said, "Oh, please, Uncle Luther, I won't be afraid. I want to go with you so much. I've always wanted to go with you on the first mad run of the winter. Take me, please, just this once." He lifted her in his arms, lifting her out of the sleigh, with the intention of setting her on her feet and telling her firmly that she could not go, but she kissed him, awkwardly, eagerly. Luther changed his mind.

"Run to the house and see if your mother will let you go," he said slowly, looking into her eyes while he spoke. "Tell her that I'm willing to have you come with me." He set Bertha on her feet. She turned and ran at once for the house. Lorna, who had been watching through the barn door, turned and ran around the corner of the barn before she was seen.

When Luther and Bertha returned from the ride, Lorna was waiting in the hayloft. May Castle was able to give me a good idea of what Lorna saw:

> Oh, she thought it was quite a hilarious scene. Well, she was half-frozen by the time they came back, and she was just terribly frightened too, because she could tell that something was up that shouldn't be up. Well, and she was just exhilarated too, of course, since she knew she was likely to see something worth seeing.
>
> So there she was, up above them, in this hay thing, terrified that she would be discovered, but she could hardly keep herself from laughing. It seemed to her that they were doing the most outlandish things. Of course, she hardly saw a thing in the flesh, so to speak. It was winter, of course, and her uncle and sister were bundled up because of the cold. This was—well—around 1910, I would think. People used to wear much more clothing then than they do now, at any time of year. Well, her uncle Luther had all but disappeared under her sister's skirts, and Lorna thought she would surely burst out laughing. Then they were turned this way, and then that way, but the blankets and clothing kept her from seeing exactly what was going on.
>
> Lorna was not—well—innocent. No, I didn't mean to say that. Snip that out. Snip! I mean to say that she was innocent, but she was not ignorant. This was country living! The Hubers had some chickens

and goats and dogs and such. Lorna had seen plenty of rutting, and
she was quite sure—in a little girl's way—that rutting was what her
sister and uncle were up to, but she couldn't tell exactly how they were
going about it. She put together an idea, a very complicated and
rather kinky idea, from what she knew about the farm animals and
what she knew about—well, about herself. Oh, she told this story
once so very well, when she got a little tipsy. That was rare for Lorna,
but whenever she and Herb and Garth and I got together, well, Garth
would always do his best to get her a little looped. And now and then
he succeeded. He always had a new drink for her to try, something
exotic, with fruit juice and rum. She never knew how much rum she
was getting with all of that juice and—oh, I don't know what else—
an orange slice, and a cherry, and so on. Well, she would get quite
giddy after a while. She always became giddy when she drank. Herb
became serious. Garth became flirtatious. Well, he was always flir-
tatious—more than flirtatious. If he hadn't been so charming, he
would have gotten himself slapped many a time. And punched many
another. As it was, well—oops, I'm straying. Well, that's when she
told the story about Bertha and Luther. Oh, but the best part of it was
that she mimicked their expressions, and it was just the most lascivi-
ous performance. She never behaved like that at any other time. And
don't think that Garth didn't try to get her to tell the story again and
again.

Lorna thought that Uncle Luther's affections had been parceled
out quite satisfactorily. What Bertha had received Lorna didn't want,
and what Lorna had received Bertha must certainly, she supposed, be
willing to let her have. For the most part, Bertha *was* willing to let
Lorna have what now seemed to her nothing more than an indulgent
uncle's fondness for a talented child. She didn't mind his praising
Lorna's talents; she had discovered talents of her own. She did, however, mind the time that Luther spent with Lorna. Time spent with
Lorna was time that might have been spent with her. It was hard
enough for Bertha to find times and places to be alone with Luther
without arousing her parents' suspicions, though it was certainly
easier now that Bertha was working in the mill and had developed
friendships with young women who had no one but themselves to
whom they had to account for the way they spent their time. Bertha

began demanding more and more of the time that Luther would have spent with Lorna.

After a while, though, Lorna didn't miss Luther's teaching. She had already surpassed him in modeling ability, and she could see that she was learning more from her own work than he could have taught her. She was working in other materials now—clay and plaster—and she had begun to make a little money doing jewelry work at home, doing piecework on links and studs, mounting glass in cheap settings of tin or pinchbeck, work that was far below her abilities.

As soon as she persuaded her parents to let her work for an hour or two each day in the mill, she was able to work with much better stuff, mounting mother-of-pearl and garnet and onyx in silver and gold. In a very short time, she had gone beyond mere mounting to fabrication, fabricating link swivels, the interlinked projecting wires that join the two parts of old-fashioned cuff links and shirt studs. The ends of the wires are turned into loops and joined in the manner of the Chinese puzzles that so frustrated me when I was a boy, puzzles that I have taken care to avoid ever since I learned, as an adult, that there are some things I do not have to be able to do. Making these link swivels was skilled work, work that lay on the border between the mechanical operations—setting the stones and other ornaments, cutting, stamping and buffing—and the artisanship of those who actually made the gold and silver settings or those who carved figures in ivory.

One could become good at making swivels in a way that one never could at gluing or buffing. There was room for style and grace here. The pliers could be manipulated in an individual manner. The loops could vary slightly. A swivel maker could vary the styles of loops from oval to round, could even introduce triangularity or, if very adept—and Lorna was—attempt squarish loops now and then. Any variation had to be accomplished within formal constraints. There was the constraint of time, indirectly applied through the piecework method of payment. There was the constraint of length, since the managers of the link-and-stud works railed against the women who used too much of the wire that formed the swivels.

When I examined the link-and-stud collection at the Chacallit Historical Society, my first reaction was that fabricating link swivels must have been boring work, but I've come to understand that there were elements of dance (in the movement of the fabricator's hands), of sculpture (in the shaping of the swivels themselves), and of mathematics (in the geometry of the loops and in using just the right length of wire). I can see how it led to Lorna's exacting work in the slide-rule factory later on, to her affection for logic and for recreational mathematics, and, of course, to the making of erotic jewelry.

Did Luther plan Lorna's entire career as soon as he saw that she had talent, or did he improvise as he saw her talent and interest grow? No one can say with certainty, but I think he improvised. I suspect that Luther was too cautious about his coarse-goods work and too concerned abut his standing in the family to have permitted himself even to imagine his brother's daughter as an apprentice in coarse-goods making when he first recognized her talent at the age of four. On the other hand, he was too calculating a sort not to have considered from the start what an asset she could become, with the right training. In any event, Luther saw that she got that training. He moved her through every aspect of jewelry making at a quick pace, always in the direction of the more skilled, the more aesthetically demanding.

By the time she was sixteen, Lorna had become one of the best ivory carvers in Chacallit, which made her one of the best in the men's jewelry business. The work required all the skills that Uncle Luther had taught her. The carvers sat around a circular table at the center of which was the archetype of the product that was currently required—a rampant lion, say—constructed by Luther, in papier-mâché, several times larger than what the carvers would produce. The ivory carvers would duplicate the archetype as precisely as they could in the form of, for example, insets for a set of shirt studs.

One afternoon, Uncle Luther came to the carving room and stood behind Lorna while she worked. He said nothing until the day's work was done, and then he asked her to wait until the others had left. When they had, he picked up one of the pieces she had carved, looked at it closely, and sighed. "Lorna," he said, "you are an astounding copyist. Do you know that?"

"I have a good eye," she said.

"A good eye, a good hand, a good imagination. You seem to understand how to adjust the proportions in a miniature so that the apparent proportions of the original are preserved."

"Thank you," she said.

"Lorna," he asked, looking into her eyes, "how would you like to carve human figures?"

Luther was taking a great risk in leading Lorna into the shadowy underworld of the men's furnishings industry, but Lorna's talent led him to believe that the rewards would be worth the risk. Events were to prove him correct. Lorna became as good at copying the human figure in ivory as she had been at copying lions and horses and such. Lorna's work had more than precision; it had a warmth that came from the pleasure she found in the work itself. This pleasure had had its origin in Lorna's desire to please Luther, to win his approval, to do work that was worthy of his approval, and some of that impulse remained, but far stronger now was the desire to please herself, to do difficult work and do it better than she had done it before, to do work that was worthy of *her* approval.

Luther had two reasons for thinking that Lorna was likely to be, and to remain, circumspect about the new work he gave her to do. First, he recognized the pleasure she took in the work itself, and he knew that she wouldn't want to lose the opportunity to work at this level of her craft, the most challenging. Second, he knew that the Lorna who sat at home of an evening, in front of the fire, playing anagrams with her sisters and her mother, would be embarrassed by the subject of, the content of, the purpose of, the work she did in the small room behind an unmarked door, where she and two other carvers sat at a circular table at the center of which was one of Luther's oversized papier-mâché models of a naked woman and a naked man, intriguingly entangled. Luther thought that he had a third reason for trusting Lorna to be circumspect, but in this one he was wrong. He thought that he detected in Lorna signs of the awakening of a desire for him of the sort that Bertha felt.

Had Luther had all his fingers, he would probably have been Lorna's first lover. It nearly happened one moonlit spring night, when Lorna was eighteen. Luther took her for a ride in a rowboat, on Lake Serenity, not far from Chacallit, where there was a large ballroom that extended out over the lake. The night was one of those warm, hazy ones in spring that anticipate summer and lift the spirit.

When Luther helped Lorna into the boat and pushed off, Bertha and Clara were standing on the dock with several of the young men who hung around the Huber girls because they were enchanted by Lorna's elusive beauty. Each stroke Luther took, each set of circular ripples the blades left in the wake, made Bertha feel more furious, more horribly betrayed, more determined to get even, at least to show Luther that he wasn't the only object of her desire. She thrust her hip against the hip of the young man beside her, Richard Reuter. Richard was surprised; Richard was pleased. He was a frequenter of the Serenity Ballroom, a poor dancer, a young man too shy to approach young women alone. He usually stayed in the company of other young men who were too shy to approach young women alone and so stood on the fringes of the flirting and dancing and gaiety, making remarks about the others and trying to appear, instead of shy, bored. This evening he had wandered outside with Bertha and Clara because many others had. He didn't consider Bertha one of the more attractive young women, but she *was* a young woman, and that was what he wanted. He glanced at Bertha, and he almost put his arm around her. He caught himself, however, and kept his hands to himself, remembering the startled reactions he'd occasioned in the past by that sort of impulsive grabbing. When Bertha repeated the pressure of her hip, however, he was emboldened to return the pressure, tentatively. He felt, unmistakably, an increase in pressure, and—there could be no doubt about it—he felt Bertha turn so that she rubbed herself against him, just enough so that the gesture could be understood as intentional before she pulled away. By the time Bertha had grown angry enough to link her arm with Richard's and lead him off into the shadows, Richard had decided that he was in love.

Clara watched her sister walk off with Richard Reuter and felt much as she had felt when she had watched Bertha heaping her plate with potato salad so many years before. She was frightened and impressed. She intended to show Bertha that what Bertha could do, she could do. And she did, with Harold Russell, a much better catch.

Luther pulled at the oars with steady, sure strokes. Lorna was careful not to look at the hand with the missing fingers, and she was careful not to praise Luther's rowing ability because she was afraid that if she did, Luther would think that the unspoken qualification to whatever she said was "for a man who has only seven fingers." So careful was she not to praise his rowing ability that Luther had to do it himself. He said, at a lull in Lorna's talk about the stars twinkling through the haze, the mild weather, the breeze that drifted through the tiny, pale, spring-green leaves, the bright half-moon, the light and the shadows and the reflections, "I'm not doing bad for a fellow with only seventy percent of his fingers, am I?"

Lorna laughed and turned away.

"What do you say we just drift for a while?" asked Luther.

"Oh, yes," said Lorna at once, glad to relieve Uncle Luther of what she felt certain must be a difficult and painful labor. "I'd like that—just to drift and look at the stars."

"Do you know the constellations?" asked Luther.

"I know some," said Lorna. "Let's see. There's Orion." She pointed, and Luther turned his head to look at the sky.

"That's right," he said. "Do you know Cassiopeia?"

It all happened so quickly, was accomplished with such fluidity of movement, that the boat never rocked in the water and Lorna didn't even have time to be surprised. Truly before she knew it, Uncle Luther was by her side, they were reclining against the cushion in the stern of the boat, Uncle Luther was pointing to Cassiopeia with one hand, and the other lay idly, just resting on her dress, as if it had fallen there of its own accord and Luther had no idea where it had gone to, along the inside of her thigh.

Lorna's heart began to pound. A number of emotions and sensations raced crazily through her, dashing this way and that, like clowns at a circus. She was curious, certainly. What Luther might be on the way toward doing did intrigue her, after what she had seen in the barn and had elaborated so often in her imagination, at night, lying awake in her bed. The rosiness she saw in Bertha's cheeks after she'd spent some time with Luther, and the smiles Luther put on the faces of his papier-mâché couples, suggested that what Uncle Luther seemed to be proposing would be a pleasure.

She let her hand drop onto Luther's leg, and she allowed it to slip a couple of inches downward along the inside of his thigh. Luther was surprised. He looked at Lorna. The color was high in her cheeks. He kissed the blush along her cheekbone. She couldn't trust herself to say or do anything, so she just kept looking upward, at the stars. Luther talked on, but his voice had become merely a low mumble, a part of the evening sounds on Lake Serenity: whispering breeze, lapping wavelets, chirping crickets, mumbling Luther. Lorna was paying no attention to what he was saying. All her attention was on her hand

and his. When his hand moved, her heart leaped, and she moved her hand. When his hand stopped, she drew a breath and stopped hers. When his hand flexed, her whole body stiffened, and she squeezed Luther's leg, so slightly that he may not even have noticed it.

Lorna was thrilled. She felt the anticipatory thrill that she felt before anything that she expected to be pleasant, but more intensely than ever before. There was the nervousness she knew, the burning tremulousness in the muscles of her hands and arms and face and belly. The coldness in her chest. The flutter in her heart. There was the familiar sense of floating, intensified by the fact that she *was* floating.

Luther was fussing with his trousers, she realized, and then quite suddenly he had taken her hand with his other and pushed it into his trousers and folded her fingers around his erect penis. This was so surprising and welcome a development that Lorna smiled un-thinkingly in her delight. Her curiosity, always great, had become enormous since Luther had added couples to the cuff link line. So tightly were the couples coupled that Lorna couldn't see much of the man, though she examined the papier-mâché models thoroughly, and she carved faithful representations of what she saw, something like an inverted mushroom, its button top between the man's legs, a bit of stem, and dark mystery where it disappeared in the woman. Lorna seized the opportunity Luther had given her and began a thorough exploration, running her fingers along and around his penis, feeling for details with a sculptor's touch. She drifted into an abstracted exploration, an exercise in genital cartography. It was as if the rest of Luther had disappeared, and she were alone with his penis and the lake and the night and the stars, and she hardly noticed that he had pulled up her skirt and brought his hand between her legs.

Luther was ecstatic. He hadn't hoped for this eagerness. He began poking and probing with his forefinger, and a rush of pleasure ran through Lorna, and she drew a sharp breath and raised her hips al-most involuntarily, rubbing herself against Luther's hand, Luther's forefinger, and that's when things began to go wrong.

It was *that* hand. The one good finger was in her, the thumb was poking around, hunting for her clitoris, and the three stumps were tickling her. A wave of revulsion ran through her, but the tickling made her want to giggle. She seemed to see the whole thing, as fully and clearly as if she had to carve it, and she imagined carving the thumb, and the forefinger, and the stumps, and herself. She turned toward Luther with terror in her eyes, her mouth in a twisted grin. He misinterpreted her look. "Now, Lorna," he began, "don't be frightened. Don't cry out. I won't hurt—"

And then she was ashamed. She shouldn't be revolted by his hand, she told herself. Even if she were, she shouldn't have let him see it. "Oh, Uncle Luther," she said. "I'm so ashamed—"

"There's nothing for you to feel ashamed about, Lorna," said Luther. He began pulling his trousers down, and then he was on top of Lorna, pulling at her clothes. "Just relax yourself," he said. "Look at the stars, and think lovely thoughts, and it won't hurt. I promise—"

But the feeling of abstraction, of detachment, had vanished, and Lorna was suddenly aware of everything and full of doubts and fears, like a person who is awakened by a thunderclap, frantic, sure that everything is about to fall apart. Out of all the questions she was asking herself, one of the unlikeliest came through loudest: *What about Bertha?*

"What about Bertha?" she said. "Bertha loves you, Uncle Luther. I know she does." To her surprise, Lorna found that she felt horribly disloyal. *Poor Bertha,* she thought. *She's homely, and she's in love with Uncle Luther. She must have been afraid of me for years—*

"Bertha! Bertha is nothing. She's— Lorna?"

Lorna was pushing him away, struggling to her feet, reaching for the oars, calling out, "No, no. Stop it! Get away from me!"

Bertha and Clara were married to Richard Reuter and Harold Russell in the summer, in a dual wedding. Richard Huber grumbled publicly over the expense but savored a secret satisfaction, since the expense of a dual wedding had been much less than the expense of two would have been. The following year Bertha and Clara each gave birth to a boy, conceived that warm spring night when Luther took Lorna for a row on Lake Serenity.

Lorna built a wall between herself and Luther. She spoke with him at the mill or in her parents' house—he was a rare visitor now— but she had no more to say to him than what was necessary to keep people from suspecting that something was wrong. He had spoiled everything she had felt for him. Her memories of his kindnesses to her, of the way that he had taught her to model in papier-mâché and to carve ivory, were pleasant ones, but they were difficult to recall when he was present. She knew all the gossip about him now; she heard it from other workers at the link-and-stud mill. She knew that he took girls riding in his new automobile, a Studebaker Big Six, and she knew—or guessed—that many of the papier-mâché models that Luther made for the ivory carvers to copy in the room behind the unmarked door recorded his own amorous experiments. Worst of all, she knew that what he had felt for Bertha—and for her—was nothing more than what the rooster felt for the chickens or the boar for the sows.

On a cold and rainy night the next September, Richard and Lena and Lorna were sitting in their living room, in front of a fire in the stone fireplace that was set into the north wall. The air was still heavy with the aromas of dinner—fresh ham, sauerkraut, boiled potatoes, turnips, and rye bread. Richard Huber was dozing in his chair; Lena was darning socks. Lorna was playing anagrams alone.

From outside came the sound of a car on the steep road beside the house. The car stopped, and from its sound Lorna decided that it must have stopped at the bend, in front of the house. It might be Uncle Luther. Lorna decided that she would go up to her room if it was.

She went to the window. There was a car outside, but it wasn't Luther's. Footsteps on the porch. A knock at the door. Lena looked up. Richard snorted.

"I'll go," said Lorna.

She pulled the curtain aside and looked out through the glass before she opened the door. A young man was on the porch, collapsing his umbrella. He was wearing a wool suit, and he seemed nervous. It was Herb.

3
In Which Herb Is Born to the Pipers of Boston

My grandfather, Herb Piper, was born in Boston, into a family that was broke. For generations the Pipers had exhibited two outstanding characteristics: a cool-headed talent for selling and a gullible ineptitude for investing. It was quite possible for a Piper to accumulate a tidy nest egg over the course of a week of selling and lose it in an hour by buying into a scheme that he thought would double his money overnight—a land deal, say, that he had overheard two fellows talking about downtown while he was having lunch, a deal that, he allowed himself to be convinced, involved virtually no risk whatsoever, a deal that was as sure as sure can be. Like a dog biting its own tail, a Piper at his worst turned his talent against himself, selling himself on the wisdom of his folly. This type of self-deception, self-injury, has been known in my family for generations as "doing a foolish Piper thing." When imprudent Pipers found that they had done a foolish Piper thing, when the land, the development company, and the two fellows vanished, some Pipers would brood and curse themselves and the foolish Piper giant who seemed to dog their steps, but others would shrug and chuckle at themselves and their inherited folly. Herb's grandfather was of the chuckling type. "Well," he had said when he broke the news about the land, the development company, and the two vanishing fellows to Herb's grandmother, "I've gone and done a foolish Piper thing, haven't I?"

Once, however, there had been a substantial Piper fortune, thanks to Herb's great-grandfather, Thomas Piper, and his association with Frederick Lewis Tudor, the finest flower ever to blossom on the vine of American marketing genius. In his essay "The American Drummer," Wilhelm Huber wrote, "I am among those who hold that a genius for *selling,* that curious alliance of art, ingenuity, inspiration, cupidity, and fraud, is *the* American genius." Certainly it was a genius for selling that made the United States, for a while at any rate, the commercial giant of the world, indeed the model for what a commercial giant might be. Just what was the nature of that genius that made America a great commercial nation, that genius that was so pronounced in Frederick Lewis Tudor and in the Piper family? Edward Huxtable has attempted to describe it, in *The Person in Your Mirror Is You:*

> *The inept salesman or saleswoman has the wrong mental image of himself or herself and his or her product, something like a huckster at a sideshow in a traveling circus might have: he or she feels that what he or she sells is inferior, an embarrassment. He or she imagines that he or she could be a much better huckster if the fat lady were fatter, the rubber man more limber, the dog-boy more slavering. But the best huckster, the genius huckster, begins by selling him- or herself on the merits of his or her commodity and so finds it not merely easy but intellectually satisfying, even morally gratifying, to persuade the rubes or inform the consumers that slim fat ladies are the rage, arthritic rubber men the rarest, dry-mouthed dog-boys the marvel of the age. The* natural genius *salesperson, whether he or she peddles books, cars, furniture, jewelry, pocket calculators, or investment schemes, is a carrier of his or her own infectious self-deception.*

Frederick Lewis Tudor was the man who established the international ice trade, cutting ice on the lakes of New England and shipping it virtually all over the world. This remarkable enterprise captured the imaginations of so disparate a trio as Henry David Thoreau, Gabriel García Márquez, and the Marx Brothers.

In the winter of 1846–1847, when the ice trade was in full swing, Thoreau watched a crew of immigrant Irish ice cutters at work on

Walden Pond and recorded in his journal these remarks about the extent and influence of the ice trade:

> The sweltering inhabitants of Charleston and New Orleans, of Madras and Bombay and Calcutta, drink at my well. . . . The pure Walden water is mingled with the sacred water of the Ganges.

A hundred years later, Márquez described the arrival in nineteenth-century Macondo of what may well have been some Walden Pond ice:

> There was.a giant with a hairy torso and a shaved head, with a copper ring in his nose and a heavy iron chain on his ankle, watching over a pirate chest. When it was opened by the giant, the chest gave off a glacial exhalation. Inside there was only an enormous, transparent block. . . .

Surely the ice trade, based as it was on teaching people to want something that they hadn't even known existed before, selling something for which there was no demand, marks the dawn of modern marketing, and the Piper family, in the person of Thomas Piper, was there.

What was Thomas Piper like? My mind's eye's image of him is an inaccurate but appealing one. It comes straight from the movie *Cracked Ice,* in which the Marx Brothers romp through a series of madcap adventures loosely based on the events leading to the establishment of the ice trade.

In *Cracked Ice,* we first meet the flamboyant Frederick Lewis Tudor (Groucho) at a dinner party in a fashionable home on Beacon Hill, in Boston, in 1805, where he is sitting between the wives of two of his brothers. The brothers, successful, sober men, sit opposite him. Tudor inclines toward one of the women and whispers in her ear. She looks startled, then smiles coquettishly. Tudor inclines toward the other (Margaret Dumont) and whispers in her ear. She squeals and slaps his face.

"Really, Fred," says one brother, "be reasonable, won't you?"

Tudor, demonstrating the mercurial temper and physical agility for which he was noted, leaps upon the table and begins berating his brothers for their unimaginative reasonableness, gesticulating with the leg of a roast duck as he does so.

"The difference between us, brothers," he declares at the end of his tirade, dropping himself into the lap of Margaret Dumont, "is that you have hearts of *ice*. Not mine, brothers! My heart burns! (It must have been the horseradish.) I say *phooey* to being reasonable. Give me imagination! It's men with imagination who leave their mark on this world!" He looks at Margaret Dumont and bats his eyes. "Am I right, toots?" he asks.

"That sounds like hubris to me, Fred," says one.

"Hubris, schmoobris," Tudor fires back. "I tell you the man with imagination can do anything he puts his mind to. Anything!"

"How about—selling water?" suggests one of the brothers with haughty composure, idly turning the stem of his crystal goblet. The others laugh. Tudor storms out of the house in a rage, and from the street he shouts, "I *will* sell water, and I'll make my fortune at it, too!"

Striding across the street, blinded by rage, he is nearly run over by a wagon (not a Studebaker; Henry and Clem Studebaker built their first wagons in 1852). The driver, young Tom Piper (Chico), stops his horses and rushes to pick Tudor up from the cobblestone pavement. Still in a fury, Tudor waves him off. "When I need your help, I'll ask for it," he shouts.

Tom climbs back up to his seat and is about to pull away. Tudor notices the lettering on the side of the van: WENHAM ICE. His face lights up. "Help!" he cries.

Tom climbs down again and helps Tudor to his feet. "What's your name, fellow?" Tudor asks.

"Huh?" Tom replies, surprised.

"That can't be it," says Tudor. "Think, man! What does your mother say when she wants you to come to dinner?" He wears a look that suggests he thinks he's dealing with an idiot.

"Come and get it!"

"Well, if it's good enough for your mother, it's good enough for me. Cumangetit," says Tudor, throwing his arm across Tom's shoulders, "tell me about ice."

"Well, itsa real cold—" begins Tom.

Tudor rides along with Tom Piper, pumping him for information about the ice business. Suddenly, Tom seems suspicious. "Just a minute," he asks, "why you aska me this?"

"Cumangetit," says Tudor, chewing on his cigar, "I'm going to start an ice company of my own."

Tom begins laughing. "You?" he says. Suddenly he stops laughing. "You got a vice president?" he asks. Tudor shakes his head. "How much does it pay?" Tudor shrugs. "Okay, I take it," says Tom. They shake hands.

Tom brings Tudor to his home. There we meet Tom's wife, Lavinia, and her beautiful sister, Katherine, who is visiting from Savannah. Tom warns Tudor that there isn't much room for another ice company in these parts. Tudor, who is lying with his head in Katherine's lap, batting his lashes at her, asks coyly, "Do y'all have many ice companies in Savannah?"

Giggling, blushing, Katherine replies that there are none.

"Well then!" declares Tudor. "We'll sell our ice in Savannah. We'll sell our ice where it's most wanted, in the sultry climes! We'll sell it in Savannah, and we'll sell it in Havana, and we'll sell it in Bombay!"

"'At's an ice idea, boss," says Tom.

They all toast the start of their enterprise.

A mad scramble begins. Tudor must raise money, obtain ice-cutting monopolies on lakes and ponds, find ships, hire workers, build icehouses, and so on. At one point, Tom and Tudor recruit the help of Nathaniel Wyeth (Harpo), who has invented a more efficient way of cutting ice. They pay him in stock.

Tom Piper is always at Tudor's side, and Katherine, who stays on in Boston to help, grows daily more smitten with the stubborn genius. Tudor grows so obsessed with what he now thinks of as his mission in life that he begins to sound like a madman, not the sort of person in whose venture one would be likely to invest. Tom Piper, however, is able to lay the whole scheme out before a potential investor in a stream of compelling words, to make it sound like a sure thing, as sure as sure can be, and he is the one who brings the investors in.

Against all odds, the enterprise is in place and operating when winter arrives. In a curiously balletic scene, we watch a swarm of workers cutting ice in a light snow: small, dark figures moving against a seamless white background under the direction of Wyeth, who scoots around, directing their work by waving, whistling, clapping his hands, and honking a small horn. It's a strange interlude, one that European audiences in particular seem to find oddly moving.

Suddenly, we're at sea! The great ice-filled schooner *Tuscany* noses

[3 9]

through the waves. The *Tuscany* arrives in Savannah, and Tom goes to work at once. He sets up a little stage right on the dock, gathers a crowd, and pulls aside a curtain to reveal Wyeth, stripped to the waist, his cheeks puffed out as if he were straining under a great weight, carrying a huge Chinese lacquer chest. He sets the chest down, unlocks it, opens it, and reveals a gemlike piece of ice inside. The crowd is delighted. Ice! Here in Savannah! They clamor to buy. "Boss, it'sa go like hotcakes," Tom reports to Tudor.

On the sea again, the *Tuscany* is now bound for Cuba. During a storm, Tom Piper entertains the crew with some snappy tunes on the ship's piano, and Wyeth, alone in his cabin, falls into a contemplative mood and plucks a harp he has brought along. At last, they arrive in Havana, and Tom goes to work again, but just as Tom and Tudor are about to conclude a deal with the Spanish governor, the captain of the *Tuscany* rushes in, upset, flustered, worried. Glancing anxiously at the governor's guards, he blurts out, "The arrangements must be canceled! The ice has melted!" Wyeth tries to muffle him with a scarf.

Calmly, taking his cigar from his mouth, Tudor says to the governor, "This must be your lucky day! Now we can give you a better price."

At sea again, the three pace the deck at night, in step, Tudor in the lead. "We've got to find a way to keep ice from melting!" he cries. "I won't be defeated! I will find a way!" All three pound their fists into their open hands.

Back in Boston, Tudor begins the experiments in preserving ice that will occupy him for months. In a quick sequence of scenes, we see that things are going badly. Tudor flings open the doors of an icehouse and water rushes out. "Blankets won't work," he says in disgust. He flings open another. Water rushes out. Wyeth staggers out with wet feathers stuck all over him. "Feathers won't work, either," Tudor says. Katherine is seen in her office, trying to keep creditors at bay. Wyeth is seen trying to sell his shares in the company to passersby. Tom Piper is seen trying to raise more money and being turned down. Katherine tries to persuade Tudor to abandon the project. They are walking along the line of icehouses set up for testing. Water is running from each one they pass. "Perhaps you're right," admits Tudor. Suddenly Wyeth rushes up, whistling like mad, carrying a huge saw. He begins sawing at one of the icehouses, still whistling like crazy, smiling and bobbing his head up and down.

"Perhaps you're right," says Tudor, misinterpreting Wyeth's message. "I'll put all this behind me and become a lumberjack."

Wyeth grabs Tudor by the coat and drags him to an icehouse from which no water runs. Tudor's eyes light up. He flings the door open. "Sawdust!" he cries.

At sea again, the *Tuscany*, with a load of ice packed in sawdust, is bound for Bombay.

In Bombay harbor, Tom, Nathaniel, and Tudor pace the deck, anxiously awaiting the arrival of the sultan of Gujarat and representatives of the British East India Company. When they arrive, Tom, in an inspired scene, delivers two simultaneous sales pitches, one directed toward the interests of the Indians, one toward the British. The final disclosure of the ice is a huge success with both. Tom offers a sample piece to the sultan as a gift.

The cargo of ice is being unloaded when hundreds of fierce, armed Indians arrive and surround the wharf. The sultan himself arrives, in high dudgeon, and appeals to the British for justice. He's been tricked. The ice he was given yesterday is gone. Much chuckling about this on the part of the British, who explain that this is melting, something ice always does, but that fortunately Tudor has leased to them the exclusive rights to build icehouses in Bombay, following the secret methods discovered in America after long and arduous effort.

Back in Boston, some time later, on the wharves, Lavinia and Katherine wait, and watch, and worry. Lavinia, peering through a spyglass, suddenly cries, "There!" It's the *Tuscany!* Both peer through their spyglasses, looking for a sign that will tell them whether the trip has been a success or a failure. At last they spot Tudor, Tom, and Nathaniel, standing in the bow of the first ship, decked out in flamboyant outfits. For some reason not made clear in the film, the sultan of Gujarat, his attendants, his guards, a bevy of girls in harem pants, four elephants, and a delegation of British colonial officials have come along with them. They are all singing "Hooray for Freddie Tudor," a number that is, it must be admitted, a pallid reworking of "Hooray for Captain Spaulding." It is sung to the same tune.

> *Hooray for Freddie Tudor!*
> *Yo ho! The iceman cometh!*
> *"Did someone call me goniff?"*
> *Yo ho! Yo ho! Yo ho!*

[4 1]

◆   ◆   ◆

The triumph didn't last for the Pipers, although ice made Tom Piper a wealthy man. When he died in 1852, he left a considerable fortune, including stock in Tudor's ice business, but within two years his two sons and two daughters had lost it all.

Tom Piper's eldest son, Eleazer, visited a palmist on the day after his father was buried. The thrust of the palmist's remarks was that Eleazer was about to go through a key pivotal time in his life, and that prospects were not good, but that Eleazer could make the best of things by trusting his intuition. Eleazer left the palmist's with his head reeling. In the course of his walk home, he decided to act in accordance with a hunch he'd had for some time. For some time he had been keeping an eye on a British patent medicine, Tono-Bungay. Its sales had grown phenomenally. Eleazer had tried to persuade his father to invest in it, but Thomas Piper's interest in ice had been so consuming that he had paid little attention to his son; Eleazer suspected that his father thought little of his business abilities. The Tono-Bungay company was just beginning to make a serious move toward expansion beyond the British Isles, and Eleazer's intuition told him that now was the time to strike. If he could persuade his siblings to invest, they might obtain an American monopoly in Tono-Bungay, which ought to put them on a surer footing in the coming turbulent times the palmist had predicted, surer than ice, as sure as sure can be.

The sons and daughters of Thomas Piper agreed, swept up by the force of Eleazer's conviction and his hereditary gift for salesmanship. They divested themselves of everything ice had brought them and bid for and won exclusive rights to the American market for Tono-Bungay.

Within a month, Tono-Bungay collapsed. The Ponderevos, who had launched the business in Britain, and the Pipers, who had hoped to advance it in America, were paupers. The palmist, confronted by a blubbering, drunk, and disheveled Eleazer Piper, told him that he had actually been extremely lucky. "If you hadn't followed your hunch in this matter," she said, "there's no telling *what* might have happened. Of this, however, I am certain: things would have been far worse."

In the years that followed, the Piper fortunes rose and fell within a narrower range on the scale of success and failure. When they rose, they rose only to the level where there was enough for dinner and a little extra in case someone dropped by; when they fell, they fell to the level where there wasn't enough for dinner, and if someone dropped by, one of the children would answer the door and say that Father was out.

4

In Which Herb Is Recruited for the Coarse-Goods Trade

Herb's father, Lester, was the least successful Piper of his generation, though he had the most talent, the best ideas, and the greatest ambition. As a young man, he experienced one short period of relative prosperity, when he not only had no debts, but had some real prospects for a comfortable future. At the time, he represented a Portuguese cork company in and around Boston, selling cork on commission. He was, then, bright-eyed and eager, bursting with ideas and high spirits. He wooed and won Millie McDougal, sweeping the girl off her feet with his obvious affection for her, his stream of hopes and dreams and plans and schemes, and his genuine desire for a quiet, settled middle age lived soberly at the center of a happy family. When Lester and Millie were married, there wasn't a person at the wedding who didn't sigh at the warmth and pleasantness of it all and beam at the brightness of their future.

However, Lester Piper's dreams and ideas, his ambition and impatience, and the Piper talent for doing the foolish Piper thing proved his undoing.

Almost from the start of his work for the cork company, he had reasoned that if there were more uses for cork, he could sell more of it and make more money. He had sold himself on the idea that his future was in cork, that everything depended on his expanding the market for it, and that a slip in his first attempt would send him on an accelerating downward path. He had undertaken a careful and deliberate examination of his surroundings, looking for everyday objects that might be made of cork, but nothing struck him as quite the right thing on which to stake his future. He bided his time, hopeful that the right idea would present itself.

After Lester and Millie were married, they moved into two rented rooms above a bakery. Up the narrow stairs they carried their belongings, their gifts, and some furniture that had been given to them by Millie's family and Lester's. Among the pieces of furniture was an enormous heirloom bed, made entirely of oak. The bed was plain and solid, painfully heavy even when disassembled. At the end of the moving day, Lester sank into an overstuffed chair; he had wobbly legs, an aching back, and what he thought was a good idea: cork furniture. It would be sturdy but light, easy to move, easy to rearrange. Over the course of the next three years, he allowed himself, in the Piper manner, to become cozened by his own idea. He invested every penny he could scrape together, every penny he could borrow, every moment he could steal, in establishing a company to manufacture a complete line of cork furniture, including sofas and armchairs, dining room tables and chairs, armoires and highboys, and, of course, beds. Millie was by nature a cautious young woman, with a skepticism that might have saved them from ruin, but Lester was so good a salesman that he sold his young wife on the soundness of his plans, with the result that, when Piper's Patented Featherweight Furniture failed, Millie's parents, a sister, and a cousin were ruined along with Lester Piper and his little family, which by then included a son, Herb.

Lester Piper watched his dreams fall apart, and when the last possibility of success was gone, when everything had been taken away from him, when the auctioneer's gavel fell for the final time, Lester went home with Millie and Herb to his brother Benjamin's apartment, where they were now forced to live, and sank into a cork armchair in a corner of the front room. He spent most of his time slumped in that chair, brooding on his past mistakes. He did, of course, get up to eat and sleep and so on, but his attitude even when out of the chair was forevermore that of a man slumped in a chair, brooding on his past mistakes, and he wore exactly the same hangdog look when he was out of the chair as he did when he was in it. Millie tried to rally him, tried to get him to get up and try again, to get another selling job, but it was no use. Lester had decided that he was a defeated man, and so he was.

Millie went to work as a seamstress, assisting a tailor in a men's clothing shop, making repairs and doing small, repetitive jobs: sewing on buttons, letting out the seats of pants, and the like. Herb began working when he was eight. His first job was ripping seams out of pants that his mother brought home from the shop, so that she could work more quickly. By the time he was fourteen, he had found several other ways to make money. He had a secondhand wagon, a Studebaker Junior, a toy that was modeled after the most popular Studebaker farm wagon. Every morning he loaded the wagon with newspapers, muffins, fruit tarts, and rolls, which he sold from a street corner before going to school. Every evening, at the same street corner, he sold newspapers and meat pies, a type of meat pie that the boys who sold them called, among themselves, "rat pie." On his way home, he visited every neighbor, looking for mending his mother could do or broken household gadgets that he could fix.

Lester's brother Benjamin had little tolerance for Lester's defeated-man-slumped-in-a-chair attitude. Benjamin was a tireless worker, unceasingly optimistic. He sold from door to door, and he had over the years taken on more and more lines, so that when he found an especially susceptible client he could return month after month with something else to sell. Among the lines he sold was the series of books distributed by Alonzo Clapp, of Albany, the jobber to whom Luther Huber had turned for the distribution of coarse goods, and when Clapp approached Ben with the idea of selling erotic jewelry, Ben took the line on eagerly, with exactly the same eagerness with which he would have added a promising line of cookware.

Every evening, when Ben came home, his eyes fell on his brother, the defeated man, slumped in his lightweight chair. Ben couldn't stand seeing his brother so. With the help of some of the other Pipers, he managed to find and subsidize a shabby and cramped apartment where Lester, Millie, and Herb could live on their own, out of Ben's sight. One evening, in Herb's fifteenth year, Herb was sitting on the floor of the larger room of that apartment—a room that served as living room, dining room, kitchen, and Herb's bedroom—fixing a meat grinder. Millie was setting the table for dinner. The sound of footsteps on the stairs made Millie and Herb start and look at each other with concern.

"Someone's coming up the stairs, Lester," Millie said. Lester Piper didn't move. He sat slumped in his chair. Millie sighed. "It's sure to be Mrs. Lightner," she said to Herb. "I owe Mr. Lightner for two weeks' worth of meat, and she doesn't like him to give credit. She knows he never asks to be paid. You answer it, Herb."

There was a knock at the door, and Herb answered. He opened the door a crack and said before he looked through it, "My mother and father aren't home."

"The hell they're not," said a breathless, wheezing, masculine voice from the hallway. "Your father's sitting in the cork chair in the corner, and your mother's standing beside him, wringing her hands."

"It's Uncle Ben," said Herb. He opened the door, and Benjamin Piper lurched into the room, placing a heavy hand on Herb for support.

"Good evening, Benjamin," said Millie, her eyes down, her hands nervous. Benjamin was a creditor, even if he was Lester's brother and never made demands. "It's always good to see you."

Ben grunted. "Good evening to *you*, brother," he shouted at Lester in an attitude of false good humor. "Any prospects?"

Lester raised his head and squinted at his brother. "I'm ruined," he said.

"And you've been ruined for more than ten years," said Ben. He turned to Herb and said, "You ought to sell tickets to see him. The Ruined Man. I'll bet you could do it, too. You've got a good tongue, Herb." He boxed the boy playfully on the ears.

"Stop it, Uncle Ben," said Herb. He twisted away. Ben held him with his large hands.

"All right, all right," he said. "That's why I'm here, though. I've got something for you, Herb, something to sell. Better than newspapers. Better than those rat pies."

"What is it?" asked Herb. He had acquired a skepticism much stronger than his mother's about the Piper enthusiasms. He recognized a tendency in himself toward dreaming and scheming, and he fought it back with skeptical questioning. Whenever one of his Piper relatives got a certain gleam in his eye, Herb got an uncomfortable feeling in his stomach, like hunger.

Millie came forward, put a hand on Herb's shoulder, and drew him to her. It was a protective gesture, and Ben recognized it. He chuckled.

"Now don't be frightened," he said. "It's nothing foolish, and you don't have to put any money in or anything like that. It's one of my lines. A guaranteed success. Such a success for me that I've got more than I can handle with it. I'm going to get you into it, Herb. Of course, I'll take a cut, but we can go through all of that later. Don't look so skeptical, Herb! It's a regular company, and they offer a straight commission arrangement. I'll even buy your samples for you."

"What is it?" asked Herb.

"Books," said Ben.

"Books?" asked Herb.

"Yep," said Ben. "Books. Professor Clapp's Five-Foot Shelf of Indispensable Information for Modern Times. It's a great sche—"

He saw the fear in Millie's eyes, and he raised his hands quickly, waving them in front of her as if to erase what he had said.

"It's a great arrangement," he corrected himself. "You go to a house, show the books, and you make the people want them, even though they can't afford to buy them and probably wouldn't get around to reading all of them if they did. Now here's the beauty of it. You pipe up with, 'Mr. Whoosis, I wonder if we might step outside for a smoke?' When you get Whoosis alone, you say, 'Please, Mr. Whoosis, let me spare you any embarrassment. The cost of the entire five-foot shelf of books is indeed quite high, as I'm sure you've guessed from the quality of the books themselves. Suppose I were to tell you that the first book can be yours, right now, for just five cents.' He can't believe it, of course. But it's true. You give him the first book for a nickel and get him to sign a paper saying he'll buy another book every month for fifty-nine cents a book until he's bought the whole five-foot shelf."

"Oh, Ben," said Millie disapprovingly.

"Now, Millie," said Ben, "what on earth is wrong with it? These people are getting a chance to enjoy some of the best books of our times. Why, just think how easily that fifty-nine cents would be wasted on useless things! No home should be without books."

"What books are they?" asked Herb.

"Oh, I don't know," said Ben. "Clapp buys them from the printers and booksellers; whatever they can't sell, they sell to him by the crate, cheap."

"Ben," said Millie, "you're a scoundrel."

He shrugged. "Come with me, Herb," he said. "I've got your books downstairs."

When Herb and Ben reached the street, Ben grabbed Herb's shirt and pulled him toward the cab of the delivery van he was driving, a Studebaker "20."

"Come here, Herb," he said. "I've got something to show you. Come here."

There was in Ben's voice the breathless quality that Herb recognized in the voices of his other Piper relatives when they had a scheme to sell. A cautious reluctance anchored Herb to the spot where he stood.

"Come on, Herb," said Ben. "I'm not going to get you into anything. You've got a lot of your mother's caution in you, Herb. That's probably good, but it certainly does make you a difficult person to talk to. Now *come here*." He tugged Herb to the door, opened it, and all but shoved Herb into the passenger's seat. Then he puffed his way to the driver's door and climbed in. From a pocket of his coat he took a small, round, white object. He held it up and turned it in the light of the streetlamp.

"What is this?" he asked Herb.

"A button," said Herb.

"Very good," said Ben. He chuckled. "But not quite correct. It's a shirt stud. Look at it more closely." He handed it to Herb.

Puzzled, wary, Herb was reluctant even to take the stud from his uncle Ben. He knew how many Pipers in the past had been undone by being smitten with a scheme at first glance.

"Take it!" said Uncle Ben. "Look at it!"

Herb obeyed. He was surprised by what he saw. The face of the stud was made of a fine grade of ivory. Carved into it, in high relief, was the figure of a woman, a naked woman, reclining against the disk that was the button part of the stud. She was toying with herself in a way that had brought a smile to her face and made Herb's heart pound and his palms sweat. Ben poked him in the ribs.

"Here," said Ben. He handed Herb a magnifying glass. "Look at the workmanship."

The glass revealed details that Herb had only imagined heretofore. Once, he had stood in a semicircle of boys in an alley and watched Elsie Campbell raise her skirt for a nickel an inch. He had contributed his share, but what he'd seen hadn't told him everything he wanted to know, and since the money he had spent on the elevation of Elsie's skirt had been money he should have brought home to his mother, the whole affair left him frustrated and ashamed. He left the alley thinking that he'd done a foolish Piper thing with the thirty cents he'd pitched into the pot. Here, on the instructive shirt stud his uncle Ben had handed him, was an education that, figuring at the rate Elsie had been paid, would have cost him more than he earned in a week.

"Gee, Uncle Ben," said Herb, "where'd you ever get a thing like this?"

"You like it, do you?" asked Ben.

"Well, sure," said Herb. He blushed. The thought had struck him that he ought to be embarrassed by what he was looking at.

"This is what you're going to sell," said Uncle Ben.

"What about the books?" asked Herb.

"The books are your answer," said Uncle Ben, chuckling again.

"Answer to what?" asked Herb.

"To the question, 'How'd you make all that money?'" said Ben.

"I can't sell these, Uncle Ben," Herb said, still examining the shirt stud through the magnifying glass. "What would Mother say if she found out? And who would I sell them to? They must be expensive, more expensive than what anyone I know could afford, and I can't very well sell them on the street."

Uncle Ben grasped the nape of Herb's neck in one large hand. "Tell me, Herb," he said, "what did your mother eat for dinner tonight? Rat pie? She can't *afford* rat pie. The only time she gets to eat that well is when you drop one on the street and have to bring it home."

"Please, Uncle Ben," said Herb.

"You listen to me, Herb. Your father is never going to get out of that chair. If you want to do something for your mother, you'll take this offer."

"But how can I find men to buy them?" asked Herb.

"Herb!" cried Ben. "Wake up! That's the other thing the books are for. The books are going to get you into situations where you can sell the jewelry. And you sell the jewelry the same way you sell the books! You get a fellow to buy one piece for nineteen cents and agree to take another piece every month on approval. You let the fellow have the piece for a week, with no charge. By the end of the week, he's gotten used to having it, he's won the admiration of his friends when he wears it at his lodge meeting or whatever, and he doesn't want to give it up. You collect for it. It's a thing of beauty, Herb."

"I don't know, Uncle Ben," said Herb.

"*I* know, Herb," said Ben. "This is your opportunity to do something for your mother—and for yourself, too. You can make something of yourself, Herb. And you can make your mother proud. She'll be proud of you because you've worked hard and you've been successful. She won't know how you did it; she'll think you did it by selling books. So will everyone else."

Herb drew a breath. It seemed worth a try. He did want to make his mother's life easier. If he was careful to keep his head, he ought to be able to get out before anything went wrong. "All right," said Herb. "I'll do it."

From the day that Herb sold his first piece of erotic jewelry, he had ambiguous feelings about the product he sold. On the one hand, he was proud of its quality, and he had reason to be, as Cecelia Pecksmith, chronicler of the American coarse-goods trade, notes early in her *Collector's Pricing Guide to Under-the-Counter Jewelry*:

> *Mass production never cheapened the quality of erotic and porno-graphic jewelry, because the market for these goods was never large enough to justify mass-producing them. Its craftsmanship was, for some buyers, sufficient justification for their buying it, and well-to-do collectors often professed to buy "coarse goods" only because they represented the last vestige of the kind of craftsmanship that had been commonplace when they were in their prime, the level of which, they were sure, succeeding generations were not likely to attain again, since each generation is inclined, in its late years, to see itself as having represented, in its prime, if not the end of civilization, the civilization's highest ascent, the pause before its accelerating downward slide.*

But if the jewelry was of good quality, it was also, for its time, obscene, and so Herb was at once proud of and ashamed of the studs, links, fobs, stickpins, buttons, and buckles he sold.

Herb never tried to sell the jewelry on the basis of its prurient attractions. To have done so would have been too risky; there was the possibility that the customer, offended by the thought that Herb took him for the sort of man who bought such things, would be aroused to anger or to the pretense of anger. Instead, Herb sold it on the basis of the quality of its workmanship. To give himself a means of introducing the topic of workmanship, he carried a cheap pocket watch that he never wound. When he had maneuvered the man of the house onto the porch for a smoke and had completed the book deal, he would take his pocket watch out, shake it, mutter under his breath, and then say aloud, "It should be a criminal offense to sell a shoddy piece of goods like this. A new watch, and it simply won't work. I tell you, it's becoming impossible to find really fine workmanship today. Don't you find that that's so?"

The man was likely to say, "True, true," or something of the sort.

"Now you take this shirt stud," Herb would say, handing one to the man. "Just look at the workmanship on that. It takes your breath away, doesn't it? Take a closer look. Here, use this glass."

Because Herb was one of the best salesmen the Piper family had ever produced, he simply couldn't keep himself from selling his cover. He sold Professor Clapp's Five-Foot Shelf of books with a degree of success that not even his uncle Ben had ever achieved. Nor could Herb resist putting his predilection for tinkering to the service of the goods he sold, and that was how the Piper nemesis, the misdirected enthusiasm, caught up with him. He invested considerable time and money in designing and manufacturing a shelf that expanded as his customers received their monthly books, eventually reaching a full five feet, but he lost money on each one he sold. He developed clever hideaway boxes and false bottoms for dresser drawers, which allowed his coarse-goods customers to keep their collections out of sight, but on these too he lost money.

Said May Castle of Herb's affection for tinkering:

> Herb loved to make things and fix things—oh, he'd make a stab at fixing anything that was broken, well, just anything! He was not always sucessful, mind you, but he'd give a try all the same. Garth couldn't fix a thing and didn't care to try—he could fix martinis, but that was about it. Garth would always manage to get Herb to try to fix something whenever he and Lorna came to visit. Well, this

wasn't difficult to do. I mean, all Garth had to do was say, "Herb, what do you think is the matter with the doohickey that makes this mixer go?" and right away Herb would have the mixer apart and spread out all over the kitchen table. And then he always wanted to make some new gadget or improvement. It wasn't enough for him to try to fix something; he always had an idea for something new. He concocted some twisted-wire thingamabob so that Garth could use the mixer to mix paint, I think. Well, that's about the last thing Garth had any use for, something to mix paint. Now something that would shake up a cocktail, well, maybe, but paint!

The selling went much as Ben had predicted. The system of selling a large set of items one item at a time was a stroke of genius. The customer found it easy to agree to purchase the first book or shirt stud; not much money was involved, after all. However, in agreeing to purchase the first, the customer had struck a bargain—not only with Herb, but with himself—to continue, to fill out the five-foot shelf, to complete the set of links and studs. Most customers did. Some of the customers for Professor Clapp's Five-Foot Shelf of books continued to buy beyond five feet, and a few became serious bibliophiles. Some of Herb's link-and-stud customers went on to buy fobs, stickpins, and belt buckles, and a few became serious collectors of erotica.

Herb was soon successful enough to be able to tell his mother to stop working, and he even managed to move the family to a new and larger apartment, on the ground floor, with a large, sunny, pleasant front room where his father, who slumped lower in his cork chair with each of Herb's successes, sat in the only dark corner. Despite Herb's losses on the expandable shelves and the jewelry caches, the Lester Pipers ate well, were well supplied with books, and were able to afford a few luxuries: a meal in a restaurant now and then, excursions to seaside amusement parks, evenings at a moving-picture house, and even an automobile.

Among the books that Herb sold was *The Automobile: Its Selection, Care, and Use.* Herb read and reread this guide, and he cast a critical eye about for a car that would suit the needs of his expanding business, since it was now necessary for him to call on a lengthening list of established customers and to continue to find new ones. He also wanted a car that he could use for pleasure, one that he could use to take the family on outings, with his parents seated in the back, his mother savoring the sun and fresh air, his father slumped morosely by her side. He also wanted a car that he would look good in, something with a little dash, something that suited a young man who already enjoyed a modest success and had every hope of enjoying more in the future. He couldn't afford a car that would do all of that, so he settled for a used Studebaker four-cylinder Model SA Touring Car.

5

In Which Herb 'n' Lorna Meet but Are Separated by War

Their meeting almost didn't occur, because Herb met Tessie Norris first. He met her at a gas station. He was stopped at a pump, leafing through his appointment book while he was having his tank filled and his oil and water and tires checked. An antiquated touring car pulled up on the opposite side of the pumps, its arrival heralded by a flourish of rattles, pings, and wheezes that made Herb look up from his book. In the passenger's seat, he saw Tessie. She looked like a pastel portrait. That she was picking distractedly at the hem of her dress Herb couldn't see; that her eyes darted about like those of a frightened bird he didn't notice; that she was biting her lower lip he overlooked. He was smitten by her pale, perfect face.

Herb had had little experience with girls or women. In school he'd had his share of crushes but little opportunity to do much about them. Now, sitting in his own car, with some money in his pocket, wearing a new suit, he not only noticed but felt in a position to act.

He got out of his car and walked around the pumps. He seemed to be on his way inside the station, perhaps to inspect the inner tubes displayed in the tiny office, but then a sudden determination seemed to come over him. He looked at the car and at its driver, and he seemed to waver in his course. The driver had by now noticed Herb, and Herb grinned sheepishly, shrugged his shoulders, and stepped briskly to the driver's side of the car.

"Excuse me," he said. "I've noticed that your machine is—well, heck, it needs some repair, doesn't it? I hope you won't mind my giving you some advice that may save you considerable frustration and unnecessary expense."

"Huh?" said the driver.

"Hello," said Herb, leaning to his left so that he could see past the large driver to the young woman beside him. He touched the brim of his hat.

"You selling something?" asked the driver.

Herb chuckled. "As a matter of fact, I am," he said, "but that isn't my reason for stopping to talk with you. I wanted to tell you that my machine, when I bought it, was, well—"

"As bad as this?" asked the driver.

"Yes," said Herb, grinning. "I'm glad you said it. Would you like to know something? I made all the repairs myself." He leaned toward the man and spoke in a low voice. "Who's willing to pay what a professional mechanic asks today? I know I'm not. Even if I were, you and I both know that workmanship today is not what it once was." Involuntarily, Herb reached for his pocket watch. He stopped himself.

"You're a mechanic?" asked the driver.

"No, no," said Herb. "I learned everything I know about the automobile from a book! A remarkable book by a fellow named Robert Sloss. I keep it in my machine all the time now. I'd be quite willing to lend you a copy, and I'm sure that by following Mr. Sloss's advice you could achieve remarkable results. Why, one chapter alone—I'm thinking of the chapter called 'How to Find the Motor Trouble'—would make the book worth its price."

The man at the wheel of the car was Arthur Norris. Herb lent him a copy of *The Automobile: Its Selection, Care, and Use* and got his name and address, insisting that it was no trouble at all for him to stop by in a week or two to pick the book up. Herb drove away, humming, planning that in a week he would drop by, during the day, in the hope that Arthur Norris would not be at home, but that the young woman, whom he supposed to be Arthur Norris's daughter, would be.

She was not Norris's daughter. She was his wife. She was distracted, nervous, and unhappy. Marriage had been a terrible disappointment to her, a disappointment that had metastasized and now affected every aspect of her life. She wandered through her days picking at her clothes, biting her lips, mumbling to herself, discovering new disappointments. All days seemed gray, all music seemed monotonous, all birds resembled pigeons, all food tasted like lima beans. Had Herb ever gone to the Norrises' house, as he had planned, Tessie would have grabbed him, clung to him, would have poured out everything to him in the incoherent volubility of the disappointed, the drunken, the mad. Herb wouldn't have been able to take his eyes off her. Arthur might have returned while Herb was still there, and he might well have been pleased to have found Herb there, since Arthur couldn't have been getting much more fun out of married life than Tessie was. Herb wouldn't have been able to prevent himself from selling books to Arthur even if he tried. Arthur would have signed up for Professor Clapp's entire five-foot shelf. He might even have bought one of Herb's five-foot shelves.

In the months that followed, Herb might have become a frequent visitor at the Norrises'. Arthur would have liked Herb, and he would have liked the effect Herb had on Tessie. Arthur would have been quite willing to have them spend time alone together because Herb's lively, hopeful manner would have brought the light back to her eyes, and in a clumsy, uncertain way, Arthur would have tried to push them into becoming lovers, thinking that perhaps Tessie might then bring to lovemaking with him at least an echo, some tremor or ripple, of whatever pleasure she took from Herb. Had Herb become Tessie's lover, his sense of honor, of loyalty, of shame, would certainly have pushed him closer and closer to the Norrises, and the trio would have wrapped itself more and more tightly, snugly, closer and closer in its own misery and desperation as time passed. Herb would never have extricated himself, he would never have gone to Chacallit, he would never have met Lorna.

Luckily, Herb was drafted.

When he got the news, he ran to his uncle Ben's and burst into the apartment shouting, "Uncle Ben, I've been drafted!"

"Oh, Herb!" cried his aunt Louise. "Oh, your poor mother."

"I know," said Herb. "That's what I'm worried about. But I've got it all worked out, Uncle Ben."

Ben put his fork down and looked at Herb thoughtfully. He assumed that Herb was going to try to get him to support Lester and Millie while he was in the army, or even—God forbid—try to make him agree to support them forever if Herb were killed. "Now, Herb," said Ben, "you know I'd like to be in a position to take on the burden of seeing that your mother and father are cared for—"

Herb laughed. "Relax, Uncle Ben," he said. "I'm not going to ask you to support them. Go back to eating. I've got a plan that will enable me to keep right on selling."

"Oh?" said Ben, brightening.

"That's right," said Herb. "Listen. I'm going to be in a camp with a thousand, ten thousand, I-don't-know-how-many thousand men. What better place for me to sell—"

He stopped himself, glanced at his aunt and at his young cousins. They were more attentive than ever before, the new imminence of death or dismemberment lending to Herb's words a gravity and fascination they'd never had before.

"Sell books," said Herb.

"Books?" asked Ben. He wore a look of surprise and incredulity.

"That's right!" said Herb. "Those men are going to be lonely. Isn't that right, Uncle Ben?"

"Oh, yes," said Ben. "I'm certain they *will* be lonely. Frightened, too, I guess. Lonely *and* frightened. Mostly frightened."

"I see what Herb's getting at," said Louise. "All those lonely, frightened men. What would they want most?"

"Um, that's exactly right," said Herb. He turned toward Ben and risked a wink. "What is it that a man turns to to alleviate his loneliness and fear? What fire drives away the chill of fear and lights even the darkest and loneliest corners?"

"Literature!" shouted Ben. "By God, you're right, Herb! It's a brilliant stroke."

"Well, uh, yes, I'm glad you think so, Uncle Ben," said Herb. He looked at his aunt and his cousins. Their eyes had filled with tears inspired by Herb's selflessness, his thinking of the fear and loneliness of his fellow doughboys, even as he must have anticipated his own loneliness, his own fear.

"I don't see how we can miss," said Ben. He threw his arm across

Herb's shoulders and drew him close. "I don't want you telling anyone else about this, Herb," he said. "We can do this all on our own. Who needs Professor Clapp? Besides, we're going to want to pick our books especially for the young man in the trenches or on his way to the trenches, the young man about to look death in the teeth. Oh, sorry, Herb. You know what I mean. Those doughboys aren't going to want to waste their time on *Practical Poultry Keeping*. They're going to want stuff like, well, the *Aeneid* and *Julius Caesar* and *Gulliver's Travels*. Twelve books, twelve great books. The Doughboy's Dozen. We'll sell subscriptions to the folks at home and ship the books to their boys on the front lines. The same one-book-every-month idea!"

Later, when they managed to speak alone, Ben said, "I know what you really have in mind, but I'm not sure we can ship coarse goods to France. I think the army checks packages and letters. The goods would never reach the boys."

"I know, Uncle Ben," said Herb. "That's why I've got to take a supply with me, a large supply. I'm sure I can sell everything I can take, but I imagine that I'll be moving around a lot, so I probably won't be able to take much. I don't know how much I can afford to buy all at once, though. I'll bet I could get a better price if I could get some pieces without buying through the Professor Clapp people. Can I go right to the people who make the goods?"

"Of course you can!" said Ben. "They're in New York somewhere, not too far from Albany, I think. What's it called, now? Chack—? Check—? Chacallit. That's it. I'll go with you! It should be quite an adventure."

The trip to Chacallit *was* an adventure. Any motor trip of that time that went much beyond the streets of a fair-sized town was something of an adventure, one that was likely to include among its highlights plenty of dust and mud, flat tires, running out of gas, leaving the road to avoid surprise obstacles, discovering roads not indicated on any map, and failing to find roads clearly indicated on every map. Herb and Ben's trip included all of these, but it also included long stretches of pleasant rural scenery and some dazzling early-autumn days. They spent nights in farmhouses, in barns, and in fields, and when they reached Chacallit at last, muddy and tired, Ben was prepared to spring for the cost of a room in a hotel.

They took a room at the Chacallit House, Chacallit's only hotel, more a rooming house, really, which stood right on River Road, not far from the building in which Lorna worked. The dining room of the Chacallit House was one of those spots that Henrietta Drechsler, director of the Society for the Preservation of Small-Town Values, had in mind when she wrote:

> There is, in every small town, one place, most often a coffee shop, sometimes a bar, where the movers and shakers gather, where the town officials, businessmen, and shopkeepers eat breakfast or lunch and exchange bits of gossip, rumor, speculation, innuendo, ideas, and hunches. It would be an exaggeration to claim that the town is actually run from this spot—let's call it the luncheonette—but it is certainly true that many a policy has its origin there, that many careers begin and end there, and that the luncheonette is the forum within which new arrivals, people and ideas alike, are subjected to a terrifying, inquisitorial scrutiny, usually in absentia.

Ben knew, from the ripple of attention that he and Herb occasioned when they passed the entrance to the dining room on their way to the desk, that the Chacallit House dining room was such a place. After he and Herb had registered, settled in their room, bathed, and changed, he said to Herb, "Now I don't know who exactly we should see about buying coarse goods, so I want to let him find us."

"How are you going to do that?" asked Herb.

"Well," said Ben, "I'm going to start by spending a considerable amount of time drinking coffee and eating sandwiches in the dining room downstairs. That's the place to get to know people in this town."

"How do you know that?" asked Herb.

"Oh," said Ben, "I can tell by the look of those fellows who were sitting there when we came in. Those are the fellows whose pants have shiny seats. They do most of their day's work right there in that dining room, keeping track of what's what and making sure that what's what is what they *want* to be what. Do you follow me?"

"Well—" said Herb.

"You can bet," said Ben without offering any further explanation, "that they spent a half hour or so engaged in speculation about us after we came in, and you can bet that by now they know from the register where we're from, and you can also bet that the dining room will be quite full this noon in the expectation that we'll take our lunch there."

"And will we?" asked Herb.

"I will," said Ben. "I think it might be best if I handled this part of the business myself. You're, well, you're a little young, Herb." He grabbed Herb by the scruff of the neck and shook him as he used to when Herb was a boy. "I'm a little better acquainted with the ways of the world than you are, for one thing, and for another a lot of men in business don't think of a young fellow as being, well, ready."

"Ready for what?" asked Herb.

"Well, ready to do business," said Ben.

Herb shrugged. "All right," he said. "What do you want me to do?"

"I want you to set out to sell books," said Ben. "It will keep you busy, keep you out of the way, and show that we've got a good cover for selling coarse goods. You'll probably make some money for the trip home, too."

While Ben spent time in the Chacallit House dining room, drinking coffee, eating stew and sausages and potato salad, and chewing the fat, Herb sold Professor Clapp's Five-Foot Shelf from door to door. It took Ben a day to establish himself as a pleasant fellow traveling with his nephew to teach the boy the book business, to help him find his feet. In the afternoon of the second day, a Chacallitan, Axel Schweib, shot his cuffs during a conversation with Ben, as if gesticulating to emphasize a point, displayed in so doing a really remarkable pair of erotic links, and then went on to deliver a pitch for Ben's taking erotic links and studs on as a sure-to-be-profitable sideline. Ben expressed interest, with reservations. A meeting was arranged with Luther Huber for the next day.

In the meantime, Herb had found Chacallit fertile ground for book sales. So successful had he been that he kept selling nonstop, knowing that everything he made would buy more coarse goods. On the second evening, he worked right through dinner, stopping at houses along the road that wound upward from the town. Rain began to fall. He thought of quitting for the day, but he was doing so well that he said to himself, "I'll make one more stop, at that house just ahead, the one with its windows glowing."

It was the narrow house on Ackerman Hill, where Lorna sat in the parlor with her parents.

The moment when Lorna opened the door was not one of those moments in which her elusive beauty shone, so Herb wasn't dumfounded at the sight of her. He didn't stand there on the porch transfixed, with his hand to his hat, his mouth hanging open. It wasn't love at first sight. When Lorna opened the door, Herb saw a young woman with a nice-enough figure, a pleasant smile, and dark hair. She looked to him like a good prospect for books. Lorna saw a neat young man with a salesman's case. He looked to her like a good prospect for a little diversion on a rainy night.

"Good evening," Herb said. He removed his hat and smiled.

Lorna put on a look of exaggerated surprise. "You must be fond of rain," she said, "if you think this is a good evening." She returned his smile. She was looking forward to watching this neat young man try to persuade her father to buy whatever he was selling.

"I guess you're right," said Herb. "Not only rain, but wind and cold, too." He chuckled. He liked her. He liked the pert and sassy way she spoke to him. He put his hat back on, stood again as he'd been standing when she opened the door, took his hat off again as he'd taken it off before, gave a shiver, and said, frowning, "Nasty evening."

"What are you selling?" Lorna asked. She leaned against the door frame, and that's when it happened: her beauty shone, and it intoxicated Herb, befuddled and delighted him.

"What are you selling?" Lorna asked again.

Flabbergasted, Herb looked at his case. It was on the porch, at his feet. He remembered that he *was* selling something, and that he had samples of it in that case, but he couldn't for the life of him remember what it was.

"I—you—you're," he said, and stopped. He couldn't make himself say, "You're beautiful," and he felt foolish for having begun.

"Yes?" asked Lorna. She knew what had happened. She had seen it happen before. She always enjoyed it. She was enjoying this young man, too. She liked the way he looked. She suspected that he was as straightforward and friendly as he appeared, that he wasn't just putting on a salesman's front. She also liked the way she could rattle him with a quick question.

Herb stooped to open the case at his feet and find out what he was selling. With the act of stooping, when he was bent over, with his eyes off Lorna, his memory returned. He took a deep breath, got a grip on himself. He grasped the handle of the case, straightened up, and, to his surprise, laughed at himself for having been so rattled. He said, smiling broadly: "Books." He risked looking at Lorna again. He was surprised, puzzled, disappointed, and—so unsettling had the experience been—a little relieved to find that the befuddling beauty he'd seen before had disappeared. Had he fooled himself into thinking he'd seen it? Had it been only a trick of the gray light, a soft shadow that fell on her face in a certain way that would never be duplicated?

"Do you have *Ben-Hur?*" asked Lorna. She'd been wanting to read *Ben-Hur* for some time. One of the girls at the mill had promised to trade her copy for Lorna's copy of *The Life Everlasting*, but the girl was an extraordinarily slow reader, and Lorna had begun to despair of her ever finishing the book.

"Well, no," said Herb. "I don't think I do have that one."

"I saw the moving picture," said Lorna. "Did you?"

"No," said Herb. "I—"

"Lorna," my great-grandfather Huber called from the living room, "who is that you're talking to?"

Lorna leaned toward Herb, put her hand on his arm, and dropped her voice. "What's your name?" she asked. She was inviting him to join her in a conspiracy, a conspiracy of the young, of children against parents. Herb would have told her his name at once, but he saw again the beauty that he'd seen a moment earlier, and again he was befuddled by it.

Lorna poked him. "What does your mother say when she wants you to come to dinner?" she asked.

"She says, 'Supper's ready, Herb.'"

"That's nice," said Lorna. She smiled. "'Supper's ready, Herb.' You know what?"

"What?" asked Herb.

"I'll bet your name is Herb," said Lorna.

"Yes," said Herb. "Herb. Herb Piper."

"It's Herb Piper, Father," called Lorna. She spoke as if Herb Piper were someone her father had known for years, perhaps a boy she had gone to school with, and so convincing was her tone that Richard Huber reacted as if Herb Piper's being there were an expected occurrence.

"Well, tell him to come in, then," he called. "And close that door. The damp air is getting into the house."

"Goodness!" said Lorna. She looked this way and that in mock terror. "Hurry inside, Herb Piper," she said, "before the damn bear gets you." She took Herb's hand and tugged at him. "And try to calm yourself," she added in a whisper. "You're going to do a fine job. You mustn't let yourself be so nervous. Is this your first try at selling books?"

"No," said Herb, a little offended. "It certainly is not."

Lorna gave him a doubtful look. "It's no disgrace," she said. "You have to start somewhere." She liked his nervousness, and she liked his face, his open, no-tricks-up-my-sleeve face.

"I'm not pretending," said Herb. He couldn't help chuckling when he said it. "I really *am* experienced, and in fact I'm very good at selling books." Lorna liked this too, this pride in his ability. She also liked the way that, for all his apparent seriousness, he seemed always to be laughing, chuckling, grinning. She couldn't have known that he wasn't ordinarily much of a laugher, chuckler, or grinner, that it was she who made him feel like chuckling.

Lorna took his hat and umbrella from him. "I can't wait to see you sell some books to my father," she said. She turned and led the way into the parlor.

When my great-grandfather Richard looked up from his newspaper, he was surprised to find that Herb Piper was someone he didn't know. My great-grandmother Lena wasn't at all certain whether she knew the boy or not. Lorna had seemed to know him when she'd called out his name, and her manner now suggested that he was someone Lena ought to remember, but she simply couldn't place him. Richard glanced at Lena to see whether he could find on her face any hint of their connection with the Pipers. He saw there a pleasant smile. It was that thin smile we all employ when we attempt to hide our ignorance, but either Lena was too accomplished at employing that smile or the light in the Huber parlor was too dim for Richard to see it for what it was. To him, the smile on Lena's face looked like evidence of recognition, and the idea began to form in his mind that Herb Piper was the son of a fellow named Henry, called Hank, a terrible drinker, notorious for it, who had fallen face-down in a pool at the Whatsit's edge one moonless night about four years ago and drowned in three inches of water. "A terrible thing, terrible," Richard reflected. He recalled that it had happened during a drought, making it one of the bitter ironies of life.

The sight of Herb, neatly dressed and apparently prosperous, gladdened Richard's heart but at the same time made him feel that he might have done, really *ought* to have done, more for Hank's widow, and for poor Herb too, for that matter. He was glad to see Herb looking so hale, but he would be gladder still when the boy was gone. Given the pathetic circumstances, Richard thought it appropriate to stand, and he did.

"How's your mother, young fellow?" he asked, taking Herb's hand in a firm grip, grabbing Herb's elbow with his other hand, composing his features in a look of grave concern.

"She's fine, sir," said Herb, smiling, humoring this stocky burgher, who, through this sudden question, impressed him as certainly mad and possibly dangerous.

"Wonderful!" exclaimed Lena, delighted to find that Richard, at least, not only recognized this Herb Piper but knew enough about the boy to ask after his mother. Then, in the manner of many a person who, relieved to find that his ignorance has apparently gone undetected, throws to the winds his former caution, his wise reticence, and boldly, recklessly, with a certain jaunty sangfroid, puts his foot straight into his mouth, she added: "I'm so *glad* to hear that. We were concerned, weren't we, Richard?"

Richard, his notion of the boy's past now apparently confirmed by Lena, nodded gravely, guiltily, and looked at his shoes. "Yes," he muttered. "I'm sorry we haven't seen you before this, Herb. The door was always open, you know. Still," he said, brightening, "I'm glad you've come to see us now, and I'm pleased to see you looking so well. You seem to be making quite a success of yourself." He pounded Herb on the shoulder. Herb stood his ground, and he maintained the smile on his face, since he had learned from his years of street-corner rat-pie selling that a calm manner and ready agreement worked best with lunatics.

"Yes, sir," he said, still smiling. "Thank you, sir."

"Herb's selling books now," said Lorna, taking a spot at the end of the sofa. Her eyes twinkled. This was going to be even more fun than she'd imagined. "He'd like to sell *you* some books, Father."

"Oh?" said Richard Huber. "Books?" He was entirely ready to buy a book or two at once, to salve his conscience, and then to send Herb on his way. "We could use some books, couldn't we, Lena?"

"Why, I'm sure we could," said Lena, eager to surrender any further dealings with the mystifying Herb Piper to her husband, now that she'd established incontrovertibly the strength and vividness of her recollection of Herb and Herb's mother, even after what she supposed had been so long a lapse of time.

"What books have you got, Herb?" asked Richard.

"He hasn't got *Ben-Hur*," said Lorna. "I've already asked him about that."

"No, I'm afraid I don't have *Ben-Hur*," said Herb. "The books I'm offering are more of the useful than the entertaining kind." He bent to his sample case.

"Now there's a distinction I've never understood," said Lorna.

"Quiet, now, Lorna," said Richard. He was embarrassed for Herb, having to go into the homes of people who had known his father, to trade on their sympathy as a way of inducing them to buy his books. He considered it little more than a way of putting a respectable front on asking for charity. However, he wasn't offended by Herb's exploiting his acquaintances in this way—in fact, he was impressed by the resourcefulness the idea showed—but he was sorry that poor Herb had been brought to it. "Let Herb show us what he's got," he said, "and don't you interrupt him, Lorna."

"What I have, sir," said Herb, "is something no home should be without." He gave everyone his smile, and when he turned to Lorna he allowed himself to add a wink. "The books that I'm about to offer for your consideration have been chosen by Professor Alonzo Clapp, late of Harvard College, as books that are essential to the health, wealth, and savoir-faire of today's man, woman, or child. This," he said, flinging open the clever case he had designed and built, "is Professor Clapp's Five-Foot Shelf of Indispensable Information for Modern Times."

An hour later, Great-Grandfather Huber had not only subscribed to Professor Clapp's entire five-foot shelf of books and bought one of

Herb's expandable five-foot shelves, but he had also written a letter of introduction for Herb and given him the names of half a dozen friends and business associates whom he considered likely prospects.

When Lorna and Herb were standing alone at the door again, Lorna said, "Well, Herb Piper, you really can sell books."

Herb laughed. "Thanks," he said. "I didn't need your help, you know."

"Oh, I'm sure of that," said Lorna. She raised her eyebrows.

"I *didn't*," insisted Herb. He laughed again. "It didn't hurt, though. Who do you suppose your mother and father thought I was?"

Lorna couldn't keep from giggling. "I haven't any idea," she said. "They were sure they *ought* to know you, and so I suppose they made themselves remember you."

"They seemed sorry for me," said Herb. "I—I think I took advantage of them."

"Oh, no," said Lorna. "You didn't. You just—let them think what they wanted to think. You were really only being polite. They would have been terribly embarrassed if you had told them that they were wrong about you."

"You don't think there's a chance that they really *do* know me, do you?" asked Herb. The thought had occurred to him that they might have been investors in his father's cork furniture business.

"No," said Lorna. She pursed her lips. She shook her head. "They couldn't, not unless you had lived in Chacallit. My mother and father have been here forever."

"Well, thanks for giving them the impression that they ought to know me," said Herb. He grinned, and he offered her his hand to shake. She shook it. She stepped onto the porch and closed the door behind her.

"It's stopped raining," she said. She walked to the railing, leaned on it, and looked up at the sky, where a bit of moon lit the thinning clouds from behind.

"Yes," said Herb. "It has." He put his hat on, stood straight, and said, "Good evening."

"You're quite right," said Lorna.

"May I call you Lorna?" asked Herb.

Lorna was surprised to find that the thought that he was going to leave in a minute or two made her feel colder suddenly, as if a breeze had come up, though the air was still. Something told her to hide the feeling from Herb. That something, that damned something, was the sense of personal dignity that is one of our most civilized attributes, the source of many of our discontents, the cause of so many missed opportunities. I make that judgment nearly seventy years after the fact, but I have support for it from May Castle:

> Oh, you know it's just the damndest thing, isn't it, the way we hold ourselves back! Of course, in the long run it's probably for the best that we do, or we'd be throwing ourselves at half the people we meet and throwing stones at the others. But how many times have I said to myself, "Oh, damn! Why didn't I let myself go and try dancing the tango?" Well, that may not be the best example—I always do try dancing the tango whenever the opportunity presents itself, and I've gotten quite good at it over the years—which is just my point, isn't it? But I've never gone into one of those saunas, you see. There I've held myself back, because I've thought I'd look foolish. Well, that's just the way Lorna felt, I'm sure.

It's a negative desire: not to lose one's dignity, not to look foolish. It may be love's worst enemy. It made Lorna let Herb leave for the war without giving herself a chance to fall in love with him. She didn't want to look foolish, to look like an infatuated girl, so she continued to behave as if she were only playing with Herb. She said, "You can call me Cinderella if you like—that's what my sisters call me."

"Hmm," said Herb. "Cinderella." He was disappointed. He liked Lorna, and he knew that he was going to see her face when he closed his eyes that night, and perhaps for many nights to come. He knew that for days he was going to be concocting, too late, clever answers to her questions, parries for her taunts. He had had, when she stepped onto the porch with him, the crazy idea that he might ask her to write to him while he was away, and that she just might agree to do so. It seemed to him now that she had only been playing with him, that there was nothing underlying her playfulness but the boredom of a rainy evening. He put his hat on. "Good night, Cinderella," he said.

"I'll see you in a month, I suppose," said Lorna. "I'm sure I can't wait for you to bring us our copy of *One Hundred Lessons in Business*."

"You won't see *me*," said Herb. He was a little annoyed now, and he let it show. "I don't live around here. Besides, I've been called up for service."

"Oh," said Lorna, surprised at how much this news startled her.

"I'll have to find someone here in Chacallit who can deliver the books for me."

"Oh," said Lorna. She couldn't think of anything to add.

"I'd better be on my way," said Herb in a tentative way, without moving any closer to the steps. "My uncle Ben must be wondering what I've been up to all this time."

"Well, I'm sure he'll be pleased when he learns what a fine job you did selling books to the Hubers," said Lorna. The pert tone was back in her voice, but she had the sickening feeling that Herb and his uncle might laugh at her parents, laugh at her, too.

"Good-bye, Cinderella," said Herb. He turned and walked down the steps, down the walk, to his car. He got in, started it, and drove away. Lorna felt the chill, but she hugged herself and watched from the porch until the taillights disappeared.

"A shame about that boy," said Lena when Lorna returned to the living room. Lorna stood with her back to the fire, but the chill she felt came from within her.

"Yes," she said abstractedly.

"He's got gumption, that boy," said Richard. "He's going to go places, I'd say. He's a pusher, you can see that. Doesn't sit around feeling sorry for himself. Runs right at a thing. Probably a real scrapper when he was little. He'll be a scrapper in business, too. He's going to go places."

"He's going to France," said Lorna.

"France?" asked her mother.

"He's been drafted," said Lorna, still abstracted, still attending to her own thoughts.

"Oh," said Richard. "Well, good for him, and I wish him luck." He raised his paper in front of his face.

"He'll probably do just as well in the war as in business, don't you think, Richard?" asked Lena, partly just to say something, to contribute her share to the conversation, and partly because, still grateful to her husband for steering them through their interview with Herb Piper, she wanted to show him that she was paying careful attention to everything he said.

"Hmm," said Richard. "Not necessarily. He may be a little *too* plucky, if you know what I mean, a little too eager. That kind is apt to get himself killed."

Lorna brought her hand to her face, tried to speak, but found that only a strangled cry came from her. She looked at her father in terror. She ran from the room and up the stairs to her bed, which she found so cold that she shivered under her quilt. The clouds had dispersed, and moonlight fell across Lorna's bed. She lay awake, thinking of Herb—mostly of that smile of his, that honest smile. She smiled herself when she recalled his surprise when he'd seen her in the right light, the way he'd paused in folding his umbrella, the way he'd held his hat, the way he'd lost his tongue. She was also thinking of herself, mostly of things she might have said, might have done.

I could have stayed out on the porch with him, talking. Just talking about this and that. The moon even came out from behind the clouds. The perfect setting. Why didn't I? Why didn't I?

"Where are you from, Herb? Albany, I'll bet. How did you ever find your way to Chacallit? Are you afraid to go to the war?"

No, no. That wouldn't be the thing to ask. He might be killed. He's got gumption, and that can be dangerous in a war. I could have touched his hand, could have made him promise to write to me, to come back to me. That's a ridiculous idea. When he comes home from France, he won't be coming to Chacallit. He might not come home at all. He might be killed.

Father liked him, even if he had no idea who he was. "He's got gumption." He liked me, liked me even when I was teasing him, liked me even when I told him to call me Cinderella. Cinderella. Damn. I might as well have told him to go away and leave me alone. Well, he has. I wish something would bring him back.

"Do you like selling books?"

That would have been better than nothing.

"You must have stories to tell about traveling, don't you, Herb? I'll bet you have stories you wouldn't want to tell me."

Teasing again. He probably does *have stories he wouldn't want to tell. There may be girls lying awake from here to Albany or wherever he came from. All of us lying awake, with the moonlight falling across our beds, thinking of things we might have said to keep Herb from going on to the next girl. Are the others thinking that, that there are others, that we're all thinking the same things? Maybe not. Maybe there are no others. Maybe I'm the only one who's made him feel awkward; maybe I'm the only one he's wanted to talk to. But maybe not. Maybe I'm different. Maybe each of us thinks she's different, that she's the only one he's really noticed, that he'll be back. Maybe each of us is wishing that something will bring him back.*

Herb stood at a window in the Chacallit House, smoking, looking at the moon, thinking of Lorna, trying to remember everything she had said and done, every move she'd made, the way she'd looked in every slant of light, especially the way she'd looked when she'd made him lose track of what he'd meant to say.

How does she do that? It's some trick she has with the way she turns her head or the way she tilts her chin. Something. I don't know. And quick-witted? You've got to hand it to her. That business with her parents. She had her mother and father thinking I was somebody else. What did she say? "They were sure they should know you, so they decided they did know you." Something like that. I'm not sure how she did it. Maybe they had been expecting someone else, but I don't think so. It was the way she conducted herself, as if they ought to know who I was, and she confused them. She does that to many people, I imagine. She must have the fellows in Chacallit following her in a line. How many, I wonder? Too many for her to bother with me, I guess. Why not me, though? There's nothing wrong with me. Mr. Huber liked me; I'm sure of that. He seemed sorry for me somehow. He made me wonder whether my coat was torn or something. Still, I could tell he liked me. The mother, too. Why shouldn't she, then? I've got good prospects. I probably make more money than most fellows my age in this town. Oh, don't be foolish. She doesn't know anything about me. I can call her Cinderella. Cinderella. Why did I let her get away with that? Aaaah, because it wasn't worth pursuing. I'll be gone tomorrow, and there isn't much chance that I'll ever be back. Good God, I didn't mean that. I'll be back. Knock on wood. You look out for yourself, you keep your eyes open, and you do just what you have to do, chances are good you'll get through all right. I might get killed. I might get hurt, lose something, lose a leg, a hand, fingers. Suppose I do get killed. Suppose I do? I might. Here I am about to get killed, and I don't have the courage to go back and talk to her, ask her to write to me. I will go back, first thing in the morning.

The next morning, Herb left Ben at a table in the Chacallit House dining room, bent over eggs and sausage and kartoffelpuffers, the potato pancakes that would forever be Ben's second-fondest memory of Chacallit. His fondest would be the deal he had made with Luther

Huber for dozens of pieces of coarse goods, a deal of that satisfying kind in which each party feels that he's getting the better of the other. Ben was pleased because he'd been able to get a price spectacularly lower than what he'd been paying to the Clapp people. Luther was pleased because Ben had paid a good bit more than Clapp paid. Both men looked forward to doing more business together in the future.

While Ben ate, Herb drove up the steep and winding road to the Hubers'. Lorna heard a car stop in front of the house, but she was rushing to leave for work and didn't give it much thought. Herb bounded from the car, strode up the walk, mounted the steps, and stopped in front of the door, uncertain whether to turn the knurled knob to ring the bell or not. He had no idea what he'd say when the door opened. Ever since he had decided, in the moonlight, to return to the Hubers', he'd assumed that inspiration would come to him at the last moment, that as soon as he had to speak, he would know what to say. He'd slept well, eaten heartily, and driven the winding road with a song in his heart, all because he expected inspiration to come to him. Now he found himself at the door, still uninspired; he felt a damp chill in his chest and a dryness in his mouth.

For Lorna's part, once she had decided, in the moonlight, that Herb would never return, the things that she would say to him if only he *would* return had come to her easily. In the morning, she stayed in bed longer than she should have, and then she had to rush to leave for the mill in time. She bounded down the stairs, dashed into the kitchen, drank the milk her mother had poured for her, and started for the door, licking her upper lip.

Well, here it comes at last, the moment that would have occurred the night before, had everything gone as these things ought to go. Lorna opened the door and found Herb staring into her face. Her beauty flared and transfixed Herb, with his hand to his hat, his mouth hanging open.

"Good morning, Herb Piper," she said without a moment's hesitation. "Did you find anybody to deliver those books for you while you're in France?" She had said exactly the right thing, and she knew it. She beamed.

Herb was astonished, ecstatic, euphoric, drunk on love, and he was, all at once, inspired. He beamed right back. "No," he said. "I didn't. In fact, I came here this morning hoping that I might persuade *you* to take the work on."

"I'll do it," said Lorna. "I don't care about the terms. I think it's important for you to know that your business in Chacallit is being looked after while you're in the—in the trenches." Her voice threatened to fail her, but she swallowed hard and went on. "You can't afford to be distracted by business worries at a time like that," she said, pressing right on with the argument she had prepared without reading in Herb's expression the fact that none of it was necessary.

"You're right," he said, speaking straight from the center of his thoughts, without any face-saving deviation. "I could get killed if I'm not careful, but they say if you look out for yourself, if you keep your eyes open, chances are good you'll get through all right."

They didn't speak for a moment, just looked at each other across the possibility of death.

"I have to go to work," Lorna said at last. She frowned.

"Let me drive you," said Herb. "I've got my own car."

"I *see* you do," said Lorna. She walked beside him to the car, and he opened the door for her, and when, to steady herself, she reached for the edge of the door that he held open, her hand touched his.

"Of course, I'll write to you often," she said, "to keep you informed about the progress of—things."

"Oh, yes," said Herb. "I hope so. Once a week, at least."

"At least," she agreed. "There are so many things for us to discuss," she said suddenly, noting with alarm how quickly they were approaching River Road. "I wonder if you could come by this evening to explain it all to me. You might come for dinner—if you like."

"I'd like to," said Herb, "but my uncle Ben and I have to get back to Boston, and we were going to leave right after breakfast."

"Boston?" Lorna asked. "Is that where you're from?"

"Sure," said Herb, grinning. "Can't you tell?"

"Tell?" she asked.

"From the way I talk?"

"I never knew anyone from Boston before," said Lorna. "I thought you were from Albany."

They made a couple of selections from the catalog of little giggles, titters, chuckles, and chortles that timid would-be lovers use when they don't know how to say, or can't bring themselves to say, what they want to say. They approached the center of town, and Lorna was reminded of work. She thought with horror that a young man from Boston wasn't likely to approve of a girl who carved improper subjects on men's jewelry. She didn't want him to see where she worked. She had Herb stop when he reached River Road. They shook hands. Lorna said, "Good luck, Herb. I hope you don't—have a hard time."

Herb grinned. "I hope I don't get killed," he said. Lorna got out. Herb put the car in gear. "So long, *Lorna*," he said.

6

In Which Lorna Becomes a Legend and Herb Is Decorated

One cannot leave oneself behind. Emerson and Huber were right: one's giant always tags along. When we say that success or divorce or war changes people, and mean by it that it makes great changes, we are likely to be commenting not on the people, but on our perceptions of them. In war, certain traits sometimes appear with a prominence that they do not have or cannot have in peacetime. The bookkeeper who becomes the fabled hero of his regiment, who astonishes us with his valor and nobility, may have stoutly but quietly refused to juggle his employer's books the week before he enlisted, but that civilian demonstration of valor and nobility may have gone unsung, may have cost him his job. Of Herb's traits, the one that came to prominence in the Great War was his mechanical ingenuity.

Training in the muddy woods of North Carolina, Herb learned to fire a rifle and jump into a trench and breathe through a gas mask and throw a grenade and thrust a bayonet through a stuffed sack. He worried about his mother, and he dreamed about Lorna, and he was drawn with all the foolhardiness of a Piper toward the schemes that flourished in the camp. He was ever wary, though, of doing a foolish

Piper thing, and his wariness kept him out of lotteries and pyramid plans and, most of the time, whorehouses. He brought his talent for salesmanship with him, but he found that he hardly needed it to sell coarse goods among his fellow draftees and recruits. When he realized how large the demand was, he decided, knowing how short the supply was, that he could increase the price by exaggerating the shortage. He invented a mysterious character who, he claimed, brought him the goods a few pieces at a time, from an orphanage, where young girls carved the items to earn their keep, using one another as models. To provide the unlikely detail that lends verisimilitude to a lie, he gave the man a mutilated right hand.

When he had time to kill, he often killed it, as he always had, by tinkering. He found plenty to keep him occupied. There was always something to fix, and there was always something that could be improved. By the end of the war, his love of tinkering had made him famous. He was known among the doughboys as "that guy from Boston" who found a way to fix the handle on the mess-kit cup.

Each infantryman was issued a cleverly designed mess kit that combined all the essential containers and implements in one package. In fact, it became its own package, the pan mating with the plate, like the two halves of a clamshell, and the handle of the pan rotating to hold the two together. One component of this kit was a cup with a folding handle. This coffee cup showed how ill prepared America had been for war: the folding handle had never been tested under combat conditions, or even under rigorous training conditions. The handle couldn't be depended on to stay in the open position, and it was most likely to fail when the cup was full. The first time Herb's failed, coffee spilled down his right leg. He wasn't alone in having this happen; it happened to many. He was, however, alone in his reaction to it. He immediately began thinking of a way to make the cup handle work as it should. He wore a little grin while he ate, though his leg was scalded and his food was insipid, because he was turning over in his mind ways that he might solve the problem the army had given him to keep him from feeling miserable.

Lorna also threw herself into work. All over America, women answered the call to do the work of men who had answered the call to war. In Chacallit, there was much work to do.

In the years before the United States entered the war, Chacallitans gave the outward appearance of favoring neutrality, but in fact neutrality had made everyone nervous, since Chacallitans of German and British background distrusted one another's private convictions. When the United States had finally decided to go to war, Chacallit had rushed to support the decision. Several of the young men of Chacallit had enlisted at once, and the town was surprised to find itself fuming unanimously with anti-German sentiment and puffing with pride in America and Chacallit. When the draft began, Chacallit showed none of the resistance shown in some other small towns—towns that answered the call with ruffians, drunks, and layabouts—nor was there any of the grisly pettiness of towns where officials on a local draft board, handed the power to administer fear, pain, even death, used it to revenge lost boundary disputes or arguments over rights-of-way, to return, horribly inflated, schoolyard taunts, to exact satisfaction for cuckoldry. Chacallit sent its best, and the draftees were treated in the *Chacallit Sentinel* as if they'd already won the croix de guerre.

The gentlemen's furnishings industry converted to production of bits and pieces for uniforms: buttons, buckles, snaps, grommets, hooks, clamps, straps, bandoleers, and such. Since women had long been employed in the mills of Chacallit, replacement sometimes meant advancement, when women moved into positions their supervisors vacated. Such was Lorna's case. She had been the only woman in the carving section of the coarse-goods operation. Two of her co-workers enlisted, and her supervisor, John Caldwell, who had always kept to himself and rarely spoke to any of the workers on any subject but their work, surprised them all by announcing that he was leaving to assist in the work being done by the Young Men's Christian Association in France. Said he, in part:

> When this terrible war is over, who will return to us? Will the men who return to our shores prove to be a greater menace than the Prussian bullies? Will they be the sons and husbands and brothers we sent over there, or will they be a syphilitic horde of Frenchified monsters? I am going to France to do my part to see that when our boys return we can embrace them without fear and loathing. I'll counsel abstinence, but I will also provide protection, for no doughboy should be without his three safeguards: his helmet, his mask, and his condoms.

Luther wanted Lorna to take over as supervisor of the coarse-goods division, but she demurred, for two reasons. One was personal: with Herb so much on her mind, she was embarrassed by her work and afraid of his finding out about it. The other was patriotic: she thought that she should be working on uniform fittings.

"Uncle Luther," she said, "I can't do what you want." She took a deep breath. "In fact," she said, "I think we should suspend production of specialty items and put all our efforts into things that are necessary for the war." She took another breath and pressed her lips together to keep herself from smiling with pride. She had been afraid to say what she felt she had to say, and she was proud and relieved to have said it. Luther stood and folded his arms across his chest.

"Necessary for the war," he said, nodding his head. "Necessary for the war. And you know what is necessary for the war, do you? Do you think wars are won with bullets? Do you think wars are won with gas or grommets or belt buckles? Ha! Let me tell you something, Lorna my dear: wars are won with spirit! Wars are won with the will to win! I'd rather see the women of America writing lascivious letters to our boys than knitting socks and canning carrots! Spirit is what we want, and specialty jewelry helps build spirit." Turning partly away and taking his chin in his deficient hand, he said, "I wasn't planning to announce this just yet, but I suppose now is the time. We're going to begin producing specialty uniform buttons. They should be a wonderful morale booster." He turned to look at Lorna again. "The tide of war turns in mysterious ways," he said. "Who can say whether these buttons might not be enough to turn the tide in France?"

Luther gained the advantage, for the time being. He succeeded in making Lorna doubt herself and her motives. She hung her head and, with ambiguous feelings, agreed to take the supervisor's job.

The Woman's Committee of the Council of National Defense produced a long list of efforts that they considered worthwhile contributions to the war effort, but the writing of lascivious letters to soldiers was not among them. A woman in Chacallit was likely to be asked to join the Back Yard Gardeners (though the steep slope of the land in Chacallit limited the efforts of this group), the Picklers and Canners (who specialized in sauerkraut), the Children's Bureau (which sought to "keep the living standards, spirits, and chins of the children of

Chacallit's men-in-arms up"), the Chacallit chapter of "America First" (which, lacking immigrants to instruct in English and citizenship, had cast about for another project and had been steered by Ben Piper's original contact in Chacallit, Axel Schweib, whose wife headed the Chacallit chapter, in the direction of the Doughboy's Dozen and so put its efforts into purchasing for departing soldiers subscriptions to the entire series of books), or the Red Cross Knitters and Stitchers (who specialized in bed socks). However, of all the kinds of volunteer work that women were doing to support the war effort, the one that most appealed to Lorna was the assembling of Red Cross Comfort Kits. In *American Women and the World War*, Ida Clyde Clarke describes these Comfort Kits as "bags made in three styles with pockets containing comforts, buttons and sewing outfits, games, soap, socks, and the like." In the kits assembled in Chacallit, "the like" included money clips, cuff links, and collar stays, donated by the manufacturers in town, who also donated brochures describing their other products.

Lorna was also kept busy by her duties as Herb's representative for Professor Clapp's Five-Foot Shelf of Indispensable Information for Modern Times. These duties were sweet, for they required her, she had decided, to write to Herb more and more frequently. She began her early letters with news about the book business, as she did this one:

> *I finished delivering* The Automobile: Its Selection, Care, and Use. *I'm sure you'll be pleased to know that everyone is quite satisfied with the book. Reverend Binder even stopped me the other day to say that he had been reading the chapter called "Housing the Automobile," and that it has inspired him to build a garage. I knew you would enjoy hearing that.*

Soon, however, she would turn from business to other matters:

> *With those deliveries finished, I will go back to my work for the Red Cross, putting together Comfort Kits. Have you gotten one of these kits? I think about you sometimes when I'm working on them, because sometimes the thought strikes me that you might get one of the kits that I put together. What do you think of that? I think it would be quite a coincidence if you did. It has become a great game*

among us girls to slip some personal token into a kit, just some little thing that could only have come from the girl who put it together. Some of the girls write a little note. Others put a picture in or something else. . . .

The "something else" that Lorna began putting into the kits she assembled made her a legend among the troops in France, anonymous, but the object of fantasies in miles of trenches.

One evening, when she gathered with the other women who worked on Comfort Kits, she brought with her, in a pocket that she had sewn into her skirt, a tiny ivory figure. It resembled the jewelry she carved, but this figure was not meant to be attached to anything else. It was not an ornament; it was a tiny piece of sculpture. Lorna had worked on it at home, in the evenings, alone in her room, using herself as a model, carving ivory that she had persuaded Luther to donate to the Comfort Kit effort.

She slipped her hand into her pocket and removed the carving. Working below the table while she kept up her chatter with Adelaide Hooper, she slipped the carving into a packet of tobacco. She let the packet rest in her lap until Adelaide turned away to get another sack of buttons; then she brought the packet up to the table and put it into the Comfort Kit she was packing. She couldn't help smiling at the thought of its being discovered.

At that moment Herb was in a field hospital, recovering from a wound that would keep him hors de combat for the rest of the war.

The evening before, as the sun began to set, Herb had been lying in a trench just west of a wood outside the village of Quelquepart-sur-Marne. The sun was going down, and its golden light lit a low serpentine ridge between the trench and the wood, about two hundred yards from where Herb and his fellows crouched, waiting. The ridge was strongly fortified, and so was the wood. In a moment, Herb and the others expected the order to charge the ridge, to charge out of the blinding light of the setting sun.

Herb crouched below the lip of the trench, waiting for the call to go up and over, to try to take the ridge and, beyond it, the wood. Before the call came, a shell burst in the trench, to Herb's right, and the explosion pushed him backward, just as if someone had tackled him around the legs and shoved him backward, against a timber that supported the muddy walls of the trench, and then spun him around it, as if he were in a revolving door.

May Castle recalled hearing Herb tell the story:

> *Well, of course, if you know someone for as long as Garth and I knew Herb and Lorna, you're bound to have to listen to the same stories quite a few times—you can count yourself lucky if the stories are at least interesting. Garth told his war stories over and over and over, God knows. Well, poor Herb really didn't have much to tell. You had to twist his arm to get him to tell about being praised by Pershing, it embarrassed him so, and he only had one other story to tell—that one about the shell that exploded in the trench. Well, there he was in a trench at Someplace-or-other-on-the-Marne, and of course it was all just ghastly. Well, it was all ghastly, wasn't it? Herb and his trench-mates or whatever you call them were supposed to come dashing out of the trench and overrun some Germans who were holding some damned hill or other. Well! Suddenly this shell exploded and Herb was tossed around pretty badly. "It was the darnedest thing," he said. "I kept thinking that someone had hold of me by the leg and was shaking me. There I was spun around and flat on my back, and I reached down to try to push away whoever was holding me by the leg. Well, no one was holding me by the leg at all. I'd been hit, and my leg was opened up from the knee to the hip, just the way you'd cut open a baked potato."*

Herb passed his time in the hospital, as soon as he was able, assembling kits to improve the drinking cup handle catches. He taught others of the recovering wounded how to make these, and soon he had a group of some fifty men working on them. The work was useful in more than the immediately obvious ways; the men who did it probably benefited as much as those for whom they made the kits. In *Terror and Tedium*, his important but neglected study of the psychology of war, Major Edward Keefe wrote of the work that Herb initiated:

> *The typical field hospital was behind the lines but barely beyond the range of the shelling. The war was still so close, such a constant*

presence, that there was no emotional escape from it. Added to the whole catalog of feelings that the war inspired in these wounded men was an almost overwhelming sense of frustration, of impotence, of not being able to do anything about it, not being able to participate. (We see another example of the effect of this feeling of impotence, by the way, in the flourishing traffic within the hospitals in pornography of all sorts—photographs, drawings, literature, even pornographic jewelry and tiny netsuke-like carvings.) Those on the mend would sometimes plead to be sent back into the fighting, even when they were obviously unfit. They worked at various tasks in and around the hospitals, of course—orderly work, supply-train work, and work on the "ice flotillas," the trucks and ice-making equipment that kept the hospitals supplied with the ice so necessary for their operation. But this was not enough. A sense of distance developed among the wounded, a sense of being a class apart. The work they did was most often work for other wounded. They felt that they weren't doing anything for their fellows who were still fighting, and they began to think of themselves as not belonging to the same group, not worthy of belonging to it. The cup handle repair kits were something that they could do for the men who were still fighting, and the wounded were eager to get in on the action, so to speak.

In his letters to Lorna from the hospital, Herb began to devote more space to matters other than business, including personal matters:

A lot of the other guys complain about the food, but I've had worse. We generally have boiled potatoes and onions, and sometimes we have rice or stew. Breakfast might be just crackers and coffee, but it wasn't many years ago that I didn't have any breakfast. Lots of times, when I went to school, for lunch I would just take a potato. Sometimes I'd have an onion sandwich, which didn't make me too popular with the other kids! I used to sell papers on the street and also a thing that my buddies and I called rat pie. We got these pies at a bakery so we could sell them, and we used to joke that they were made of rat meat. I think all of us thought it was probably true. If a rat pie got wet in the rain or if somebody dropped one on the pavement, I'd take it home, and we'd have that for dinner. Many nights we'd have just potatoes. So I don't mind this food at all. In fact, sometimes when we have just bread and onions, I make an onion sandwich and it reminds me of home. The truth is, I like onion sandwiches. . . . I'm glad that the books are arriving on time. I'd be pleased if you would continue to write to me to let me know how things are going, if it isn't too much trouble.

One of Herb's letters to his mother was much like another, and they all included something like this:

So, you mustn't worry about me, because, as I said, I'm all right. My leg is healing just fine, and everyone says that I probably won't walk with a limp or be able to predict rain. I've arranged to have some money sent to Uncle Ben for you. I don't need any money where I am, so don't you worry about taking it.

One of his letters to Ben was much like another, and they all ended in the manner of this one:

I've had a good week—prices are climbing. Please give Mother an extra twelve dollars. I know you're keeping track of everything you give her, and you can rest assured that I will be able to pay all of it back and then some.

In one, however, he had a couple of interesting questions to ask:

Here's a funny thing. Some of the fellows here have been buying special carved buttons for their uniforms. Where do you suppose they're buying them? Do you think we have competition? Some of the fellows say they heard that sometimes special carvings—not buttons, but very special carvings—come in packages from the Red Cross, but I don't think that could be right, do you?

Early one afternoon, about two months before the Armistice was signed, Lorna sat in the lunchroom in the mill, reading a pamphlet. What she read struck her with such force that she pounded her fist on the table, spilling her soup and startling the women around her.

"Damn!" she said.

"What's the matter?" asked Elsie Hensel.

"Oh, I'm furious with myself for being so—so—childish!" cried Lorna. She stormed out of the lunchroom and strode through the building. She hesitated for only an instant outside Luther's door; then she knocked, with sharp, rapid taps.

"Come in," said Luther. Lorna opened the door and went inside.

"Uncle Luther," she said in a rush, knowing that if she hesitated, she would surely waver in her resolve, "I want you to tell me how much you were paying John Caldwell to do the work I'm doing." She took a long breath. Behind her back, she rolled and twisted the pamphlet in her hands.

Luther drew a long breath of his own. "Lorna," he said, "I'm surprised at you. That's not a polite question to ask."

"Politeness doesn't have anything to do with it," said Lorna. She hoped that the anger and fear rippling through her wouldn't make her voice quaver. "I've been reading this pamphlet." She brought it out from behind her back, untwisted it, bent it back to flatten it, and held it out to Luther with both hands. "It's about women's working conditions."

"Lorna, Lorna," said Luther, rising and moving toward her. "You mustn't let yourself get into such a state. These are difficult times, Lorna dear," he said. He put his hand on her shoulder, and Lorna stiffened. "We all have important work to do, and we all must make sacrifices. This is not a time when any of us should be thinking about personal gain."

"I'm not thinking about personal gain," said Lorna. She had to work to keep the *p* from betraying her anger.

"Now, really, Lorna," said Luther. "What other name can we put on it?" He took the pamphlet that Lorna held out to him. "'The National Women's Trade Union League of America,'" he read. "Now who are they? Do we know anything about them?"

"I know something about them," said Lorna. She was surprised (and, she would admit to herself later, pleased) to find that Luther's attitude incensed her, made her bolder than she would have been. "I know that I like what they say."

"And what do they say?" asked Luther. He smiled. Lorna thought that she might kick him if he didn't stop smiling. She snatched the pamphlet from him and flipped through its pages to the place where she'd been reading when she'd struck the table with her fist.

"They say," she said, " 'Equal pay for equal work.' " She swallowed.

"Oh, now, Lorna," said Luther.

"Uncle Luther," said Lorna, pressing her feet together so that she wouldn't kick him, "I don't want to argue with you. My mind is made up. I'm going to—"

"Stop," said Luther with maddening calm. He looked at her for a moment, deciding what he wanted to do. He had begun to consider Lorna a liability in coarse goods. Her work was wonderful, of course, superior in every way, but as a carver she had been bad for morale. She had set a standard that the others couldn't attain. Half of them strained to measure up, taking pains that wasted time without improving their work, and the other half fell into grumbling and loafing. Production had fallen off. As manager, she was an even more imposing presence. The others in the specialty department feared or resented her ability, and Luther, though he admired her talent, wondered if he wouldn't be just as glad to see her go. "Perhaps you're right," he said. "I have an idea. Why don't you quit the specialty goods and go onto the regular line in suspenders or buttons? I shall be pleased to pay you just what everyone else is getting there."

"I—" Lorna began, surprised and confused.

Still smiling, quoting her, Luther said, "I don't want to argue with you. My mind is made up."

Lorna stood straight and clenched her fists at her sides. "I think I'll just quit work altogether," she said.

"Lorna, Lorna," said Luther with an exaggerated look of offense and disappointment. "There's a war on, remember? I'm sure you want to do your part."

"Uncle Luther—" Lorna began.

"You know, Lorna," said Luther as if the idea had just occurred to him, "it would break your parents' hearts if they knew what you'd been up to here."

Lorna took two steps backward, as if she'd been pushed. In an instant, she understood how rough a fight she was in, and she struck back with the kind of blow she'd been dealt.

"And it would make your brother furious if he knew what you'd been up to with his daughters," she said with a calm like that she'd seen in Luther.

On the way out she repeated to herself, *Do not slam the door; do not slam the door*, and because she couldn't trust herself not to slam it, she left it standing open. Luther slammed it.

Lorna did go to work in the suspender fitting section. It doesn't seem likely to me that she actually feared Luther's spilling the beans about her erotica work if she didn't do what he wanted. She must have known that their standoff was stable. It's more likely that she took a place on the main floor, where an American flag was mounted on each of the machines, at each of the benches and tables, because she knew that more hands were always needed and because she would have missed the company of the other women. At her cutting machine, she worked among women who gave their work only the necessary effort. She made herself work in the same manner, letting her hands perform while her mind wandered. More and more often her thoughts were of Herb.

Herb had been assigned to a prisoner-of-war camp, where he and other recuperating men supervised German prisoners who were put to the task of fabricating cup handle repair kits. The men who ran the camp were a mixed lot, thrown together from among the wounded of many divisions. They were a group that represented the whole fabric of American society, including men from the warp and men from the woof, the only truly integrated group of soldiers in the American Expeditionary Forces.

About three weeks after the Armistice was signed, a tremor of excitement rippled through the camp. Herb was stretched out on his bunk, writing a letter, when Ezio Corelli, a wisecracking, curly-haired pastry chef from Brooklyn, burst in with startling news.

"Hey, Piper!" he shouted. "You better polish your fucking shoes and practice your fucking salute—they're gonna make a fucking hero out of you."

"What?" said Herb. He grinned at Corelli, anticipating the gag that was sure to come.

"Yes, Herbie, that's right," said Jo Jo Washington, a serious-minded cornetist from Chicago. "That certainly is right. No jokes this time, Herbie. They are going to *recognize* you. That's the truth."

"What is this?" asked Herb, his amusement and caution growing.

"Herb! Herb!" called Anton "Boom-Boom" Delacroix, a big-hearted fisherman from New Orleans. He burst into the bunkroom, lumbered to Herb's bunk, and lifted Herb to his feet. "You are one damn lucky son of a bitch, you," Boom-Boom boomed.

"What on earth are you talking about?" asked Herb, wriggling in Boom-Boom's bear hug.

"Herbert!" called Izzy Moskowitz, a devil-may-care dental student from South Bend. "I certainly hope you are prepared for this. This is going to be one of the most memorable moments of your life." He stood in front of Herb, regarding him with evident pride, as a brother might.

Herb put his hands on his hips. "All right, all right," he said. "What are you—"

From the doorway, Seamus O'Brien, a freckle-faced barkeep from Alabama, cried, "'Tennnnnnshun!" and in a moment, without other fanfare, Black Jack Pershing himself strode into the bunkhouse.

"Which one of you figured out how to fix the coffee cups?" asked the general.

"Here, sir," said Herb. For the first and only time since it had healed, his leg gave him some trouble. A queer flutter ran through it, and he was afraid it would fold under him.

"Herb Piper," said Pershing, "it's a pleasure." He saluted Herb and then held out his hand. For a moment, Herb thought that Pershing wanted to shake hands with him. Then, pointing with the other hand to a spot on the extended hand, Pershing said, "See this scar?" Everyone craned his neck to see. "A damned cup of coffee did that. Before you came along." He paused, stared at his hand, and said reflectively, "You know, it's a funny thing how life doesn't really change much in a war—how the little things are still annoying." He took a deep breath and frowned at the bitter mysteries of war. "I've seen a man with one leg gone—torn away—prop himself up so he could keep firing, and I've seen men just as brave scream in pain and lose all their will to fight when they were burned by one of those damned collapsing coffee cups." He put a hand on Herb's shoulder. "Piper, you've done more for the morale of our men than taking Quelquepart-sur-Marne did." Grinning, he reached into his pocket. "Now, what you did," he said, "isn't the sort of thing I can give you a medal for, you understand, but you ought to get something, so—"

He extended his hand, and Herb cupped his under it.

[8 7]

"—here's something for what you've done."

Into Herb's hand he dropped a pornographic shirt button.

"Sew that on your shirt, Piper," said Pershing, "and if anybody complains, tell 'em I gave it to you."

Herb did what Pershing told him to do. He sewed the button onto his shirt, and he wore it with some pride while he was still in France. On the way home, however, he tore the button off. It embarrassed him, and it frightened him. He couldn't help feeling, though he knew that the feeling didn't make sense, that the button would somehow give him away. When asked, he claimed to have lost it, and he even suggested that it might have fallen overboard somewhere in the Atlantic. In the next forty years, he showed it to only one person, his uncle Benjamin, who said when he saw it, "Will you look at the workmanship on that!"

7
In Which
Herb 'n' Lorna Ignite
the Flame of Passion

Herb's uncle Ben met his train when Herb returned to Boston. Millie Piper couldn't trust herself to meet her son in public. She was determined not to cry, absolutely determined, but she knew that she *would* cry, and she didn't want to cry over him with everyone watching—if she was going to cry and make a fuss, and she was afraid that she was, she wanted to do it at home, where she could do it without embarrassing Herb.

And cry she did, but not at all as she had supposed she would. Silent tears began running down her cheeks when she heard Herb's rapid footsteps on the stairs. Herb meant to keep her from crying. He intended to burst into the room and fill it with noise, fling his cap against the wall, pick Millie up, and whirl her around the room, but when he opened the door and saw her there, he couldn't even say hello. All he could do was clear his throat. His hands and feet seemed suddenly so much heavier than normal, like the puffed and clumsy hands and feet we sometimes find attached to us in dreams. He couldn't move. Millie had imagined herself running to him the moment he opened the door, but her feet seemed to have undergone the same nightmarish transformation, and for a minute she couldn't move, either. They stood across the room from each other without moving or speaking. Herb began to sniffle. He held his arms out to Millie and began shuffling toward her. She held her arms out and began shuffling toward him. Slumped in his chair in the corner, Lester Piper watched. There wasn't a sound in the room but Millie and Herb's sniffling and the shuffling of their feet. Lester felt something unfamiliar. He had a sudden awareness of his chair, the presence of it behind his back, under him, the worn spots on the arms, the burnished, darkened cork in the places where he rested his hands. He seemed to be able to feel every tiny fissure in the cork, to feel the floor through his shoes. He seemed to be able to taste the air he breathed, to hear the crunch of individual grains of grit beneath the shoes of Herb and Millie as they shuffled toward each other. What was this odd sensation? It was—it was—joy.

"Herb!" he shouted. He leaped up from his chair. "Herb!" He swept Millie off her feet and carried her in one arm to Herb, where he crushed them together and began whirling them around the room, crying, "What a wonderful day, a wonderful day!"

Ben appeared in the doorway, red-faced and sweating. "All right, all right, all right," he said. "He's home. You're out of your chair. It's a wonderful day, but I'm holding the bags, remember? How about a hand?"

Millie sat Herb at the table and made him eat. While he ate, she stood behind him with both hands on his shoulders, crying as quietly as she could manage, her tears running down her cheeks.

Herb had planned, as soon as things settled down, to go to the tobacco shop, where there was a telephone, and call Lorna, but before he could get out, Ben's wife, Herb's aunt Louise, arrived with his cousins and a friend of his cousins', Alice Mills. Alice was sixteen, a girl of striking beauty, with wide eyes, a lively, laughing mouth, and waves of fine golden hair that cascaded over her shoulders and caught and gilded even the poor dim light in the Pipers' apartment. She was a quick blusher. She had voluptuous lips, and she kept them slightly parted in a look that made her seem naïve and vulnerable. She couldn't take her eyes off Herb. She had fallen in love with him while he was in France.

Before she had fallen in love with Herb, Alice had already developed a romantic attachment to the general idea that young men were fighting in France, suffering unspeakable horrors, and pining all the while for the girls they'd left behind, who pined in turn for them, sighing through slightly parted lips in a way that made them seem naïve and vulnerable. How Alice wished that she had been one of the girls whom the boys had left behind, so that the poignant ache she felt in her heart might have some specific object, and so that, in his turn, the object of her heartache, some doughboy lying cold and miserable in a trench somewhere in France, might pine for her, specifically for her. Alas, the boys she knew were all too young for war, so none of them was likely to be heading over there with his heart full of her. She needed someone *already* over there, and so she chose Herb, her best friend's cousin. She'd seen him before, but her memory of him was fuzzy enough not to interfere with her fantasy. She wrote letters to him but found that they never struck the note she had intended them to strike, and so she never sent them. She prayed for his safety. She promised herself that, once he returned home, and they were firmly in love, she would always be faithful to him. She sat on the window seat at home, looked wistful, and sighed for him through her voluptuous lips. She stood in front of her mirror and admired the way she was maturing, touched her lips with her fingertips and tried to imagine what kissing her would be like for Herb, touched her breasts and tried to isolate her fingertips, tried to make them Herb's, to feel her nipples tighten as he would, and, in bed, tried to remove herself from herself, put herself beside herself, be Herb beside her, caress herself as Herb would, beg herself to give herself to him as Herb would, tried to imagine climbing atop herself as Herb would, and slowly, gratefully, tenderly, reverently, augmenting her imagination with the handle on a darning egg, penetrating herself as Herb would. She succeeded well enough to convince herself that she was in love with Herb. She had never had a serious doubt that, given the opportunity, he would love her.

When Herb saw Alice he was astonished. She wasn't at all the little girl he remembered. She was beautiful. She was alluring. She seemed to adore him. What he felt for her he immediately took for love. He put off telephoning Lorna.

When Andrew Proctor returned to Chacallit, more than two thousand people were waiting on the platform at the railroad station to greet him. He was Chacallit's hero. He had, single-handedly, taken a hill, saved his captain, and captured a German officer, but his exploits were already being exaggerated, so that in the conversation of Chacallit he had, single-handedly, taken a hill, a ridge, a bridge, and the bank of a river, saved his captain, a trio of buddies, and a nurse, captured a German officer, a patrol, a regiment. No one in Chacallit would have dared correct the exaggerations. Nor would anyone have cared to correct them. Chacallit was proud to have a hero, and the more heroic he was, the better. Andrew was carried from the train on the shoulders of two stout men, and within an hour a dozen men were claiming to have been one of them. The men set Andrew down at the side of the mayor, who recounted the version of Andrew's deeds that he favored. No one was in any mood to quibble about the accuracy of this version—certainly not Andrew, who was so overwhelmed by the admiration of his townsfolk that he couldn't trust himself to speak and was happy just to smile and wave. Standing directly in front of Andrew was Lorna. When Andrew looked at her, he caught her in one of her moments. Lorna struck him as so beautiful a young woman that he stepped away from the mayor, put his arm around her, and kissed her. It was an extraordinary thing to do, but this was an extraordinary occasion, and Andrew was being honored because he had done extraordinary things. It seemed, once he had done it, like exactly the right thing for an extraordinary young fellow to do. No one minded, not even Lorna, who blushed but considered this a kiss inspired by nothing more than exuberance. Andrew had hardly noticed Lorna before he left Chacallit, but at just that moment he decided that he was in love.

Andrew was an immediate success with Richard and Lena Huber, and Lorna was quite taken with him herself. He wasn't bad looking, after all, and he was the talk of the town.

Almost at once, Andrew and Lorna were considered a couple. Andrew's father was pleased by his son's choice. Mr. Proctor was wary of girls who were too pretty, since they were likely to be as attractive to other men as to their husbands. Lorna seemed just right to him. He considered her looks ordinary—pretty enough, but ordinary. (True, he admitted to himself, every now and then she struck him as positively dazzling, but that, he thought, was probably the effect of certain desires of his own that ought to be suppressed.) Mr. Proctor was a successful man, and his success enabled Andrew to employ the courting arsenal of a successful man. He was able to give gifts and arrange outings, surprises, and treats. Lorna enjoyed being courted so lavishly, enjoyed being part of Chacallit's favorite couple, and enjoyed being the envy of the other girls in town, and she began to think that she was in love with Andrew.

"I want you to tell me about the war," said Alice. She was sitting beside Herb on the sofa in the living room of the Millses' apartment, over Alice's father's saloon. The Millses' place wasn't much grander than the Pipers', but Alice and her mother put a lot of effort into making it "cozy," and Herb enjoyed the shabby clutter they had created.

"I don't have much to tell," said Herb. He looked at Alice and shrugged.

"I know it must be hard to talk about it," said Alice. She brought her hand to Herb's cheek and looked into his eyes with great compassion. She had often imagined this time, when her Herb would have come home at last, when they would be alone and he could confide in her all the terrible things he had experienced and describe for her how often he'd thought of her in the midst of the horror, how often he'd dreamed of sitting beside her like this.

"It's not that," said Herb. "It's just that I don't have many stories to tell. I didn't do much of anything."

Alice brushed a tear from her cheek. This was even better than she'd hoped. Sitting alone with her was, apparently, so intoxicating that Herb could hardly speak, couldn't find the words to tell her how much it had meant to him to know that she was waiting for him. "I understand," she said. She let her head rest on his shoulder.

Prohibition might have deprived the Millses of their livelihood if Mr. Mills hadn't been as resourceful a man as he was. He reasoned that many people came to his saloon for companionship rather than, or as much as, for liquor, and that, if he kept the saloon open as a gathering place, without liquor, he stood a good chance of hanging on to some of his old customers and even drawing some new ones. He might even get them to bring their families. If he sold food and soft drinks and charged a membership fee, the place should make a small profit, he decided, and it would be a dandy cover for a speakeasy in the cellar. The idea worked brilliantly. He called the place Mills's

Family Club. It was hailed as a model of what temperance might do for family and community. The Millses prospered.

Herb put off visiting Chacallit, and put it off again, and thought less and less about it. He began spending time in the club, upstairs and down, not only because Alice often worked there, but because Herb enjoyed the people who gathered there. He'd never had much time to relax and talk before. He discovered how much he liked being with people, listening to their stories, laughing at their jokes. He noticed the way other young men looked at Alice, but he didn't notice how little he cared.

Before Alice had fallen in love with Herb, her mother had worried that Alice would flirt away the years when her beauty was most marketable. "Nothing's sure, is it?" she said to Alice one day. "Who's to say you'll get prettier? You might be as pretty right now as you'll ever be. You may even be on the way down."

"Oh, Ma," said Alice.

"'Oh, Ma' nothing," said Mrs. Mills. "Look at your friend Annie. We all thought she'd grow up gorgeous. Now she's a fright."

"Oh, Ma," said Alice.

"She is. She's a fright. It could happen to you. Then you'd have to settle for whatever men're left."

"Oh, Ma," said Alice.

"Worse yet," said Mrs. Mills, "you might *never* marry. You might become a nuisance and a burden."

Mrs. Mills had another worry, one that she kept to herself. She worried that Alice's beauty might go on improving forever, while her own declined. At those times, she could imagine herself spending the rest of her life in the shadow of her daughter. It was this worry that most made Mrs. Mills like Herb. She liked Herb's prospects. He seemed ambitious to her. She liked the idea that if he married Alice, his ambition might lead to his taking Alice away somewhere, somewhere far enough away so that she wouldn't visit too often, so that she wouldn't be a burden or cast a shadow.

To help move matters along, Mrs. Mills left Herb and Alice alone whenever she could arrange it. After several evenings of petting that ended with Alice's whispering, "We mustn't, my darling, we mustn't," Alice apparently succumbed to the heat of passion. At the point in their petting where (her blouse off, her bra undone, so much smooth, pale skin glowing in the dark, Herb's shirt open, his belt loosened, Herb tugging at one of her nipples with his lips, she felt Herb's hand reach above the tops of her stockings, felt him rubbing her thighs) she ordinarily pressed her legs together and whispered, "We mustn't," she sighed instead and seemed to melt, let her body drop slowly backward on the sofa, as if she were putting her head back to let herself float on a wave, and whispered, "Take me, my darling, please take me."

When Herb did, the little cry that escaped from her and the expression on her face when she looked deep into his eyes (an expression that she intended to say, "I feel pleasure, my darling, a new and thrilling pleasure, but my deepest pleasure comes from giving to you something wonderful and precious, something for which I know you must certainly be very, very grateful") had been rehearsed. In anticipation of this grand moment, Alice had practiced often, in her bed, manipulating the darning egg handle with one hand and sighing, panting, smiling, and grimacing into the mirror that she held in the other. She had gotten rather good with the darning egg handle and had developed a repertoire that pleased her: ease in, eeeease out, sliiide in, sliiide out, thrust, retreat, thrust, retreat, thrust, retreat, in, out, in, out, eeeease in, eeeease out, eeeease in, eeeease out, thrust, thrust, thrust; repeat as needed. She was a little disappointed to find that Herb didn't follow this satisfying pattern, but, still, this *was* the moment she'd been waiting for, and she was determined to try to make the best of it.

"Oh, my darling, my darling Herb," she said. "My poor darling. How often you must have dreamed of loving me like this, in the war." She sighed and smiled. "Are you happy, Herb? Are you happy right now?"

"Yes," said Herb. "Yes, I'm happy." He was lying. He certainly wasn't *un*happy, but Alice didn't make him happy. At some time after he had penetrated Alice, while he was moving in her, he had felt a curious sensation come over him, a sense of detachment, something like the disembodiment he had felt when he was hit by that shell fragment in France. Then, his mind had taken him aside, as a protector might, pulled him a step or two away from the place where that poor body, which happened to be his, was being ripped and splayed. His leg had suffered the pain; his self had stood apart. Now, his mind had taken him a step or two away from pleasure. His penis was having a wonderful time, the time of its life, slipping, sliding, slurping back and forth in Alice, delicious, lubricious Alice, but his mind had begun to wander, and in a vague sort of way it seemed to be headed for Chacallit.

"Oh, so am I, Herb," said Alice. He heard her, but he'd forgotten what she was talking about. Alice swallowed, and her eyes grew misty. The truth is that her mind had begun to roam around a little, too. She was puzzled and annoyed by the fact that, although Herb was, certainly, enjoying her, he didn't seem to be enjoying her as much as he had enjoyed her when Alice had imagined herself as him enjoying her. With a little inner sigh, she admitted to herself that, therefore, Herb must not really be the right man for her after all. She was going to have to let him go. A lump formed in her throat when she thought about the pain she was going to cause him, the sadness he was sure to feel. She resolved to be very kind. And for now, she would make the best of things, not only for herself, but for Herb, too. She owed it to him, after what he'd been through, for all the time he'd yearned so for her, and— A surprise. A surging rush of sensation, a thrust, another, thrust and thrust again, lively and—oh—lively and—*hot-headed* compared to that darning egg handle, and a shudder ran through Herb, that ecstatic shudder, and his thoughts came dashing back to join his penis in its happy pop, its rip, its roar, its hip-hooray!

And then, slowly, quietly, while Herb lay with his head on Alice's breast and she ran her fingers through his hair and wondered whom she might try next, Herb's thoughts wandered off again, to Chacallit, and brought him another ecstatic thrill, the thrill that comes when one is surprised by a truth, in this case the truth that he would rather be with Lorna.

"I guess you want me to tell you some more about the war," said Andrew. He and Lorna were sitting on the sofa in the Hubers' parlor, as they had on many evenings since Andrew's return. Richard was standing, filling his pipe. Lena was sitting in her accustomed chair, knitting. Before she quite realized what she was doing, Lena let a sigh escape from her. When she discovered herself sighing, she tried to disguise the sigh as a yawn. When she realized that a yawn was every bit as bad as a sigh, she became confused about what to do next, and she burst out giggling. She glanced up from her work and saw that she had become the focus of attention.

Lorna rose from the couch and walked to her mother's chair, where she stood behind her and squeezed her shoulders.

"I'm sure we'd *love* to hear some more about the war," Lena said with a hearty eagerness that made Richard wonder whether she needed a long rest.

"You needn't feel that you have to tell us everything, my boy," said Richard. "I'm sure that there are many things you'd rather keep to yourself."

"Oh, no," said Andrew. "Not at all. I've got a million stories to tell!"

"Ah," said Lorna, barely audibly, "only half a million to go."

Lena giggled again. Richard, who had heard Lorna well enough, gave her a stern glance. Andrew, who told himself that surely she could not have said what he thought he'd heard, gave her a bewildered look.

"What was that, Lorna?" he asked.

"I said, 'We really have to go,'" said Lorna. She gave her mother another squeeze and smiled at her father, who applied himself to the tamping of his pipe.

When Lorna and Andrew had left, Lena let her knitting drop into her lap and said, looking straight ahead, "He really is a very nice boy."

"Yes," said Richard. "He's a fine boy. A brave fellow." He puffed at his pipe.

Lena said, "I only wish——"

"Yes," said Richard, "so do I."

Lena went back to her knitting, and Richard stood puffing on his pipe and looking at the newspaper. He reminded himself, again, that Andrew was a good prospect. With the end of the war and the return to normal production, a wonderful optimism had spread through Chacallit. Hindsight allows us to see that this optimism was, insofar as it was based on the expectation of growth in the gentlemen's furnishings industry, ill founded, but for the time being there seemed to be no reason to doubt that the industry on which Chacallit depended would prosper or that Andrew Proctor, who would one day ascend to the presidency of Proctor's Products for Men, was a good prospect. So it was difficult for Richard, who wanted to see Lorna securely settled, to admit that he would really rather not have her settled on Andrew Proctor.

It was even more difficult for Lena to admit. She had seen the war take some of the best young men of Lorna's age and had watched Lorna pass what she considered her peak. She had watched Lorna grow less and less interested in the men who might have been interested in her. She felt that Lorna expected too much, and she was afraid that if Lorna drove Andrew away, there might be no one left. So, a little ashamed of what she was doing, she had begun to push Lorna toward thinking seriously about marrying Andrew, even though, whenever Lena watched them walk away from the house together, she admitted to herself that she was glad not to be the one who would have to listen to Andrew for the rest of the evening.

Lorna tried to convince herself that Andrew's failings didn't matter, that she was imagining some and exaggerating others, that he really was good enough, but the truth struck her on the night when Andrew made love to her, on the back seat of his car, a Chevrolet. To be fair, her expectations may have been too high. Lorna was a nineteen-year-old virgin who in the last two years had spent approximately twenty-six hundred hours scrutinizing sexual performances of great diversity and sophistication and replicating them, in ivory, with painstaking exactitude. Though she didn't yet know what she liked, she knew much about the art. When she decided that tonight might just as well be the night, her imagination summoned all the couples she had carved, all their frozen moments of sex. Lorna came at Andrew as a flame licks at tinder, and if Andrew had noticed that Lorna's eyes burned brighter than his, that her breathing was quicker, her hands were hotter and bolder, and if, when she took his penis in her hands and inched herself toward him so that just the tip touched her, he had taken the time to notice her luscious concupiscence, then he would have cried out, "Oh, Lorna, take command, burn me up, *consume me.*" But Andrew didn't notice any of that and wouldn't have understood it if he had, so when she approached him he thought she meant, "Take me, conquer me," and he threw himself into the task with the cold-blooded single-mindedness that had made him a hero. He wrapped his arms around her, pressed her backward against the seat, and pushed himself, with one quick, grunting effort, as far into her as he could. Lorna hadn't anticipated that, and she didn't welcome it. Andrew began a steady humping progress toward his satisfaction, something like a forced march. A thought crossed Lorna's mind: *If there's a medal for this, he's determined to get it.* She started to snicker, but she covered it with what she hoped sounded like a startled exclamation prompted by an unexpected pleasure.

Andrew stopped moving in her. Just stopped. He extended his arms and raised himself up so that they could look each other in the face and said, "I'll bet you've wondered what this would be like. I know I have." He grinned and winked and went back to his huffing and puffing and fucking. Lorna looked at the mouse-colored fabric lining the roof of the car and let her mind wander away from Andrew's fuss and hubbub, and on its own her mind wandered back to the rainy night when Herb stood on her front porch shaking his umbrella. And just as Andrew reached the end of the march, fired his salute, and collapsed in the shade, a shiver ran through her and she realized that she wanted more than anything else to be with Herb.

The next morning Herb went to see his uncle Ben. "Uncle Ben," he said, "I want to go back to Chacallit."

"Good!" said Ben. "So do I. I've got an idea that is going to revolutionize the coarse-goods business."

Herb looked at his uncle with the wariness he'd inherited from his mother. "This isn't going to lose you money, is it, Uncle Ben?"

Benjamin colored, thrust his hands into his pockets, and cleared his throat. "It's not kind of you to ask a question like that, Herb," he said. "The Doughboy's Dozen was a dandy idea, and I should have made out all right with it." He pressed his lips together for a moment. "Commerce is a matter of subtleties, Herb," he said, shaking his head. "Subtleties and chances. And luck. You've got to take chances if you're going to get anywhere. You've got to understand the subtleties. You've got to have luck. I wasn't lucky."

"I don't follow you, Uncle Ben," said Herb.

"I made a little mistake, Herb," said Ben. He held his hand up, showing a small gap between his thumb and forefinger. "A little mistake. I thought the war would last longer. I figured we'd still be in it now. If it had lasted another five months, just five months, we'd have come out all right on the Doughboy's Dozen. If it were still on now, we'd be comfortable, Herb, very comfortable."

"Uncle Ben!" said Herb.

"Oh, don't get me wrong," said Ben. "I don't mean I *wish* it had lasted longer. I just mean that *if* it had, we'd be comfortable." He shook his head. "*Very* comfortable," he added. There was a silence between them for a while. Then Ben said suddenly, "But never mind that! It's all over and done with, and I've got a *terrific* idea! Not only is it a good idea, but it doesn't take any of our money."

"That sounds like a *great* idea," said Herb. "What is it?"

Ben grinned and reached into his pocket. He brought out something that he quickly concealed with both hands. He held his hands out, one cupped over the other, hiding and protecting something precious, as he might have held a tiny bird. Slowly, he opened his hands. There, cupped in Ben's hands, was the world's first piece of animated coarse goods.

Herb burst out laughing. "Gosh!" he said. "Will you look at that workmanship!"

Ben's prototype was a crude piece of work. The two wax figures were badly modeled, thickset, lumpy, graceless. The mechanism was nothing more than a pair of heavy wire forms joined by a loop (not unlike the link swivels that Lorna once fashioned) and kept apart by a tiny coil spring. A crank turned a cam against the wire on which the man, the upper figure, was molded, and the action of the cam provided the jerky up-and-down motion that was all the animation of which the couple was capable. The act they performed was crude and basic. The woman just lay there; the man pounded away at her, up and down, in and out, grimly, mechanically.

"It needs work," said Ben. "I know that. I don't have the talent to do anything better than this. But you do. You do, Herb. You're mechanically inclined. This kind of thing—much better than this, mind you, but this *kind* of thing—could be very successful, Herb. It could fit into a little case, like a pocket watch. It could go onto a chain just like a watch. Or it could take the place of a fob. Or maybe it would just be something a guy would carry in his pocket. The stem could make it work. You'd turn the stem instead of this crank, and—well, you see what I'm getting at, don't you?"

"Yes," said Herb, his mind already occupied with a set of interesting ideas prompted by the clumsy little couple. "I do."

Ben's idea *was* a good one, and Herb saw that it was immediately. Animated coarse goods could sell for much higher prices, at a much greater margin of profit, than static carvings. If Ben could get such things manufactured in Chacallit without risking any money, he might recoup the losses he'd taken on the Doughboy's Dozen. Herb worked night and day for a week to produce a more successful prototype, fabricated from two female figures that had been part of a shipment of conventional, static coarse goods from Chacallit. First, he had to make the tools his work would require. Then he had to transform one of the figures into a male. He wasn't entirely pleased with the success of this operation, but he knew that he wasn't likely to achieve anything better, so he went on to the articulation of the figures.

Painstakingly, he cut the figures apart at the elbow, shoulder, hip, and knee joints and across their abdomens, so that he could achieve more versatile and fluid movement than Ben's figures had been able to manage. As far as it was possible to do so, he concealed the articulating mechanism within the figures, which required him to drill through the arms and legs and to carve cavities in the figures where his tiny wires, cables, and pulleys could be concealed. The challenge to his ingenuity was exhilarating, much more so than designing the expandable shelves or the secret drawers or devising a repair for the mess-kit cup handles had been, and Herb took great pleasure in the work. In a week he had finished, and, on the whole, he was pleased. Ben was overjoyed.

"Brilliant work, Herb!" he said. "Brilliant! You're a genius at this, my boy. You've got a great future! Collectors are going to be after these, and they're going to want different positions, different ways of—well—moving, and so on. You're going to be able to name your price. You've got talent, Herb, real talent."

Herb shook his head. "No, Uncle Ben," he said. "I did this for you, but I won't do any more. I'm getting out of coarse goods. I'm in love with Lorna Huber. She's a wonderful girl, and I'm sure she'd be ashamed of me if she knew about this."

When Herb and Ben checked in at the Chacallit House, Ben, full of eagerness and confidence, certain of success, sure of the value of what he had to offer, went off to see Luther at once. Herb, who was not as confident, not at all certain of success, hesitated. He hadn't told Lorna that he was coming. He'd tried to write, but he hadn't been able to find a way to say the things that he wanted to say.

He unpacked. He took a bath. He shaved. He dressed, considered the effect in the mirror, didn't like what he saw, changed, and didn't like what he saw any better than he had before. Doubts breed rapidly, and they breed fastest in front of a mirror. Herb sighed and let his shoulders fall. He went off to see Lorna reluctantly. What he had to offer her seemed of little value.

He stopped his old Studebaker in front of the house, and he sat for a moment, with both hands on the wheel, trying to think of something to say to Lorna—no, not *some*thing, *the* thing, that remarkable thing that would tell her everything he felt—the word, the phrase, the sentence, the declaration that she would never forget, that she would, years from now, tell their children, their grandchildren. "I'll never forget," she would say, "the day that Herb came back to Chacallit. I opened the door, and there he was. He smiled and said—" What? What?

By the time he reached the Hubers' door, Herb had begun to think that he should have stayed in Boston. He caught sight of his reflection, and to himself he looked like a thin guy holding a battered hat, wearing a shabby suit and scuffed shoes, with an old heap parked behind him.

Lorna was at home, since she was now unemployed. When the war ended, Lorna had been among the first of the Chacallit women Luther had let go from the main floor. Her parents were puzzled when she didn't return to ivory work, but at dinner one Sunday Luther had provided an explanation, one that was false when he offered it but became true in time: he said that the market for expensive jewelry for men was declining, and that he couldn't very well keep Lorna at work when there were returning veterans without jobs. "Perhaps," he said, giving Lorna an unwelcome pat on the arm, "things will change, and I'll find a way to bring Lorna back to work." She was in the kitchen chopping cabbage when Herb turned the doorbell. She started for the door in her apron, but the thought that had come to her so often came to her again, the thought that this might be Herb, and she quickly untied the apron and threw it onto the kitchen table.

"Herb Piper," she said when she opened the door, not daring to add what her heart hoped: "You've come back to me!"

"I didn't get killed," said Herb. They were the first words that came to him, and by them he meant, "I came to see you because you're always on my mind, even when I'm with someone else. You're always there. The idea of you comes flickering through, like sunlight through the leaves on a tree."

Lorna burst out laughing. "I know," she said. "You used to write to me, remember?" By it she meant, "When you stopped writing, I was afraid I'd never see you again, and then I knew how much I wanted to see you again."

"I don't know why I said that," said Herb. "It was the first thing that came to me." He meant, "I didn't have the courage to say any of the things that I wanted to say. To tell you the truth, I'm not even certain just what those things are. I just said whatever popped into my head. Please, please, don't think I'm a fool."

Lorna pushed the screen door open and stepped out into the spring air. "I'm glad to see you," she said, meaning, "I think I love you, Herb."

"And I'm glad to see you," said Herb, looking down at his hat in his hands, embarrassed, because he was sure she must be able to tell that he meant to say, "I think I love you, Lorna."

"How's your leg?" Lorna asked, instead of saying, "Gee, Herb, you look wonderful! I'm so happy to see you again that I could cry."

"It's all right, thanks," said Herb. "You look well." (Instead of, "You look beautiful.")

"Oh, I've been fine." ("I missed you.")

"Good." ("I missed you.")

"Yes."

"You—um—didn't get married or anything like that, did you?"

"No. I would have told you so if I had."

"You would?"

"Well, I—I would have because, well, because you're my employer, and you might need to know."

"Employer?"

"The books," said Lorna.

"The books," said Herb. "Of course, the books. How are the books going?"

"Fine. Just fine. Everyone's pleased. No complaints."

"Good. Good."

For a moment, they just stood and smiled at each other.

"So you didn't get married, then?" Herb reached for her hands.

"No." Lorna put her hands in his.

Too quickly for fear to stop him, Herb leaned forward and kissed her cheek. It was hardly a kiss at all. His lips brushed her cheek. As the years passed, Lorna would become less and less sure about her memory of what Herb had said to her when he returned, but she never forgot that wisp of a kiss. It was the unforgettable statement Herb had hoped to make.

Lorna was surprised and suspicious when, on the day after her reunion with Herb, Luther asked her to come to his office at the mill, but her curiosity was aroused by Luther's conciliatory attitude. She agreed to go because she wanted to find out what Luther wanted from her.

"Lorna!" said Luther, rising from his desk and rushing to greet her. "How are you?" He took her hands in his and looked her up and down. "No need to answer, my dear, I think you've never looked prettier. You're glowing! Positively glowing."

Lorna turned away. She knew that what Luther said was true, and she didn't want him to begin speculating about why her cheeks had that rosy glow, why she was so quick to smile. She didn't want him to have anything to do with Herb; if it could have been arranged, she would have kept him from knowing anything about Herb at all.

"It's the springtime, Uncle Luther," she said. She gave him a knowing look. "Surely you've noticed that girls glow in the spring."

"So I have," said Luther. He set his jaw and narrowed his eyes.

"Well, that's enough of that, wouldn't you say?" Lorna suggested.

"Yes," said Luther. "That is enough of that. Sit down, Lorna. I want to show you something." He waved her toward the leather wing chair in front of his desk. He settled himself in his own chair, paused for dramatic effect, and lifted the top from a small box on his blotter. From the box he produced Herb's animated couple. He held the object out for Lorna to examine.

"Why, Uncle Luther!" she exclaimed.

"Spring seems to be advancing in your cheeks, Lorna," said Luther. "We'll be in high summer in a moment."

"Who made this?" Lorna asked. She took the gadget from Luther.

"That's not important," he said. "Turn the little wheel at the side."

Lorna gave the wheel a turn. "Oh, my," she said. There was

admiration in her voice, and Luther was encouraged. "Who carved these figures?" she asked.

"Originally? Sally Hirsch, I'd say," said Luther.

"You're probably right," said Lorna. "They look like her work. Who on earth performed the—ahhh, modifications?"

"To tell you the truth," said Luther, "I don't know. Nobody with any talent in that line." He smiled and brought the tips of his thumbs and index fingers together. "Clumsy work," he said, "but a brilliant idea, and a fine, fine job mechanically. Don't you think so?"

"Yes," she said. She twisted the wheel again, slowly, while she observed the little copulating couple from various angles. They enchanted her. In part, they won her over with their fluid agility and their cunning construction, but most of all, a small gesture won her: a gesture that Herb had supplied by shaping one tiny pulley with an eccentricity, the slightest little bump, like the lobe on a cam, so that at one point in the performance the man brushed his lips against the woman's cheek. It was a tiny gesture, one that Lorna had to see several times before she could be sure that it wasn't accidental, that it wasn't caused by the way she held the figures or the way she turned the wheel. When she satisfied herself that it happened every time, with the precision of all the other gestures and exertions that composed the performance, when she was certain that it was intentional, that whoever had made the little couple perform had considered this sign of affection an essential part of the performance, she was charmed.

"Interested?" asked Luther.

Lorna looked at him, but a moment passed before what he had said registered. "In what?" she asked then, taken aback.

"In returning to carving," Luther said. "None of the others could do this kind of thing the way it should be done. Trumbull, maybe. But not as well as you. Aren't you intrigued? Think what you could do with movable joints. Imagine—"

"No, Uncle Luther," said Lorna. "I'm through with all that. Forever."

"It's a wonderful night, isn't it?" said Lorna. "It's one of those nights when sweet scents are in the air."

"That might be my hair tonic," said Herb. They were in Herb's car, heading for the Serenity Ballroom. Herb wound his window down. "I might've put too much on."

"Herrrrrb——" said Lorna, drawing out his name in a way that meant, "Don't be silly!" (This would in years to come become one of Lorna's most-frequently-uttered remarks.)

"I wish I'd had time to get a new suit before I left home," said Herb. "Well, I had time, but I didn't take the time."

"I'm glad you didn't," said Lorna.

"You mean you like this suit? I got this before the war, long before the war." He was suddenly struck by the fact that a great deal of time had passed during which ordinary things like buying a new suit hadn't even crossed his mind, and by the idea that his suit and the new awareness he had of his suit, marked two points—the moment when he'd chosen the suit and the moment just passed when he'd been reminded of that moment—between which lay a huge bubble of time: all the time he'd been in the war, all the time it had taken him to begin to recognize love, all the time it had taken him to realize that he loved Lorna. "This is a *very* old suit," said Herb, meaning all that.

"I didn't mean that I like the suit," said Lorna. "I meant that I'm glad you didn't take the time to get a new one. I'm glad I didn't have to wait any longer for you to come back. That's what I meant."

Herb looked at her and smiled, but the smile faded quickly. "Does that mean you don't like the suit?" he asked.

"No, it doesn't," said Lorna. "I think you look just fine. Your suit is fine. Your shirt is fine. Your tie is beautiful."

"Beautiful?" said Herb. He looked at Lorna with his face twisted in a worried grimace. "It's wrong, isn't it? It's too loud. Calls attention to itself. I should've worn something different. Brown. A brown tie."

Lorna burst out laughing. "Herb," she said. "It wouldn't make any difference what you wore. All the girls I knew in school, everyone I worked with in the mill, all the boys I've ever danced with, everyone who knows my family, anybody who's ever known me, would have something to say about it anyway."

"You mean they'll be looking for something wrong with me."

"I'm afraid so. They'll all want to know what it is about you that makes you more—well——"

"Yes?"

"More interesting or more——"

"Desirable?"

"All right. More desirable." She assumed the air of an outraged matron, mother of one of the young men of Chacallit; "I ask you," she said, "what makes him more desirable than the young men right here in Chacallit?"

"Uh-oh," said Herb. "I have the feeling that there's one young man in particular."

"I'm afraid there has been," said Lorna.

"Will he be there tonight?"

"I suppose so."

"How will I recognize him?"

"He's tall and good-looking—"

"Mmm."

"—with dark, wavy hair and a strong jaw and big hands—"

"Oh, boy."

"—and he usually has a circle of admirers around him."

"I should have worn a brown tie."

When Herb and Lorna walked into the ballroom, everyone fell silent, and everyone turned to stare.

Herb had no difficulty identifying the particular young man. Andy Proctor hopped up from the table where he was sitting with a group of friends and admirers (a couple of whom were, to be accurate, neither friends nor admirers but young men and women who were broke and out of work and entertained hopes that Andy would get them work at Proctor's Products, lend them money, or at least pick up the tab for the evening). He bounded to the door to greet Herb and Lorna, producing exactly the effect he'd hoped for: a ripple of admiration for his big-heartedness ran around the room, and Andrew was a hero for the second time. (Elsa Burch, who had been inclined to think of him as an egotistical braggart, developed a fondness for him on the spot. Four months later they were engaged; they married the following spring. They lived together in Chacallit all their lives. Their youngest son still lives in Chacallit today. He owns the gay bar, 24-Karat Studs.)

"So you're the better man," Andy said when Lorna introduced Herb. "What do you say we step outside?"

Outside, Andy leaned against the railing on the open porch that reached out over Lake Serenity. Moonlight flickered on the rippling water. He reached into his jacket pocket and produced a small sterling flask manufactured by Proctor's Products. The flask was a little outside the usual catalog of the company, but it was doing very well for them; Andy had suggested it, and the suggestion had confirmed for his father the wisdom of grooming the boy for a future at the helm.

"Drink, Herb?" Andy asked. He smiled a cheerless smile, a challenging, bellicose smile.

"I will. Yes. Thanks," said Herb. He wiped his palms on his jacket and accepted the flask.

Other young men began drifting out of the ballroom and taking positions along the railing. Most made some attempt to appear to be talking among themselves, but it was clear to Herb that they had come outside not for a drink or a smoke, but to see what would happen between him and Andy.

"Thanks," Herb said, returning the flask and the smile.

"Don't mention it," said Andy. The smile again. He drank. "You enjoying yourself in Chacallit?" he asked.

"Yes," said Herb. "Yes, I am. It's a nice place." He leaned on the railing, looking out over the lake, wishing he could think of something snappy to say.

"Hey, Bump," Andy called out. "Come over here and meet somebody."

Herb turned from the lake and saw that the invitation to "Bump" had drawn not only a large sandy-haired fellow—Bump, he supposed—but all the other young men on the porch, who drifted in his direction behind Bump.

"Hello there," said Bump. He gave Herb a nod. No smile.

"This is Herb Piper," said Andy. He smiled at Bump—the same humorless, antagonistic smile.

"Herb Piper," said Bump, pronouncing the name as if he thought it should be familiar to him. "Herb Piper," he said again. His expression (pursed lips, twisted mouth, eyebrows drawn together) suggested that he was searching his memory for some information about Herb Piper that ought to be there. "I think I must have known a Herb Piper. You don't look familiar, but the name sounds familiar. Ever live in Albany?"

"No," said Herb.

"Baltimore?"

"No."

"Didn't work for the B and O, did you?"

"No," said Herb. "I've lived in Boston all along."

"Boston? Herb Piper. Herb Piper. Were you in France?"

"Yes. I was in France."

"Where?"

"Quelquepart-sur-Marne."

"Holy jumping Jesus!" exclaimed Bump. "Are you the guy from Boston? The one who fixed the cup handles?"

"Yes," said Herb. "That's me."

"This is an honor!" said Bump. He grabbed Herb's hand in both of his and began pumping it. "An honor!" He raised Herb's arm in the air and said, turning to the crowd, "This is Herb Piper!" There wasn't much of a reaction to this announcement: puzzled looks, some mumbled speculation. "Herb Piper!" Bump said again, a look of incredulity on his face. "The guy from Boston who fixed those goddamned cup handles," he said. He turned to Herb. "Boy," he said in an apologetic tone, "*sic transit gloria mundi*, huh?" But the others remembered now, and they began to draw nearer in a circle around Herb.

"Shake the hand that shook the hand of Black Jack Pershing himself," said Bump, waving Herb's arm above the others, who pressed in for the chance to do so.

"I—uh—knew you'd want to meet him," said Andy, tugging at Bump's sleeve.

"I didn't actually shake hands with—" Herb began. Good sense made him stop. He shrugged and let the claim stand. He reached for the hands extended toward him.

A couple of hours later, after they had chatted with Lorna's friends and danced and eaten pieces of lemon cake, Lorna whispered to Herb the suggestion that they rent a boat and row around on the lake in the moonlight for a while. They excused themselves, left the crowd that had gathered at their table, skirted the dance floor, and left by the door that led onto the porch.

Adelaide Hooper and her sister Priscilla watched them go. When they were gone, Addy sighed and gave Priss a look that Priss understood at once. It was a look they had exchanged often, ever since they had become interested in boys.

"Don't you wish——?" asked Addy.

"Oh, don't I," said Priss.

"Hey, wish what?" asked Zack Mitchell. He gave Addy a squeeze. "You're not wishing you were her, are you?"

"No, it isn't that," said Addy. "I just wish we were more like them. They're so—well—they kind of understand each other."

"We don't?" asked Zack.

Addy sighed and frowned. "Did you see the way he looked at her when he came back into the hall with Andy Proctor and all those other guys? Just a little grin, but she knew what he meant by it. Priss and I can do that, but you and I—well—I wish we—I wish we—understood each other like that."

"And the way they dance together," said Priss.

"Come on," said Zack. "They don't dance well at all."

"I know," said Priss, "but they—oh, I know this doesn't seem to make sense, but they don't dance well the same way—the way they don't dance well is just right for them."

"I know just what you mean," said Addy.

"Well, I *don't*," said Zack. He went outside for a pull at his flask.

Arnold Abbot Adler, leader of the resident dance band at the Serenity Ballroom, Arnold Abbot Adler's Triple-A Orchestra, stepped to the edge of the bandstand and said, "Now, folks, we'd like to try something a little different, something that the boys and I have been working on for a long time, something we call 'Lake Serenity Serenade.'"

Lorna, holding Herb's hand to steady herself, stepped into the rowboat. The first notes drifted out over the lake just as Herb pushed off from the dock. And—what luck!—"Lake Serenity Serenade" turned out to be lilting and beautiful, and the sax section of the Triple-A Orchestra outdid itself. It was a great stroke of luck, one of those happy accidents we discredit when we hear an account of their happening to someone else, although they figure so prominently in our dreams and daydreams and are sometimes our only reason for hope.

In *Time and Free Will*, his essay on the immediate data of consciousness, Henri Bergson remarked that joy and passion are "very like a turning of our states of consciousness toward the future. As if their weight were diminished by this attraction, our ideas and sensations succeed one another with greater rapidity; our movements no longer cost us the same effort." That is precisely what Herb, in his joy and passion, experienced, though he didn't give it a thought. He just found the rowing remarkably easy. The water seemed as insubstantial as the moonlight that played upon it. Herb took long, languid strokes. When he lifted the oars, silver droplets fell from the blades, leaving silver circles on the surface, circles that widened in the wake of the little boat. The boat glided on, as easily as if it were floating above the lake, through the clear air of the Whatsit Valley. Lorna reclined in the stern and looked at the stars. She let her fingers brush the surface of the water on either side of the boat. They left rippling wakes of their own. Herb couldn't see where he was going. He had his back to the bow; he saw only Lorna. He was quite content. He saw her smiling, and he was delighted to see her smiling. This was a smile of contentment, of serene joy.

"Lorna," he whispered, "close your eyes."

Still smiling, she closed her eyes. Herb went on rowing.

"Imagine that you see your future," said Herb. "Tell me what you see."

Lorna drew a breath, and the air she inhaled thrilled her. For a moment she could hardly believe that she was breathing ordinary air, the effect was so intoxicating. She had imagined so well that she seemed to have taken a breath from her future, and her smile widened because she'd tasted her future and found that she liked it. Herb was rowing toward the future; the past was in their wake.

"It must be good," said Herb, watching her.

"It is," said Lorna. "Close your eyes, and I'll tell you what I see."

"If I close my eyes, I won't be able to see where I'm going."

Airy laughter, almost giggles; silvery, moonlit laughter.

"Of course I can't see where I'm going," said Herb. He swallowed and dared to say, very softly, "But I can see my future." Then he closed his eyes. "I closed my eyes," he said.

"I see *you*," said Lorna.

Herb drew a long breath and found it so intoxicating that he gripped the oars tighter to steady himself. "Does that mean what I hope it means?" he asked.

"I hope so," she said.

"Do you want to know about my plans?" Herb asked.

"Of course I do," said Lorna. "But it won't make any difference what they are; it's you I love, Herb, not your plans. Do you want to know mine?"

"Wouldn't make any difference to me either," said Herb.

Lorna sat up suddenly. "Are we engaged?" she asked.

"I hope so," said Herb.

The crowd inside the ballroom called for an encore of "Lake Serenity Serenade" and got it, and during the encore Herb and Lorna made love. It was, compared to what either had tasted so far, a feast. All the senses were invited, and there was no reason this time to leave the mind, the heart, or the imagination out of the fun; there was something for all of them—some rocking rowboat, rocking, rocking, beneath their tentative caresses, balsam scenting the air, moaning saxophones, Lorna leaning over Herb, running her hands over his chest, imagining modeling him in clay, tugging, pushing, kneading at his skin as if it *were* clay, pushing him backward and pulling his pants down, laughing, the rowboat rocking, rocking, *rocking*, whooops, rocking, grabbing for the gunwales, ouch, ooh, a splinter, thin sliver in the palm of Lorna's hand, Herb's slow, cautious extraction, drawing the sliver out so slowly that the sweet pain made Lorna run her hand between her legs, salty taste of Lorna's blood, fluttering tickle of Herb's tongue in Lorna's palm, Lorna stretching out, her slow undressing, moonlight turning her to ivory, Herb imagining her in ivory, articulated here, here, here, here, wavelets lapping the sides of the boat, distant voices, laughter, a call, a shriek, stars twinkling in the night sky and bouncing in the water, Lorna's foot dangling in the water, Lorna twisting around and settling onto Herb, wiggling to feel Herb in her, the long curved edges of the gunwales pressing into Herb's calves, his feet dangling in the water, the wavelets tickling the soles of his feet, and at the moment of his coming the tickling becoming too much to bear, his laughing, laughing, laughing, their collapsing into the boat like fish landed after a struggle, flopping over the seats, bruising themselves on the edges and corners and oarlocks, and laughing, laughing, and subsiding, and lying with their arms around each other, just looking out over the water, the flickering water, silver with moonlight, but now, oddly, gold here and there, and even red, and—

Lorna lifted herself on one elbow and looked back toward the ballroom. It was in flames. They hurried into their clothes and began rowing back, sitting side by side, pulling at the oars, keeping their course by keeping their fire-formed shadows in the boat, and Lorna, who was so giddy with the promise of the future they had tasted that she couldn't resist her happiness, even though she worried about the fire, turned toward Herb and asked, "You don't think *we* did it, do you?"

8
In Which Herb 'n' Lorna Move to Babbington, New York

The fire at the Serenity Ballroom was caused, an investigation disclosed, not by Herb and Lorna's ardor, but by a kitchen fire. According to May Castle, Lorna considered the burning of the ballroom the symbolic end of her girlhood, the end of her life as a child:

> *Oh, yes, it was the burning point of her life. Oh! I didn't mean that, not at all. I meant to say "turning point," I honestly did. Stop. Rewind. Start again. That night was the turning point of her life, you see. And everything just happened all at once. Here she was engaged, and she'd just made love to this wonderful man—the man she was destined to live her life with—and, oh, I don't know, she may have had her first orgasm. Well! Then, to top it off, there was this perfectly spectacular fire! It was quite a night. It doesn't surprise me a bit that she decided right then that she and Chacallit were fini.*

"Close your eyes, Herb," said Lorna, "and I'll tell you about our future." She and Herb had driven to the top of Ackerman Hill, or as far as the road went, and they had stopped in the turnaround there.

Herb had his arm around Lorna's shoulders, and she reclined against him. He closed his eyes.

"All right," he said.

"Now imagine this," said Lorna. "Six months have passed. We've been married for four. Four months ago, my father gave you a job in the sales department, and there was some talk, which you and he and I ignored as well as we could. From your very first day on the job, though, you impressed everyone, and now even the people who resented you most when you arrived have to admit that you're the best salesman they've ever seen."

Herb gave her a little squeeze.

"They still talk about you behind your back, but now they usually say something like, 'You know, I hate to admit it, but that Herb Piper is one heck of a salesman.' My father is very proud of you. So am I. I've stopped working at the mill, because you don't want my old friends to think that you can't support me. My father approves, since he never wanted me to work at the mill in the first place. I spend all day at home. My mother won't let me cook, since that's her job. However, I *am* permitted to wash the dishes. Every day my mother asks me if my marriage is happy and if there's anything I need to ask her about.

"You and I are still living on the third floor, and we have to whisper when we talk in bed at night. We eat dinner with my parents every evening, and after dinner we all sit together in the parlor, except on weekends, when you and I go out. Every time we go out, we run into Andy Proctor. You and Andy have become great pals. Every time he greets you he pounds you on the back, and every time he greets me he winks.

"My mother and father celebrate our six-month anniversary by opening a bottle of champagne. My father announces that you've earned another promotion. We're all delighted. Then he clears his throat and tells us how happy he and my mother are about the way things have turned out. He makes a joke about the misunderstanding when they first met you. My mother laughs. We all laugh. He says something sentimental. We all shed some tears. We eat dinner. We sit in the parlor. The clock ticks. My father nods in his chair. You and I go upstairs. We slip into bed. We are very quiet. In the dark, I whisper in your ear, 'Herb, let's get out of here.'"

She sat upright, took Herb's face in her hands, and said, "Herb, why wait? Let's get out of here now."

"Okay," said Herb.

"Chacallit is about one hundred seventy-eight and a half miles from Boston," said Lorna, looking up from the map that she had spread out on the kitchen table.

"'About'?" said Herb. He poked her. She bumped him with her hip.

"About," she said. "Here. Let's try something." From a drawer, she took a ball of string. She stretched a length of it from Boston to Chacallit. She held the Boston end in place, and with her pencil at the other end, she scribed an arc. Then she held the Chacallit end in place, put her pencil at the Boston end, and scribed another arc.

"What have we got?" asked Herb.

Together, they bent over the map.

"Well, we've got West Burke, Vermont," said Lorna, pointing out the northern intersection of the arcs, "or"—turning to the southern intersection—"Babbington, New York. On Long Island."

She looked at Herb. He looked at her. "I like the ocean," he said.

"I've never seen it," said Lorna, beaming.

Separately, each of them knew that they'd need money to move, and, separately, each of them knew how to get it, and neither of them wanted the other to know how it would be gotten, so each of them concocted a lie, and the lies, like the arcs Lorna drew to find a place to go, overlapped and intersected, and they concealed truths that overlapped and intersected, too.

"I have some money—" Lorna began.

"So do I," said Herb.

"But my uncle Luther is—holding it," said Lorna.

"My uncle Ben has mine," said Herb.

"I—I invested it—that is, he invested it for me," said Lorna.

"I lent it to Uncle Ben to help him out, but I'm sure he can pay me back now," said Herb.

"It will take a little while for me to get it," said Lorna.

"I'll have to go home and explain to Uncle Ben," said Herb. "It could take—a while."

♦   ♦   ♦

In Boston, Herb told his uncle Ben what he had in mind. "Here's what I have in mind, Uncle Ben," he said. "I'll make eleven more prototypes. That'll give you a dozen models. Okay?"

"Okay," said Ben. "I'll work out an arrangement with the people in Chacallit so that you get a certain percentage of the sales."

"I need money now, Uncle Ben."

"Maybe I can get them to advance you some money. I'll have to see."

"Why don't I just *sell* you the designs, Uncle Ben? Outright. Then you make whatever deal you want with the manufacturer. How about that?" (Herb felt a little ashamed of himself for what he was doing, because he thought that he might be taking advantage of his uncle Ben. An outright sale of the designs seemed to Herb the only prudent course to take. It would have seemed so to his cautious mother, too. A bird in the hand certainly *seems* to be worth two in the bush. But, as it turned out, Herb was, at the very moment when he was feeling guilty about taking advantage of Ben, doing a foolish Piper thing. He was convincing himself that the coarse-goods trade was a poor financial risk. He was talking himself into taking sure money instead of the royalties that might have made him rich.)

"Well, I'd be taking a risk," said Ben.

"Oh, right," said Herb. "You're right. I understand that—"

"I wouldn't be able to give you too much for them," said Ben, "on account of the risk."

"I understand," said Herb. "I know you're taking a risk."

"How much did you think you'd want?" asked Ben.

"Three thousand dollars," said Herb.

"Oh," said Ben. He was genuinely disappointed. He had hoped that he'd be able to let Herb have everything he wanted, that he would be able to be both generous uncle and good businessman. "It's more than I can put out," he said. "I've got an idea, though. I can give you half of it in cash and half of it in goods."

"What kind of goods?"

"Coarse goods."

"Aw, Uncle Ben," said Herb.

"It's the best I can do, Herb," said Ben. "I mean it."

"All right," said Herb. He paused. "Uncle Ben, you have to promise me something. You have to promise me never to tell anyone about this."

"Hell, you shouldn't be ashamed of this, Herb. There's lots of people who do worse things than——"

"Uncle Ben, you have to promise."

"All right, I promise."

"And I mean never."

"Never."

When Lorna arrived at Luther's office, he greeted her with a thin smile. "This is an unexpected pleasure," he said.

"Uncle Luther," said Lorna, "I'll do it."

"Do what?" asked Luther, smiling unctuously.

"You know what," said Lorna.

"Why, you don't mean——" said Luther, raising an eyebrow to complete his question.

"Yes, I do, and you know it."

"Now must be never, then."

"I guess it must."

"What changed your mind, my dear?"

"Herb and I are going to leave Chacallit, and we'll need money to get ourselves settled.

"Oh, I'm sorry to hear that."

"Uncle Luther, let's talk about my terms."

"Terms?"

"I'll work for two months."

"Two months?"

"That's all. I want your word that you'll never tell anyone about this and that you'll never ask me to work on coarse goods again."

"Does this mean that your young man doesn't know about your craft?"

"He doesn't know anything at all about it, and I want you to promise that he'll never know anything from you, directly or indirectly. No accidental slips. No hints. No winks. Nothing."

"He will never know from me, dear," said Luther, raising his hand. "I wonder, though, whether deception is a good beginning for a marriage."

Lorna went right on. "I want twenty-five percent more than John

Caldwell's getting now," she said. "You can tell people I'm getting less, if you want, but that's what you're going to have to pay me."

"My, my, isn't it amazing the way time changes people. It seems as if it was only yesterday when you came into this office full of righteous indignation, waving a pamphlet from the Women's Socialist League or something like that—"

"The Women's Trade Union League."

"Oh. The Women's Trade Union League. You were quite taken with what they had to say back then. Wasn't it 'equal pay for equal work'?"

"It was."

"Well, what happened to that idea?"

"Why, Uncle Luther," said Lorna, "you know very well that John's work was never the equal of mine." She turned and walked out of the office, leaving the door open behind her. When she was halfway along the corridor, she heard its satisfying slam.

It took more than two months for Herb to dispose of the coarse goods Ben gave him, develop eleven new couples (and how he yearned for Lorna while he worked, how much his imagination was enlarged by thinking of her), sell his list of Five-Foot Shelf customers, sell his old Studebaker Four, and buy a new-to-him Studebaker Series 19 "Light Six." Lorna carved coarse goods for Luther while she waited for Herb's return, and together, though apart, they accumulated a nice little nest egg.

At Herb and Lorna's wedding, Lester Piper appeared to have regained all of his old spark. He so charmed Richard Huber that Richard spent hours trying to persuade Lester to leave what he supposed was a fairly good position in Boston and move to Chacallit, where the air was clear and the rushing waters of the Whatsit were mellifluous and pure, and to try breathing some life into his sales department. To Richard Huber's surprise (but much more to the surprise of Millie and Ben Piper), Lester accepted.

There was some talk in Chacallit when Lester and Millie arrived and put up with the Hubers until they found a place of their own, and there was some resentment when Lester assumed his duties, but in a few months even the people who had resented him most when he arrived had to admit that Lester Piper was the best salesman they'd ever seen.

Herb and Lorna arrived in Babbington on a cold and rainy Sunday night. The town looked deserted. Main Street was nearly dark; the only light came from night lights in a few shops, from the streetlamps at the intersection of Bolotomy and Main, from the police station, and from a garage across the street from the police station. Of these, the first that Lorna and Herb saw, coming into town from the west, were those at the police station and the garage.

"Well," said Herb, "it's not quite what I'd imagined."

"How can you tell?" asked Lorna. "I can't see a thing."

"That's what I mean. I had imagined a clear night, a moon, moonlight on the ocean, something like that."

"Sounds like the night we burned the ballroom," said Lorna.

"There's something," said Herb. "Looks like a police station up ahead."

"I'll take your word for it," said Lorna.

"And a service station across the street. Speedy's Reliable Service."

Herb pulled into Speedy's and dashed through the rain into the station. There, at an oak desk, bent over a copy of the *Babbington Reporter*, was Officer Dan Whitley, youngest son of the renowned scoundrel and noted angler Andy Whitley, the mayor of Babbington at that time. After a moment or two spent standing, patiently, just inside the door, clearing his throat and shuffling his feet now and then, Herb decided that Dan was asleep. He retreated soundlessly to the door, opened it, backed out into the rain, and reentered, this time with a heavy tread and loud exclamations.

"Whoo!" he exclaimed. "It's not a fit night out for man or beast!" He stamped his feet and shook the rainwater from his hat.

Dan, startled, sat up straight, shook himself awake, and rubbed his eyes.

"Say, I didn't startle you, did I?" asked Herb.

"Me?" asked Dan. "Heck no. You just kind of surprised me. I was pretty intent on what I was reading here, that's all."

"What's that?" asked Herb.

"Obits," said Dan.

"Uh-oh," said Herb. "Nobody close to you, I hope."

"Hm? Oh, no. Not anybody special. Well, there is a cousin in here today, kind of a distant one, though. Couple of other people I knew enough to say hello to. I read 'em all, though. Don't matter to me who they are. It's kind of a study with me, a study of human nature. You find out a lot about people this way. 'Course, you have to know how to read between the lines sometimes, but it's funny how much you don't know about somebody till he's dead."

Herb and Dan spent a moment in silent contemplation of that idea, and then Dan looked at Herb as if realizing for the first time that Herb was someone he didn't know at all, not even to say hello to.

"Say," Dan said, "what're you doing out on a night like this? You in some kind of trouble?"

"No," said Herb, "no trouble. My wife and I——"

"Lost?"

"No, I——"

"Passing through? Want some gas?" A toilet flushed somewhere behind Dan, and he jerked his thumb in the direction of the sound. "Speedy'll be right out. I'd pump you some myself, but I'm on duty."

"That's okay. I don't need gas," said Herb. "I need some directions."

"Said you weren't lost," Dan pointed out. He narrowed his eyes.

"No. Yes. That's right, I'm not. Lost. I——we——we're going to settle here."

"Here? In Babbington?"

"Yes, in Babbington."

Dan inspected him. Behind him, a door opened, and a squat man in coveralls emerged from it. Herb smiled and nodded at him. "You related to the Feasters?" Dan asked.

"No," said Herb. "The name's Piper, Herb Piper. I don't have any relatives here——I don't even know anyone here." He extended his hand. Neither Dan nor Speedy made a move to shake it.

"The wife?" asked Dan.

"No, no. We just came to Babbington because——"

Herb had been about to describe the method that Lorna had used to choose Babbington as a place for them to live, but he thought better of it. It would, he knew, seem ridiculous, and, worse than that, it might seem insulting. After all, wouldn't he be saying that he and Lorna had come to Babbington because they knew that they could be happy wherever they went, that their love, their benevolent giant, would follow them anywhere? *You can't say that to a person,* Herb thought, *say that this place, the place where he lives, seems to you only as good as any other place—no better, no worse.*

"Because what?" asked Dan. There was a new chill in his voice.

"Well, because we heard nice things about it," Herb lied. He certainly didn't want to begin his life in Babbington by offending the civic pride of, or arousing the suspicions of, the police. "That is, my wife did," he said, his mind racing. "See, my wife is from Chacallit, upstate, not far from Albany, and—um, when she was a little girl some people from Babbington were passing through, and—"

"That would be the Sutphens, I'll bet," said Speedy, folding his arms across his chest.

"The Sutphens!" said Herb, eager to establish some link between Lorna and himself and the town. "It probably was! Yes, it probably was. The Sutphens."

"Went to Canada," said Speedy. Herb nodded enthusiastically.

"*Fled* to Canada," said Dan. "Probably passed through this place your wife's from—Whatchamacallit—"

"Chacallit."

"Right. Wilfred and Elizabeth Sutphen. Wilfred was accused of embezzling, went to trial, wasn't convicted."

"Not guilty," said Herb, nodding again.

"Not *convicted*," said Dan.

"Uh-huh," said Herb, who was beginning to wonder how long it would take to drive to West Burke, Vermont.

"Nobody ever found the money," said Speedy.

"I read where Wilfred died just a few weeks ago," said Dan.

"Fell off a horse in front of a truck," said Speedy.

"I remember the headline on his obit," said Dan. He held his hands in front of him with his thumbs and index fingers spread and drew them apart to suggest a banner headline. "'Former Babbingtonian Dies in Wolf Snout, Manitoba,' it said. And then under that, smaller, it said, 'Wilfred Sutphen, fifty-eight, Alleged Embezzler.'"

"Well," said Herb, "I'm sure it was somebody else, then, not the Sutphens, but whoever it was, these people made the town sound so wonderful that my wife fell in love with the place."

"She fell in love with it without even seeing it?" asked Speedy. He didn't look like a man convinced. Herb asked himself why he hadn't just told the truth. He was backing farther and farther into a corner. This was not getting off on the right foot.

"She—" said Herb. He sighed. He didn't know what to say next. The door opened. Lorna walked in. "Lorna!" he said. "Lorna. I—was just trying to explain to—um, Officer—um—and Mr. Speedy how it was that we decided to settle here in Babbington, why it had to be *this* town and no other. Not as if we just picked out any old town on a map—and they were wondering how it was that you fell in love with the place without ever having seen it."

"I saw it in my mind's eye," said Lorna, "in my imagination. The little seacoast town. The neat houses." She stopped. They wore looks that said they expected more.

"The—uh, church steeples," offered Herb. "The—red and yellow leaves on the trees in the fall."

"Schoolchildren on their way to—school," said Lorna.

"The glowing streetlamps," said Herb.

Lorna held her hands up as if calling for silence and half closed her eyes. "The night, the glowing streetlamps, the people asleep in their cozy beds, in their neat houses, safe and warm, while trusty guardians keep watch through the night." She smiled. She wore the look of an enchanted child, envisioning her Shangri-La.

Dan and Speedy smiled back. They looked enchanted themselves. "And after all these years, here you are at last," Dan said.

Lorna smiled her answer.

"Well, I hope you won't be disappointed," said Speedy. "A lot of times, you find out that things aren't everything you were hoping they'd be, you know? You get an idea all worked up in your mind about how something is going to be and then, brother, are you in for a surprise. Take right now, for instance. I'll bet you didn't imagine that when you got to Babbington, you'd be caught in a rainstorm like this, did you?"

Lorna couldn't resist. "Oh, I did," she said, breathless, her eyes shining. "I imagined it just like this."

"What?" said Speedy, his eyes widening. "Howling wind, driving rain, and you all wet and shivering—that's the way you imagined it?"

"Yes," said Lorna, still the enchanted girl.

"And you fell in love with it?"

A nod full of charm, those bright eyes.

"Boy, oh, boy, love is a crazy thing," said Dan, grinning and shaking his head. "A woman can fall in love with the—" he began. He caught himself. Confused, he looked at Lorna. He found no help in her smile. To change the subject, he asked, "Where—um—where did you imagine you two were going to stay?"

Lorna closed her eyes. "A small hotel—" she said.

"Mm-hm," said Dan.

"Yeah," said Speedy.

"—where salesmen stay sometimes—"

"Mm."

"Yep."

"—with a small dining room—"

"Gosh."

"Brother."

"—not far from here."

"That's got to be the River Sound Hotel!" said Dan. His eyes were wide.

"Couldn't be anyplace else," said Speedy. He let his mouth hang open.

After Lorna and Herb were settled in their room at the River Sound, they went out for a walk. Through the rain and the dark, they walked in the direction in which Lorna supposed the ocean to be. They walked along River Sound Road, then along Bolotomy Road, until they reached the Municipal Dock. Storm-driven waves pounded the dock, and spray washed over the bulkheads. Lorna cried, "The ocean!"

It was not—it was only Bolotomy Bay—but Lorna felt exactly the surge of excitement she had imagined she would feel when she first saw the ocean. She ran to the edge of the dock. Clinging to a piling, she leaned out over the dark water and let the spray splatter her. She licked the water from her lips and tasted the salt. She ran to Herb and hugged him.

"Let's go back to the hotel and see if we can burn it down," she said.

At that time, the economic foundation of Babbington still rested on the bottom of Bolotomy Bay, on the bay's clam beds. The clamming industry and related industries—boat building and repair, the manufacture of clamming equipment, clam processing, clam by-products, tartar sauce preparation and packaging, and so on—employed most of the men of Babbington and nearly all of the women who worked. The Babbington Clam Council, an industry group, was a powerful force in local politics, and clamming-related fraternal orders—notably the Mercenarians, the Order of Littlenecks, and the Secret and Mystical Fraternity of Fun-Loving Baymen—were important in the social life of the town. A casual stroll along Main Street, like the casual stroll that Lorna and Herb took on their first full day in town, provided ample evidence of the importance of the bay and the clam.

At first glance, Main Street, Babbington, looked much like Main Street in any other small town of that time; the street was lined with banks, lunch counters, a hardware store, a five-and-ten, a movie house, groceries, shoe stores, clothing shops, and such, and above the shops were offices occupied by insurance companies, the *Babbington Reporter*, lawyers, dentists, a gypsy reader, and other professionals— the assortment of enterprises that one would expect on Main Street just about anywhere. A closer look, however, discovered signs of the dominance of clam fishery: the clam-digging equipment displayed in the window of Babbington Diggers' Gear, the "Stages in the Life of a Clam" exhibit in a window of the local office of Continental Clam, the "treading booties" offered in the window of the Superior Shoe Shop, the clam chowder, clam broth, clams casino, baked stuffed clams, clam fritters, clam cakes, fried clams, steamed clams, clams on the half shell, and "clamburger" on the menu at Louise's Lunch, and so on.

They walked the length of Main Street. They stopped across the street from Continental Clam to watch some schoolchildren on a field trip make their way from panel to panel in the stages in the life of a clam. The children seemed fascinated by one panel in particular. Lorna took Herb by the arm and pulled him across the street. They stood behind the children and looked over their heads. Large blue letters at the top of the display announced:

FERTILIZATION TAKES PLACE OUTSIDE THE SHELL!

A diorama depicted a submarine orgy. Several female clams were discharging puffs that reminded Lorna of her father's pipe smoke.

FEMALE RELEASES A HUNDRED MILLION EGGS AT ONCE!

Several male clams were releasing thin whitish streams in random directions.

MORE THAN TWO BILLION SPERM PER EJACULATION!

The children were giggling. One girl noticed Herb and Lorna's reflection in the window. She turned and looked at Lorna and blushed. Lorna smiled and, quite aware of the implications of what she was doing, winked at the girl. She squeezed Herb's arm tighter, and when they walked away she stopped after a couple of steps, put both arms around Herb, hugged him, and kissed him. She hoped the girl was watching, and she hoped she'd get the message Lorna meant to send: it's a lot more fun than that.

In the days that followed, Herb looked for work, and Lorna looked for a place to live. As it happened, Lorna found a job, and Herb found an apartment.

The job that Lorna found, through a conversation with a woman in a drugstore, was a job for Herb. It wasn't much of a job. It was a job as a culler in the Babbington Clam packing plant. Cullers picked through the clams, sorting them by size and quality. Cullers' work was boring work. It didn't pay much. The woman who suggested it to Lorna was a clammy's wife; she had thought of culling as work for Lorna, work to bring in money until her husband got a job, work that would assure her that some money would always be coming in, even when her husband was out of work, work to help make ends meet, work to earn her some mad money, perhaps, but not a breadwinner's work, not work for bringing home the bacon.

Herb took the job at once. He and Lorna didn't need money right away; they had put together enough to keep them for a while. Herb knew, though, from his selling experience, how important, persistent, and difficult to alter a first impression is, and for that reason he wanted to get to work right away, and the meaner the job, the more it suited him. The first impression that people have of you, even when it is a mistaken one (and I'd be willing to bet that three first impressions out of four are mistaken), becomes a part of your past as perceived (or misperceived) by those who have formed the impression (or mis-impression), a part of the past that pursues you forever, that dogged giant who's always on your heels. Bob Mintner, in his overpriced videocassette series *You Could Make a Million If You Would Stop Acting Like a Jerk*, says, on the subject of the first impression:

> You can NEVER overcome the first impression. If you get off on the WRONG FOOT, you can NEVER get back in step. You may think that tomorrow, if you wear a new jacket and tie, change your hairstyle, sprinkle your remarks with some of the latest "SNAPPY" expressions, and put a new SPRING in your step, people will see you in a NEW LIGHT, that they'll say, "Say, I've been ALL WRONG about Fred! Why, it's as if I'm seeing him for the FIRST TIME." Well, FORGET it. You're WRONG. They may look at you, but they won't SEE you. The man they are going to see is the man who matches the IDEA THEY FORMED OF YOU when they FIRST MET YOU. Compared to you, that guy is a GIANT! The only thing you can do if you've gotten off on the wrong foot is pack your bags, get out of town, change your name, and start ALL OVER AGAIN.

"What I want to do, Lorna," said Herb, "is make a good first impression. I want to impress on people the idea that I'm ready to work. I want them to think of me as a hard and willing worker. Later on, I can find a good selling job, I'm sure of that. When I do, I'll have a reputation around town. People won't think of me as a guy who came into town as a salesman. They'll think of me as a guy who came to Babbington with nothing but ambition and a willingness to work and who, by God, worked himself up from a job culling in the clam plant to a good job as a salesman. I'll be a Babbington success story, a local hero, and people will be happy to buy from me."

Lorna wasn't sure whether to laugh or not. She saw that there was wisdom behind Herb's idea, but even so it sounded like a laughable scheme. "Where did you get those ideas?" she asked.

"Well," said Herb, "I thought of the details myself, but I got the basic idea from one of the books in Professor Clapp's Five-Foot Shelf."

"What one was that?"

"*Sixty-six Steps up the Stairway to Success—Starting at the Bottom.*"

The apartment. Well, the apartment might not have seemed much better than the job. Herb found it while he was walking along Bolotomy Road, on his way to the area in the southernmost part of Babbington, along the bay, where, he had learned, most of the messier work was done. He intended to wander through the area and see what the businesses looked like, see whether there were any jobs to be had. He had already fixed his mind on the notion of demonstrating to Babbington a rise from obscurity by dint of labor, so that he would be admired and trusted, and he had decided to take any small, mean job at the scruffiest of the plants.

Bolotomy Road began at the heart of Babbington, the only intersection lit by streetlamps on the dark night when Lorna and Herb arrived in town: the intersection that Babbingtonians of long standing always referred to as "Bolotomy and Main," though in fact only the northerly reach of the road that intersected Main Street there was officially called Bolotomy Road. The part of it that ran to the south, toward the bay, had been renamed Bella Vista Boulevard, a name that the progressive faction of the town council had advocated as a step toward attracting touring motorists to Babbington. Bella Vista Boulevard was one of the shibboleths that identified newcomers; it was ignored by all Babbingtonians whose residence in Babbington predated the change or who wished to appear to have been living in Babbington before the change. Old-timers always referred to Bella Vista Boulevard as Lower Bolotomy and Bolotomy Road as Upper Bolotomy, or simply as Lower and Upper.

Along Lower, as he walked south from Bolotomy and Main, Herb passed a couple of blocks of shops, shops that didn't require the visibility of Main Street locations (or didn't desire that visibility—it was in this stretch, about twenty-five years after Lorna and Herb came to Babbington, that Head Cheese, Babbington's first psyche-delicatessen, opened, displacing a candy-and-tobacco store called Maxie's). Farther along, he passed large, handsome frame houses, most of them painted white, many the homes of professional people—doctors, lawyers, accountants—some of whom had offices in their homes and hung their shingles on metal brackets that projected from the sides of their front porches. He continued walking, past blocks of smaller houses, into a stretch where the houses were very small, not much larger than cabins, and tumbled together, like sugar cubes spilled from a box. The little houses were separated by narrow strips of sand in which, here and there, hardy patches of crabgrass grew, and in odd corners there was the happy surprise of a wild rose.

In the window of one of these houses was a sign:

APT TO LET

Herb couldn't imagine where the apartment could be. The house presented such a tiny, pinched face to the street that it seemed too small to house the landlord, let alone a tenant. Curious, he knocked.

In a moment, the door opened a few inches. A gaunt, bent man with sunken eyes looked out.

"Hello," said Herb. "I saw the sign. 'Apt to let.'" He smiled.

The eyes looked Herb up and down. The man's tongue popped out one side of his mouth, as if acting on its own initiative, and waggled. The man's mouth moved as if in speech, but no sound came from it other than something like "Dut, dut, dut." The man's head nodded, and the door closed. Herb wasn't sure whether he'd been told to wait or to go away. He waited. In a moment the door opened again, fully this time. Standing in the doorway was a short, scrawny woman. She had wild hair; it looked as if she'd given each of the phrenological regions of her scalp a hairdo of its own. She looked at Herb for a moment without saying anything or altering her blank expression. Then, suddenly, she burst into a frenzy of welcome.

"Come in! Come in!" she cried. She reached out and grabbed Herb's sleeve and began tugging at him. She bared her few teeth in a smile. "I'd be happy to show you the apartment. Happy." Herb let himself be drawn inside, and she closed the door behind him at once.

Herb followed her down a narrow hallway that ran along one side of the boxy little house. On his left was an outer wall. It was covered with wallpaper that must once have been bright and pretty, a pattern of wild roses, but was now so darkened and stained that the roses barely showed. On his right were curtains, improvised from old bedspreads, worn and soiled, that provided the only separation between the hallway and the living quarters beyond. These bedspreads didn't quite meet. Through the spaces between them, Herb saw a dark sitting room and a dingy kitchen. In the kitchen, seated at a small table, was the man who had come to the door when he first knocked, now bent over a copy of the *Babbington Reporter*, straining to read in the dim light, rocking slightly while he read and repeating to himself, "Dut, dut, dut."

At the end of the makeshift hallway was a door, and beyond the door was another very narrow hallway, without any light at all, and at the end of that was another door. The shrunken woman opened the second door, and the effect was as if she had opened a door to the sun. Herb stepped inside a small room, almost a perfect cube, a box of yellow light. It was a tiny room, but it had been scrubbed and polished and whitewashed, and there were windows all around it. In one corner was a rudimentary kitchen; in another was a living room (two upholstered chairs arranged on either side of a wobbly table); in the third was a bed—crudely built, the honey color of old pine, enormous and inviting; in the fourth corner was a bathtub on ball-and-claw feet.

"Is there—uh—?" asked Herb.

"Uhh?" asked the white-haired woman.

"Uhh—" said Herb.

"Uhh?" she asked again.

"Uh, that is—"

"Ahhh!" said the woman. "Ohhh, yes, yes, right out here." She opened a door beside the tub and, to Herb's relief, disclosed a flush toilet.

"Remember," said Herb, "you have to wear the blindfold."

"All right," said Lorna. Actually, she liked the idea of wearing a blindfold, liked the mystery, looked forward to the surprise, loved Herb's obvious delight over the apartment he'd found, took pleasure from his pleasure, and took pleasure from the fact (and there was no doubt, could be no doubt, that it was a fact) that he wanted to please her, wanted her to be as happy with the place he'd found as he was. She tied the blindfold, Herb's scarf, around her head and arranged it so that she couldn't see.

"You're smiling," said Herb.

"I'm happy," said Lorna. "This reminds me of closing my eyes when we were out on the lake the night we burned the ballroom."

"Here we are," said Herb. He stopped the car, leaped out, ran around to Lorna's door, and helped her out. He led her to the door of the house. He didn't have to knock. Mrs. Mixup—so she called herself, giving in to the inability or unwillingness of the people she met to pronounce Mikszath—had been watching for their arrival. She opened the door silently, and silently Herb led Lorna along the hallway, through the first door, through the narrow hallway, and through the second door, which he closed behind them.

"And now," he said, working at the knot Lorna had made in his scarf, "we can take the blindfold off." He pulled it away, and Lorna gasped. For a terrible moment, Herb thought that he'd failed completely to see the place through Lorna's eyes, thought that her gasp was a sign of revulsion, but that passed, passed as quickly as it had come. She clapped her hands, she whirled around, she moved from one part of the room to another, drawing deep breaths, beaming.

"It's so bright!" she said. "And it's so—tiny."

"It *is* small," said Herb, uncertain again.

"Not small," said Lorna. "*Tiny.* It's wonderful. It's like playing house, *just* like playing house. And look! Roses outside the window!"

"You like it," said Herb.

"I *love* it," said Lorna. She ran to him and threw her arms around his neck.

"There *is* a drawback," said Herb.

"What?" asked Lorna.

Herb reached behind him and opened the door. In the dark, narrow hallway, Lorna saw a bony white-haired woman, wiping her hands on an apron, and, behind her, a bent man who bobbed slightly and moved his mouth but said nothing. Herb grimaced and shifted his eyes from Lorna's. "I'd like you to meet the Mikszaths," he said.

"Why, hello," said Lorna.

"Such a lovely girl," said Mrs. Mikszath. She rushed forward and took Lorna's hands. "A lovely girl, isn't she, Miklos?"

"Dut, dut, dut," said Miklos.

"I think I should show you—um—the entrance," said Herb. He took Lorna by the hand and led her into the narrow hallway. The Mikszaths retreated before them, backing toward the front door.

"Lovely," said Mrs. Mikszath, again and again.

"Dut, dut, dut," said Mr. Mikszath.

Herb and Lorna moved in the next day, but while they were unpacking, Herb began to feel that he'd been unfair, that he'd forced Lorna to share, or at least to try to share, his enthusiasm for the apartment. He began to feel that he should have left the apartment hunting to her, that she should have been the one to choose the place where she would live, and that, if she *had* been the one to choose, she would never have chosen a place like this, would certainly never have chosen any place where she had to walk through her landlords' home and home life to get to her own.

"I know it isn't as private as you'd like," said Herb.

"It doesn't matter," said Lorna. "I love it here."

"It's going to be awkward walking through their place every time we come and go," said Herb.

"I don't mind," said Lorna.

"It isn't too late to change our minds," said Herb. He came to her and took her face in his hands. "I'll tell them that we really have to have a larger place, and that I talked you into taking this place, and it wasn't fair to you—"

"Dut, dut, dut," said Lorna. She wrapped herself around Herb and kissed him quiet. "Ignite me, please," she whispered.

When they got back to unpacking, Herb watched with amusement and surprise while Lorna unpacked with great care a lurid papier-mâché duck and tried placing it in several locations around the room before settling on a windowsill in the kitchen as just the right spot for it.

"Lorna," said Herb, "where did you get—"

"Don't say anything nasty about it," said Lorna. "I know it's not beautiful, but it's important to me." She held the duck in front of her with both hands, elevated it, rotated it, examined it. "I've had it since I was a little girl." She paused. "A very little girl," she added distractedly, struck by an appreciation of all the time, so much time, that had passed since she'd thought that the duck was beautiful and that it stood for Uncle Luther's love. How much more it meant now. And yet how much uglier and smaller it seemed, now, here, removed from childhood and Chacallit, distant in time, space, and understanding. "*This,*" she said, meaning all that, "is a *very* old duck."

Their stay in the one-room apartment at the Mikszaths' would, Herb and Lorna agreed, be temporary, and it would do just fine for a while, till they found something bigger, something better, while they were learning their way around Babbington, while Herb was establishing himself. It would be just fine until they found someplace that they really liked.

They stayed for five years. During those five years, Mr. Mikszath, who had been the victim of a stroke, never said anything but "Dut, dut, dut." Herb and Lorna learned to interpret his pointing, his sketching in the air, his twisted facial expressions, and the various emphases he put on his "duts," and they made his vocabulary of "duts," grimaces, and gestures a part of theirs. Mrs. Mikszath's affection for them grew and grew, but she also developed a romantic interest in Herb. She began wearing makeup, elaborate costume jewelry, and gauzy, nearly transparent, blouses. Her remarks took on the style of double entendres, even when they were not so intended, so warmly burned the fire in her heart. Once a week, at least, she would come to their door in the evening, soon after Herb had returned home, with a tray on which she'd laid out dinner for two, insisting, always, that she'd made too much for Miklos and herself, or that this was a dish she'd eaten as a girl—full of memories, they had to try it—or that Miklos couldn't eat because his stomach was "stormy." Whatever she brought was provided in his-and-hers sizes: a large plate for Herb, almost a platter, and coffee in a mug; a small plate for Lorna, and coffee in a tiny cup, an heirloom, a precious cup of the thinnest, finest china, offered as an apology for the way she felt about Herb, an acknowledgment of Lorna's femininity, and a reminder of her own.

Herb's work at the clam-packing plant was noticed from the start; he seemed to have a talent for culling, and he was so dexterous that he came to be regarded with the kind of awe and envy that athletes inspire when they perform feats so far beyond the capabilities of the average person that they seem by performing them to be enlarging the aspirations of the species, to be outlining a new bulge along the frontier of human endeavor. Herb enjoyed his growing reputation, and he was surprised to find how content he was to do this work, this work that required so little of him. He hid his true ambitions well, so well that Lorna hardly saw any evidence of them herself. She saw him reading the *Reporter* every day, but never looking at the help-wanted ads, and she wondered whether he really meant what he said when he told her that he'd been inspired by what Dan Whitley had told him that very first night when they arrived in Babbington: that it's amazing how much you learn about a person from an obituary, amazing how much you didn't know or didn't notice when the person was alive. From that, Herb had gone on to the realization that in a small town the key to selling, or any kind of advancement, was information, information that an outsider had to make a special effort to acquire. Much later, when he and Lorna were retired in Punta Cachazuda, he put the idea this way: "You've heard people say, 'It's not *what* you know that counts; it's *who* you know.' Well, that's not quite right. I found that it's what you know about who you know that counts." Herb was finding out a great deal about the people of Babbington, but the more he found out, the more he found there was to find out. He began keeping notes, on cards.

His affection for tinkering, for fixing things, improving things, served him as well in Babbington as it had in Quelquepart-sur-Marne; he was always ready to do anyone a favor of the tinkering type, and an unanticipated reward of his doing these little favors was that he obtained, incidentally, close-up glimpses into the lives of many Babbingtonians. His very first repair job in Babbington was his work on the Mikszaths' sagging front door. When he had made the door as good as it once had been, he went on to make it better: he added a secret lock, a spring-loaded bolt, that could be opened by pushing an ordinary-looking nail that projected slightly from the door frame, just to the right of the doorknob. This arrangement allowed Miklos, for whom the effects of his stroke and of arthritis made manipulating a key nearly impossible, to lock and unlock the door on his own.

When Herb demonstrated his ingenious handiwork to the Mikszaths and Lorna, the women, moved by the generosity of thought that underlay Herb's work, hugged him in turn. Mrs. Mikszath blinked away her tears; Lorna let hers run down her cheeks. Miklos locked and unlocked the door again and again. He turned to Herb, and the strength of his emotion was clear on his gaunt face. He clapped one gnarled hand on Herb's shoulder and squeezed it as well as he could. He swallowed hard.

"Dut, dut, dut," he said.

"Aw, don't say that, Miklos," said Herb. "It was fun for me. I like doing this sort of thing."

Mrs. Mikszath could not be prevented from telling the story of Herb's work on her front door. She broadcast the news of Herb's generosity and tinkering talent far and wide, and she described in

precise detail just how the ingenious lock worked. A welcome consequence of her advertising was Herb's being called upon to fix and
improve things all over town; an unwelcome one was the visit of a
burglar, who, after overhearing Mrs. Mikszath's precise description
from the other side of the vegetable counter at the Main Street Market one morning, found himself irresistibly tempted to make use of
the knowledge. Several days later he crept into the house in the middle of the day, when it was empty, and made off with everything he
could find that was of any value—some silverware and china and
knickknacks of the Mikszaths' and a sack full of Herb and Lorna's
wedding gifts.

Like an artist who finds, to his excitement and terror, that he's come
up with an idea so large and consuming that he may have to spend the
rest of his life trying to realize it, who wakes in the night terrified and
thrilled, having seen in his dreams a vision of his busy future, Herb
saw how much work he was going to have to do before he made even
the smallest of public steps in selling, because his move into selling
would create the first impression of him as a salesman, an impression
that had to be the right one if the enterprise was to prosper. So he
studied and listened and watched, and, in his mind, he practiced
selling, while he was lying awake in bed or daydreaming at the culling
table where most of his mind was free, while he was fixing or making
some little thing, or while he was relaxing in the tub at night while
Lorna read to him. He practiced selling to the people he knew, using
what he knew about them. What he imagined himself selling—because it was the most difficult thing he could imagine selling, something the burglar hadn't even disturbed—was Lorna's duck.
    If Lorna suspected that perhaps Herb had lost interest in selling,
lost his ambition or shifted the object of his ambition to some position
in the clam-packing plant, she was nonetheless determined that he
should follow his inclination, do whatever it was he thought best. The
future she had envisioned when she'd closed her eyes that night on
Lake Serenity had been a future with Herb, not a future with Herb in
a specific place or with Herb doing a specific kind of work or support-
ing a specific way, level, or style of living. If she had to, *she* would
provide the things that Herb's clam-plant salary couldn't. After the
burglary, without telling Herb, she approached Joseph the Jeweler,

who had a shop downtown, about working on an as-needed basis, repairing ivory pieces, restoring cameos, and doing engraving. She got a little work, and when her skill and talent became clear, she got a great deal more. She was able to stay as busy as she wanted, and she brought in money that made a big difference in the way she and Herb were able to live.

Herb noticed; he noticed every dollar she brought into the household (even the dollars that she tried to hide by spending them on meat of better quality or out-of-season vegetables, things she hoped Herb wouldn't notice or wouldn't think of as expenses), and he counted those dollars as debits against his future earnings. Every now and then, however, when an Occasion was approaching, he'd feel that paying Lorna back in the future wasn't good enough, that it wasn't fair of him to make Lorna wait to have the things he wanted her to have or do the things he wanted her to be able to do, and at those times he would suggest a trip to Boston to visit his uncle Benjamin.

9

In Which Herb Becomes a Studebaker Salesman

"This is—this is—*astonishing*, Herb," said Ben on the first of Herb's visits. In his hand he held one of Herb's prototypes.

This one, the first Herb had created since his marriage to Lorna, represented something quite new. It set a style that would define the course of development for animated coarse goods for nearly two decades. Inside a silver case, very much like the case of a pocket watch, a tiny couple was couched. Slowly, very slowly, Ben twisted the stem and observed the couple's performance. What the couple did as Ben turned the stem was affectionate, inventive, clever, difficult, and surprising. Herb had spent countless hours developing the routine, doodling on scraps of paper, constructing mechanisms in his imagination, building tiny frameworks of wire and bewildering assemblies of gears and shafts and pulleys and belts in moments stolen from work at the clam-packing plant.

Ben looked up from his examination of the couple in the watch-case and grinned. "This is very—um—creative, Herb," he said. "Very creative." He glanced at Herb and then turned his attention back to the couple. "I wonder where you get your ideas," Ben said.

Herb colored, and he chuckled to try to hide his embarrassment. Ideas came to him from his imagination, from his dreams and day-dreams, from that never-ending lust that a man feels for the girls of his youth, and from observations of women around Babbington. He might notice in a woman a certain way of walking, say a certain swing of the hips, and see it as a manifestation of the woman's peculiar style, just as one might recognize in the use of a certain blue or a certain recognizable brush stroke a manifestation of a painter's style, or recognize in the frequent use of a certain grammatical technique a certain manner of thought that underlies a writer's style. While Herb observed the woman's walk, he made some inferences about her style, and he asked himself some interesting questions: *How would that style show up in the woman's lovemaking? How would it affect her movements in bed?* Such pleasant speculations occupied Herb for many hours every day; they were the salacious equivalent of the kind of speculation that helped make him such a superb salesman: *I know certain things about this person. From them, what can I decide about his attitudes, his desires? What can I predict about his resistance to my selling?*

"You must be enjoying married life," Ben said without looking at Herb.

Herb looked at his hands and said nothing. He was enjoying married life, and he was enjoying sex with Lorna, but something was missing. He was a restrained lover in the big pine bed in the room behind the Mikszaths', less imaginative, less daring, than he was in his gear-and-pulley work. When Herb was at work on his coupling mechanisms, he couldn't help wondering whether some of the techniques and alignments he developed were entirely original, whether he had invented anything that had never had an in-the-flesh trial in all the history of mankind. Sometimes he wondered whether some of his inventions were humanly possible. Always he wondered how they would feel. Many struck him as too far removed from the simple and obvious ever to be widely accepted, and many struck him as unacceptable for home use. And sometimes he was afraid that, because these were the products of his imagination and his desires, they might be things that only he could enjoy, things he ought to be ashamed of, and this feeling applied not only to the things that might have been too bold, but to those that might have been too sentimental or too silly.

"Dut, dut, dut," Herb said as a way of avoiding having to explain to Ben any part of all that he thought and felt.

"What?" asked Ben.

"Oh, nothing," said Herb. "It's just something our landlord says.

What do you think you can give me for this couple, Uncle Ben? I want to get Lorna a coat for her birthday."

A month or two later, while on a visit to Chacallit, Lorna accepted Luther's invitation to visit the mill one morning to "say hello to the girls in Links" and to see "some of the new products we're going to be making in ivory." She knew what he must have in mind, and she was curious to see what the unknown designer of animated coarse goods had been up to lately.

"Lorna," said Luther, holding the prototype enclosed in his hand, "what I'm going to show you is a work of genius. I want you to appreciate that, and I want you to consider very carefully whether you shouldn't be adding your talent to it." He put the case in Lorna's hands, pressed them together around it, gave them a squeeze, and said, in a hushed and reverent voice, "I'm going to leave you to contemplate it on your own." He left the office, and Lorna, bursting with curiosity, opened the lid.

She watched the couple for a long time. She found, while she watched, that she began wishing she could show them to Herb. She wished that what they were doing could be put to trial in the big pine bed. She sighed and closed the lid. It wasn't likely. She was a restrained lover, restrained by the fear that she might give herself away, by being ashamed of the work she did, and by the generations-old Huber conviction that it was safest not to appear extraordinary. Now and then she dared to surprise Herb with something, but only something small. She was usually careful, very careful.

"Herb," she whispered that night when they had retired to her old room in her parents' house, "I think I'd like to do a little work for my uncle Luther now and then."

"What do you mean?" asked Herb.

"Well," she said, beginning an explanation that she had practiced during her walk up Ackerman Hill from the mill, "when I saw the work that he's getting from people in the ivory department, I realized something. This is going to sound very immodest, but I have to say it. I realized that I was the best ivory carver Chacallit has ever seen. Everyone who was working there in the ivory section knew it."

"Uh-huh," said Herb.

"And you know what else I realized?" she asked, rolling onto her side and bringing her lips close to Herb's ear.

"What?" he asked.

"I realized how much I liked the work. I really liked doing something that I could do so well. It made me feel—it made me feel—" She stopped, unable to say what she had felt.

"I know," said Herb. He turned to face her. "I know what you mean. It made you feel—better—better than anybody else."

"That's right!" whispered Lorna.

"It's hard to admit, but it's nice, a nice feeling, to feel that you're the best at something."

"Yes," said Lorna. "Yes, it is."

"But how could you manage to work for your uncle? You don't want to move back here, do you?"

In a rush, Lorna explained the plan. She would do everything by mail. From time to time, Luther would ship her some ivory and a list of the subjects she was to carve—tiny roses, leaves, animals, and the like. She would set herself up with a place to work. She wouldn't need nearly as much space as she would need for, say, a sewing machine. She would work during the day, while Herb was at work. She wouldn't work too much—he didn't have to worry about that, and no one would even know that she was working. He didn't have to worry that it would look as if he couldn't support her. Now and then she would get a package from Chacallit—nothing unusual about that. And now and then she'd send a package to Chacallit—nothing unusual about that, either! "Oh, Herb," she said, "you wouldn't mind, would you?"

"Will you promise me one thing?" he asked.

"What?"

"I want you to spend the money on yourself."

"I—"

"Promise?"

"Promise."

She nuzzled him and, silently because they were in her parents' house, pressed herself against him. She remembered the little couple she had seen that afternoon. *Do I dare?* she wondered.

Herb drew a deep breath, slowly. He thought about the routine he had devised for the little couple. *Should I try?* he wondered.

It's really just a matter of arranging myself in a slightly different way, she told herself.

It's a delicate matter, he reminded himself. *It can't seem like something I've thought out or—even worse—something that I've done before.*

I can't let him think that it's something I learned from someone else. It has to be just a little touch here, a little turn this way, like that—

It has to be just sort of like going for a stroll, when you're enjoying the walk and not paying too much attention to where you're going and then you look up and find you're in a part of town where you've never been before.

Oh, my, she thought. *I would never have thought it would be so easy. Or so, so—*

She doesn't seem startled or—upset. It's—

—wonderful.

—wonderful.

They astonished each other. Lying in the dark, later, when each thought the other had fallen asleep, Herb asked himself the question Lorna had feared: *Where on earth did she get those ideas?* He couldn't help wondering whether Lorna had had more experience than that provided by Andy Proctor, the hero of Chacallit. He knew about the back-seat session with Andy because Lorna had told him one evening, the same evening when he told her about Alice Mills. It had been one of those "damned confessional evenings that lovers insist on torturing themselves with," according to May.

Gad! Why do they do it? I mean—why don't they have the sense to keep quiet about things that they ought to keep quiet about? Well—it was an evening when they went rowing on the bay in the moonlight. A favorite thing of theirs to do, of course, since it reminded them of the night the ballroom burned. But of course it reminded Lorna of that night in a rowboat with Luther, too. So! She was of two minds on such occasions, as you can well imagine. Oh, anyway, Herb kicked things off. Why is it men need to confess things? Clear the air! Get things out in the open! Lay my cards on the table! Get this off my chest! Brrrr! I get chills when I hear words like that. "May, I want to get something out in the open." No thank you! Good night!

Perhaps it's just boasting, do you think? Well. Anyway, Herb told her about Whatever-her-name was, that girl who fell in love with him while he was in France—Alice Mills. And then he told her about that strange couple—the ones he met at that gas station—you remember them. Oh, you *know. Herb assumed the woman was Whoosis's daughter, but she turned out to be his wife? Arthur and Tessie Norris. Well, Herb told Lorna all that. Lorna* told *Herb that he didn't have to go into all of this for her sake, but he* insisted. *He said—and he honestly* believed *what he was saying—that he hoped that as the years went by Lorna would learn everything about him there was to know, since he thought it was important for a married couple not to hide anything from each other. Oooh. A* ghastly *idea.* Ghastly. *Well, Lorna—poor thing—felt she had to give something in return for all this honesty, so she gave him Andy. So to speak. Now what do* you *suppose happened? I'll tell you what I suppose. What always happens. They both wound up thinking,* Well, there must be more. Nobody would confess everything, so there must be more. *Honesty is* very *dangerous.*

As time passed, Herb and Lorna began, little by little, to invite imagination into the big pine bed. Though Herb wondered about the sources of Lorna's inspired lovemaking, he never recognized what should have been obvious, that some of the ideas had been his. Nor did he recognize Lorna's inventiveness. Jealousy made him suppose that her ideas must come from other experiences.

A curious kind of cottage industry sprang up in the sunny room behind the Mikszaths'. During the day, while Herb was away, Lorna would work for a couple of hours at a little folding work table that Herb built for her. Building the table had been a labor of love, two loves: love of Lorna and love of tinkering. Along the back of the table, in tiers, were small bins that held all of Lorna's tools and supplies, and this entire section pivoted when the table was collapsed, so that nothing would spill, since the bins were always level, whether the table was open for work or folded to stand against the wall. During the day, while Herb was away, Lorna would unfold the table and spend three or four hours at work. She would begin by spending a little while working on innocent carvings, delicate rose blossoms or sinewy horse heads that would be used for expensive sets of links and studs but that served primarily as decoys. She spent most of her time on the exacting work of carving the intricately articulated figures that went into the animated coarse goods that were becoming known as "Watchcase

Wonders" and were, though Lorna didn't know it, making Luther a wealthy man.

It would have been impossible for Herb to find time or a place to work on his designs if it hadn't been for his meeting Garth Castle. Garth was at the time a young man to watch at Babbington Clam. He was only three years older than Herb, but he had about him an air of worldly sophistication that made him seem much older. This air was only an air—Garth had been born in Hargrove, the next town, and had never traveled farther from Hargrove than New Jersey. To give himself the air, he drew on his imagination and his careful observation of men who seemed to him to be truly worldly and sophisticated. Some actually were; others were merely successful at business, and that only on a local scale.

Garth wanted to be, in Babbington, a New York gentleman, or what he took to be a New York gentleman. He behaved as he supposed one would if he were, for reasons unknown but probably just a little bit scandalous, rusticating in Babbington. He succeeded admirably. He was tall, wiry, and handsome. Success in this pretense brought Garth confidence and a relaxed style, and in time he appeared so at ease in the role he'd written for himself that he seemed to many Babbingtonians to be a man making the best of having been banished to Babbington, a man who'd risen above being resigned to his lot and was now—and with what grace!—actually enjoying it. He was a model for every ambitious young man in town.

Herb attracted Garth's attention by designing a new culling table. Formerly, the culling table had been nothing more than a large wooden table, about waist height, covered with a sheet of zinc, placed in front of an opening in the bin into which the clams were dumped like so many lumps of coal. Cullers stood alongside the table, and one of them, the "doorman," slid a small wooden door upward, releasing clams from the bin. When the table was covered with clams, the doorman, with great difficulty, slid the door down again, and the cullers began work. Each sorted the clams that came immediately to hand, tossing them according to size, without looking backward, into crates arranged along the walls behind the cullers. This method had many faults: the doorman's job was difficult and frustrating; the cullers often interfered with one another, straying across poorly defined boundaries in their zeal to cull; and, though the cullers were (after much training and practice) very good at getting the clams into the crates without looking, and even knew from the sound of the clams clattering against their crated fellows how nearly full a crate was, clams often collided in midair and ricocheted into the wrong crates, and the concussion of one clam against another, in the air or in the crate, occasionally cracked or crushed them.

Herb was intrigued by the problems the table presented. He began lingering in the carpentry shed after work to put in some time on an idea he had for an entirely new kind of culling table. He worked alongside one of the carpenters, Andrew "Swifty" Switt, to build it. When it was finished, he and Switt installed it one night in place of the old table.

Herb's table was much longer than the old one. At the head, in place of the sliding door, was a cylinder with an opening in one side of approximately the same dimensions as the opening behind the old door. A crank allowed the doorman to turn this cylinder. As the opening rotated past the opening to the clam bin, the cylinder filled with clams, and, as the opening rotated over the table, the clams tumbled from the cylinder onto the table. The doorman could vary the rate of rotation to suit the pace of the cullers. The table was slanted so that the clams would be inclined to slide toward the far end. Herb and Swifty had carved the surface to create a system of valleys, through which the clams could be urged, by the cullers, to go. From the largest valley, at the head of the table, the clams might, with the assistance of the first group of cullers, pass into either of two smaller valleys, and then, from each of those, with the assistance of the next rank of cullers, into either of two still smaller valleys. The cullers used this system of branching valleys to sort the clams into their four sizes: undersize (that is, too small to sell legally), littleneck, cherrystone, and chowder clam. The system had the great virtue of allowing the use of apprentice cullers at the head of the line, since they merely had to distinguish the relatively smaller clams from the relatively larger clams. The more seasoned cullers who were stationed farther along made the subtler distinctions, and they did it with little wasted motion, merely nudging the clams a little to guide each into the proper valley. Toward the end, the table fanned out, and the valleys diverged, each ending above a crate, into which the clams tumbled fairly gently.

When Garth Castle saw the new table in operation, he was astonished as much by the fact that Herb had undertaken its design and construction for pleasure as he was by the results. Here was someone out of the ordinary. He was impressed, too, by the ease with which Herb had gotten Swifty to build the table, working after hours, and by the cooperation he got from the cullers, who were generally considered to be a hidebound lot, resistant to change, second only to the clammies themselves in stubbornness. Here was a leader. Garth offered Herb the foremanship of the culling section. Herb asked instead that Garth arrange for him to move into sales. And, as if it were an afterthought, he asked that Garth set aside for his exclusive use the area of the workshop where he had developed the culling table, so that he could tinker. It was there, in an hour or two after work, any afternoon when he could spare the time, that Herb developed the prototypes of the Watchcase Wonders.

Herb's moving into sales had a painful consequence, though: he had to be away from Babbington, and Lorna, for days (and sometimes for weeks) at a time. As soon as he had experienced the first of these separations, he began racking his brain for a way to get out of traveling. He had wanted the job for only one reason: to earn himself a reputation. He had imagined that a year or so traveling for Babbington Clam wouldn't be so bad, but he'd found instead that to be without Lorna was to be in an almost constant state of need. When he was away he seemed to lack everything. No matter what he ate or how much he ate, he was hungry; when he woke in the night and his mouth was dry, the water he drank didn't quench his thirst any more than do those glasses of water we drink in our dreams; boredom and loneliness sent him to bed early, but he never seemed to get enough sleep; and, without Lorna, he sometimes felt cold, especially at the tips of his fingers and across his shoulders, even in the warmest weather.

"How, how?" he asked himself, again and again, when he lay awake on lonely nights in half-empty beds in faraway places. How could he get out of this misery he'd brought himself? He couldn't quit so soon; he'd appear unreliable, disloyal, fickle. He couldn't use the truth as a reason. Love and loneliness weren't suitable reasons for a man to abandon a job that was a step up, especially not when he was performing so brilliantly that he'd attracted the attention of everyone who had the power to improve his future.

Garth provided the solution. One day, when Herb was between trips, Garth asked him to meet him after work. They drove to the rattiest section of the ratty wharf area of Babbington.

In *Seafood and Sex*, his study of life in "a small coastal town somewhere in America," T. Wallaston (Stretch) Mitgang, the pioneering psychohistoricosociologist, wrote:

> The waterfront area—that is, the area near the working waterfront, the poorest area of town, the messiest, the rattiest—is its true social frontier, a miniature of the social frontier of American society at large. Here are tiny clusters of representatives of ethnic and racial groups who haven't yet made their way downtown (or haven't been permitted to) and who may never make their way (or be permitted to make their way) to one of the shady streets of comfortable houses along the pleasant canals away from the sound and smell of men and women at work, unless it is to make a delivery, mow a lawn, or wash a floor. To spend time in this part of town, with its diversity of colors, tongues, religions, pasts, plans, and dreams, is to see that the melting pot, with its suggestion of a homogenized mush, is the wrong metaphor. Better would be something like a stewpot. If we are concocting an American social dish, this is where it's cooking, and it's something like a hearty stew or chowder, with chewy bits in every spoonful, not all of them familiar.

Garth took Herb to a place that Herb had heard of but never visited before: Corinne's. There were two parts to Corinne's. In plain sight, almost at the end of Lower (that's Lower Bolotomy Road, remember), was a fish house with the name CORINNE'S on a painted sign that ran along the ridge of the roof, and behind the fish house, concealed in a warehouse, was the other Corinne's, the one sometimes referred to in speech as Corinne's Warehouse, a name delivered with a wink, a raised eyebrow, and a sly elongation of the first syllable of the second word—this was the speakeasy and whorehouse.

When they entered the warehouse, Herb found himself in a chaos of crates and boxes and pallets and skids and barrels. Garth followed what seemed to be a familiar pathway through this chaos, and Herb tagged along. Suddenly, for no apparent reason, Garth stopped and stood perfectly still for a moment, listening. Satisfied that there were no following footsteps, he pushed the side of a large crate, and it swung inward. Garth motioned Herb into the cabinet he had revealed, followed Herb inside, and pulled the door closed behind them. From his pocket he took a small silver penknife engraved with his initials, and he pushed it through a knothole on the opposite side of the crate. In a moment, that side of the crate swung open, and a small, bent old man in a brown suit welcomed Garth and Herb. As they passed him, Garth held out his hand, and the old man dropped Garth's penknife into it.

Herb tried very hard not to notice who else was in the place. He understood that Garth's gesture in bringing him here was a statement of trust, and he wanted to show that it wasn't misplaced.

"Herb," said Garth, "I'm going to tell you something that you have to keep under your hat."

Herb nodded, just once.

"Good," said Garth. "I'll come right to the point. I'm going to leave the company, and I want you to come with me. Some important people—I can't say who just yet—have gotten together to buy a Studebaker distributorship, and they want me to manage it. Herb, how would you like to sell Studebakers?"

"Here in Babbington?" asked Herb.

"Well, yes," said Garth. "I know it might seem a little—well—boring to be in Babbington all the time, but you could really build a future here, Herb, and—"

Herb raised his glass and nodded, and Garth smiled.

"Good," he said. "Good."

10

In Which
Herb 'n' Lorna's
Daughter Is Born

When Dr. Stickler gave them the news that Lorna was pregnant, Herb and Lorna felt, immediately, that this made everything just perfect—not that either wanted things to remain forever as they were, but each felt that for now, with a baby on the way, everything was perfect. But then Herb began to worry. He worried that Lorna might not want a child now, while they were living with the Mikszaths, while he was trying to make a start at Babbington Studebaker. More than anything else he wanted Lorna to be happy, and he thought that he had to *make* her happy. And then Lorna began to worry. She worried that *Herb* might not want a child now, while they were living with the Mikszaths, while she was working to make ends meet. She wanted him to be happy; she thought she had to *make* him happy.

"Do you mind?" she asked when they were back at home.

"Mind?" said Herb. "Mind! I'm overwhelmed! Overwhelmed with joy, I mean."

Overwhelmed, she thought. *Overwhelmed by the idea of three of us living in this room?*

"Do you—do *you* mind?" Herb asked. He wondered whether her question was a way of asking whether he agreed that they'd be cramped with a baby.

"Oh, Herb," she said, "I love it. Her. I love her already."

"Her? You're sure?"

"I have a hunch."

"You won't feel cramped here, Lorna?"

"Not if you won't."

"*I* won't if you won't."

"You will, won't you?"

"No! Oh, no. Not if you won't."

"Are you being honest with me, Herb?"

"I *am*. I *am*. *You're* the one who isn't."

"You want to move, don't you?"

"No! *I* don't want to move. I think *you* want to move."

"And *I* think *you* want to move."

"All right, let's move."

"Fine! If that's what you want, let's move."

"It *isn't* what I want! It's what *you* want. Why don't you just admit it?"

"I will not admit anything of the kind. You're doing this because *you* want to move."

"Lorna, I'm doing this for you."

"I don't *want* you to do it for me. I don't want you to do *anything* for me. Not like this. I don't want you giving anything up for me. Or for Ella."

"Ella?"

"Ella."

"Ella. Hm. Ella."

Do you like it?

"I—"

"You don't like it."

"I *do*. I *do* like it. Ella Piper. It's easy to say—that's important. People remember your name if it's easy to say, if it's catchy. Ella Piper. It's not short for anything, is it?"

"Cinderella."

"You're not going to call her—"

"No, no. Of course not. She'll never even know. Only you and I will."

A pause.

"You—you do want to move, don't you?" said Herb.

"*You* want to move!"

"Only if *you* do."

And so they decided to move. Lorna wanted to tell Mrs. Mikszath herself, when they were alone. She invited her for coffee, sat her down, and fussed over her, putting a pillow behind the small of her back, insisting that she kick off her shoes and put her feet on the ottoman, buttering a roll for her, putting a third lump of sugar in her coffee. And then, when she thought that the pillow and ottoman and buttered roll and extra sugar had provided enough of a cushion, she delivered the blow: "Mrs. Mikszath," she said, looking into her cup, "Herb and I are going to move. We don't *want* to go, but we have to have more room for the baby, for Ella."

Mrs. Mikszath said nothing. She stirred her coffee. She looked at the roll. She put her spoon on the saucer. She sighed. "I'm sorry," she said. A tear fell from her right eye, struck her cheek, ran along a wrinkle. "I wish you wouldn't go."

"Oh, so do I, Mrs. Mikszath. We've really liked it here, really. We just—"

"Miklos and I—"

"We need more room."

"Miklos and I, we, we are in the way."

"In the way?"

"You have to go past us. In the living room. When we—we're in the living room—you have to go by us. We hear you, at night. On tiptoes. You don't feel at home."

"Oh, no. No, Mrs. Mikszath. That's not it. We do feel at home. It's just the space. That's all."

"Maybe Miklos and I could move in here!"

"What?"

"Sure! We could move in here. You and Herb move in our place. Living room, regular kitchen, whole big bathroom, bedroom, plenty of room. What do we need, anyway?" She looked around. Her shoulders dropped. She frowned and shook her head. "No," she said. "Miklos wouldn't stand it. It's too small. It would make him feel bad to be in just one room." She smiled at Lorna, a weak smile, as if the idea had been Lorna's and she was sorry to have to disappoint her. "I can't make him feel bad," she said.

Thomas Piper, Frederick Lewis Tudor, and Nathaniel Wyeth (*arrows*) oversee the ice-cutting operation on Lake Wenham, Massachusetts, in 1845.

Herb (*arrow*) behind the lines, somewhere near Quelquepart-sur-Marne, about 1920. Note cluster of doughboys behind Herb, examining mess-kit cup with noncollapsing handle.

Lorna (*arrow*) working at a cutting machine on the main floor at Cole & Lord's Gent's Accessories, in Chacallit, about 1920. Note flags mounted atop machines at Luther Huber's suggestion, to remind the women that belt buckles could win the war.

Clam shuckers at work in front of Shucking Shed Two at Babbington Clam, about 1925. Herb (out of sight in shed at extreme right) is at work constructing the new culling table.

Clamdigger known as Bitzer, with two baskets of clams, "over south," about 1929.

May Hopper and Garth Castle, out for a spin in May's new Erskine sport roadster, encounter an unidentified equestrienne, somewhere on Long Island, about 1928.

Herb (*lower right*) demonstrates the stability of the "Rigid Rockne" (even on three wheels!) to a skeptical customer outside Babbington Studebaker in the dispiriting days of 1933.

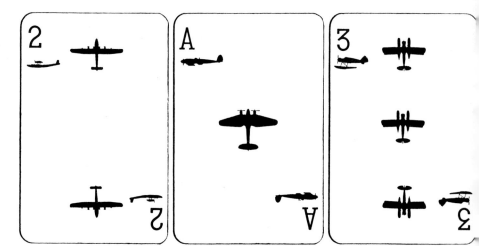

Cards made by Herb and Lorna, from spotter's cards, for use in Piper Poker, about 1942.

A portion of the illustration in *LIFE* magazine, January 31, 1938, that inspired Lorna to create erotic charms with moving parts.

A proud family of Babbingtonians, typical of Herb's satisfied customers, shows off a brand new Champion to admiring in-laws and envious neighbors, 1950.

Greetings from Punta Cachazuda!

Sunset over the Gulf of Mexico, seen from Punta Cachazuda, from a postcard that Lorna sent to Ella, 1963.

"Of course not," said Lorna.

Mrs. Mikszath touched the handle of her cup as if she was going to lift it and drink from it, but she paused, thought, made a frail fist, nodded once, and raised her head to look at Lorna. There was mischief in her eyes. "So," she said. "In this case, I want to tell you. Something I have to say. A secret, you understand?"

"Yes. A secret."

"A secret for women, okay?"

"Okay."

"At night, Miklos and I, we hear you. Always, you and Herb, we hear you."

Lorna looked puzzled. "I'm sorry if we——"

"Oh, no, no. I mean we hear you——" She nodded toward the pine bed. "——in bed."

"You do?"

"From the first night!" She clapped her hands. "We try not to listen. I wash the dishes, make noise, but we can't help it. You are— very *busy* in bed."

"Mrs. Mikszath!"

"You are, you are, very—alive! Bouncing. Giggling. Squealing. Sounds very good, very nice. We try not to listen, but we can't help hearing, and I tell you, most things we don't hear so well. Finally, we give up trying not to hear. We start hearing. After a while, we *listen*."

"How—often?"

"All the time!"

"All the time?"

"Sure. All the time. I tell you. We wait for you. At night. When we hear you start, I pour Miklos his beer, and a little for me. We turn the radio off, put out the lights. We sit, and we listen."

"You listen."

"Yes, and—I have to tell you this. We——"

"You don't have to tell me, Mrs. Mikszath."

"We—oh—we—we this and that. I'm sorry. I——"

"Oh, Mrs. Mikszath," said Lorna, "don't be sorry." She sat beside her and put her arm around Mrs. Mikszath's shoulders. "I'm not upset. I'm glad. I'm glad you and Miklos—this and that."

"Not what you think, I think. Miklos—Miklos—I'm afraid for Miklos. He might have an attack. Miklos is afraid too, but he doesn't say it. So we don't do much——" She put her hand on Lorna's. "But

[1 5 1]

you do. Oh, do you! And we—we remember. And we have—our little pleasures." She looked at Lorna and blinked. "There, I told you. I'm glad I told you." Then she burst out laughing. "Miklos and I are going to miss you," she said.

Lorna sat for a moment. She looked at Mrs. Mikszath. She pursed her lips. She thought. She grinned. "Mrs. Mikszath," she said, "I'd like to give you something. Something to remember us by." She got up and, from the windowsill in the kitchen, took the papier-mâché duck that Luther had made for her. Carefully, she separated the top from the bottom, along a nearly invisible seam. She removed what looked like a pocket watch and brought it to Mrs. Mikszath. She squatted in front of her and held the watchcase in both hands. She pressed the stem, and the lid opened. An ivory couple lay on rumpled sheets in a pine bed. Mrs. Mikszath said "Ah!" and brought her hand to her mouth.

"A secret," said Lorna. "For you and Miklos only." Slowly she began to twist the stem.

Lorna profited from the move in an unexpected and wonderful way. She found a lifelong friend: May Castle (then May Hopper).

Oh, good! It's time I stepped in. Well, there I was, all alone in the handsomest house in Babbington, because, you see, my parents were dead, poor things. They had died in Paris—well, just outside Paris—in a train wreck, a disaster, really. Hundreds killed. And they left me absolutely everything—well, nearly everything—including the house, of course, and I had the entire place to myself. Well, nearly to myself. I had a wretched aunt living with me, because she had no permanent place to live, and you see, I was only a girl. Was I nineteen yet? No, I don't think so. I may have been seventeen. No, that's not likely. I must have been eighteen. Now the less said about this aunt, Auntie Phipps, the better. Ooooh! She was awful!

I'm quite certain that when the family went looking for a companion for me, someone must have said, "Oh, how about Auntie Phipps?"

"Oh, yes! She'll be just perfect! Where is she?"

"Oh, I don't know, she must be in the back of a closet somewhere. We'll just dig her out and make her go and live with little May."

I'm sure that's where they found her, in some closet. Well, I couldn't stand having her around all the time, and having no one else to talk to. That's why I decided to rent the guest house. We always called it the guest house, but it was actually attached to the house, the main house, so it should have been called the guest wing, I suppose. Well, I ran an ad, and Lorna showed up at the front door. I liked her at once, and she liked me, of course. She was lively and attractive, and she was young! Actually, she was eight or ten—I don't know—say eight—years older than I, but she was, well, no older than an older sister. And yet, she hadn't really been anywhere or done much of anything, so that put us on a more equal footing. Oh, we were friends from the start.

May's was a pretty place: shady patios, ivy-covered trellises, trim lawns, a rose garden, a long gravel driveway. The guest house was linked to the main house by a porte cochere, "attached," as May said, but quite private. There were two bedrooms, a living room with a view every bit as good as that from the front rooms of the main house, and a small kitchen tucked into a corner in the back, with a view over a patch of lawn behind the garage, where a rope swing hung from a twisted apple tree, a swing that May's father had hung for her.

The years that Herb and Lorna spent at May's were exciting ones, years of progress and innovation, rising expectations and increasing prosperity. At the Massachusetts Institute of Technology, Vannevar Bush and a team of scientists and engineers constructed an electromechanical calculator that nudged the slide rule a little closer to death. Tutankhamen's tomb was opened. Lindbergh flew to Paris. Paul Whiteman bought Arnold Abbot Adler's arrangement of "Lake Serenity Serenade," added a vocal by the Rhythm Boys, and made a hit of it. Studebaker introduced the pretty little Erskine Six sport roadster and ran a pair of President Eights around the Atlantic City Speedway for nineteen days nonstop at an average speed approaching seventy miles per hour.

At May's, Herb and Lorna enjoyed luxuries they would never have found anywhere else. May employed a gardener, handyman, housekeeper, and cook; the gardener tended the grounds outside the guest house just as carefully as the rest, the handyman kept the guest house in as good repair as the main house, and the housekeeper cleaned Herb and Lorna's quarters once a week. More often than not, May insisted that Herb and Lorna eat dinner with her. Her generosity had a simple motive: she wanted Herb and Lorna, especially Lorna, to be free to be her friends and boon companions.

Ella was adorable from birth. She had the robust good health and pink plumpness that one sees in rubber baby dolls, a resilient firmness that real flesh doesn't ordinarily exhibit, the rubber-doll bounce of bouncing babyhood. Herb was hugely proud of her. At work, he recounted each of her little triumphs. Several times. The small occurrences in our lives sometimes mean the most to us, and offering to share them is an invitation to the most intimate friendship, but because they don't make exciting stories, they don't often interest other people, not even people we think of as friends. Everyone at Babbington Studebaker thought of Herb as his friend, wisecracked with him, slapped him on the back, but Herb with a story to tell about Ella, Herb with that glow on his face, Herb with his proud-papa look, was someone to avoid.

Take, for example, the morning when Ella seemed to wink at Herb. Herb rushed to work, practicing the story of her winking as he drove. He parked in the lot behind the showroom and trotted toward the door. Hal Tripp saw him coming.

"Uh-oh," he said, tapping Dick Barber on the shoulder, "here comes Herb, with that little grin on his face, and he's talking to himself. You know what that means."

"Yep," said Dick. "He's got a story about some damned cute thing Ella did."

"What say we scoot out back and see how Old Randolph's doing?" suggested Hal.

Herb came through the door exclaiming, "Wait till you hear this! She winked at me!" There was no response. No one was in the showroom. A Dictator, a Commander, and an Erskine sat there alone. Herb went to his desk, disappointed. He hung his coat and hat and stood for a while with his hands in his pockets.

"Old Randolph!" he said suddenly. He dashed out to the service area, where he found Old Randolph in the grease pit, under a Big Six. "Wait till you hear this!" he exclaimed. "She winked at me! Little Ella winked at me!"

"No kiddin'," said Randolph.

"Nope, no kidding," said Herb. "She was so cute! Lorna had just

changed her, see, and she was lying on the rug in the dining room—
Ella was—while I was drinking my coffee, and I looked down at her
and I made that little sound out of the side of my mouth, the way you
do with babies, chk-chk, like that, chk-chk, and she giggled the way
she does when I do that, and then—she winked at me! Just like that!
It was the damnedest thing I ever saw!"

From somewhere in the grease pit, but not from Old Randolph,
came snickering. Curious, suspicious, Herb tiptoed around the Big
Six. He found Hal and Dick huddled together, bent over, trying to
keep from laughing aloud. Herb trudged off, his heart hardened.

In later years, whenever Herb began an anecdote of the small and
personal variety, the kind that might be taken as insignificant, he
would say, first, "You might want to slip off to the grease pit before I
start this story."

Herb sold quite a few Studebakers. The work he had put into making
himself known and respected began paying off. He began capitalizing
on the store of knowledge he'd accumulated about Babbingtonians.
He also had the Piper talent, in such abundance that he became, in an
important sense, his own best customer. He sold himself on Studebaker, and by studying the cars and the prospective buyers, he
found pairings that he sold himself on, too. His pitches rang true
because he was convinced that his pairings of prospects and cars were
right. When a man or woman or couple came into the showroom,
chances were that Herb had already picked a car for them, and when
he described the satisfaction that someone was going to get from, say,
a Standard Six, it sounded like a fact, not a prediction. Herb had
another quality, one that struck everyone but Herb himself as his
strongest: he was a nice guy, the genuine article. Some people bought
a Studebaker from Herb rather than another car from someone else
just because they liked Herb and didn't want to disappoint him. Even
May, who informed Herb when he first suggested he had a car that
might interest her, "In my family we have always owned Chryslers,"
eventually gave in and bought an Erskine roadster. (She refused to
abandon her loyalty to Chrysler entirely, however; she went on buying
Chryslers for as long as she went on buying cars. Herb suggested,
often, that she bought Chryslers just to get his goat. She would ask,
"Is it working?")

When May's Erskine arrived, Garth Castle delivered it in person.

Oh, that was a day. That was a day. Herb telephoned to say that Garth was bringing the car over, and I thought that was a nice touch, but I asked Herb why he wasn't going to bring it himself. Well, Herb was never particularly good at lying. He mumbled something I couldn't make out, and I asked, "What?" and he said, "He wants to meet you." Well, Garth was not the sort of man I would have had a chance to meet when my parents were alive, because he gave the impression of being terribly fast, and Auntie Phipps would certainly never have allowed a man like Garth to call on me. If she had her way I would never have met anyone who wore long pants. But here was an excuse, you see. Well, when I saw Garth come up the drive at the wheel of that adorable car, wearing that big grin of his, I fell in love. Head over heels. Just—wham!—like that.

May had to elude Auntie Phipps to go out with Garth. She pretended that she went out only with Herb and Lorna, but they all went off to meet Garth, and a foursome was established that would endure for more than twenty years. They went to dances at the Boat Club (which, years later, became the Yacht Club without a noticeable increase in the size or opulence of the boats that belonged to its members). They went picnicking, hiking, swimming, sailing, and rowing. They played cards, talked, drank, ate. They went to movies together, and occasionally they drove into New York together. Once they even drove to Chacallit together.

The trip wasn't entirely successful. In the Hubers' parlor, Garth looked like a city slicker, and Richard Huber refused to carry on a conversation with him. Lorna's sisters, Bertha and Clara, spat venom from the start.

"Lorna!" cried Clara as soon as she saw her. "You look so pale! Have you been sick?"

"And so thin!" said Bertha. "I'm worried about you. Are you taking care of yourself?"

May recognized all this for what it was. She was surprised only by the crudeness. She expected to see some fight in Lorna, but she was disappointed. "I'm fine," said Lorna. "Just fine."

May appointed herself Lorna's champion. Eyes wide, lashes flapping, she said, "Yes, it's the fashion now to be slim. At home, *all* the women are slim."

May claimed to find Chacallit enchanting, but she found it considerably less so after she slipped, while stepping from stone to stone, and fell into the chilly Whatsit. Only Lester Piper really enjoyed the visit; he enjoyed it thoroughly. He was delighted to be able to show Herb that he had made a success of himself in Richard Huber's sales department, and he was quite taken with May. Millie Piper, on the other hand, found May shocking, and she feared that there might be goings-on within the quartet of young people, of a type that she had hoped she'd never have to concern herself with.

Of course, the grandparents, Richard and Lena and Lester and Millie, adored Ella. She was curious and quick, and in the course of a morning she did a hundred little things that seemed to be worth telling. When Bertha and Clara arrived with their fat and stolid children, they had to listen to a hundred annoying little stories. Though they smiled, one could see in their eyes the look of an employee at Babbington Studebaker who hadn't managed to slip off to the grease pit.

During this visit, May noticed something unsettling about Ella:

> She—she fell in love too easily. She fell too hard, too fast. I had had an idea of this before, I had seen it a bit, back at home. We often took her with us, of course, when the four of us went here and there, and she seemed to think I was her mother sometimes. I mean, she seemed to feel toward me just as she felt toward Lorna. It bothered me. It did. It didn't seem right. She didn't seem to know the difference— oh, how can I put this—she didn't have the idea of degrees of love. Well, now I'm talking about later, of course. But there, in Chacallit, she just got this mad crush on that man—that Clara's husband. Why? Who can say? One never knows. She fell for people that way— too quickly—too strongly. No apparent reason. You can't tell sometimes.

On the Babbingtonians' final day in Chacallit, Richard and Lena served a buffet supper for everyone: Lester and Millie Piper, Luther Huber, Bertha and Richard Reuter, Clara and Harold Russell, Garth and May, Herb and Lorna.

Bertha was nervous. She was dressed in something she had made herself, without benefit of a pattern, after studying an illustration in a magazine. It was meant to be daring, but it had been an act of desperation and it looked it. Over the course of the Babbingtonians' visit, Bertha had come to feel like a lumpy bumpkin, and she blamed this feeling on Lorna. Bertha was envious, horribly envious. She envied Lorna her legs, her clothes, her baby, her life, her luck, her friends. She didn't realize that the Babbingtonians weren't a very sophisticated bunch. Garth seemed to her exactly what he wanted to be taken for: the Arrow collar man. He seemed to live in a world Bertha had inferred from magazines and novels, frightening, possibly evil, immeasurably pleasurable. And May! Everything about May suggested a life of ease, lived on the gentle horizontal, not the tough slopes of the Whatsit Valley, ease that left legs slim and smooth, as May's short skirts boasted. To Bertha's envious eye, Lorna and Herb glowed with May and Garth's reflected light, especially Lorna, who even wore May's hand-me-down silks.

Garth had brought liquor from Babbington. He passed cocktails around. Lena and Millie refused, and Bertha and Clara refused at first, but Bertha changed her mind when May and Lorna took theirs, and Clara changed her mind when Bertha took one. "Wouldn't you rather have something else, girls?" asked Lena. She wrinkled her brow.

"Mother, really," said Bertha.

"She's right, Mrs. Huber," said May. "They're not girls any more."

Bertha looked hard at May, then at Lorna.

"After all," said May, "you girls—oh, now *I'm* doing it—you and Clara *are* Lorna's *older* sisters. I'm sure Lorna doesn't think of herself as a girl any longer, and—"

"May," said Garth. "Why don't you give me a hand in the kitchen?" May gave a little shrug, as if to say that she couldn't imagine why Garth couldn't handle the cocktails by himself, and followed him into the kitchen.

"May," he whispered, "don't you think you ought to—"

"No, I don't," said May, struggling to keep her voice down. "That woman has been horrible all week." She left the kitchen, apparently composed, and she sprinkled light and glittering conversation around the living room while she hunted for Bertha. She found her at the table in the dining room, spooning potato salad onto her plate.

"Bertha, I'd put some of that potato salad back, if I were you," whispered May. "It looks dreadfully fattening."

Bertha glared at her.

"Well, perhaps you're right," said May. "It can't make *that* much difference." She walked off, beautifully. Bertha watched her go. When May got to the living room, she took Bertha's husband's arm and whispered in his ear something that made him laugh. May succeeded, in a way: she hurt Bertha, made her angry. But May wasn't the object of Bertha's anger, Lorna was—Lorna, who was slim, who had a lively, bouncing baby, who seemed to have stumbled into a life so much better and easier than Bertha's, who didn't even have to fight back when she was taunted, because she had a clever friend to fight for her. All the old hatred came back. Methodically, Bertha began eating her potato salad.

When it was time to go, and Herb lifted Ella from the lap of Harold Russell, Clara's husband, Ella clung to him and cried furiously. She kicked and screamed and called out for Harold in the car. She sobbed herself into exhaustion. After half an hour of feeble whimpering, she fell asleep. Everyone was silent for a while. Then May said, in Bertha's voice, "Lorna! You look so thin! I hope you're taking care of yourself! Have a plate of lard, won't you? I'm having my second!" Lorna tried not to laugh, but she couldn't help herself. She began giggling, and soon all four were burlesquing Bertha and Clara, laughing till tears ran down their cheeks.

Bertha lay in bed, awake. The rest of the house was asleep. Cocktails, potato salad, and envy had unsettled her stomach. She felt dizzy in bed, so she got up and went into the kitchen for a glass of warm milk. While the milk was warming she buttered a slice of bread and sprinkled it with sugar, making the treat she called in childhood "bread-and-butter-sugar-bonnet." She had heartburn, and she thought something rich and sweet and comforting would cure it. She belched. Acid caught in her throat. It tasted of potato salad. She took a piece of paper from a drawer. She poured the milk and began eating the bread-and-butter-sugar-bonnet. She looked at the paper. Acid rose in her throat again. Brashly, she began a letter to Herb.

One rainy evening not long after, Garth and May and Herb and Lorna were settled in front of a fire in May's living room, and Herb was telling the story of the arrival at the showroom, that morning, of Miss Decker.

"She took me by surprise," said Herb. "She was the last person any of us ever expected to buy a car. We used to joke about it."

"That's right," said Garth. "It was already a stale gag. We'd be having a cup of coffee and someone would look up as if something had caught his eye and say, 'My God, I don't believe it! Here comes Miss Decker!' The idea was to make someone turn to see if she really *was* coming—you know, just to see if you could get a rise out of someone."

Herb said, "We used to do the same thing with, umm, a pretty girl, or—"

"Yeah," said Garth. "I'd give a whistle and say, 'Ooooee,' or something like that, and see how many heads would turn."

"Life must be pretty boring at Babbington Studebaker," said May.

"Anyway," Garth said, "we had a name for those gags. What do you think we called them?"

"I can't imagine," said May.

"'Miss Deckers,'" said Garth.

"So when I looked up from my desk and saw Miss Decker," said Herb, "I said, 'My God, here comes Miss Decker!' Garth called out, 'You're not getting me to come out of my office, Herb.' Well, I went to the door and held it open for her and said, 'Good morning, Miss Decker.'"

"I was sure he was trying to pull a Miss Decker on me," said Garth. "I called out, 'What on earth brings *you* here, Miss Decker?' I really exaggerated it, so Herb would know I hadn't been taken in. I thought I was just going along with the gag."

"And Miss Decker called right back to him, bright and cheery, 'I thought I might buy myself a car.'"

"I thought I was going to have a heart attack," said Garth.

"I heard Garth's chair crash to the floor, and then I saw him in the doorway of his office, red as a beet, stammering and harrumphing."

"I tell you, I couldn't talk," said Garth. "She had pulled the biggest Miss Decker of them all."

"It got worse," said Herb. "She wanted to buy a President tourer. Now, I had given a lot of thought to what kind of car would be best for her, just in case she ever *did* happen to walk into the showroom, and a big President was all wrong. I explained that a nice lightweight

Erskine delivery car would be much more convenient for carrying the pies she makes, and that I was sure people would quickly become accustomed to her driving a delivery car.

" 'I would look ridiculous,' she said.

" 'Oh, no,' I told her. 'You wouldn't look ridiculous.' "

"And this is when I almost ruined it," admitted Garth. "Ordinarily, I never interfere with a sale, but this was no ordinary sale. I came out of my office onto the floor and said, 'Oh, no, Miss Decker, you wouldn't look ridiculous at all! In fact, one of those big Presidents might make you look, well, not ridiculous exactly, but as if you were overreaching yourself.' Well, *overreaching* was the wrong word, I guess. All I meant was that the damned car was too big and impractical, but after all, she does sell pies, doesn't she? You would have thought I'd called her a tramp.

" 'Overreaching!' she shouted. 'Overreaching! Why, why, why—'

"And I said, 'Well, that may have been the wrong word.'

"She began reciting the family history. 'The Deckers have been among the first families of Babbington since before there *was* a Babbington. Why, Ephraim Decker built the first house to have a stone-and-mortar foundation!' "

"They were one of the *last* families to have indoor plumbing," said May.

"I began backing toward my office," said Garth. " 'I'm terribly sorry, Miss Decker,' I said. 'I'm not myself today. I may be coming down with something.' And you know what she said? 'I should hope so!' "

When they stopped laughing, Herb said, "Now for the funny part."

"Oh, she didn't!" cried Lorna.

"She certainly did," said Herb. "A seven-passenger tourer."

They laughed. They repeated the best bits. They laughed some more. Garth made more drinks. After he had handed them around, he set his down and dropped to one knee in front of May. He said, "If you're ready for something *really* funny, I'd like to ask you to marry me, May."

Well! I laughed. To tell you the truth, I thought he was pulling a Miss Decker. So I thought I'd pull one right back. I said yes.

[1 6 1]

They drank their drinks and made plans for the wedding, and, very late, they went to their beds. Herb made such tender love to Lorna that she thought the proposal-and-acceptance scene must have touched him, and she smiled in the dark at his sentimentality. There was, however, another reason for his tenderness. He hadn't mentioned, in telling the story about Miss Decker, the fact that when he had looked up from his desk, surprised by Miss Decker's arrival, he had had on his desk a letter from Bertha, the letter she had begun writing the night they left Chacallit. She had taken a long time deciding to send it, but the bitter taste she associated with Lorna kept coming back, and sweet foods wouldn't drive it away. Finally she decided that there was only one way to eliminate it. She mailed the letter.

Dear Herb,

It pains me to have to write this letter, but now that I have gotten to know you a little bit, I know that it would be wrong not to tell you what I think you should know. I think you should know that when Lorna was a girl she did things she shouldn't have done with our uncle Luther. I know you're wondering how I know this, and I have to tell you that I know because I saw with my own eyes. I should have spoken up at the time, but I couldn't bring myself to do it. I was just a girl myself naturally. I wouldn't even have known what words to use. I hardly know what words to use now. What they did was what the rooster does to the hen. It was what the bullock does to the cow. I'm sure you know what I'm getting at! Even if you never lived on a farm! But I'm sorry that I have to tell you that they did much more than that. I know you will understand how hard it is for me to say these things. And how shocked I was as a little girl to see these things. How can I put it? The cow does not try to swallow the bull's pizzle, does she? Well, that's one way Lorna didn't behave like a cow, if you take my meaning. I'm sure I don't have to go on. You must be able to imagine the things that went on between Lorna and our uncle Luther. And I'm sure it wasn't Luther who started all of this. In fact, now that I think of it, I remember that it was Lorna who started it all. I remember her begging Luther to take her for a ride in his sleigh, and he didn't want to, of course, because it was dangerous. She kept asking him please, please won't you take me? And he kept telling her no, that it was too dangerous. *So she took his hand and put it right under her dress. I remember it now. I remember seeing it. They were in the barn. It sent a chill up my spine because it was Uncle Luther's hurt hand, the one that doesn't have all its fingers, and I could imagine what it must feel like to have that hand there. It wasn't Luther's fault, though. Men are weak. I'm sorry that I had to bring you the pain of this news. I just thought that you should know.*

Hoping you are well,
Bertha Reuter

Herb had sat, staring at the letter, not at all certain what he thought of it. Then Miss Decker had arrived. After she had gone, he looked at the letter again, and he decided that what Bertha said must be true. It was the chill down the spine, Bertha's revulsion at the thought of having Luther's damaged hand between her legs, that made him believe it. He sat looking out the window for the rest of the afternoon, and by the time Garth called out that it was time to close up and head for home, Herb had decided that Luther must have been the man who taught Lorna the things that surprised him in bed. He couldn't agree with Bertha that Luther hadn't been at fault. Luther was a man; Lorna was a child. Nor could he agree with Bertha that the things she said were things he ought to know. *What made her write this?* he asked himself. *What* really *made her write it? This is the sort of thing a person does to get even. Get even for what? For May's teasing? That doesn't make sense. Nobody would write this because of some teasing. There's got to be more to it. Jealousy, I'll bet. She must have been jealous of Lorna and Luther. That must be it. Bertha wanted Luther. God, how she must have taken it out on Lorna when they were kids. Poor Lorna. And poor fat, miserable Bertha. She made herself crazy.*

Herb was wrong in nearly all the particulars, but right in nearly all the essentials. He destroyed the letter. He was determined never to mention it or its assertions and never to let it affect his feelings for Lorna. In all the rest of his life, he never did mention it, but it did affect his feelings for Lorna. Every now and then, when he saw worry in Lorna's puckered brow, he was reminded of the suffering he supposed Bertha had inflicted on her, and he embraced Lorna with a comforting tenderness that surprised and delighted her. Whenever he saw Bertha, he treated her with maddening solicitude, as an object of pity, and on the one occasion when Bertha dared whisper a reference to her letter, Herb patted her hand, smiled the smile we smile when we're listening to the incomprehensible babbling of toddlers, and said, "Dut, dut, dut," which baffled and infuriated her.

11

In Which Curiosity Leads Herb 'n' Lorna to a Misunderstanding

At May and Garth's wedding, Herb was best man, Lorna was matron of honor, and Ella was flower girl. As a wedding gift, Garth gave May a cottage on the beach.

At that time, the narrow barrier beach across Bolotomy Bay from Babbington was only sparsely developed. Strung along the bay side were a few shacks, shelters for clamdiggers, where they could get out of the weather when the weather was foul, stay close to their work when the clamming was good, or hide out among their fellows when the door was locked at home. Attracted by the carefree bohemianism that a shack on the beach suggested, a few people who were not clamdiggers bought shacks, but since life in a shack is more rough than romantic, they enlarged and civilized them into weekend out-posts of their mainland homes, where on weekends they led barefoot versions of their mainland lives.

Among the clammies, this stretch of shacks had no real name; most called it "over south," as in:

"Where's Bitzer these days? Haven't seen him in a week or more."

"He's holed up over south. The woman locked him out, you know."

However, to the people who thought of their cottages as retreats, where they might escape the cares, routines, conventions, and restrictions of life in town, "over south" was "the beach."

The shack Garth bought for May was small and rough, but with it he gave her a sketch he'd made of what it might be. By the following summer it was a comfortable little cottage, thanks to May's money and Herb's handiwork. The island was accessible only by boat. It was nearly a mile long, but less than a hundred yards wide. From a narrow dock on the bay side, a narrow boardwalk led to the "main street" of the settlement: a somewhat wider boardwalk that linked all the shacks. At its westernmost end was a small store, a shack much like the others, except for its sign: NECESSARIES. At its easternmost end was a bar, which, since Prohibition was still in force, looked *just* like the other shacks, without a sign; if it had had one, it would have read NEWSOME'S. Said May of the bar at the beach:

> *Oh, nobody called it Newsome's. If there had been a sign, it should have said "Nosy's." But Nosy wouldn't have liked that. Not a bit. That bar was just a scream. Mr. Newsome—he ran it—had been a schoolteacher and a prizefighter, or an amateur boxer, anyway. He wanted everyone to call him Mr. Newsome, but every called him Nosy, because he had a big broken nose pushed flat on his face. Nosy Newsome. Well, at first the bar was just too quiet. It was dull. Then one evening I said, "Mr. Newsome, I'm going to make a contribution to the atmosphere in this establishment: I'm going to give you my piano." Well, I had an old upright in the cottage—not very good, but a piano. It was a* grand *gesture—giving the piano to Nosy. There was applause. I took bows. It's talked about to this day. I suppose it is. The piano is still there. I think. I haven't been to Nosy's for years. I don't think it's even called Nosy's now. Well, that doesn't matter, does it? Oh, anyway, a dozen fellows went right over and carried the piano from the cottage to the bar. Well, they didn't actually* carry *it the whole way—they pushed it quite a bit—did it have little wheels?— I think so. I rode on top. We were all a little drunk. Well, we got it into the bar, and we sang some songs and danced, but we had to dance outside, on the boardwalk, because there wasn't enough room for a piano* and *dancing.*

The beach was a wonderful place. It offered the pleasures of sea and sand and bay and the entertainments of people at their ease who are dependent on themselves and one another for their amusements. The clammies welcomed the vacationers, since they were openhanded and their pockets were deep. They liked to have a good time and did. It was the prosperous and fun-loving Babbingtonians who bought shacks and spruced them up or built new cottages. They enjoyed the insularity, the loose, unbuttoned life, and one another's company. They knew the same songs, the same dances, the same jokes, the same bootleggers.

Herb and Lorna and Garth and May spent a lot of happy hours at the beach. A couple of cottages away from May's was one owned by a couple with a small boy called Tippy, who was two years older than Ella. He was spoiled, willful, selfish, and nasty. Ella fell in love with him. She and Tippy were together for hours at a time, and Tippy teased and provoked her relentlessly, but she always came back for more, and she pressed little gifts on Tippy—toys of her own, candies, kisses. Snapshots from those days show Lorna and May on a blanket, chatting, Ella dozing beside them, Lorna's hand resting on the small of Ella's back; May lying on the sand in the sun, reading *The Bridge of San Luis Rey*; Ella and Tippy building a sand castle, Tippy raising a shovel threateningly, Ella smiling; Herb, Lorna, and May sitting in white wicker chairs around a card table in the cottage, rain streaking the windows, anagram tiles on the table, condensation on their drink glasses, running down in wandering droplets, Garth's chair pushed aside, not to block the camera; May in a wide-brimmed straw hat; Garth striking a pose in a woolen bathing suit, saluting the viewer with his upraised glass; Garth with his arm around a succession of young women guests; Ella walking along the boardwalk between Herb and Lorna or between Garth and May; Lorna holding Ella in the surf; Herb holding Ella in the surf; Garth holding May; Herb holding Lorna; Garth holding Lorna; Herb holding May.

When Garth turned thirty, May threw a birthday party for him on the beach. Guests arrived in a festive little flotilla, their boats decked out in bright bunting and paper streamers.

> *Oh, it was a perfect day, just a perfect day, perfect. Clear and hot, with a light breeze, just enough to keep one from sweating unattractively. We swam, of course, and we played some ball game or*

other—baseball, I suppose—and we played badminton, and we
played tag. That was quite a lot of fun, tag. Delicious, really. You see
we'd been drinking *all day, and so there was a lot of hugging and*
*squeezing and—well—*fondling *involved, and people would chase*
one another into the water, and—well—romp. Frolic. Gambol.
When it began to get dark, we built a gorgeous bonfire. We played
charades in the firelight, and then we ate. Lorna and I had arranged a
marvelous clambake. After dinner, there was a certain amount of—
well—drifting off. Couples began wandering off into the dunes or just
into the dark, and—well.

You'll have to turn this off, Peter, this recorder. I'll tell *you the*
rest, and you may put it in, but you may not quote me.

May wandered away from the fire, alone. She wanted to stretch
her legs, look at the stars and moon, think, clear her head a bit. She
walked to the water's edge, where the foam shone with phosphores-
cent whiteness in the moonlight. It was so pretty that she wanted to
call the others to come down there with her, to see what she saw, but
the people around the fire were loud and animated, and just now she
wanted quiet and calm. She saw Herb, standing apart, looking out
into the darkness. If he were to come down to the edge of the water
with her, alone, that would be fine, but she didn't want to go back and
ask him, or anyone else, to come and walk in the glowing foam with
her. She kicked off her shoes and walked in the shallow water, kicking
at it, making the bright foam scatter in front of her. She turned back,
saw with surprise how small and isolated the fire and the group
around it appeared, how large the sky and sea. She didn't see Herb
anywhere. She struck out for the dunes above the beach, where she
could sit alone and watch the sea roll in under the moonlight.

Atop a dune, she sat with her arms around her legs, watching. A
figure was walking along the water's edge, as she had. It was a man.
Herb? He was directly in front of her now, and he had stopped. He
was turning this way and that. Had he followed her? Was he looking
for her now? He lit a cigarette, and May saw that it was Herb. She felt
a ripple of curiosity and excitement. "Up here," she called softly. "Up
here, in the dunes."

She watched him walk toward her. She could read his walk, could
see that the appearance of ease, even lack of interest, was false. She

knew that he *had* followed her. He stopped, not quite sure which way to go.

"Here," she called again. He corrected his course. At the foot of her dune, he still couldn't be sure where she was. "Here," she said in little more than a whisper.

He looked up, and now he could see her. "Hi, May," he said. He scrambled up the dune and sat beside her.

"Looking for some peace and quiet?" she asked.

"No, not really," said Herb. "I was looking for you." She put her hand on his, and he kissed her cheek. She felt a flutter of excitement. She wondered what Herb had in mind. Herb had begun to wonder, too. When he had followed May—and he had followed May—he hadn't thought about his motive. Perhaps he had avoided thinking about his motive. Now that he was at May's side, alone in the moonlight, hidden in the dunes, her presence so palpable and inviting, he felt a guilty thrill, and he asked himself what on earth he was up to.

Lorna had seen May walk off into the darkness. She had seen Herb watch May go. From the way he watched her go, Lorna thought she could tell what he was thinking. When, just a while later, she saw him walk off, as if he had no other object than to see what the sky looked like from outside the circle of firelight, Lorna was sure she knew what he was up to. He was a little drunk, she knew, and might have forgotten his fetters. She felt a jab of jealousy and fear, and something that surprised her: curiosity. She had for years been exercising a professional sexual curiosity. Nearly every man she saw had been its object, some the objects of fleeting guesses, others of protracted speculation. Garth had been on her mind for quite a while. She acted on impulse. She walked to a group where Garth was telling an anecdote. She stood close and listened to him talk. She brushed against him, jostled him, as if accidentally, but she didn't move away. She pressed her hip against him, her breast, still so lightly that it might be unintentional. When Garth finished, and the laughter was done, and someone else began another story, Lorna said, "I'm going to look at the stars," and walked away.

Garth wondered whether that was an invitation. From Lorna? It didn't seem likely. Still, there was a possibility. He waited a bit and then said, to no one in particular, "I think I'll fix myself another drink," and walked off, out into the dark, toward the water. He found Lorna looking out to sea, letting the water wash over her feet. "Hello," he said.

"Hello," she said. She held her hand out to him. "Let's walk a little."

They walked along in the direction opposite to the one May and Herb had taken, holding hands and talking about the luminous sea. Garth put his arm around Lorna's waist. She put hers around his. They walked slowly, attentive to the pleasure of feeling their bodies touch. Then Garth stopped, turned Lorna toward him, and kissed her. It was much as she had imagined. They embraced, and Lorna ran her hands along the long muscles in Garth's back, making mental notes. He pushed himself against her, Lorna noted his tumescense, and a very specific problem arose: Lorna was enjoying herself.

May put her head on Herb's shoulder. "I wondered what you were up to," she said. "I saw you walking along the edge of the water and I said to myself, 'He wanted to be alone for a while, like me,' and then I said, '*Maybe* he came to look for me.'"

"Do you want me to leave you alone?"

May looked into his face and grinned. "No," she said. "I want you to stay here." She kissed him. *She likes to lead,* he thought. *She likes a man who follows her lead. If I were animating her, I'd put her on top. And I'd make her very lively. And clever. Clever? Maybe not. But daring. I've always thought she would be daring. I wonder——* The opportunity to test a hypothetical animation was at hand. Herb was thrilled, thrilled twofold, intellectually and sexually. The sexual thrill made him feel guilty, made him feel that he ought to go. The intellectual thrill made him want to stay. May began unbuttoning his shirt.

Garth heard the nervousness in Lorna's laugh. "Second thoughts?" he asked.

"Oh, yes," said Lorna. "Many."

"You're lovely in the moonlight," he said. As luck would have it, this dangerous moment was one of those when the moonlight brought out Lorna's astonishing beauty. She was in water up to her waist; Garth was nearer shore, and the wavelets rhythmically hid and exposed him, his penis bobbing in the moonlight. Lorna hugged herself to hide her breasts.

"Oh, Garth, stop." She noted his bobbing penis. *Like a little fish,* she thought, *swimming in front of him.*

"Well, you are," said Garth. "Put your arms down—I want to see you."

"No. Let's get dressed, I—"

Garth put his finger to his lips and shushed her. He waded toward her, slowly, slowly, and she let her lips part and her arms fall. Closer, closer. He reached out for her, embraced her, drew her toward him. Something poked at her underwater. *A fish? No, silly, it's Garth.* She brushed at it and touched it. Garth's penis. But the fish idea wouldn't leave. She grabbed it, underwater, and palpated it, running her hand the length of it, investigating with her fingers, noting details.

"Oh, Lorna, Lorna," said Garth.

He surprised her. For a moment she had been aware of only part of him. "It's like a fish," she said without thinking.

"What?"

She let go of it and laughed. "Oh, I'm sorry," she said. "It's just—" She put her hand over her mouth, still laughing. "Just for a second, I thought it was a fish."

"Lorna—" said Garth.

"Garth, would you—" She thought, *Would you be willing to—just stand still—on the sand, where I can see you—and let me see you—and touch you? I'm just—curious. Just curious.*

"Yes?"

"Would you—"

"Do you want to do something unusual? Don't be embarrassed. We can do it any way you want. Do you want to do it here, in the water? I'll be Neptune, and you can be a mermaid. How do mermaids make love, do you think?"

Make love? Oh, Garth, I don't want to make love. I just want to— "Oh, Garth, could we just get dressed and go back? This is—foolish. Really. Isn't it?"

"Thank you, my dear."

"Oh, Garth, I don't mean you. I mean me. I feel foolish—silly—and I wish you'd help me out of this—this spot I've gotten into."

"Well—"

"Please, Garth. Please."

"All right," said Garth. He waded toward shore. Over his shoulder, he said, "Don't look, now."

"Oh, I intend to look very closely," said Lorna.

"Ahhh—" Garth turned toward Lorna again.

"But that's all," said Lorna. *Unless you'd be willing to let me just—poke around a little.*

Garth walked back to his pile of clothes and began dressing. Lorna watched.

Herb ran the tips of his fingers over May's breasts. *I shouldn't do this. I shouldn't do this. But I want to see her move, I want to see what she does. I want to see how she does it. But Lorna—what will I say to Lorna?*

May pushed him, nudging him onto his back. "You just lie back," she said. "I want to do something to you." *I knew it.* He flopped onto his back, ready, eager. *This is going to be great. Fascinating.* May ran the tip of her tongue the length of his penis. *Interesting. This is going to be very*—she straddled him—*very hard to tell Lorna.*

"May?" She brought him to her and inserted him, just barely.
"Mmmm?"
"I want to go back, May." She lowered herself, just a bit.
"Why?"
"Because I'm—scared." Just a bit more.
"Of me?"
"Of you. Of me. I shouldn't have followed you." She stopped.
"Gee, mister, you got me all warmed up, and now you're going to walk out on me? Just feel how fast my heart's beating." She took his hand and pressed it to her breast, and as she did so she let herself settle on him.
"May—" *Please let me go. Please don't let me go.*
"I see you smiling. You don't want to go."
"No, I don't." *I do. I don't.* She began rocking, ever so slightly. "Stop. Hey, May. Stop that." *Don't stop. Stop.* "Please, May."
"You mean it, don't you?"
"Yeah. I do."
"Oh, Herb, you're sweet. You know that? Come on, we'll go back." She lifted herself up, so abruptly that they slurped in disengaging. She giggled.
"Thanks, May."
"You're sure now?"
"I'm sure—I think."
"All right. We'll go back. Where are my shoes?"
Garth took Lorna's arm suddenly and held her back, before they returned to the firelight. "Lorna, wait a minute. I want to ask you something."

"What?"

"It wasn't me, was it?"

"Oh, no. It wasn't you. It was me."

"Do you think that, if things had been different, you would have—"

"I'm sure I would have."

"Thanks. I was afraid it was me."

He threw his arm around her, and she threw hers around him, and they returned to the firelight laughing.

Herb took May's arm and held her back, before they returned to the firelight.

"May," said Herb, "before we go back, I want to—I want to tell you—"

"You're not changing your mind, are you? You want another chance?"

"No, no."

"Oh, you don't want another chance."

"Oh, I do—"

"You *do* want another chance. All right, let's—"

"That's not what I meant. You're teasing me. You know that wasn't what I meant to say. I meant that—if things had been different—I—I would—I would have loved to—"

"Oh, Herb, thank you! That's very nice. I think that's the nicest thing anyone has ever said to me. I'll remember that forever: 'If things had been different—I—I would—gosh—oh, gee.'"

"Aw, May."

She gave him a cuff on the ear. "Let's get a drink," she said, and she took his hand and ran off toward the fire, calling, "Let's go down to the bar, everybody, and wake up old Nosy." They came back into the circle of firelight just as Lorna and Garth did. Lorna and Garth walked into the firelight with their arms around each other, flushed, a little out of breath, laughing. When Herb saw them, they looked like lovers to him. Lorna saw Herb and May run into the light hand in hand, flushed, a little out of breath, laughing. They looked like lovers to her.

As Proust probably says somewhere:

How surprising we find it that, numbered among the many atten-
dants of Love, we do not always find Understanding, the pervasive

*understanding which we suppose ought to be a prominent member of
the procession of Venus. We suppose, and certainly it seems to us
perfectly reasonable so to suppose, that love begets, among the many
offspring that we suppose it to beget, Understanding, and, so well do
we convince ourselves that in so supposing we are correct, we persist in
believing that we must be correct, even when we are confronted with
contradicting evidence, as a blind man, who, feeling on his face a
comforting warmth he takes to be the familiar effect of the sun, walks
in the direction he supposes to be sunward and persists in his mistaken
belief that he feels on his cheeks not the calescence of a terrestrial fire
toward which he advances but the radiance of the sun, and still persists
even when, at the last instant, benevolent hands prevent him from
walking into a heap of flaming fagots.*

And if he does say that somewhere, then, as is sometimes the case,
Proust is right. Love sometimes leads to misunderstandings. Neither
Herb nor Lorna ever said a word about that night. Neither dared ask,
"Did you—?" Neither dared say, "I was just curious, you see." Lorna
supposed that she understood what Herb had done and why, and
Herb supposed that he understood what Lorna had done and why.
Each loved the other too much to ask for an explanation, so they
provided their own. Each was too timid to ask for a description, so
they provided their own. They were faithful to each other for the rest
of their lives, and each forgave the other for that lone transgression,
which they blamed on the heat of the moment, supposing that heat to
be the heat not of knowledge's flickering lamp, but of lust's consuming flame.

12

In Which Coarse Goods Help Herb 'n' Lorna Survive the Great Depression

For a while, the nation, the Studebaker Corporation, and Herb and Lorna were doing well. Herb sold Studebakers with the zeal of a fanatic. Because he loved selling for itself, it was a far stronger affection than the money he made could have inspired; it was the kind of affection that people develop for leisure activities, for following a basketball team, tending a garden, trying to turn a lawn into the lush carpet pictured on bags of grass seed. Add to his love of selling his fondness for Studebakers, which grew and grew. He couldn't seem to get enough of them, know enough about them. In idle hours at the showroom, he read and reread the sales brochures, and he even read all the technical and repair manuals. He knew the cars so well that other salesmen brought potential customers to him to have their questions answered and gladly gave Herb a part—a small part—of their commissions when he helped with a sale. It wasn't unusual for one of the mechanics, even for Old Randolph himself on occasion, to come in from the shop wearing a puzzled look and holding some doohickey or other.

"Say, Herb," he might say, "what the Sam Hill is this thingumabob supposed to do? God knows I never saw the like of it before now."

"This?" Herb might say, giving the part the once-over. "This gadget is part of the free-wheeling assembly. Brand new. We've only sold two cars with it so far. You don't have one in for repair already, do you?"

"To tell the truth, I'm not sure if it's broke or not. Just makes a funny kind of noise."

"Whirrrr-ticka whirrrr-ticka?"

"Yep, that's it. Kind of a whirrrr-ticka whirrrr-ticka."

"That's normal," said Herb. "Button her back up."

It was at this time, when Herb had some money to spare, that tinkering for the sake of tinkering became his consuming leisure-time occupation. Earlier, the little projects he undertook had practical ends, however meandering may have been the routes he traveled to attain them. At this time, though, perhaps symptomatic of his infection by the attitudes endemic at the time—freedom, daring, aimless whoopee—Herb began undertaking more and more projects for the intricate work they promised, without much regard for the practicality of the result.

He was at a critical point as a tinkerer. On the one hand, he had discovered how to increase the salutary distraction that comes from fiddling around, the distraction that, to take woodworking as an example, comes from cutting and sanding, producing a bunch of smooth rectangles and a nice pile of sawdust. On the other hand, however, Herb was losing sight of the need to justify such fiddling around by producing something that had enough utility to keep one from being considered a loony. (Just think of all the happy guys across America who are passing this moment making the chips fly with powerful and noisy routers. If asked by a neighbor, "What the hell are you up to, making all that racket?" they don't have to be so frank as to say, "Oh, just fiddling around." They justify the time they spend in their cozy workshops by making signs for the homes and cottages of their friends and neighbors, thereby demonstrating their generosity and, quite frequently, their reckless disregard for the plural and possessive forms of surnames.)

Herb designed and built, to consider one example of his work during this period, an insert for kitchen drawers that, when the drawer was fully opened, raised itself from the drawer and presented the contents at an angle of about forty-five degrees. When one began pushing the drawer closed, the gadget began collapsing into the drawer again, its rate of collapse matching the rate at which one closed the drawer. Hour after happy hour went into the design, the construction of prototypes, the modification of the prototypes. They were hours when Herb whistled while he worked. Lorna, who loved his projects, sometimes sat beside him and talked or helped while Ella played with scraps and rejects, keeping always close beside her a Raggedy Andy doll with which she had fallen in love. Lorna took pleasure from Herb's pleasure in the work, and she admired his ingenuity, his mechanical cleverness, which she considered the equal, in its way, of the work of the anonymous coarse-goods animator. These were wonderful, contented, worry-free hours, but the product of those hours was, May recalled, almost useless:

> Well, that folding-drawer gadget was an absolute scream. Herb outfitted our entire kitchen with them! Every time you opened a drawer, this handsome—and they were very handsome—wooden whatchamacallit would riiiise up—very gracefully—and tillllt forward—and dump everything on your feet. But it was a beautiful thing to look at, just the same, and it worked like a charm. It didn't do anything that anyone in her right mind would want a gadget to do, but it did it remarkably well.

It was also at this time that Herb began leaving projects half-finished. The most pleasant part of the work ended, for him, when he was going to have to turn out a product. Often, Lorna would step in at this point and finish up, while Herb went on to something else. She was curious to see how the project would turn out, and she loved adding her work to Herb's.

Because they were doing so well, they turned away from coarse goods, though their respective uncles tried nearly identical arguments to make them change their minds.

"Herb, Herb," said Ben, "you're making the biggest mistake of your life. You are a mechanical *genius,* Herb. Will you just listen to me for a minute, please? You've been doing all right. Fine. But not long ago you weren't doing so well, remember? Whenever you were a little short or you wanted something for Lorna, or you needed something for Ella, where did you turn? To me! You turned to me, Herb. And I was happy to see you. Now you're selling cars, and that's fine, just fine. You're making some money. Everybody's making some money. Now is our big chance. While everybody's got some money, it's our chance to expand! This is your chance to build a nest egg, Herb—put some money away for little Ella."

"I'm sorry, Uncle Ben," said Herb. "I know there's sense in what you say, but—you have to understand—I look at it the opposite way. This *is* my big chance. It's my big chance to get out, get out of coarse goods forever. I'm making money now, and I've got a good future. I don't want to jeopardize that. I don't want anyone, especially Lorna, to find out what I've been doing, and the longer you keep at something like this, the harder it is to hide. This is the end, Uncle Ben. The end."

"Lorna," said Luther, "forgive me for saying that I've heard this before."

"I know you have, Uncle Luther," said Lorna. "This will be the last time, though. Herb's doing fine now, and I know he's going to—"

"—just do better and better!"

"Yes. He is. And you have no right to ridicule him for doing what he does. He *will* do well. I'm sure he'll do well. And he'll do it without resorting to—what I've done."

"Lorna, you ought to be *proud* of what you've done. You're an artist! Your work is admired by some of the most discriminating collectors in the world."

"Don't treat me like a child, Uncle Luther."

"Do you think I'm lying to you?"

"I—"

"I assure you, I'm not. You are—"

"Never mind," said Lorna. "I don't want to hear it. It doesn't matter anyway. I'm finished. Finished."

Lying in bed at night in those moments when even the closest lovers turn to private thoughts in the privileged solitude of those about to fall asleep, Herb and Lorna felt—this is the honest way to put it—purer for having renounced something that had always been a guilty secret; they felt (individually, privately, secretly) proud of having put this bit of the past behind them and secure in the idea that if things *did* get bad, or if Ella needed something that cost an awful lot of money, if there was an emergency, then (*"A mechanical genius,"* he said, thought Herb), but only then (*"An artist,"* he said, thought Lorna), coarse goods would pull them through.

And then along came serious trouble: the stock market crash, bank holidays, business failures, unemployment, bread lines, declining Studebaker sales. Garth began letting people go: a mechanic, a salesman, the bookkeeper, two more salesmen, two more mechanics, the janitor, another salesman, until only he and Herb and Old Randolph were left. Old Randolph kept busy keeping old cars running, and Garth filled his time keeping the salesroom and the display cars tidy. Herb pursued potential buyers with undiminished fervor, but fewer and fewer bought. One day, Garth asked Herb to take a walk with him at lunch time.

"Herb," he said. "We're in big trouble."

"Sales have been slow," said Herb.

"Worse than slow," said Garth. "I don't know how long we can keep going."

"It's that bad?"

"I'm afraid so. We put a lot of money into remodeling the showroom. When cars were selling fast, we made a lot of deals that didn't make us much but were—"

"—good for the future," said Herb.

"Yeah," said Garth, "good for the future. Well, the future's here, and we need cash. We're not selling enough cars to pay the mortgage, Herb. Hell, we can't even pay the light bill."

"I didn't realize—"

"The partners were going to close the place, Herb."

"They—they were? How—why did—why did they keep it open?"

"May's been paying the bills."

"Oh."

"I can't keep going back to her again and again. It makes me feel—like a kid—like asking my mother for money for a show. I don't know what to do."

"Maybe I could help out," said Herb. "Lorna and I have a little. We—"

"No. I can't take your money, Herb. You've got Ella to look out for."

"You won't be taking it. I'll be investing it—to save my job."

Herb and Lorna invested everything they had saved in Babbington Studebaker. Six weeks later, the Studebaker Corporation went bankrupt. The company was placed under the control of court-appointed receivers. The owners of the Babbington dealership locked the showroom doors, and Garth began spending his time at the beach, in Nosy's bar. Herb cursed himself for having done a foolish Piper thing. Lying awake at night, he vowed that Lorna and Ella wouldn't suffer for his foolishness. He would do what he had to do. He would design some new prototypes for coarse goods and he would get Ben to let him have some goods to sell. Lying beside him, Lorna vowed that Herb would not suffer for having done what he had thought it best to do. She would do what she had to do. She would telephone Luther and tell him—*ask* him—to take her back.

The years that followed were difficult ones. The Studebaker Motor Company began clawing its way back. The Babbington dealership reopened, for three days a week, with a staff of two: Herb and Old Randolph. Herb was working on straight commission. Garth Castle did not come back. He lived at the beach, avoiding the company of anyone who made him feel that he ought to shake off this setback, pick himself up, dust himself off, get a grip on himself, pull himself together, get back to work—especially May. Whenever Garth looked at her, he saw in her face, in her eyes, the admiration she still had for him, and that look of trust and confidence made him feel like a fake and a failure. In fact, he *had* been something of a fake, but May had never objected to that quality in him; she'd considered it part of his charm.

The truth was that Garth was afraid to go back to work. He was afraid of failing again. The world, the nation, and Studebaker had pulled a dirty trick on him, letting him get his hopes up and then letting him fall, like some wiseacre who pulls a chair out from under a guy. Garth wasn't going to fall for the same nasty gag twice; he wasn't even going to risk falling for it.

At the beach, Garth hung around with the clammies. He preferred the ones who were living "over south" because they weren't comfortable on the mainland, especially the failures, and among the failures he preferred those who had managed to make failures of themselves despite innate ability, good fortune, helping hands, and powerful friends, the ones who had failed because they were too lazy to succeed, those of whom he could say to himself, "I may be next to nothing, but at least I'm here through no fault of my own. This guy— why, this guy is nothing but a lazy bum." He acquired the manner of a failed clammy as quickly and thoroughly as he had the manner of a New York gentleman, with this difference: he'd had to invent his New York gentleman, since he hadn't had the opportunity to observe any very closely, but he had opportunities galore to observe failed clammies, so his emulation was in this case a far better one than before. He spent more and more time at Nosy's; the drinking that in the past had made him seem charming and witty now only made him sullen and dismal.

May tried again and again to win him back from the beach. At first, she visited him often. She brought Herb and Lorna and other friends, and she tried to re-create the happy times they'd enjoyed in the cottage. Garth hid from these attempts to resuscitate the old gaiety. Most often it was Herb who tracked him down, dragged, pushed, and tugged him out of Nosy's and delivered him to May. As Garth grew worse, fewer of May's friends were willing to make themselves available for these embarrassing excursions to the beach, and as the Depression grew worse, fewer could afford to maintain their cottages. The places fell into disrepair. They began to look like their former selves: the shacks they had grown from. Garth got the isolation he had sought, and in Nosy's he advanced a twisted Emersonianism: the notion that a bum was born to be a bum and would be a bum forever, "just like those shacks—those old shacks that we tried to fancy up! Shacks again! They were always shacks under the skin."

May was determined not to give up on Garth, but one frightening visit nearly drove her away from him. She had tried romance as a lure before and failed, but she had run out of ideas and so tried again, hoping that something, anything—a difference in the weather or the phase of the moon—would change her luck. She brought candles and wine and a good dinner to the cottage. She brought her filmiest nightgown. She managed to get Garth out of Nosy's and into the cottage, and for a while she thought she was making real progress. Garth picked up a shrimp, stared at it for a while, and then ate it, and May hoped that he might still have an appetite for food. He looked May over and attempted a wolf whistle, and May hoped that he might still have an appetite for her. But then he picked up the bottle of wine and a glass and dropped into a chair, and it was clear that he had an appetite only for failure.

"May," he said, "I've been thinking."

"Yes," she said. Her voice was lifeless and hollow. She was looking out the window, at nothing in particular.

"Let's live here," said Garth. "Here at the beach. I like it here, May. You'd like it here, too. They're swell people here, not like those people we used to know. Swell people—the guys who work the bay."

"You mean the guys who *don't* work the bay," said May. She stubbed out her cigarette.

Garth chuckled. "Maybe I do," he said. "Maybe I do. Maybe they're the smart ones. They have nothing to lose. They *had* nothing to lose. They're no worse off than they were before. Isn't that smart? Come on, May, come on and live here with me. Forget about all—" He stood, wobbled, and, with the hand that held his glass, indicated Babbington by flinging a stream of wine in its direction. "—*that!*" he said.

Well, it was horrible, *simply horrible. You have to understand that he wasn't inviting me to sail off to Tahiti to join him in living some idyllic island life, some carefree existence—coconut milk and mangoes and grass huts, that sort of thing. No, nothing like that. He was asking me to be a* bum, *like him, like those smelly,* lumpy *men. A bum! He wanted me to join him so that he'd know it was all right to be what he had become. Well, not on your life! I ran from there,* ran.

She did. She bolted for the door in her nightgown. Garth made a grab for her as she went by, a drunk's try at an embrace, but she stepped aside, and he lost his balance and fell. May pushed the screen door open and ran along the boardwalk toward the boat. Behind her, she could hear Garth laughing.

I cried all the way across the bay. I was running away from him. I was disgusted by him. And I was furious with him. The bastard was still so handsome. I can close my eyes now and see him slumped in that chair, asking me to live at the beach, and he looks like a damned movie star. I think I ran because I was afraid I might stay. Well. Maybe. Who knows?

Lorna and Herb sat up with May and listened to the whole horrible tale. "This is the end," May said. "It really is. I can't do anything for him, he won't *let* me do anything for him, and he won't do anything for himself. There's nothing that *can* be done, nothing."

"May," said Herb, "let me try just one thing." He took her hands and squeezed them. "Hear me out, May," he said. "Hear me out. My father was a failure, you know. He lost everything in cork furniture. When he knew he was ruined, that there wasn't any hope, he sank into a chair. He wouldn't get out of that chair, just sat there. He wouldn't leave it except, well, you know."

May smiled despite herself.

"Let me go to see Garth," said Herb. "Let me go to see him alone, and tell him the whole story about my father. Maybe if he sees someone else's mistake, he can benefit from it."

Herb went to see Garth, but he didn't say anything about his father. He found Garth at Nosy's, and when Garth suggested that Herb have a drink with him, Herb said, "Gee, Garth, it's pretty early in the day for me." From his pocket he pulled what looked like a pocket watch. He flipped the case open and said, "Oops, wrong one."

"Say, what is that?" asked Garth. He leaned across the table.

"This?" said Herb. "Oh, sort of a toy." Herb had never before taken such a risk. He had never even shown a piece of coarse goods to anyone he knew. He winked. He extended the Watchcase Wonder toward Garth and began turning the stem slowly. "Just look at the workmanship," he said. Garth watched, amazed. "You think you could sell these, Garth?"

Garth lifted his eyes from the animated couple and looked at Herb. He was wearing a twisted grin, and in his eyes, behind the blankness that had settled there, Herb could see an ambitious gleam.

"Now, here's the way I see it," Herb said on the trip to Boston. "Since the dealership's open again, you ought to come back. Start selling Studebakers again."

[1 8 3]

Garth drew back from him and looked at Herb with suspicion.

"Sure," said Herb. "You've got to. You've got to have something else to sell beside this stuff. When I first started, it was books. For you it might as well be Studebakers."

"Why?" asked Garth.

"Well," said Herb, "the books, or the Studebakers, are your answer."

"Answer to what?" asked Garth.

"To the question 'How'd you make all that money?'" said Herb. They burst into invigorating laughter, hopeful laughter.

On the first of July in 1933, Albert Erskine, who had been president of Studebaker when it went into bankruptcy, killed himself. The news sent a shudder through Garth, who imagined, unrealistically, that he might have felt driven to such an act if Herb hadn't halted his downward slide. Herb and Garth heard the news about Erskine while they were in Boston, picking up a supply of coarse goods from Uncle Ben.

From the start, Garth enjoyed the coarse-goods trade in a way that Herb never had and never would. He liked the backslapping and elbow nudging that went with it, and he loved the secretiveness it engendered. He liked having things to hide from May, being out on false pretenses, meeting clients in dark corners of bars. Herb sold a piece now and then, since Studebaker sales were still poor, but he never sold to a Babbingtonian, only to men passing through. Studebakers were what Herb wanted to sell, and he turned to coarse goods only to make ends meet. Garth put nearly all his effort into coarse goods and almost none into Studebakers. He spent part of every day in the showroom, but Herb virtually ran the operation.

May and Lorna believed what Herb and Garth told them: Herb had delivered such a moving account of the suffering his father had visited on his mother that Garth shook himself sober and pulled himself from the Slough of Despond. They allowed themselves to believe the stories Herb and Garth told about successful sales, though most seemed to be to out-of-towners who were never seen driving their Studebakers around Babbington. But both May and Lorna were wary. May was surprised to find herself wondering, now and then, what life would be like on her own, having to look out for herself, having only herself to look out for. Lorna found herself planning and scheming, devising ways to make some money, to put some distance between them and the edge of the dark valley Garth had slid into.

Now that Ella was in school, Lorna could work undisturbed and undetected for several hours every day. She went back to work for Luther. To disguise what she was doing, she also went back to work for Joseph the Jeweler, for whom she had done repairs when she and Herb were living at the Mikszaths'. She sat Herb down one evening and confessed that she had worked for Mr. Joseph.

"I knew," said Herb. He chuckled and tousled her hair.

"You did?"

"Sure. I didn't know who you worked for, but I knew you were working."

"You did?"

"Sure I did. You were careful, but you gave yourself away."

"How?"

"You never went over your budget. You always had enough. You never had to ask for a little extra for the household, the way you used to."

"But you never said anything."

"I was going to," said Herb. "The day I figured it out, I was going to, but, you know, you were humming while you were cooking, and kind of bustling around, full of life, and I didn't want to—I didn't want to change that."

"Thank you, Herb. So you won't mind if I go back? He doesn't have a lot of work for me—I wouldn't be putting in more than a couple of hours a day. Say you won't mind."

"I won't mind."

Lorna spent a couple of hours every day working for Mr. Joseph, and many more hours working for Luther. She enlisted May's help in deceiving Herb about those extra hours. She told May that she didn't want Herb to know how hard she was working, so May concocted joint shopping trips, afternoons spent swimming and sailing, and hours idled away gossiping over coffee.

Working on the sly and deceiving each other, Herb and Lorna got by. They didn't prosper, but they got by.

13

In Which
Coarse Goods Buy
Herb 'n' Lorna a
Home of Their Own

In time, prosperity, at least relative prosperity, returned. The new management at Studebaker strengthened the company by eliminating weaknesses. They gave up on their unprofitable line of small, economical cars named for Knute Rockne, the football coach at Notre Dame, and sold the Peirce-Arrow company, which Studebaker had owned since 1928. By 1935, Studebakers were selling well again, and the company was turning a profit. The Babbington dealership was sold to out-of-towners who paid its debts, and Herb was able to smile and pretend that he agreed with Lorna when she told him that events had proved that he hadn't done a foolish Piper thing after all. The new owners built a modern showroom down the street from the original site, and at the grand opening Garth gave a good imitation of his old charm and verve.

Studebaker then took a step the importance of which can't be exaggerated. The company hired Raymond Loewy, the gifted visionary, as its chief designer. Loewy's arrival ushered in a period of daring, distinctive design that set Studebakers emphatically apart from other makes. In 1950 he and the team he directed would produce the famous bullet-nosed models and, a few years later, the beautiful Starliner coupes. But in the opinion of more than one Studebaker historian, the Loewy designs would lead, ultimately, to the demise of the company. Ina Schildkraut, for example, writing in *Those Fabulous Studes,* says of Loewy's impact on the fortunes of the company:

> *Loewy's was a classic case—the case of the artist (an artist whose medium was the sheet-metal skins of automobiles) with ideas too avant-garde for mass taste. From the very first, Loewy's designs disturbed the hidebound Yahoos who, sad to say, bought most of the cars produced in this country. Their reaction was the familiar one of halfwits everywhere when confronted with something they don't understand. They shielded themselves with ridicule, mockery. Philistines from coast to coast found that Loewy's designs inspired them to commit humor. Typical: the gas jockey's exaggerated puzzlement over which end of the car was supposed to receive the gas. Droll, no? Add any number of variations on "Say, Bub, how can you tell if you're comin' or goin' in that thing?" Loewy's designs for Studebaker were among the most exciting in the history of the automobile, but (sad to say, oh, sad to say) hiring him and giving him his head may well have been the* worst *business* decision *in the history of the company.*

The ultimate failure of Studebaker was still a long way off, however, and for the time being Lorna and Herb were enjoying the feeling that they had made it through difficult times. They were doing all right again, and they felt that they needed, and deserved, a reward. The reward that occurred to both of them was a home of their own.

A coolness, a distance, had developed between May and Garth that made life at May's less than pleasant. Lorna and Herb were always, awkwardly, in the middle, listening to the confidences of one or the other, trying to offer the right advice, trying to bring back the happiness that had been in the house not so long ago. They couldn't keep it up, so Lorna and Herb decided, in the flush of optimism that their returning prosperity brought with it, to buy themselves a house. To provide a down payment, each of them, in secret, got from the appropriate uncle an advance on future coarse-goods work.

One night, when Herb had his money in hand, he burst through the door wearing one of those ear-to-ear grins. "Lorna," he said, "I've got great news."

"Why, I have, too, Herb," said Lorna.

"Me first," said Herb. "Mine's too good to keep. You don't mind, do you?"

"No. I don't mind at all. You go ahead."

"I—no, you go. I can see you want to. Go ahead."

"It's all right, Herb, really. You go."

"No, you, Lorna. It wasn't fair of me to—"

"Herrrb!"

"All right. Look at this!" He took a wad of bills from his pocket and fanned them in front of Lorna.

"Herb!" said Lorna. "Where did you—?"

"From the Studebaker company!"

"The Studebaker company?"

"That's right. I never said anything to you, because I didn't want to worry you, but they held back part of my pay during the bad times. I never thought I'd see a penny of it, and then all of a sudden, today, Garth called me into his office and handed me this."

"In cash?"

"Sure, in—well, no. No, not in cash. Of course not. A bank draft, but I cashed it. I cashed it right away because—because—I guess it was because I must have been worried that they'd go out of business before I could cash it. That must have been it."

"Well, wait till you see this," said Lorna. She produced a similar wad of bills.

"Where'd you get that?" asked Herb.

"From Mr. Joseph. The jeweler."

"What for?"

"Why, the same as you. I hadn't told you either. Mr. Joseph held back some of my pay, when he wasn't able to pay me sometimes."

"He did?"

"Isn't that a coincidence?"

"It's practically unbelievable," said Herb.

"It is, isn't it?" said Lorna.

"He paid you cash?" asked Herb.

"Yes," said Lorna. "Yes, he did. Cash. This cash. Just like this."

"Hm," said Herb.

"What luck," said Lorna. "You know, I think we have enough to look for a house."

"Oh, I'm sure of it," said Herb.

In the western part of Babbington, the part they had first entered on that rainy night when they arrived from Chacallit, they found a house that suited them. It was on an unnamed street off Bay Way, the road that led from Main Street to the bay. At the corner of this unnamed street was a sign, erected by the Babbington Department of Public Works, a sign with a temporary look, not the job of a practiced sign painter. It read CAUTION NO BRIDGE.

The little street ended, abruptly, as the dozen or so little streets parallel to it ended, at a canal that reached inland from the bay, providing access to the water for an area that would otherwise have been landlocked. For years after the canal was dug, no one considered building a bridge over it, since nothing was available on one side that wasn't available on the other. In the twenties, however, Fred and Shirley Mintz bought a piece of land along the bay front and created Fred and Shirley's Shore Club, a nice spot with a smooth beach, a lifeguard, an outdoor shower, a small lunch counter, and a pleasant pavilion where one could relax at a table in the shade. The Mintzes reasoned that their enterprise would better prosper if families on the other side of the canal could get to it more easily, so they began agitating for a bridge across the canal.

At that time both the mayor of Babbington, Andy Whitley, and the head of the Babbington Department of Public Works, Walt Whitley, lived on the Fred and Shirley's Shore Club side of the canal. Both Andy and Walt enjoyed complimentary family memberships in the club, which they had won, Fred and Shirley assured them, in a random drawing. Andy and Walt didn't want to upset the Mintzes and lose their complimentary family memberships, so, in their capacities as mayor and head of the BDPW respectively, they decided that the Mintzes should get their bridge as soon as possible. On the other hand, neither Andy nor Walt wanted the quiet streets in that part of town to become congested with Fred and Shirley's Shore Club traffic, and neither wanted the club to become crowded with people from the other side of the canal, so they decided to take "as soon as possible" to mean "never." Walt had the BDPW conduct a study to determine the best location for a bridge; they chose the narrow, unpaved street, and Walt launched a flurry of activity designed to keep the Mintzes happy. He had the street surveyed, widened, and paved, and then he and Andy set the project adrift in studies and committee meetings and budget hearings, where it has languished, as idle as a painted ship upon a painted ocean, to this day. The sign—CAUTION NO BRIDGE—was erected to suggest to the Mintzes that though there was no bridge *yet,* there would be one *soon,* and the street came to be called, by everyone who lived nearby, No Bridge Road.

On No Bridge Road, on the north side, about midway between Bay Way and the canal, was a pretty little stucco house that struck Lorna and Herb as just right. It had a tile roof and a large, solid front door with a rounded top. The door opened into the living room, a long room with a fireplace. To the right was a dining room, and beyond the dining room, toward the rear of the house, was the kitchen. Two steps up at the rear of the living room was a hallway. Off this hallway, on the right, was the bathroom. Across from it was a small bedroom for Ella. At the end of the hall was a large bedroom for Herb and Lorna. The house was owned by a Mrs. Stolz, who had been living in it alone for a year and a half, since the death of her husband. She had finally decided that she could no longer support it.

"A house needs a man to keep it up," she said while she was showing Lorna and Herb through it. "Things have to be fixed, and I can't do it. I don't know how. I never knew how."

"Can't you find someone to keep it up for you?" asked Lorna. "A handyman, a carpenter?"

"Oh, I can't afford that," said Mrs. Stolz. "And it isn't the same. A man doesn't keep up a place the same if it isn't his. You can't blame him, really. His heart isn't in it. He's only working for money."

"Where will you go?" asked Lorna. "Do you have children to live with?"

"Oh, I wouldn't bother them," said Mrs. Stolz. "Your welcome doesn't last very long if you're planning to stay forever, if you know what I mean. I'm going to get a room at the River Sound Hotel. It will suit me just fine, I think."

That night Lorna and Herb lay awake in the dark, each thinking about the house, trying to remember it precisely, imagining life there, and trying to be still about it, in order not to wake the other, but neither was breathing like a person asleep, and finally the thought of crocuses coming up in the little lawn in the spring became so vivid in

Lorna's mind's eye that she giggled from the pleasure of it. She tried to stifle the giggle, and she did muffle the sound, but still she made the bed tremble with the rhythm of a giggle.

"You're awake, too," said Herb.

"Mm," said Lorna.

"What do you think of it?" asked Herb.

Lorna snuggled up to him and kissed his ear. "I think it's just right," she said.

"That's what I think," said Herb. "It's just right."

"The little bedroom could be very pretty with some new wallpaper and ruffled curtains," said Lorna.

"We can build a garage on the east side of the house, with a grease pit and space for some tools, welding equipment, and stuff like that," said Herb.

"Do you think we could paint the dining room green?"

"We could put a screened porch between the garage and the house, with movable blinds, so that we can have sun or shade, whichever we want."

"Could you build a corner cupboard for the dining room, for that corner in the front, away from the living room?"

"Sure. I could build a workshop in the cellar, too."

"I want to plant flowers everywhere. Crocuses in the lawn, roses beside the steps, morning glories along the fences."

"And we could build a den in that ell between the kitchen and our bedroom, with a door off the hall, a secret door, set into the paneling, with a hidden latch, or maybe a door hidden behind a bookshelf," said Herb.

"Oh, Herb," said Lorna. She was laughing.

"That's a dumb idea, isn't it, a hidden door?"

"Oh, no, Herb. It's not a dumb idea. It's not a dumb idea at all. I'm not laughing at what you want to do. I'm laughing because I'm happy."

The weeks before they moved were busy ones for Herb. He and Lorna had little furniture of their own, since the apartments they'd rented had been furnished. Herb had made Lorna's work table and a crib for Ella. Now he made a bed for him and Lorna and a smaller copy of it for Ella, who was seven now, dressers for all of them, and a dining room table. They bought several other items from Mrs. Stolz, who was pleased not to have to move them or find out how little they interested her children. Among these items was an upright piano that stood at the far end of the living room. Herb visited Mrs. Stolz one day without Lorna's knowing and arranged to buy it and make weekly payments. May gave them a sofa and a pair of wing chairs from the guest house, and she lent them four dining room chairs.

On the evening of their moving in, after the furniture was all in place, after they had eaten the cold dinner that May had had her cook pack for them, after Ella was tucked into bed, with the kitten that was her current love curled up at her feet, Herb built a fire and Lorna sat at the piano and picked out "Lake Serenity Serenade." If you'd been standing outside, with your nose pressed to the window, you would have said that what you saw was a perfect scene of domestic peace. Herb stood behind Lorna with his hands on her shoulders. The tune and the firelight gave the room the erotic buoyancy of a rowboat on Lake Serenity. Herb touched Lorna's cheek. It was wet with tears.

"Lorna!" said Herb. "What's the matter?"

"I can't help thinking of poor Mrs. Stolz! We've taken her house from her! Here we are in her living room, in front of her fire, and I'm playing her piano—"

"We didn't *take* it from her, Lorna, we—"

"Oh, I know we didn't really take it from her, but didn't we take advantage of her, wasn't her loss our gain?"

"Well, no, not really, I—no—at least I don't think so—"

"Oh, Herb, just imagine her living the rest of her life in that miserable hotel!"

"It's not so miserable. We liked it when—"

"Herb," cried Lorna, "we can't let her stay there!" She leaped to her feet, and in a moment she was at the door, in her coat, with Ella beside her, wrapped in a blanket, waiting for Herb to warm up the car.

Mrs. Stolz was settled in her favorite chair, wrapped snugly in her old robe, eating, in small, luxurious bites, a chocolate cream from a box on the table beside her. A copy of *Life* was open in her lap, but she had stopped reading to watch the raindrops run down the window pane, and she was thinking how pleasant it was to be in such cozy quarters, in a place as snug as her old robe, a place that gave her so much comfort but asked so little of her, when Lorna and Herb knocked at her door.

"Oh, my," she said when she saw them dripping in the hallway, "what's wrong?"

"Mrs. Stolz," said Lorna, tears streaming down her face, "we've come to take you home."

"If you *want* to come home," said Herb. "Of course, you may be happy right here—"

"Herb," said Lorna. She stepped into the room and took Mrs. Stolz's hands in hers. "We know how much you must miss the house," she said, "and we don't feel right about it. We feel as if we've taken your home from you."

"You want me to take it back?" asked Mrs. Stolz. Fear made her suddenly so cold that she began wringing her hands. She had the chocolate cream in one of them.

"We were hoping you would come to live with us," said Lorna.

"Live with you?" said Mrs. Stolz. The idea sounded preposterous to her. She wondered what could have brought them to such a strange desire. She stared at the sticky goop on her hands. She couldn't quite imagine what it was.

"Yes," said Lorna. She fought to control herself. Why hadn't she seen how far gone the poor woman was? Here she was rubbing chocolate on her hands. She needed watching. "We want you to be back in your own home again," said Lorna.

They must need money, thought Mrs. Stolz. "Do you need money?" she asked. She looked around the room for something to wipe the chocolate from her hands.

"Oh, no," said Lorna. "We wouldn't charge you anything. We just want you to be happy." She handed Mrs. Stolz her handkerchief.

From behind Lorna's back, Herb winked at Mrs. Stolz. He intended his wink to mean that it was perfectly easy for him to imagine her preferring to stay at the River Sound. He put his arm around Lorna's shoulders and gave her an affectionate squeeze. He winked at Mrs. Stolz again, and he meant her to understand that he had come along to humor Lorna in her conviction that Mrs. Stolz would want to return, but that Mrs. Stolz should feel free to disburden her of this misperception, taking into account the tenderness of her feelings and the generosity of her motives. Mrs. Stolz thought he was telling her that Lorna was insane.

"Oh!" said Mrs. Stolz. She brought her hand, with Lorna's handkerchief, to her mouth. She was startled and saddened. Compassion swelled in her breast; tears welled in her eyes; dabs of chocolate spotted her chin. She gripped Lorna's hands. "Of course, my dear," she said, nearly sobbing, "of course. If it's what you want, I'll come home."

Lorna, smiling tenderly, squeezing Mrs. Stolz's sticky hands, said, "It's what we want."

Ella threw her arms around Mrs. Stolz and hugged her with granddaughterly affection. Herb said nothing.

Herb began work on the new room at once. He persisted in referring to it as "the den," in the hope—which he never expressed in any other way, not through any dropping of hints, not through any irony or the slightest ambiguity in his tone of voice—that before he had actually finished the new room Mrs. Stolz would have decided that she'd really rather return to the River Sound Hotel, and the room would in fact become his den. For the time being, Mrs. Stolz slept in the room that had been intended for Ella, and Ella slept in the living room, on the rose-colored sofa.

As the odd arrangement developed, it seemed likely to make everyone but Herb quite happy. Ella loved Mrs. Stolz with the comfortable old-shoe, familiar-sweater, cuddles-and-hugs kind of love that a child comes to feel for a grandparent if the child and grandparent are fortunate enough to be able to spend a lot of time together from day to day. She had developed her own explanation for Mrs. Stolz's presence in her family: Mrs. Stolz had come with the house, like a fixture, the fence or the oven, and this was the way such things ordinarily happened. (The little girl who formed that notion was the one that Ella most liked to recall from her years in the stucco house on No Bridge Road, and when, five years after her marriage, she had a house of her own, the girl in her was disappointed that it was new, with no previous owner lingering on.)

Mrs. Stolz adored Ella, and she was pleased to find that she showed a respect for Mrs. Stolz's opinions that Mrs. Stolz had never seen in her own children or grandchildren, who seemed to regard her as hopelessly out of touch, a relic of another time. Mrs. Stolz was astonished to realize how much she enjoyed the feeling that in this household she was needed, desperately needed. To her great relief,

Lorna had apparently lapsed into a period of rational calm. Certainly there were odd things abut her, though—the way she slipped off to the cellar to work at her table for hours every day, for one thing. Mrs. Stolz knew, from snooping, what she worked on.

One afternoon, about a year after Mrs. Stolz had come to live with them, a telephone call from Ella's school had sent Lorna rushing off to bring Ella, who'd been sick in the lunchroom, home. Mrs. Stolz had, after a couple of minutes' battle with her scruples, convinced herself that in order to be better able to help Lorna, she really *needed* to know what was in the locked work table, why Lorna insisted that she not be disturbed while she was at work, wouldn't even permit Mrs. Stolz to come down the cellar stairs when she was working. Mrs. Stolz accepted in general Lorna's explanation, that she worked on jewelry—she had seen the jewelry, after all, and she admired Lorna's work and marveled at the way God sometimes bestows a compensating asset on those He's burdened with pitiable liabilities—but she felt a need to know Lorna's work in all its particulars. She felt a need to know what she hadn't been permitted to know.

Mrs. Stolz descended to the cellar and found Lorna's work just as she had left it. In the center of her work table was a large magnifying glass, mounted on a swivel, that Herb had rigged up for Lorna, to make her jewelry work easier on her eyes, which were beginning to show the strain. Mrs. Stolz bent over the glass and looked through it. She saw two beautiful, though unfinished, figures, engaged in an activity that made her gasp.

"Oh, my goodness," she said aloud. The sound of her voice frightened her. She rushed back to the foot of the stairs. She held her breath and listened. When she was sure she was still alone in the house, she returned to the work table and studied the little ivory couple through the glass. She became so absorbed in her study that she almost failed to hear the door. She was out of breath and perspiring when she greeted Lorna and Ella in the kitchen, and she was so flabbergasted by what she had seen that she forgot why Lorna had brought Ella home, offered her no comfort, didn't even notice how pale and tremulous she was.

In bed that night, Mrs. Stolz said to herself, "The poor child," meaning Lorna. "I suppose she needs that sort of thing somehow. It's crazy work, but at least she keeps it out of sight." She vowed to carry the burden of her discovery alone, since Herb—poor soul—had enough to worry about already. She fell asleep wondering whether there really were any men with tongues as long and agile as the one she'd seen the little ivory man employing in so fascinating a manner.

Except for Lorna's work in the cellar, Mrs. Stolz found that Lorna behaved as if she were as normal as anyone else. Mrs. Stolz considered this a miracle. Every night since her return, she had fallen to her knees beside her bed and prayed for Lorna's sanity, and it seemed to her that her prayers had been answered—at least there were no screaming fits or mad scenes. Mrs. Stolz tried not to give herself credit for Lorna's relative sanity, but she had to admit to herself that it was, most likely, her calming presence, her maturity, her regular habits and set ways, that kept Lorna on an even keel.

Lorna was pleased just to see how pleased Mrs. Stolz was, and her pleasure lasted as the years went by. Every morning, when Lorna came into the kitchen and found Mrs. Stolz bustling around, fixing breakfast and listening to Ella gush about her teachers, for each of whom she developed a heartfelt crush, Lorna was sure that she and Herb had done the right thing, that Mrs. Stolz had missed her home horribly, still considered herself the mistress of it, and was so grateful to Lorna and Herb for bringing her back that she felt she had to bustle about, cooking and cleaning, to show her gratitude and earn her keep.

As more time passed, Mrs. Stolz began to think of herself as a saint, a small and insignificant saint, perhaps, but a saintly woman just the same. She acquired a serenity from the conviction that she was filling each day, each passing year, with good works, that the dusting and cleaning she had always done, the dishes she had always washed, the meals she had always cooked, now had a point, a value, beyond merely keeping a home tidy and a family fed. She was working for someone who, she assumed, could not work for herself, and it was an elevating experience. She became so serene and self-satisfied that her old friends couldn't stand her anymore and saw less and less of her. That suited Mrs. Stolz. She had more and more to do at home, she found. Keeping everything just right, making the home as perfect and as smooth running as could be was, she became certain, the key to Lorna's keeping a grip on herself, confining her madness to the cellar. It was critically important, Mrs. Stolz thought, for her to listen to Ella's descriptions of the boys with whom she fell in love in junior high school and high school, to discuss with her every possible interpretation of every smile, frown, nod, note, whisper, and argument. Knowing what she did about Lorna's secret work in the cellar, Mrs. Stolz felt that Lorna couldn't be trusted to take the proper attitude toward Ella's fervent infatuations. That burden was, like other Piper family burdens, entirely on her shoulders, but it was, she felt, absolutely crucial that she not show the strain but continue to bustle with undiminished energy, whistle a happy tune, wear a smile.

Lorna began to think that Mrs. Stolz was lapsing into senility. She seemed to go at the most tedious household task with the unblinking good humor of the feeble-minded. She bustled about the house as if there were twice as many dusty corners as there were, and she developed rigid ideas about where every furnishing should be placed and how it should be aligned. She straightened the antimacassars several times a day. Lorna thanked goodness that she'd had the intuition to recognize that Mrs. Stolz needed her home, that she needed *a* home, and Lorna was enormously grateful to Herb for going along with her and providing it.

After a while, not even Herb really had any objection to Mrs. Stolz's living with them. The ménage was a happy one, and he wouldn't have done anything to disturb it. Within the first year, he had the den in habitable shape; Mrs. Stolz moved in, and Ella was able to sleep in the room that Herb and Lorna had intended for her. It took Herb another eight years to finish the den completely, but finally he did finish it, and it made a comfortable sitting room and bedroom for Mrs. Stolz. His last piece of work was the hidden entrance. In the hallway, between the door to the bathroom and the door to Herb and Lorna's bedroom, he built a set of bookcases, recessed into the wall. Among the books on the shelves was a leather-bound edition of *The Thousand and One Nights*.

"How do you suppose you get into the room?" asked Herb. He had assembled the household for a viewing of the completed room, but he had kept many of the details and special features secret, none more carefully kept than the method of opening the secret entrance. "How do you suppose you open your door, Mrs. Stolz?" he asked.

"Oh, I'm sure I don't know," she said. "I'm sure I don't know at all."

"I don't *see* any door," said Ella. She was fourteen. For everything but romance, she had a literal mind.

Herb chuckled. "Oh, yes, you do," he said. "You just don't recognize it. Things aren't always what they seem, you know. The truth is, you're looking right at the door."

"I am?" said Ella. "Where?"

"This bookcase is a door," said Herb. "Watch." He removed *The Thousand and One Nights*. In doing so, he released a hidden latch. He opened the book as if he were going to read from it. He flipped a few pages until he apparently found what he wanted. "Open, Sesame!" he boomed, and he replaced the volume on the shelf, thereby activating a hidden spring. Slowly, one section of the bookcase swung open.

"Gosh!" said Ella. She was wonderfully impressed, not so much by the door as by her father's ability. She applauded.

Lorna, charmed by Ella's reaction as much as by the door, reacted just as Ella had. "Oh, Herb," she said, "it's magic!" She clapped her hands together like a girl and hugged Herb.

Over Lorna's shoulder, Herb winked at Mrs. Stolz, and Mrs. Stolz, convinced that Lorna, batty as she was, really believed Herb had made magic, reacted as Lorna had, the better to keep the illusion alive, or to strengthen it. She clapped her hands like a girl. She was really applauding Herb's compassion. Her heart went out once again to this wonderful man, this saintly man, who put so much effort into building a crazy world for his crazy wife, a world that seemed to have magic in it, a world where doors were hidden in bookcases and drawers lifted their contents when they were opened, a world with nonsense built into it so that his wife would feel at home in it, a world with unlikelinesses to match her irrationality, a world where she could feel sane.

From then on, whenever Mrs. Stolz went to her room, she would open the door by removing the leather volume, flipping through it as if she had forgotten the command and had to find it again, come at last to "Ali Baba and the Forty Thieves," and, apparently reading from the book, command the bookcase, "Open, Sesame!" replace the volume, and seem to marvel again at the magic she worked. Lorna, whenever she saw Mrs. Stolz go through her rigmarole at the bookcase, would swallow hard at the poignancy of it and think to herself, *The poor old woman has really lost her marbles.*

14
In Which Lorna's Soap Carvings Entertain a Hundred Calculating Women

In the spring of Ella's sixteenth year (Herb's forty-first, Lorna's thirty-ninth), when Ella began to look more like a pretty young woman than a pretty young girl, Dudley Beaker, a bachelor for whom this was the spring of his twenty-eighth year, bought the house next door. Dudley was, for the neighborhood into which he had moved, something of an exotic. He was slim and clever, worked in an office, and had been to college. Whenever he visited the Pipers, he spent some time chatting with Mrs. Stolz about the day's news, and since he listened to what she had to say, Mrs. Stolz decided that Dudley Beaker was a man of sophistication and taste. He asked Herb's advice about repairs and improvements to his house, and he always took the advice that Herb gave. He bought a Studebaker from Herb, one of the striking Loewy-designed Commander coupes, and he was a willing audience for demonstrations of Herb's gadgets. Herb thought Dudley was a swell guy.

Dudley was an amateur student of logic, and he loved springing "puzzlers" and "posers" on Herb and Lorna. The first he ever sprang was the familiar "Brothers and sisters have I none."

"Here's a puzzler for you," he said one Saturday morning while he was seated at the kitchen table, trying not to watch while Herb dunked one of Lorna's fresh doughnuts.

"A what?" asked Herb.

"A puzzler. An interesting little problem in logic. Ready?"

"I guess," said Herb. Lorna dropped another ring of dough into the fat.

"All right. You're introduced to a man at a party. You ask him who he is, and instead of telling you his name, he winks and says, 'Brothers and sisters have I none, but that man's father is my father's son.' When he says 'that man,' he points to a man across the room. Now, are you ready for the question? Who is he?"

"Mm, I'm not sure," said Herb, "but he's perfect for a President convertible sedan—something snappy, peppy. He's a fellow who doesn't take life too seriously, a guy who likes to tell a joke, a guy who winks his eye. Perfect for a President convertible."

Dudley chuckled. "Herb," he said, "I've put this poser to many people, and I've never heard an answer like that before. I'm sure I never will again."

With the end of a wooden spoon, Lorna lifted a doughnut from the fat. "He's the father of the man across the room," she said.

"Noooo," said Dudley, smiling and shaking his head, "that's what everyone—" He stopped. "Did you say he's the father of the man across the room?" he asked.

"Yes."

"That's right. That's right! Look, here's another one. Stand up, Herb." Herb stood, and Dudley stood beside him. "Herb and I live on an island where everybody is either a Liar or a Truth-teller. All right? Liars always lie, and Truth-tellers always tell the truth. Okay? Now, I want you to ask us, 'Is either of you a Truth-teller?' I'll answer, Herb. Go ahead, Lorna."

"Is either of you a Truth-teller?"

"No," said Dudley.

"You're a Liar," said Lorna.

"Lorna!" said Dudley. "You're wonderful!"

"What about me?" asked Herb.

Lorna smiled. "You're a Truth-teller, of course," she said. "You always have been." A teasing pause. "Haven't you?"

"Well, sure," said Herb. He chuckled. His face felt warm. He hoped it didn't show.

Dudley was delighted to find someone with a talent for logic, and he began developing it at once. Lorna took to the logical puzzles and problems that Dudley supplied her as quickly as she had taken to modeling in papier-mâché or carving ivory. She discovered that she enjoyed doing something that required as much from her intellect as the little ivory figures required from her imagination and her fingers. Lorna decided that Dudley was an "intellectual," and once she had decided that he was an intellectual she endowed him, in her perception of him, with the attributes she considered part and parcel of an intellectual. She thought of him as distracted, forgetful, fussy, and fey.

Dudley began helping Ella with her schoolwork. He was more intelligent and better informed than any of her teachers. He did a better job of explaining what she was required to know, and he did more than that: he took her beyond what the school taught her in every subject. Ella thought that Dudley was fascinating ("dreamy") and extraordinary ("a man in a million"), and she fell in love with him.

One late-spring night, an extraordinary night, one of those nights that make you think that you might make your dreams come true, Ella came into the living room with her cheeks flushed and her biology book under her arm. She was wearing lipstick—not much, but some. Her hair was pulled to one side, and she had pinned a carnation in it. She was wearing a white cotton blouse with an elasticized neckline, a type of blouse that the girls in Ella's set bought so that they'd look like Dolores del Rio.

"Ella," said Herb, "you look just like Dolores del Rio."

"Oh, Daddy, I do not," said Ella, delighted.

"Well, I think you do," said Herb. "Do you have a date?" he asked.

"Of course not, Daddy," said Ella. "I'm going to go next door to see if Dudley can help me memorize the parts of the frog."

My God, thought Herb, *she's fallen in love with Dudley.*

Lorna studied Ella over the top of her reading glasses. *Ye gods and little fishes,* she thought, *she's in love with Dudley.*

"I'll help you study, if you want," said Lorna, testing.

"Thanks, Mom," said Ella, "but I don't want to interrupt you."

"I'm not doing anything important," said Lorna.

"Yes, you are—you're working on your puzzles," said Ella.

"They aren't important," said Lorna.

"But you like working on them," said Ella, "and I don't want to interrupt you."

"But perhaps you shouldn't interrupt Mr. Beaker, either," said Lorna.

"Oh, he told me to," said Ella. "He said that I shouldn't hesitate to come to him whenever I had a question."

"But Ella," said Lorna, "it's nearly nine o'clock at night."

"It *is* kind of late," said Herb.

"Oh, that's all right," said Ella. "Dudley's up. He's sitting in his den, reading a book——"

Herb and Lorna, simultaneously, said to themselves, *Ye gods! She watches through his window!*

"Reading," said Herb.

"Yes," said Ella. She realized, with a shudder that she hoped she kept hidden, that it might seem as if she'd been spying on Dudley, and she hadn't, she really *hadn't* been spying, she'd just been, well, *looking* at him, and she couldn't help it, really—his den was practically right outside her bedroom window. It was so close that sometimes, when she was undressing for bed, standing in front of her window, she wondered whether Dudley was likely to see her if he looked up from his book, and lately she'd begun to wonder if he ever *would* look up from his book.

"I saw him reading," she said, "because I——I was having trouble concentrating—and——I was just staring out the window—and I noticed him—sitting there—reading."

Lorna looked at Ella hard for a moment, and Ella giggled. *Ah,* thought Lorna, *it's all right. It's just a crush. Dudley probably won't even notice.* She smiled. Ella took it for a conspiratorial smile.

Lorna said, "Well, it's all right with me, if it's all right with you, Herb."

There's no reason to worry, Lorna told herself. *Dudley's an intellectual. His mind is off in the clouds somewhere. He probably hasn't even noticed Ella as a——as a woman.*

"Sure it's all right," said Herb. "She's got her exams next week. If Dudley can help her, it's fine with me."

There isn't a thing to worry about, Herb told himself. *Dudley's a swell guy, much too swell a guy to go chasing after young girls who aren't much more than half his age.*

Mrs. Stolz watched Ella walk out the door, and she said to herself,

Oh, dear, oh, dear. Dudley is a man of sophistication and taste. Ella shouldn't be alone with him in his house.

Herb and Lorna and Mrs. Stolz sat in uneasy silence for a few minutes, and then Herb said, with great calm, "She probably won't be long. She'll be back in a while."

A couple of minutes passed.

"It could take as long as an hour, I suppose," said Lorna.

"Really?" said Herb. "Do you think it'll take that long? To learn the parts of the frog?"

"I think it could," said Lorna.

Another couple of minutes passed.

"Oh, I don't know," said Herb. "She'll probably be back in a while."

Mrs. Stolz began wringing her hands. "I'm sure——" she said, and stopped. She had intended to say, "I'm sure it's none of my business, but I think Ella should not be alone with Mr. Beaker," but as soon as she began she realized that this would sound like something a meddlesome old woman would say. She said to herself, *Why, it really is none of my business.* Suddenly she felt a great sorrow. She wondered why she had ever let herself arrive at this position. How, she wondered, had she let herself be drawn into playing the part of a meddlesome old woman in someone else's home? Why had she, nearly ten years ago, let herself be lured from the River Sound Hotel, where she could have been sitting quietly now, having a nice cup of tea and reading a magazine, without a thought of Ella, without a care in the world?

"Yes?" said Lorna, with a sigh, thinking that the poor woman had forgotten what she wanted to say.

Mrs. Stolz looked at Lorna. She saw as the distracted grin of a madwoman what Lorna had intended as a compassionate smile. To herself she said, *I have to do something,* but to Lorna she said nothing. She just smiled back at her and nodded, and Lorna began to wonder how long it would be before they would have to put Mrs. Stolz in a home.

Another couple of minutes passed.

"She's been gone for quite a while, hasn't she?" asked Herb.

"It's been nearly half an hour, I think," said Lorna.

"Do you really think so?" asked Herb.

"I have to do something," said Mrs. Stolz, forgetting herself and speaking her mind.

Lorna gave her another compassionate smile. "What, Mrs. Stolz?" she asked.

Mrs. Stolz stood and announced, as calmly as she could manage, "I think I'll take a walk."

"Then we'll go with you," said Lorna. She was certain that Mrs. Stolz couldn't be trusted outside in the dark on her own. "Won't we, Herb?" she said, turning toward Herb, who, distracted, concerned, had gotten up out of his chair and was staring out the window toward Dudley's house. "Won't we, Herb?" Lorna repeated.

When the trio reached the foot of the front walk, Mrs. Stolz, their leader, paused and looked up and down No Bridge Road, as if deciding in which direction she would like to walk. She didn't want to appear to be planning to go to Dudley's to bring Ella back home. It seemed to Lorna, judging from Mrs. Stolz's hesitation, that the poor woman had forgotten where she was.

"Well!" said Lorna, trying to help Mrs. Stolz through what she felt sure must be a terrible embarrassment for her. "Here we are at the sidewalk. That's No Bridge Road, and we could walk either—to the left—or—to the right."

Mrs. Stolz shut her eyes for a moment and swallowed hard. She was afraid that she would burst into tears for the poor madwoman, her saintly husband, and their threatened daughter. "Let's go that way," she said, "to the right."

"Good," said Herb. He started off at a brisk pace. Dudley's house was to the right, and that was where Herb wanted to go. When he reached Dudley's front walk, however, he began to feel a little foolish—and a little embarrassed. *What could I have been thinking? What I've been worrying about isn't worthy of a swell guy like Dudley,* he told himself. *It's insulting. Still, Dudley's only human, isn't he?*

"Well, here we are at Dudley's walk," said Lorna.

"Yes!" said Herb, as if it were a great surprise to him. "Here we are at Dudley's walk."

"That's right," said Mrs. Stolz brightly, with a special I-understand smile for Herb. "Here we are at Dudley's."

"Where shall we go next?" asked Lorna. "Shall we visit Dudley?" she asked in the thin, bright voice one uses with children and idiots, hoping that her tone would make it seem that she wasn't seriously suggesting that they visit Dudley and yet hoping that Mrs. Stolz would take the bait.

"Oh, yes! Let's!" said Mrs. Stolz, jumping at the chance the poor crazy woman had given her.

"Well, we wouldn't want to interrupt them," said Herb. As soon as the words left him, they sounded to him like part of an off-color joke, and he reddened in the dark. "I mean—" he began, and he realized that he'd only make things worse by explaining himself, so he just stopped.

Mrs. Stolz had, on her own, begun walking toward Dudley's front door. Herb and Lorna followed slowly, silently. Mrs. Stolz stopped at the foot of the steps. Herb and Lorna stopped just behind her. Lights were burning in the front rooms—the living room and the dining room. The windows were slightly above eye level. Herb stood on his toes. From below he could see only the ceiling, the top of a cabinet, triangles of light cast on the walls by the lamps. He heard no voices.

Mrs. Stolz turned and looked at Herb and Lorna in turn. She dropped her guard. "Shall we walk around to the side?" she asked Herb.

"Well, we could," said Herb.

"Yes, let's," said Mrs. Stolz. "Then we'll know if they're—if we should—if they're busy studying. Because we wouldn't want to interrupt them if they're studying. But of course I'm sure they're studying. I mean— Oh, come on."

They walked to the side of the house.

"I still can't see in," said Herb.

"Lift me up," said Lorna.

"What?" said Herb.

"Or get down on your hands and knees, Herb," said Lorna.

"I—"

"Go ahead, Herb."

Herb got onto his hands and knees, and Lorna clambered onto his back and peeked throught the window.

"Well?" asked Herb.

Lorna was afraid to raise her head much above the windowsill, but she could see the back of Dudley's sofa and its right arm. One lamp was on in the room. She couldn't see any sign of Dudley or Ella, and she couldn't hear anything.

"I—" said Lorna, and stopped. Ella's bare arms appeared above the sofa, as if she was stretching. They waved about, languidly, prettily. Then Dudley's right arm appeared, raised as if he was stretching. It began to drop, slowly, hesitated, then fell along the back of the sofa, where Ella's shoulders would have been, then slipped out of sight.

"You what?" asked Herb.

"I see them," whispered Lorna. She noticed Ella's book on the dining room table, closed. The carnation she had worn in her hair lay beside it. "They're at the dining room table," Lorna said. *What on earth are they up to?* she asked herself.

"Studying?" asked Herb.

Ella's feet suddenly appeared on the arm of the sofa. She kicked off her shoes. *She must have her head in his lap,* Lorna thought. "Studying!" she said, almost too loudly.

"Studying!" said Mrs. Stolz. "Isn't that wonderful?"

Lorna stepped down from Herb's back. *What am I going to do about this?* she asked herself. Herb stood up and rubbed his hands. Lorna began putting her shoes back on. Mrs. Stolz chewed on her lower lip.

Studying, Herb said to himself. *I shouldn't have thought what I was thinking.*

Mrs. Stolz shuddered. Embarrassment, or shame, had chilled them all. *An old busybody,* she thought. *I'm becoming an old busybody.* Lorna put her arm around her shoulders.

"Let's go home," said Lorna. When they reached the end of Dudley's walk, she said, as if the thought had just occurred to her, "You know, it *is* late and Ella's at an age when she——"

Herb and Mrs. Stolz had stopped.

"——when she needs plenty of sleep," said Lorna. She put one arm around Herb's waist and the other around Mrs. Stolz's and urged them toward the house. "I think I'll call when we get inside and ask Dudley to send her home."

Everyone was relieved when Ella fell in love with the Leroy brothers, no one more than Lorna. Ella brought the boys home one day after school and surprised Lorna and Mrs. Stolz, who were in the kitchen.

"Oh, my," said Lorna. "Oh, my." She wiped her hands on her apron. They were the handsomest boys she had ever seen, a pair of tall, sandy-haired guys with wide smiles and shining eyes.

"Mom, this is Buster Leroy, and this is Bert Leroy," said Ella.

Lorna shook hands with them. She was surprised to find that their good looks made her uneasy. She felt awkward and shy, and she felt old. She found herself patting her hair into place and wishing that she'd worn another dress. "Hello," she said. She wished she could think of something more to say, something nice, something that would make the boys think of her as someone, not just as Ella's mother. Nothing came to her, so she just said again, "Hello," and smiled, and wiped her hands on her apron, and looked to Ella for the next remark. Ella smiled at her, a smile that told Lorna that Ella had seen and understood her discomposure. Lorna was embarrassed. She desired these boys. She was shocked to recognize it. She was more shocked to see that Ella recognized it.

"Mrs. Stolz," said Ella, "I want you to meet Buster and Bert Leroy." Lorna watched as if from a distance. Where had Ella learned this formality, where had she acquired this calm? How did she remain composed in the presence of these young men? The young people went off to the living room, and Lorna took her apron off and dropped it on the kitchen table. She thought of going to the bedroom to change her dress, put on some makeup, fix her hair, but she stopped at the door when she remembered that she'd have to go through the living room to get there. Ella darted back into the kitchen and collided with Lorna. She was beaming. She threw her arms around her mother. "Do you like them?" she asked.

"Yes," said Lorna. "They're very handsome. I—I got all—discombobulated." It was a confession, and she wondered if Ella would understand that it was. Ella winked at her, and she and Ella burst into giggles.

"Shhhh," said Mrs. Stolz.

"Can they stay for dinner?" asked Ella.

"Oh, I don't know," said Lorna. She looked around the kitchen. "I wasn't planning to have anything special, I—"

"Please," said Ella.

Lorna couldn't refuse the look Ella gave her. "The three of you can go to the store for me," she said. "Get a couple of chickens. I'll make some potato salad—and I'll—don't worry—I'll fix something. It will be nice." When they had gone, Lorna telephoned Herb to warn him that the boys would be there for dinner, and then she went to the bedroom to change.

Dinner was a success, but Lorna was nervous throughout it. Once she caught herself just sitting, wringing her napkin in her lap and watching while the boys ate, wondering whether they were just being polite in taking second helpings of her potato salad or whether they really liked it, wondering whether they liked her, wondering how old they thought she was.

At one point Herb asked, "You boys aren't twins, are you?"

"Uh, no, sir," said Bert.

"Which of you is older?" asked Herb.

"I'm a year younger than Bert," said Buster.

"Yeah," said Bert.

"*But* I'm about two years smarter," Buster said. "So I got put ahead a grade. It was when I was in the fifth grade. They moved me up to the sixth with him."

"Yeah," said Bert.

"Isn't that something?" Lorna said. Both boys turned toward her when she spoke, and she was caught with a forkful of potato salad at chin height. She hadn't intended to say anything more, but with both of them looking at her she felt that she ought to add something. She wished she could make her fork disappear. "Your parents must have been proud," she said to Buster.

"Yeah," said Bert.

"Oh, I guess they were," said Buster. He smiled, and Lorna set her full fork back on her plate. "We never talked about it much at home. Mom and Dad didn't want me to get a swelled head. In fact, to tell the truth, I think they were prouder of *Bert*."

"Yeah," said Bert.

"Oh?" said Lorna. "What for?"

"For not getting put back a grade," Buster said. It was a joke, and he winked at Lorna to show that it was.

That night, Lorna lay awake recalling the evening. When she closed her eyes she saw Buster's face, his grin, his wink. She couldn't get to sleep. She got out of bed. Herb was sleeping soundly. She put her robe on and walked down the hall. The bookcase that led to Mrs. Stolz's room was closed. The door to Ella's room was open. She was asleep, hugging her pillow. Lorna went to the living room. The embers barely glowed in the fireplace. She sat in the armchair at the far end of the room. For a while, she sat in the dark. Then she shook herself, told herself to act her age, switched the floor lamp on, and picked up a copy of *Life*. On the cover was a photograph of student nurses, apparently listening to a lecture. One caught her eye, the one in the lower right-hand corner. She wore an intent expression. She had dark, precisely plucked eyebrows, thin lips carefully rouged, and dark hair smoothly brushed.

I used to look like that, Lorna thought, *when I was her age.* She flipped the pages idly.

HOW RY-KRISP HELPED MARION TALLEY REDUCE

Reduce, Lorna thought. *I should reduce.*

WORLD'S BIGGEST BALL (200 FT.): THEME CENTRE OF THE FAIR

That will be fun. It will be fun to go to the World's Fair. There were photographs of models of statues to be erected on the fair's central mall. Lorna admired the modeling of the musculature of a naked running man who symbolized Day, especially his calves and buttocks. She didn't think much of the work on his hair, but she liked the purposeful expression on his face, the economical modeling of his lips and chin. She didn't care at all for the woman meant to symbolize Night. Her features were vague, and her arms and legs were generalized and unattractive, the result, Lorna felt sure, of careless observation. Her belly looked soft, almost misshapen. Her breasts were flat and not especially feminine, redeemed only by her small, tight nipples. *I can do much better work than that,* Lorna told herself, and she was pleased to find that she felt uplifted by pride in her talent. She went on. She read an article about Germany that concluded, "Nazi Germany faces her destiny with the greatest war machine in history. And the inevitable destiny of the great war machines of the past has been to destroy the peace of the world. . . ." She flipped past an article on basketball in Indiana, past an advertisement for Old Overholt, Old Taylor, and Old Grand-Dad whiskies, and stopped at

CAN YOU IDENTIFY
ALL THESE CHARMS?

On this page is shown another phase of the mania for jingly, conspicuous jewelry. Here are 109 charms, reproduced slightly larger than life-size. Each is different.

    Although charms are as old as mankind, the present vogue dates back to the Big Depression. Customers of top-notch jewelers like Car-

tier, Marcus, or Udall & Ballou, found it a bit difficult to commemo-
rate anniversaries with the usual precious stones. Instead they bought
diminutive charms. The ladies liked them very much, clamored for
more to string on their bracelets and necklaces. In no time at all,
charms began to appear in gold, silver and gilt. The charms on this
page range from 10¢ to $330. Most of them are of gold, cost from $4
to $28 and have moving parts.

Moving parts. She examined the picture closely. What she saw struck
her as crude work, terrible work. *Why, I could make beautiful little
charms,* she thought. She flipped back to the article on the World's
Fair. *I could even make statues. Didn't Uncle Luther say I was an artist?* She
studied the muscles along Day's flanks. She turned back to the
charms. She held the intervening pages together and flipped back and
forth between the statues and the charms. *Moving parts,* she thought.
*Moving parts. Why not? Why should I make coarse goods only for men? Why
not coarse charms for women, really beautiful ones, ones that anyone would be
proud to wear? Well, to wear on certain occasions. But why not?*

"Lorna," whispered Herb. "Lorna, are you all right?" He stood at
the end of the hall.

"Oh, Herb," she said. "I've had a wonderful idea. Look at
these—oh—" She wished she could tell him, right then, tell him that
there was something about her that made her extraordinary.

"What is it, Lorna?" asked Herb.

"Oh," she said, shrugging, abandoning the idea of telling him
everything, "nothing. I was just looking at these charms."

Herb came to her side and looked over her shoulder. "Mm-
hmm," he said.

"And I was thinking—well—I was thinking that I could do better than this. Look."

Herb looked closely. "Sure you could," he said. "Those little dogs
and horses you carved for your uncle Luther were much better than
this stuff."

"They were," said Lorna. "Yes, they really were. Herb—"

"Mmm?" he said, still studying the charms.

"The article says that most of them have moving parts."

"Mm, I can see that." His mind was racing. *These are nothing.
Children could have designed these.* He wanted to tell her what he could

do along these lines, what he had already done. *She'd be amazed, amazed. "A mechanical genius," Ben said.* He had half a mind to go to the cellar and get his Watchcase Wonders from the hidden compartment in the box on the shelf under his workbench, bring them upstairs, and show them to her. *They would give her something to look up to me for, get her mind off those grinning boys. Look up to me? Not likely. She'd be more ashamed than amazed.* "Not much to most of these," he said. "Mechanically, I mean. The propeller goes around on the plane, the wheels rotate on the wagon, the telephone dial turns, the safe door opens. I could—" He stopped and looked at Lorna. She was beaming. "I could do much better than this," he said.

"We could work together," said Lorna.

"We could," said Herb. "I could do the mechanical work."

"And I could make the little figures." Her heart was pounding. She wanted to tell him. She came close to telling him, very close to telling him. He was bent close to the pictures of charms, examining them, and reciting their mechanical attributes: "—little egg beater goes around, the fan blades turn—" The charms seemed so innocent. Herb seemed so innocent, so trusting, such a truth-teller. She felt deceitful. And lustful. She didn't dare tell him. Didn't dare. It had been those boys—surely he would be able to tell that it had been those boys. She wondered how she could even have thought of it. She had been holding her finger in another part of the magazine, marking the place where the statues were shown. She slipped her finger out.

Herb made some sketches, and together they made some prototypes—a tiny silver toaster from which two slices of burnt toast, slivers of walnut wood, emerged; a Studebaker President convertible with a folding top, a working steering wheel, and a hinged hood and doors; and a minuscule piano with four keys that actually struck notes (the first four notes of "Lake Serenity Serenade," which had become a standard)—but then the project began to wither. Their hearts weren't in it. They wanted to work together, and they wanted to work on jewelry, but they didn't want to make toasters, convertibles, and pianos. They seemed to find less and less time to work on the prototypes, and after a few months they found no time at all. The toaster, convertible, and piano became the most coveted charms worn by any

of the girls at Babbington High, where Ella wore them, on her brace-
let, every day, until the fad for charms faded and she put them into a
box in a dresser drawer where she kept other outmoded jewelry.

Ella and Buster and Bert were great chums throughout their last years
in high school. Ella was in love with both of the boys, and they were
both in love with her, and they seemed quite content to have things
stay just as they were. Herb and Lorna even thought that there was
probably some safety in this arrangement, since Ella wasn't likely to
go to bed with either of them as long as she loved both of them, and
no one, not Herb or Lorna or Ella or Bert or Buster, even considered
her going to bed with both of them. After they graduated from high
school, however, matters changed as if overnight. Apparently both
Bert and Buster had been waiting for graduation day to pop the question, and when it arrived they both did. Ella faced a dilemma that
would have delighted most of her girlfriends—she couldn't decide
between them. But they were both asking her to marry them, and it
seemed as if she must decide.
    "Mother," she said, "do you know what I wish?"
    "What?" asked Lorna.
    "I wish neither of them had asked me."
    "Oh. Oh, Ella—"
    "I wish we could have just—"
    "—gone on the way you were going."
    "Yes."
    "I'm sure you're worried about hurting them—or one of them,
anyway—"
    "And me. It's going to hurt me, too. I'm going to lose *one* of them.
And I don't want to. I don't want to lose either of them."
    "Oh, Ella—"
    "Do I *have* to choose? Do I *have* to? I've been thinking. *Imagining* is
more like it. I've been imagining what it might be like if we—if all
three of us—"
    "Ella. Ella. You can't do that. You know you can't do that."
    "Ohhhh!"
    "I'm afraid you do have to choose. You really do have to choose."
    And so she chose. She chose Buster. Bert took it gracefully. Buster
was the obvious choice, and Bert had been losing to his quicker,

brighter brother for so many years that he was almost used to it. Buster and Ella had an engagement party, the first among their friends. It was small and restrained; Buster and Ella didn't want Bert to feel that they were celebrating his elimination. They planned to be married the next spring.

In December, the Japanese attacked Pearl Harbor. Buster Leroy enlisted in the navy. Everyone tried to convince him that he could do his duty just as well in the Coast Guard, but among young men in Babbington and many another seacoast town, the Coast Guard was considered a refuge, easy duty. If you were willing to put yourself to the test, you joined the navy. Bert was no seaman. He had never liked being on the water. He joined the army. Their mother insisted that they spend their last night in Babbington at home, that this be a family evening, like Thanksgiving, and she made a Thanksgiving dinner for it. Ella was invited, of course, and she sat at the table between Buster and Bert. Buster pressed his knee against hers beneath the table, and she pressed back, but then she felt disloyal all of a sudden and pressed her other knee against Bert's, so that he wouldn't feel that he would be entirely forgotten while he was away at war. She finished the meal in silent confusion.

The day Buster and Bert left, Ella began writing to them. She wrote at least two pairs of letters a day, one in the morning and one at night, and on days when there was anything of special note to report, she wrote a third pair or even a fourth. She filled her days with housework and cooking, since Lorna was working, and she did volunteer work for the USO, passing out doughnuts and coffee, dancing with servicemen on leave. When the men asked her to go out with them, she would say she was engaged, and when they said that all the girls claimed to be engaged, she would show them her ring and a photograph of her and Buster. She would have to identify Buster as "the one on my right," since the photo she carried with her was one in which Buster and Bert had made a seat for her by clasping their forearms and were swinging her toward the camera. But something had happened to alter her feelings for Buster and Bert. It may simply have been the act of choosing, or it may have been her projecting different feelings for them into the future. She came to think of Buster—or it might be more accurate to say that she made herself think of Buster—as the love of her life, as her husband, and she came to think of Bert—or made herself think of Bert—as just Buster's brother. She continued to write to both of them, but she wrote Buster's letters first, and all her effort went into them. Bert's were just snips and snatches of news copied from Buster's.

Herb began dismantling his half-finished projects so that he could turn the metal in as scrap. In a couple of months the cellar was clean, neat, uncluttered. There were no more pieces of Studebakers behind the garage, and the garage itself was empty enough to hold the car. Herb signed up as a spotter. He and the other spotters stood watches on the roof of the police station, keeping an eye out for German and Japanese planes. Each spotter was issued a packet of cards bearing the outlines of the various planes they needed to be able to recognize, including ours. Herb learned his in an evening. He sat down in the living room and studied them in the same methodical way he studied the cards he kept for potential Studebaker buyers. The other spotters weren't nearly as quick. Herb wondered whether this was a national problem. Surely it must be. Once again, as he had in the First World War, Herb came through with a nice idea when his country was most in need of one. He reworked the cards into a semblance of a conventional deck and taught the other spotters to play poker with it. This spotter-training technique would, I'm certain, have caught on across the country and earned Herb the recognition he deserved for devising it if he had been able to fashion a congruent equivalent of the fifty-two-card, four-suit, thirteen-cards-per-suit deck, but the planes wouldn't fit that structure, and the closest Herb was able to come was a deck with ninety-seven cards in eleven suits of unequal size, with different numbers of "face" cards in each. Learning the game took weeks, and the difficulties the game presented obscured the fact that its players quickly learned the various planes and the differences among them.

Developing this game, and working through the logical oddities that such a deck presented, provided a collaboration for Herb and Lorna that was much more engaging and pleasant than what they had found in animated charms. They played game after game in quiet hours at home, throughout the war, adjusting the rules to new circumstances that arose during play, learning to accommodate changes in the deck when one nation or another introduced a new plane or retired an old one. Lorna became the world's best player of the game

that came to be called (in, I'm sorry to have to say, the tone of voice—
a kind of oral smirk—one uses when referring to a folly) "Piper
Poker."

Before the war, the best slide rules had come from Germany. Now the
need for slide rules—for calculating artillery trajectories, plotting
courses, calculating wind drift, figuring time to target, and the like—
was great and pressing. The production of slide rules became a defense industry, and domestic slide rule manufacturers scrambled to
meet the nation's computational needs. In Hargrove, the town to the
east of Babbington, Hargrove Slide Rules faced a critical situation: to
meet their quotas they had to double production. Where would they
find people with the skill and talent for the fine, exacting work that
slide rules required? They appealed for help and guidance to the
mathematics department at Hargrove University, where the department secretary, Kitty Kern, suggested that they try recruiting among
jewelers, and that's how they found Lorna.

One afternoon, after she had been with the Hargrove Slide Rule
Company for three months, Lorna was sitting alone in the company
cafeteria, bent over a slide rule, absorbed in calculating the interior
volume of her home on No Bridge Road, when Edwin Berwick, a
promising young fellow who had been put in charge of training new
employees, approached her. Beside her lay an egg-salad sandwich on a
piece of waxed paper. She had unwrapped the sandwich and eaten a
couple of bites, but then she had set it aside and ignored it. The bread
had curled. The egg salad had darkened. Her coffee, barely touched,
was cold.

"Mrs. Piper?" said Berwick.

"Oh!" said Lorna, startled from her concentration.

"I'm sorry," Berwick said at once. "I didn't mean to startle you."

"Oh, that's all right," said Lorna. "I was just—well—I wasn't
doing anything important."

"Testing the product, I see," said Berwick.

"Oh, not really," said Lorna. "In fact, this is an old rule. I was
just—"

"Yes?"

"I was figuring the volume of my house," Lorna admitted. She
smiled and shrugged.

"Just for the fun of it?" asked Berwick.

"Oh, no," she said. "Or, rather, yes—and no. Herb—my husband—wants to build a gadget to filter the air in our house—when the war is over. He has a good idea, I think: he's going to bubble the air through barrels of water in the cellar, and all the impurities—even germs—will be left behind in the water. When the house smells stale—you know how a house gets that stale odor when it's been closed up for a long time during the winter—all we'll have to do is squeeze a little lemon juice into the water or toss in some pine needles to make the whole house smell fresh again."

Mr. Berwick wore an unchanging smile throughout Lorna's explanation. To Lorna it looked a lot like the indulgent smile *she* wore so often when she was talking to Mrs. Stolz. Lorna supposed that the object of Mr. Berwick's indulgent smile was Herb, not her, and because she thought it was directed at him she felt worse than she would have if she'd thought it was directed at her. She was embarrassed for Herb. "I see that you're skeptical," she said, with ice in her voice. "It may sound like a foolish idea, but Herb is very clever, and I think he can make it work."

"He's an inventor?"

"Just as a hobby. He sells Studebakers."

"I see." That smile again. It was beginning to annoy Lorna, but if she had known what it really meant, it wouldn't have. Berwick was pleased with what he was hearing from Lorna. He'd been asked to help in recruiting for an urgent project: calculating tables of artillery trajectories for the army. He hoped he'd be able to recommend someone. It was the first time his country had asked anything specific of him, anything that he could do better than anyone else, and the army was, of course, an important client of Hargrove Slide Rules. "Let me ask you something," he said. "Why did you say, 'Yes and no,' when I asked if you were making these calculations just for the fun of it?"

"Oh," said Lorna, "because I'm *really* doing it for the fun of doing it." Now she was feeling defensive. She felt that Mr. Berwick was challenging her interests, Herb's interests, her abilities, Herb's abilities, even the way she and Herb worked toegther. The more pleased he was, the more broadly he smiled and the more condescending he appeared. Lorna wanted to make him understand her; she felt that she *must* make him understand her if she was going to preserve her self-respect. "You see," she said, "Herb needs to know the volume of air in the house, of course, but he doesn't need the precision that I'm going to give him. I could have come up with the figures he needed in a couple of hours, but instead I'm including every nook and cranny. I'm even making allowances for the air displaced by furnishings—and by Herb and me, and our daughter, Ella, and Mrs. Stolz—she lives with us—and even the air displaced by the cat. Here, let me show you. Our cat spends, on the average, fourteen hours, twenty-three minutes, and seventeen seconds in the house every day. Of course, I made that calculation last week, when the weather was good, so I'm going to have to gather data over a whole year to be really accurate. Herb made a clever little timer that attaches to the cat's door—he made the door, too, of course. The timer switches on every time the door opens from the outside and goes off every time the door opens from the inside, so it clocks the time that Tom—the cat—is inside. Tom displaces—let me see—456.19 cubic inches. *But,* since he's only in the house 59.95 percent of the time, he only represents, on the average, 273.49 cubic inches—"

"About sixteen hundredths of a cubic foot," said Edwin.

"Yes," said Lorna, just a little surprised to find that Edwin had been following her so carefully. "Then there's the air that Herb and I displace—"

"You know," Edwin interrupted, "a few months ago I built my daughter a sandbox. I had to figure out how much sand to get for it. Simple problem. Nothing to it. But a question popped into my head: How many *grains* of sand do I need? I made myself a little cardboard cube a quarter-inch on a side, filled it with sand, poured the sand out on a sheet of paper and—"

"—*counted* the grains?"

"—counted the grains. When I finished, I did it again—"

"—with a different sample of sand," suggested Lorna.

"—with a different sample of sand," Edwin said, smiling the same smile, a smile that was, Lorna found, beginning to take on a different appearance from what she'd seen before. "I kept at it until I had a reliable average figure for the number of grains in a cubic quarter-inch. My family thought I was crazy, of course, but once I had begun work, the problem took on a life of its own."

"The problem became your purpose," said Lorna.

"Yes!" said Berwick. "Thank you. I wouldn't have thought to put it that way."

[2 1 7]

Lorna was ashamed of herself for having thought that Berwick was thinking what she had thought he was thinking. She thought of apologizing, telling Berwick that she'd misjudged him, explaining why, warning him about the misleading impression his smile could give people, suggesting that he practice another smile, but he spoke too quickly for her. "Are you good at these problems?" he asked.

"Yes," said Lorna, "I am. I'm very accurate with a slide rule, and I'm fairly fast. I—I want you to know that I only do calculations during lunch—never when I should be working."

"Oh, I didn't mean to suggest anything like that," Berwick said. "No, not at all." He drew a breath. "Mrs. Piper, I'd hate to see you leave here. You're the very best of the new employees. But—"

"What is it, Mr. Berwick?"

"I think someone from the army would like to speak to you about your skill as a calculator."

Lorna used the telephone in Berwick's office to call Herb and tell him that she'd be late getting home. When she finally arrived, it was nearly nine. She was flushed with success, self-satisfaction, and appreciation of her competence and importance. She sat in the living room without taking her coat off and told Herb and Ella everything in a disorganized rush. When she finished, she was out of breath and glowing.

In *The Analytical Engine,* Jeremy Bernstein outlines the project that Lorna described to Herb and Ella:

> In 1943, the Moore School and the Aberdeen Proving Ground, in Maryland, were conducting a joint project involving the computation of artillery firing tables for the Army. The Moore School contingent . . . used a Bush analog computer and employed a hundred women to do hand computations as a necessary adjunct to the machine operations. . . .

"You'd have to go to Maryland?" asked Ella.

"Yes," said Lorna, "I would. Come here, Ella." She patted the sofa beside her. Ella sat by her side and said nothing. Ella and Lorna had never been apart for more than a night. Lorna put her arm around Ella's shoulders and tried to think of a way to tell her the simple truth: that she *wanted* to go. She looked at Herb, and she saw that he was grinning.

He knows, she thought. *He knows that I want to go, and it's all right with him.* She couldn't look at Ella when she spoke, but she found it easy to look at Herb—found, in fact, that looking at Herb gave her the steady voice she needed to speak to Ella. Herb had an admirable generosity, that readiness to say yes, to *think* yes, to give the benefit of the doubt to someone's ideas, to urge a person on. It showed in his eyes, his grin.

Lorna gave Ella a squeeze and told her the truth: "I *want* to go." Her heart was pounding, and she hoped that Ella couldn't see how excited she was about going, how eager she was to go, how exhilarated she'd been by the tests she'd been given, how thrilled she was to have a talent that she could display. A devil-may-care cranny of her mind, electrified by her success and by the anticipation of the adventures that lay ahead in Maryland, wanted her to blurt out everything, to amaze Herb and Ella with her secret life and secret talent. The counsel of wiser crannies kept her quiet, told her that it was daring enought to admit that she wanted to go to Maryland to work on the calculation of artillery tables.

In Maryland, she allowed herself to acknowledge her secret talent. At night, when the women who performed the calculations were at their leisure, they entertained themselves with cards and songs and talk. One evening, not long after the group was assembled, one of the women said, "You know what we are, don't you? Doing what we do? We're a bunch of calculating women!"

They took the name. The talk in the evenings wandered, as the talk of people who've been thrown together and have time on their hands will, but it included lots of the anecdotes that we introduce into a conversation not because they illustrate a point, but because they give us a chance to talk about ourselves. On many evenings the conversation became a string of such anecdotes, and these were the liveliest and most revealing evenings of all. One evening, the topic turned to uncles who had a more than avuncular affection for their nieces. Many of the women had interesting anecdotes to contribute on that topic, but none commanded such rapt attention as Lorna's, and the attention of her audience, the avidity with which they followed her story, made her extend it. The more she told, the more they wanted to hear. After a while, she found it easy and pleasant to say to these women things she had thought she would never be able to say to anyone at all, and she wasn't even terribly surprised when she found herself saying, "My uncle also taught me to make jewelry, carved jewelry, very special jewlery——" As soon as she began, she was so thrilled to be telling someone at last that she told it all, everything.

That very night, she began making soap carvings for the women. She found that soap was a congenial medium, so easy to work that she could turn out a carving in an evening. She had an eager audience from the start, and soon she began taking requests. The earliest requests were the obvious ones: a woman would ask Lorna to make the soap woman resemble her and the soap man resemble her husband or boyfriend. Then they began to get more interesting and more complicated. More and more of the women began to ask for men who resembled men they had never made love to, men they'd hardly spoken to, and in several cases, men who had appeared only in their daydreams, the wonderful men of their imagination. Because soap was so much cheaper a commodity than ivory, Lorna found a new freedom and artistic daring in working with it. She let her imagination range a bit more, and she also used the soap carvings to release some of her loneliness, some of her longing for Herb. This had a result that Lorna found oddly titillating: many of the men wound up resembling, in one way or another that none of the other women would have detected, Herb. Whenever a woman couldn't describe her dream man adequately for Lorna to go on with her work, Lorna would supply the required bit of Herb. Soap was in short supply, and it couldn't be wasted, so Lorna's carvings were used for washing, and the expectation that her work, the evidence of her secret occupation, would go down the drain gave Lorna a feeling of security that allowed her to enjoy the work as never before. This was also the first time she had ever come to know her audience and the first time she had ever counted women among her audience. Under these unusual, irreplicable conditions, she did some of her best work. It lacked animation, however, and Lorna felt the lack, an emptiness in the work, apparent only to her, as if the couples were hollow; it was a feeling that, if she had had a reason to describe it, she would have compared to the hollowness she felt in herself, missing Herb.

15
In Which Herb 'n' Lorna's Grandson and Biographer Is Born

Buster Leroy drowned when his ship, a destroyer escort, was torpedoed in the North Atlantic. The news came one Wednesday evening, while Herb was in the dining room at home, playing Piper Poker with the Spotters Club, some spotters who had begun getting together every Wednesday evening.

"Okay," said Dexter Rice, "what've you got?"

"Three pair. Heinkel one-elevens, Mitsubishi Zeroes, and Dornier two-seventeens," said Bob Schoop.

"Damn!" said Simon Misch. "I should've known you were bluffing!"

"Three pair. One-elevens, Zeroes, and two-seventeens. That's good," said Dexter. "That's good. But it's not good enough, I'm afraid." He spread his hand on the table. "A pair of Kawanishi Emilys, a pair of Junkers eighty-eights, and three Messerschmitt one-oh-nines."

"I don't believe it!" said Simon. "I could have taken that pot. Look at this! A double full house: Dornier two-seventeens over Mitsubishi Bettys over Stukas. I'm no good at this game."

"All right, all right," said Dexter, shuffling. "My deal. The game is twelve-card draw. Kawasaki Nicks are wild. Sturmvogels and Zeroes or better to open."

The phone rang. "Deal me in," said Herb. "I'll be right back."

It was Jack Leroy. He could barely manage to tell Herb what had happened. The Leroys had known the awful news since that morning, but they'd been enclosed in their grief. Only when the sun went down and Jack made himself a drink did he even realize that other people needed to know. Ella came to mind, and he knew that he had to call and tell her. When he had given the operator the number, he prayed silently that she wouldn't answer. When Herb answered, he thought that he really ought to ask Herb to put Ella on so that he could tell her himself, but then he realized with relief that he couldn't *not* tell Herb, now that Herb was on the phone. He told him.

"My God," said Herb. "Oh, my God." He didn't say anything else. He just set the handset in the cradle.

Dexter was finishing a joke: "—so she says, 'But this *has* to be Thursday because the iceman *always* comes on Thursday, right after the milkman and just before the grocery boy!' "

Hilarity followed. Bob Schoop, with a bite of sandwich in his mouth, kept repeating, "Tell Herb. Tell Herb."

Herb stood with his hands on the edge of the table, saying nothing. After a while everyone noticed that he was just standing there, and everyone noticed the look on his face. "What's the matter, Herb?" asked Dexter.

"That boy—Buster Leroy—he's dead."

"Dead?" said Simon, who lived near the Leroys and had had his *Babbington Reporter* delivered by Buster, his garden weeded by Bert, his car washed by the pair. "Dead?"

"Who is he?" asked Bob.

"Come on," said Simon, who understood at once. "We've got to go."

"Who is he?" asked Bob.

"I'll tell you outside," said Simon. "Come on."

They were gone in a few moments. Herb stood at the table. Bob's sandwich lay on his plate, a couple of bites out of it. Dexter had left an untouched half. *They should have taken those sandwiches,* thought Herb. He picked up his beer glass and took a swallow. The table was littered with spotters' cards. Herb gathered them up and made a neat stack. He carried the plates into the kitchen. He wrapped the uneaten sandwiches in waxed paper. He washed the dishes. He finished his beer. He wiped the dining room table with a dishcloth and dried it with the dish towel. He turned the kitchen light off, went into the dining room, where the telephone was, on a table in a corner near the living room, and called Lorna in Baltimore.

Lorna was enjoying herself, seated at the center of a group of calculating women, working on a soap carving—it depicted the woman who had requested it in the passionate embrace of Gary Cooper—when Herb's call came through. She and Herb decided that she should arrange to return home at once and that Herb should wake Ella and tell her the awful news.

Herb stood in Ella's doorway for a while, just watching her sleep and listening to her deep, untroubled breathing. He sighed and stepped to the side of her bed. He sat on the edge and put his hand on her shoulder.

"Ella," he whispered. "Ella."

She stirred, but she didn't wake up.

"Ella," he said, so softly that Ella would have had difficulty hearing him if she'd been awake, "something awful has happened, and I have to tell you about it." Ella stirred, stretched, and turned her head slightly, so that she almost seemed to be responding to him, but still she didn't wake up. "Buster is dead, Ella," Herb said, so quietly that Ella didn't stir at the sound of his voice. "It's terrible, terrible. I called your mother in Maryland. She'll come home right away. She should be here tomorrow night, so we only have to get through tonight and tomorrow without her. Then she'll be here, and she'll—"

Ella stirred again. She turned onto her back, and she rolled her head away from Herb toward the window. Herb held his breath. He could feel his heart pounding, and in the quiet of the room he seemed to be able to hear it. He waited. Ella didn't open her eyes.

"She'll know what to say, what to tell you. She'll know what to do." He put his hand on Ella's cheek. "You can't let this get the best of you, Ella," he said. "You can't let it—destroy you. You have a way of taking everything too hard. This isn't the end of the world. You still have Bert." He sighed. *Oh, God,* he thought. *I hope I can come up with something better than that when she's awake.*

The telephone rang. It startled him. He stood suddenly. Ella cried out and sat up in her bed.

"It's all right. It's all right," he assured her. He reached out to her, held her shoulders. "It's all right, Ella. It's only me."

"What's the matter, Daddy?" she asked. "What's wrong?"

"I—"

"The phone's ringing."

"Yes. It's—"

"Is it our ring?"

"I don't know. I—I didn't pay attention."

"It is. It's our ring. You'd better get it. It must be important."

"It's probably your mother, Ella. I have to—I'll be right back." Herb backed out of the room, and he dashed down the hall to get the phone.

Ella got out of bed and pulled her robe on. She stood in the hall for a moment, listening. She heard her father's voice, but it seemed to come from farther away than the dining room, and he was saying very little, not much more than "yes" and "I understand." He came back to the hall. "What is it, Daddy?" she whispered.

"It's for Mrs. Stolz," he said. He brought his hands up over his eyes. "It's bad news. Her grandson. Her grandson is dead. Killed."

"Oh, Daddy," said Ella. She felt a surge of compassion and responsibility that struck her as a more mature feeling than anything she had experienced before. "Let me go wake her up. You wait here. I'll get her." She took the copy of *The Thousand and One Nights* from the shelf and replaced it. The bookcase swung open, and Ella disappeared into the dark. In a few moments she emerged with Mrs. Stolz, who was blinking at the light and repeating, "What is it? What is it?" Ella took her to the phone and stayed with her while she spoke to her daughter. Herb stood in the hall. He felt that he could barely breathe. His hands wouldn't stop shaking. His mouth was too dry to allow him to swallow. Ella and Mrs. Stolz came back, walking slowly, bent, as if they were wearing wet overcoats. "I'll help Mrs. Stolz pack," said Ella. "You should call Mother, Daddy. Tell her. Then call about a train for Mrs. Stolz."

"I already called your mother," said Herb. "She'll be home tomorrow night."

"You did? She will?" said Ella.

"Yes," said Herb. Mechanically, distractedly, he added what he had rehearsed: "So we only have tonight and tomorrow to get through without her. Then she'll be here, and she'll—she'll help you.

She'll know what to do. She—oh, Ella—" His mission came back to him suddenly. "Something awful has happened."

Ella was a little frightened. Her father seemed to have forgotten what had just happened, forgotten that he had already told her about the something awful.

"I know," she said.

"No. No. It's—Ella, come into the living room and sit down, I—"

"What is it, Daddy?" she asked.

"Ella—" he began. His voice had the colorlessness that comes from rehearsal. "Buster is dead, too."

For one awful moment, Ella thought that her father was playing a trick on her. Then she knew that it must be true. Her legs gave way under her. She dropped to her knees beside Herb and huddled against him. "Oh, why Buster?" she asked.

May Castle met Lorna's train at the Babbington station. It was the last week of January. Snow was falling in fat, wet, heavy clumps. On the ground, the flakes turned to slush. May and Lorna greeted each other quickly, hugged briefly on the platform, and then rushed across the parking lot to May's Chrysler, threw Lorna's luggage onto the back seat, and climbed in.

"Whew!" said May. "What a night! Horrible! Just horrible! What a night to have to go through what you're going to have to go through."

"Good weather wouldn't make it any easier," said Lorna.

"No, it wouldn't," said May. "Nothing makes it any easier anymore. I used to love a nice night, a clear night, with stars. The stars used to make me happy, but now—oh, now nothing makes me happy. Everything seems so miserable. Everything seems so hopeless."

"May!" said Lorna. "Is that the way *you* feel? Does everything seem hopeless to you?"

"Well, yes," said May. "I think it does. It was different when I was younger, at least it was different for *me* when I was younger. I think I thought I was going to live forever. No. That's not it. I never *thought* about it at all—dying, I mean. Now, well, now dying is all anyone talks about. It's all I think about. I look at myself in the mirror in the morning, and I think to myself, *You're dying, May. This dying woman you see in your mirror is you.* Doesn't that seem hopeless?"

"It sounds as if you're upset about growing old, May, not about dying."

"Well. Maybe. Maybe I am. I don't know which is worse," said May. "You either die or grow old—or both. It's hopeless."

Lorna burst out laughing. For hours, throughout the train ride, she'd tried to prepare herself for Ella. She had imagined the look on Ella's face when she saw her, tried to imagine what Ella would be feeling, what Ella would need from her, and how she could come close to providing it. She hadn't expected May, hadn't prepared for her, wasn't sure what she needed or how to provide it. "I'm sorry, May," Lorna said. "I'm not laughing at you. I'm just—I'm just nervous, I guess."

She studied May's face while May peered through the snow and concentrated on her driving. For the first time, Lorna saw beyond her remembered image of May as a gay and light-hearted girl. She saw the wrinkles around May's eyes, the furrows across her brow, the vertical lines in her upper lip. She remembered the night after she had met the Leroy boys, when she had sat in the living room, alone in the dark, slumping under the weight of the feeling that she was too old to interest anyone as young as Buster Leroy, annoyed that she had lived to be older than she had ever wanted to be. "I know how you feel, May," she said.

May turned to look at her, just for a moment. Lorna put a smile on her face. "It *is* hopeless," she said. She laughed. "It's a hopeless situation, but you don't have to feel miserable about it. Maybe we *should* feel miserable about it, but I don't—not anymore."

"Oh?" said May. "Did you meet a man in Baltimore?"

"No!" said Lorna. She grinned in the dark. "I—found something to—keep me going. It was very difficult there. The work they wanted us to do was impossible. Every day we fell farther behind. We just couldn't do everything they wanted us to do. It was impossible. It was a hopeless situation. We all knew they were disappointed in us, and we were disappointed, too. But I didn't feel miserable about it. The others didn't, either. Somewhere along the line, we all decided—those of us who stuck it out—not everybody did—that we would do everything we *could* do and that was *all* we could do."

"I see those logic puzzles have paid off," said May. Lorna poked her shoulder.

"I worked as much as I could," Lorna went on, "and I got as

much done as I could. I *liked* it. I think we all liked it. We had wonderful times at night. We were all thrown together, a hundred of us, with a hundred stories to tell. We were always tired, but we were never too tired to talk. I heard stories about husbands and sisters and uncles and mothers and babies and—everything."

"But what did you find?"

"Find?"

"What did you find to keep you going?"

"Oh. Work. Work and—I—" Lorna stopped herself. She had been about to tell May about her soap carvings. Now, she decided, was not the time, but after the liberation of her work with the calculating women, she was determined not to keep her work a secret from May.

"It's too long a story, May." she said. "I'll tell you tomorrow."

"When do you have to go back?"

"Back?"

"To Baltimore."

"Oh, there isn't really any need for me to go back. The project is a failure, really. Oh, not a failure, just not a success. It's not as if I'd make the difference if I went back. They very nearly told me to stay home. I think they didn't want to actually *tell* me that it wouldn't make any difference whether I came back or not, so they told me again and again how important it would be for me to be at home with my daughter now, that they understood, and they didn't want me even to think about coming back for several months."

"Well, they were right. It *is* important for you to be home with Ella now."

"Oh, I know," said Lorna.

They had arrived. May stopped the car and sat with both hands on the wheel, looking straight ahead through the windshield. "Shall I come in with you? No, you wouldn't want me to come in with you, would you? You'll want to see them on your own first. I'll come over tomorrow."

"Will you help me with my bags?"

"Oh! Of course! Of course I will. I don't know what I was thinking of."

Together, they carried Lorna's bags to the porch. Before she let herself in, Lorna took May by the sleeve and asked her, suddenly, impulsively, "Is Garth home, May?"

"No," said May. "No. He's off somewhere. He's off somewhere quite a lot, lately." She looked downward.

Lorna put her hand under May's chin and tilted her head upward. "Why don't you go out somewhere and have a drink?" she said.

"What?" said May. "By myself? You mean to a bar?"

"Yes," said Lorna. "Why don't you go somewhere where someone is laughing and telling loud stories?"

"Where would that be?"

"Oh, I don't know," said Lorna. "There must be—"

"Someplace where I could go by myself? Believe me, Lorna, Garth and I have done time in every bar in this town, and the only women alone in any of them are women I wouldn't want to know. There is no— Well, actually, I have to take that back. There is one place. Whitey's. It's a family kind of place. Kids and everything. There wouldn't be children this late, I guess, but there are sometimes. We used to have quite a lot of fun there, to tell the truth. Whitey is quite a sketch. He—"

"Good. Good, May. Go there. Talk with some people. Laugh a little."

"Oh, but— Come with me, Lorna. Oh, of course—"

"Go on, May. You go. Go have some fun."

"But I—"

"Go to Whitey's by yourself tonight, and I promise you I'll go there with you tomorrow night. I have a wonderful secret to tell you. All right?"

"All right," said May. In the light that came through the diamond-shaped window in the front door, Lorna could see that she was smiling.

Lorna went inside, and she spent the night holding Ella, talking to her, trying to soothe her, and regretting that she had ever told Ella that she ought to choose between Bert and Buster.

May went to Whitey's. She found that she liked the place from the moment she arrived. She saw many familiar faces there, and she rediscovered a pleasure in light conversation and inconsequential flirtation that, she was surprised to find, was much of what she missed of youth.

The next night, at Whitey's, Lorna told May about her soap carvings, and then she went on to tell her all the rest, the whole story of her work in coarse goods. They were facing each other, sitting in a wooden booth, one of several along the wall opposite the bar. They became more and more animated as Lorna's story progressed and May consumed Manhattans. At last Lorna said, "I'll bet you think I'm making this up." She leaned across the table and looked hard at May. "Don't you?" she asked.

May wasn't sure what she thought. "Well," she said, pausing with her glass raised, "I'm not sure *what* I think. You *might* be making it up. It's a delicious idea, but it isn't something I'd expect you to do. You are—you have always seemed—to me—a little—well—*prim*." She giggled. Lorna smiled at her but didn't speak. May couldn't decide whether Lorna was pulling her leg or not. "Oh, I don't know. It's a wonderful thought," she said. "I know you have the talent—" She mimicked Lorna's tight-lipped smile. She sat in silence for a while, but still Lorna spoke only with her twinkling eyes. May shrugged. "Oh, I guess I believe you," she said.

Lorna reached into her bag and brought from it a silver watch-case. She held it in front of May, cupped in her hands so that the people near them wouldn't see it. She pressed the stem. The lid popped open. May's eyes lit up.

"Ohhhhh," she said, and set her glass down. She leaned closer to get a better look at the little ivory couple inside the case. Slowly, Lorna turned the stem.

"Oh, my God!" said May. The laugh she laughed was astonished, shocked, thrilled. "That's—" She leaned across the table and said in a whisper, "—obscene." She laughed again. "And *wonderful*," she added. "May I?" Lorna handed her the watchcase, and May examined the ivory couple closely while she turned the stem.

"I don't want to brag," said Lorna, "but I hope you'll notice the workmanship."

"Oh, I *am*," said May. "I certainly am noticing the workmanship." More laughter.

"My goodness," said May, "where do you get your ideas? I mean—well, this seems quite—ah—*advanced*. Do you and Herb— do you—ah—do this sort of thing?"

"Now and then," said Lorna. A thought struck her, and she voiced it without considering whether she ought to. "Not for a while, though."

"You don't mean that you have—ah—other models?"

"Oh, no. I just meant that we—don't—"

"Yes," said May. She sighed. "Well, none of us drinks champagne as often as we'd like, either."

"Anyway," said Lorna, "most of the ideas aren't mine. Most of the—um—movements, the routines—"

"Oh, *hardly* routine!"

"Well, I get models—"

May raised her eyebrows.

"Not that kind. Little stick figures, made of wire, with all the gears and all of that, the works. I get them from my uncle Luther—"

"My goodness! That man's an inspiration for us all. How old *is* the randy geezer?"

"*He* doesn't make them up. I don't know who does, to tell you the truth."

"Well! If it's a man, it's a man I'd like to meet," said May. They fell into such loud and raucous laughter that May had to hide the watchcase beneath the table, since they had attracted the attention of everyone around them.

Lorna was less successful in cheering Ella up. She had been able to lead May to what she needed, the pleasure of society, but Ella needed Buster, and that was something no one could supply. Ella spent hours lying on her bed, her hands clasped behind her head, her eyes fixed on the ceiling. When she was up, she walked through the house in silence. She went about her business as if living had become merely a set of automatic responses. When Lorna put food in front of her, she ate it. When Lorna suggested a ride, she put on a coat, got into the car with Lorna, and rode. If Lorna asked her to wash the dishes, she put an apron on, stood at the sink, and spent a silent hour working.

Lorna was just, well, shaken *by how depressed Ella was. She had this idea that it was terribly important for Ella to stop this grieving, to get on with life. Well, isn't that just how she felt about me? You know—I don't mind saying this now, but I would never have admitted anything of the sort at the time,* never—*I was in despair myself. Garth, well, Garth was being simply* awful. *It was a terrible-enough time, wasn't it, without his being such a rat. There was the damned war, and none of us was getting any younger, and everyone was depressed as hell. And Lorna—oh, Lorna. Lorna was an angel, a dear. She was determined that she was going to pull you out of your depression. She was going to figure out what would cheer you up and see that you got it. But I'll tell you what I think. I think that cheering us up was what cheered her up. By trying to make the rest of us feel not-so-miserable, she was keeping herself from feeling miserable. That's what I think.*

Lorna went back to work at the slide rule factory. She found that she had become a celebrity there. In her absence, people had exaggerated the work she had been doing in Maryland, as the people of Chacallit had, after the First World War, exaggerated the exploits of Andrew Proctor. Rumors had spread among her co-workers that Lorna's work was secret, mysterious, dangerous, absolutely essential to the war effort. No one expected her to talk about it when she returned, but everyone hoped she would, that at least she would accidentally drop a hint now and then. Whenever she did say anything about the calculation of artillery firing tables, her listeners would smile and nod, exchange a wink or a nudge, certain that they understood hidden meanings in whatever she said, certain that she was diminishing the importance of what she had done and hiding its true nature because in these frightening times no one knew who might be listening. Each evening, Lorna returned home flushed with the pleasure of her work and the admiration of her co-workers and then, just inside the front door, dropped, as if she were riding a swift elevator, into Ella's misery. Then, one evening, when she stood in the doorway of Ella's bedroom wondering what she might say to her, she noticed through the window the light from Dudley Beaker's living room, and she asked herself, *Now, why didn't I think of that before?*

"Ella," she said, "have you spoken to Dudley recently?" There was concern in her voice.

"No," said Ella. "I haven't. Why do you ask?"

"Oh, I don't know," said Lorna. She stepped into the room and walked to the window. She stood there a moment, looking across at Dudley's living room window. She sighed. "He seems awfully down in the dumps to me. I wondered what you thought."

"Do you think anything is wrong with him?" Ella turned onto her side, facing the window.

"Well, I'm not certain," said Lorna, "but I think Dudley may be feeling a little—old."

"Oh, but that's silly. Why should Dudley feel—"

"He's thirty now, you know."

"That's true—"

"And none of us paid much attention to his birthday. We haven't been paying much attention to him at all lately. He may be feeling a little neglected."

"Oh."

"He might feel that—oh, I don't know how to put it—he might feel that the romance has gone from his life."

"That's a terrible thing," said Ella. She got up from the bed and stood beside Lorna, looking in the direction of Dudley's house. "His light's on. He's home now," she said. "Do you think I should—"

"That's a fine idea!" said Lorna. "Why don't you go over and try to cheer him up."

"All right. If you think it would help."

"Don't let him see that you're worried about him, of course—"

"Oh, I wouldn't."

"And—try to show him that he's—not too old to be interesting—to a girl your age. Flirt with him a little."

"Mother!"

"It's the one thing that's certain to make him feel rejuvenated."

"Well, I—"

"Brush your hair. And put on that sweater that buttons up the back."

"I thought you didn't approve of that sweater."

"I—oh, don't bother about what I think. Dudley's sure to like it."

When she had finished the dishes, Lorna went into the living room and sat at the piano with the lights off. Herb was off playing cards with the Spotters Club, and Ella was in Dudley's arms, where she was rediscovering, to her surprise, a set of sensations that she thought she'd never experience again and learning, for the first time, that love is not a homogenized, unvarying blend. In the dark, Lorna began to play "Lake Serenity Serenade."

One afternoon a couple of weeks later, while a team at the University of Pennsylvania was hard at work on the first electronic computer (the "electronic numerical integrator and calculator," or ENIAC), thereby hastening the eventual obsolescense of the slide rule, Lorna was alone in the kitchen, whipping up a batch of potato salad and listening to *The Loves of Ellen Burch* on the radio. Dudley appeared at the back door, tapping on the window, fogging the glass with his breath. Lorna motioned to him to come in, and he did. He closed the door behind him and stood on the mat. "Lorna," he asked, "is Ella home?"

"No," said Lorna. "She's at Emily's."

"Good," said Dudley. He began pulling his galoshes off. "You and I have to talk."

"Oh?" said Lorna. "What about?"

"About Ella," said Dudley. An organ crescendo came from the radio. Ellen Burch, a young girl with dreams, had arrived at an important fork in her young life just as Dudley had arrived at the back door. Lorna wondered whether she had decided to travel to Patagonia with the darkly intriguing Reynaldo or stay in Beaverton with Dave. Two actors portraying the Bullard Brothers began an advertisement for Bullard Brothers' Double-Roasted Coffee. "It's roasted," said the first. "And roasted again," said the second. "For twice the coffee flavor," they said together. "So your second cup is almost as good as your first."

"Do you want some coffee, Dudley?" asked Lorna.

"Yes, thank you, that would be nice," said Dudley.

Lorna struck a match and lit the gas under what was left of the morning coffee.

"Poor Ella," said Lorna. She stuck a fork into one of the potatoes and found it not quite done. "I've felt so sorry for her." A male chorus sang the Bullard Brothers' jingle. "She just seemed to fall apart when Buster was killed. She simply couldn't imagine a future without him in it. Do you know what I mean?"

"Yes, I do," said Dudley. He sat at the kitchen table, a square table with wooden legs and a metal, enamel-coated top, white with black edges. With his fingernail, he traced zigzag routes through the network of scratches and knife cuts on the tabletop. The organ played the Ellen Burch theme. "It's quite odd, the way people think of the future," Dudley offered. "Some of them seem to have the expectation—the hope, I should say—that they will turn a corner one day and find that everything is new, all is changed, yet others seem to hope for just the opposite, that things to come will somehow be just as they've been before, that life will stop in a way, freeze, like a snapshot." Lorna poured coffee for Dudley.

"You're missing a chance to see the world beyond Beaverton," said Reynaldo.

"I know, Reynaldo," said Ellen, "but, well, you know what Emerson said about travel."

"People like that," said Dudley, "want copies of the same snapshot, strung out from here to eternity. They want to be able to think that they already know what they'll be pasting on the blank pages of the photo album of their lives. Do you follow me?"

"Yes, Dudley," said Lorna.

"No," said Reynaldo, icily, "I do not."

"I suppose," said Dudley, "some of those people are so pleased with their lives that they simply want to continue as they are, to 'let well enough alone,' but more of them, I think, *fear* the future. They would rather have *nothing* happen to them than to have anything else go wrong. I hope I'm not getting too philosophical for you, Lorna."

"Oh, no," said Lorna. She turned back to her work to hide her smile. "I follow you."

"He said, 'Traveling is a fool's paradise,'" said Ellen.

"This, I think, was Ella's situation," said Dudley.

"Yes, I can see that," said Lorna.

"Now I have something shocking to say, Lorna."

"Perhaps you will find that your Beaverton is a fool's paradise," said Reynaldo.

"Yes?" said Lorna. *My God,* she thought, *what if he's fallen in love with Ella?* When she had sent Ella to Dudley's, she hadn't fully considered what might result, she had just had an inspired idea for pulling Ella up from the dumps she was down in. Since then, she had begun to wonder whether she had done the right thing. Would Ella remain forever in love with Dudley? Lorna had begun to worry that she might. And now, if Dudley was serious about her—

"That's something I'll have to find out, I guess," said Ellen.

Dudley pushed his cup and saucer away from him. He put his hands flat on the table. He bowed his head. He said, "Ella has—I may as well be direct—fallen in love with me."

"Yes, I know," said Lorna, without thinking.

Dudley's face went white. "Has she—confided in you?" he asked.

"Oh, of course she has," said Lorna.

"I'm trying to be delicate about this," said Dudley.

"I'll always remember you, Reynaldo," said Ellen.

"I want you to understand, Lorna, that Ella had developed a deep and passionate love for me."

"Yes, yes," said Lorna. She turned to her work again. She stabbed the fork into a potato, pulled it out of the pot, and began peeling it.

"I think it's just as well that she has," said Dudley.

"Yes," said Lorna. She didn't turn around. She worked at the potato.

"I have no doubt about that," said Reynaldo.

"I don't mean to shock or upset you," said Dudley, "but I think that I am just what Ella needed. I think that by falling in love with me she has broken the spell, so to speak. I have played the part of the handsome prince in a fairy tale, freeing the virgin—ah—freeing the princess—from her enchantment."

Lorna compressed her lips and applied herself to the potato.

"What is necessary now," said Dudley, "is to free her from her enchantment with me."

"Good-bye, Reynaldo," said Ellen.

"Yes!" said Lorna. Hope filled her like a breath of the sweet mountain air of Chacallit. She forked another potato. *Dudley, you pompous dope,* she thought, *you're exactly right.*

"You must admit," said Dudley, "that we are not exactly a match. Ella's a darling girl, wonderfully attractive, with all the freshness of youth and so on, but I think I would be just too much for her."

"I'm sure," said Lorna.

"Good-bye, Ellen," said Reynaldo. "You were—an amusing diversion."

"I've given quite a bit of thought to this," Dudley went on, "and I've decided that it would be best for me to go away for a while. I'll be called away on family business—perhaps a death—or—no, perhaps not—money troubles, then. I'll stay away until Ella finds someone better suited to her, someone who—"

There was a knock at the door. Dudley and Lorna turned but saw no one. Ellen opened the door. "Is that Reynaldo guy gone?" asked Dave.

"It was the radio," said Lorna.

"'That Reynaldo guy' has not yet gone," said Reynaldo, "but he was just—" Lorna reached up and turned the radio off.

Dudley went on talking. Lorna turned her back on him and returned to her work. She finished peeling the potatoes, sliced them, put them into a huge crockery bowl, poured vinegar over them, and began tossing them. While she worked, she wore a small, contented smile that Dudley couldn't see, and she hummed, so softly that Dudley couldn't hear, the up-tempo novelty version of "Lake Serenity Serenade" that Kay Kyser had made popular that winter. The kitchen filled with the odor of warm vinegar.

Dudley said, "Did you hear me, Lorna?"

"What?" said Lorna. She turned around and was surprised to find Dudley at the door, with coat and galoshes on, ready to go. "Oh, I'm sorry Dudley," she said. "I did hear you. Yes. You'll go away. Fine. It's best. You're right. Ella will find someone else. We'll see you when you get back."

They were startled by a knock at the door. Standing outside, his face framed in the window, his breath freezing on the glass, was Bert Leroy.

Ella and Bert were married in a month. They had no money, and Bert had no job. They couldn't afford a place of their own, so they were going to have to live either with Bert's parents or with Ella's.

"Oh, Mother," said Ella, "I *couldn't* live there. I'd feel so *funny* if we did. I'd always be thinking about—about Buster. It *is* a nice place. They have lots of room—it's a big house—three bedrooms. But, oh, I *couldn't* do it. I mean, I know there would be more room for us there, but, gee, I'd feel I was always bumping into Buster. And Buster's bedroom is larger than Bert's. What if we moved in there? I'd feel so *queer* if we were sleeping there and—everything."

Ella proposed that she and Bert move into the room that Herb had built as a den, the room behind the hidden door, the room where Mrs. Stolz had lived. To make this possible, Mrs. Stolz would have to go. Lorna took it upon herself, since she had been the one who had insisted that they bring Mrs. Stolz home, to call her.

"This is Lorna Piper," she said when the call was answered. "May I speak to Mrs. Stolz, please?"

"Oh!" said the voice at the other end. "Oh, I—this is her daughter, Mrs. Geiger."

"Oh, Mrs. Geiger," said Lorna. "I was sorry to hear about Mrs. Stolz's grandson—about your son, I mean. I—I'm sorry, I don't know what else to say."

"Oh, that's all right. Nobody does. It's just—something you have to live with. It's part of God's plan."

"It is?"

"Why, yes. Yes, of course it is."

"Well, I— Maybe you're right. It's a grisly thought, though."

"What?"

"Well, what kind of God would— Mrs. Geiger, may I speak to Mrs. Stolz?"

"Oh, yes. Yes. I'll get her. It will just take a minute—no, not even a minute—a second. Do you want to hang up and call back?"

"No, I'll wait if you can get her right away."

"I can. I will. Just wait." There was a pause. "Don't get upset, now. Don't hang up."

"I—won't," said Lorna. "Don't worry. I'll wait."

Mrs. Stolz's daughter put her hand over the mouthpiece of the phone and called out, "Mother! Motherrrrrrrr! Hurry, it's long distance."

Lorna pressed the handset to her bosom and whispered to Herb and Ella, who were standing beside her, "Oh, Herb, her daughter is terribly distraught. She's—she's irrational."

Mrs. Stolz bustled into her daughter's kitchen. "It's that woman, that crazy woman, Mrs. Piper," said her daughter.

Mrs. Stolz put her fingertips to her lips. "Oh, dear," she said. "I—I don't know what to say to her."

"You have to say *something*—it's long distance," said her daughter. "She's—she's in a bad way, I think. She doesn't make sense."

Mrs. Stolz took the earpiece from her daughter and stood at the old phone. "Hello?" she called into it.

"Hello, Mrs. Stolz. It's Lorna."

"Is anything wrong?"

"No. No. Well, nothing more than all the things that have already gone wrong."

"Oh, dear. Maybe you should be resting, Lorna. This telephone call will be awfully expensive. Herb might be upset—"

"Herb's right here, Mrs. Stolz. Don't you worry about the cost. I—we—Herb and I—and Ella—wanted to call to see how you were."

"Oh. Perhaps I should speak to Herb."

"Certainly. You can speak to Herb in a minute. But I wanted to ask you how your daughter is doing."

"Oh, she's fine, just fine."

"Now, Mrs. Stolz, she can't really be 'just fine,' can she? She just lost her son. She must be terribly upset."

"Oh, yes. Well, yes, she is."

"Ella was, too, of course."

"Ella? Oh! I forgot. Poor Ella. That Leroy boy. The smart one."

"Well, I have some good news, though. Ella is going to marry *Bert* Leroy."

"She is? The other one? Are you sure? Perhaps I should speak to Herb."

"Of course. In just a minute. I wanted to talk to you about Ella and Bert a little more first. They're going to need a place to live."

"Oh."

"They thought of staying with Bert's family. They really have more room than we do. But——"

Mrs. Stolz saw a chance, and she took it. "Oh, I don't think they should," she said. "Have them move into my room. A girl needs her mother at a time like this. She needs a mother's advice. She's bound to have questions, you know. Questions, and doubts. Why don't you let me speak to Herb."

"I will, but I'm not finished. Are you sure you wouldn't mind if they took your room?"

"Oh, no. I wouldn't mind. My daughter needs me here. Yours needs you there. Lorna, I want you to *promise* me that you'll have Ella and her young man——"

"Bert."

"You *must* have them stay with you. They could be quite comfortable in my room. And the baby——"

"Baby?"

"Oh, there's certain to be a baby! The baby can have Ella's room. It's perfect. Now let me speak to Herb."

"She wants to speak to you," said Lorna.

Herb took the phone. "Hello?" he said.

"Herb," said Mrs. Stolz, "I can't help you anymore. I'm sorry, but I just can't. I'm too old. I need a rest. Ella and—is she really going to marry that Bert?"

"Yes, yes, she is."

"Well. Ella and Bert can help you, and the three of you will be able to keep everything going smoothly. I'm sure you can. I'm afraid you'll have to."

"I'm not sure I understand. Do you mean the housework?" asked Herb.

"Yes," said Mrs. Stolz. "The *housework,* of course. The housework."

When he hung up, Herb put his hand on Lorna's shoulder and sighed. "The poor old thing," he said. "She got so attached to the housework. It seemed to be all she could think about."

Mrs. Stolz placed the earpiece on its hook and stood still for a moment with her eyes closed. She held her breath. She felt a great sense of relief. She was waiting to see if she began to feel guilty. When she had held her breath for as long as she could and still hadn't begun to feel that she was doing something wrong, she exhaled and permitted herself a smile. "I'm sure they'll be able to take fine care of her," she said.

Herb and Lorna packed Mrs. Stolz's clothes and books and knick-knacks in a crate and delivered it to the Babbington railroad station, where they had it shipped to her daughter's home. When the crate arrived, Mrs. Stolz had it taken to a small hotel not unlike the River Sound in Babbington. There she lived quietly and happily for the rest of her days.

Bert and Ella moved into the room behind the bookcase. I was born in the fall.

16

In Which
Herb 'n' Lorna
Fan Ardor's
Still-Flickering
Flame

For the next five years, Bert and Ella and I lived with Herb and Lorna. The automobile business entered a boom period right after the war. Business was brisk at Babbington Studebaker, and Herb was able to get Bert a job there, in the service department. He and Bert left for work together every morning and came home together every night. My mother and grandmother stayed at home, kept house, and took care of me.

Bert worked hard in the service department. He and Ella opened a savings account at the Babbington Five Cents Bank, and each week they put a little something away for The House, which is to say, the house that they hoped to have someday, when Ella and Bert and I could afford a place of our own. Because Bert insisted on paying rent for the rooms that we used and contributing three-fifths of the cost of food and heat and all the other expenses of running the ménage on No Bridge Road (despite Lorna's calculations of the true, accurate, much lower percentage of those expenses that the three of us represented), the savings account grew slowly, far more slowly than Ella's yearning and disappointment. Bert took on a second job, working evenings and Saturdays at Speedy's Reliable Service, the garage across from the police station, on Main Street, the spot where Herb and Lorna had stopped to ask directions on the rainy night when they first arrived in Babbington more than twenty years before. This garage is, in my memory, a trim, exciting, happy place. It was the place where my mother and father and I spent our Saturdays. Because Bert came home late at night during the week, neither of us saw much of him then. Saturdays and Sundays were our only chance. On Saturdays Speedy took the day off, and Bert was in charge of the station. My mother and I would spend the day at the station, watching him work. My mother would buy bottles of Coca-Cola from a machine that resembled a squat red refrigerator, and sometimes she would let me buy a scant handful of nuts or a gumball nearly too large for my mouth, from machines that stood side by side on steel poles. My mother called these machines Mr. Nuts and Miss Gumball, because they looked like a pair of busts, one male, one female. Mr. Nuts seemed strong, hard-working, and opinionated. He had a thick neck, a head of cubic stolidity, and a gaping rectangular mouth. He wore a cast-metal cap that resembled the ones workingmen wore in those days. Miss Gumball was smaller. She had a slender neck, a spherical head, and a mouth shaped in an O of surprise. Her head was filled with a riot of colored balls. If they'd been able to speak, he would have groused and grumbled, and she would have been light-hearted and witty.

I remember well the sounds and smells of Saturdays in the garage, and, because the days I spent there were so uniformly pleasant, I developed a lifelong affection by association for the odors of gasoline, brake fluid, and motor oil and for the sounds of the bell that rang *ching-chang* when a car drove over the pressure hose, the quite different bell that rang *ding* at widening intervals from the air pumps when someone was filling a tire, and the bell that rang *bing* (pause) *bing* (pause) *bing* with measured regularity when Bert pumped gas. I realize now, recalling those days, that they couldn't have been as pleasant for Bert, not only because he was at work, but because my mother's favorite topic, about which she could chatter tirelessly for entire Saturdays, while Bert fixed flat tires, pumped gas, changed oil, and so on, was The House.

◆　　◆　　◆

Herb built me a model of Speedy's Reliable Service. It was wonderfully complete. There were wooden cars, gas pumps with little rubber hoses, an air pump with a thinner red hose, cans of oil and antifreeze on the shelves inside, a grease rack, tires, tools, a trash heap of engine parts and old tires in the back, and best of all, miniatures of Mr. Nuts and Miss Gumball. Tiny pebbles that Lorna had collected at the beach, each selected for its nutlike shape, filled Mr. Nuts's head, and BB's, painted in gumball colors, filled Miss Gumball's.

The five of us ate, I calculate, two hundred fifty Sunday dinners at the dining room table, making allowances for Sundays when we were on vacation and Sunday dinners we ate as guests in other people's houses. Of these, about eighty were pot roast with string beans and Lorna's warm German potato salad, seventy were fricasseed chicken and dumplings, sixty were sauerbraten with red cabbage and potato dumplings (*Kartoffelklösse*), ten (Thanksgivings and Christmases) were turkey, and the remaining thirty were a miscellany.

Sometimes we went to May's cottage at the beach. I particularly enjoyed playing under the boardwalks, where the sun shone through in thin, brilliant lines that wrinkled on the wind-rippled surface of the sand. Often, on clear nights, we would all lie on our backs on the sand, listen to the surf, and look at the stars.

These were wonderful years. They were the ones during which I formed the notion of Herb and Lorna as cuddly and comforting, as Guppa and Gumma. I didn't notice anything that might have suggested to me a life for them without reference to me. I certainly didn't notice anything to suggest that my grandparents lived secret lives, that they were secretly burning with passion, that they were the geniuses behind the art of American erotic jewelry.

But it is amazing to me, when I cast my memory back to that time, to discover how much I saw but did not notice, how much I noticed but ignored. I remember, for instance, a time, on one of those nights at the beach, when May got to talking about Garth and began to wonder what had become of him, and began to cry. Bert said to me, "Peter. Come here. Take this." He gave me a bottle. "Go carry this over to the other side of those dunes and bury it."

When I had finished, and I came back over the top of the dune, May and Herb and Lorna were walking away together, toward the cottage, and my parents were waiting for me alone. Herb and Lorna were on either side of May, with their arms around her. She stopped and turned around to face the sea, forcing them to turn with her. She gesticulated toward the dark water. "He's dead!" she cried. "I'm sure of it now! He's dead!"

Well, I can't say that I recall that particular *occasion, but I certainly did go through a period when I was* quite *a tragic figure. When Garth—*took off—*he left a note behind. Well, it was positively embarrassing. "I love you—you're an extraordinary woman—you're beautiful—but a man has yearnings—I'm not the husband type, I guess—" That sort of thing. My God! He actually wrote that—"I'm not the husband type, I guess." Well, I mean* really! *He might have done the decent thing. He could have written, "Darling, I* have cancer *and I can't* bear *the thought of being a burden to you, so I'm going off to* kill *myself."* Yearnings! Not the husband type!

I tried to pretend that something awful had happened to him—shanghaied, you know, or a victim of amnesia, wandering in Calcutta *somewhere in a stupor of pathetic confusion. Well, not even I could believe it, so I began telling people that he had died on a business trip, in Baltimore. I don't know why I chose Baltimore. Well. I began dressing in black. Loose, robelike things—quite attractive getups, really. I was a striking sight—sort of Greta Garbo playing Georgia O'Keefe.*

I began spending weekends at the cottage, alone, just drinking by myself. I was all right when I was with other people—at Whitey's, or anywhere, as long as I wasn't alone. But at the beach I would just fall apart. *Herb and Lorna saved me. I mean that they absolutely* saved me. *They caught on, you see, and then they* wouldn't *leave me alone.*

I certainly couldn't have understood all of that at the time, not even if anyone had wanted to try to explain it to me, but I knew that something awful had happened to May, and I could see that all the others were affected by it. Perhaps I shouldn't be surprised to see, looking back, that my little self wanted nothing to do with it.

Nor did I see that there was tension in the house. I was happy there. I supposed that everyone else was, and supposing it to be so, I saw it as so. I would never have imagined that, one night, Herb lay in bed, awake, imagining how Bert and Ella must feel, at night, lying in bed in the room down the hall, inhibited by the fact of their living in his house, forced to be so quiet, so contained, constrained to whisper, so tense and awkward. He realized that the feelings he ascribed to them were those he felt himself.

"Lorna," he whispered. "Lorna, are you awake?"

"Mmm."

"It must be awful for them, Lorna."

"What?"

"Living here with us."

"Oh. I know."

"You remember how you felt about living with your parents?"

"Indeed I do."

"This is worse."

"I think you're right."

"Back then, neither of us ever thought about what it might have been like for your *parents* if we had lived there. I mean, well, I never thought that they would feel—inhibited."

Lorna sat up. "I never thought about them at all. I suppose I thought they were too old to care. I suppose I thought that when they went to bed they just went to sleep and that was that."

"Now we're finding out," said Herb. "We have to whisper at night, just the way we would have if we had lived at your parents' house."

"And we have to be careful about not having one drink too many."

"We have to talk in code."

"And we haven't set fire to anything for quite a while."

"We're hiding from them."

"And they're hiding from us, too."

"They're so quiet at night that sometimes I catch myself straining to try to hear something."

"I know what you mean. Sometimes I worry that their marriage is breaking up. I never hear any—crackling flames. If it weren't for Peter, I would have wondered whether they ever—well—"

"—struck a match."

"We've got to get them out of here, Herb."

"How much do you think they have saved?"

"Oh, I don't know, but it can't be much."

"I think I could raise some money pretty quickly, Lorna."

"You could?"

"I could—I'm sure I could. There are—a couple of people who are going to be coming due for new cars that I could kind of hurry along, I think, and the—I forgot to tell you this—the company is having a contest—it's a contest for top salesman in the country—they haven't announced it or anything yet—and the whole thing is going to be kept quiet—no ceremony or anything like that—no hoopla—just a cash award, and—"

"I have an idea, too!" said Lorna. "Mr. Berwick—"

"—wants you back at the slide rule factory?"

"No—better than that. He wants me to make some jewelry for Mrs. Berwick—very special. He's been after me about it for some time. I don't know why I never mentioned it. I guess I was a little afraid of it—it's a bigger job than I've ever tried before. Well, I'm going to do it! He's willing to pay very well."

They lay there in silence for a while, contented, scheming, each planning how to return to the coarse-goods trade, which they had long neglected. Herb planned some bogus business trips. Lorna planned to enlist May's help. But then another thought came to them. How would they get Bert to accept the money? It was easy enough for them to imagine duping each other, but they didn't immediately see how they could fool anyone else.

"Lorna—" said Herb.

"I know. How are we going to get Bert to accept the money?"

"Yeah. He's so damned stubborn about it."

"I'll think of something," said Lorna. "Let me worry about that part."

Herb kept a metal box on the shelf under his workbench in the cellar. It was painted green, with a white skull and crossbones painted on the top. Once, he opened this box for me and explained, with firm seriousness, that I must never open it because the jars and tins and bottles in it held acids and other chemicals that could burn me, even kill me. In a tray on top, like the tray in a toolbox, there were containers of muriatic acid, soldering paste, lye, and so on. He didn't lift the tray to show me what was in the space under the tray, but I supposed, as I now understand he intended me to suppose, that it held more of the same. It was here, I'm sure, that Herb kept his coarse goods, sketches for new ideas that came to him from time to time, and a few experimental prototypes.

Lorna kept some of hers, I believe, in her kitchen canisters, under the flour, the sugar, the corn meal, the rice, and the oatmeal. I remember a moment that puzzled me when it occurred but now, in the light of what I've learned, makes sense at last. Once, not long before my parents and I moved into our own little house, I startled Lorna while she was fussing with those kitchen canisters. She was emptying them into paper bags.

I called out to her, "What are you doing, Gumma?" She nearly dropped the canister she was holding.

"Oh!" she said. "You startled me, Peter. Close your eyes. Quickly! You mustn't see what I'm doing."

"How come?"

"Just close your eyes," she said. "It's a surprise. I'm—going to bake something—something special. I don't want you to see it before I'm done."

"But why are you dumping everything out?"

"I had to empty these canisters so that I could give them a good cleaning. When they're nice and clean I'll fill them back up again, and then I'll make something special."

She sent me out of the room. I think, now, that she was retrieving pieces of erotic jewelry from the bottoms of the canisters, that these were her caches and that I had very nearly discovered her secret. That night, for dessert, we had pineapple upside-down cake, which was a favorite of mine at the time.

Lorna returned to Chacallit and visited her uncle Luther. She was able to sell him everything she had on hand, but Luther was seventy-three now, ill, and nearly blind. He hadn't been active in the coarse-goods business for nearly thirteen years. He squinted through an enormous magnifying glass at the pieces Lorna had brought, and he told her that he didn't consider these anywhere near the quality of her best work. The prices he offered Lorna were thirteen-year-old prices, but Lorna had no other outlet for her work, so she took what he offered her. He had made some inquiries before she arrived, so he had several prototypes for new couples to show her. Lorna examined them, closely and carefully, and as she studied them her stomach grew cold, her throat tightened, her eyes moistened, her fingers began to tremble. "These——" she said, and she was astonished to find that she was about to cry. She took her handkerchief out and coughed in it, dabbed quickly at her eyes. "These aren't very good," she said. She swallowed. "They're not from the same person—the same man—are they? They're not. I can tell they're not."

"No," said Luther. "There are quite a few people doing this stuff now. But, to tell you the truth, they're not as good as they once were. None of this stuff is today. No one takes pains. No one——"

"What—what became of the other one—the other man—the one who was so good?"

"Became of him? I don't know. How *should* I know? I certainly never knew who he was or ever wanted to know. If I *did* know, I wouldn't tell you, Lorna. You know that. Discretion is the foundation of business. I have always made that my watchword. One of my watchwords. You can be thankful of it. I'm sure you wouldn't have wanted me to going telling anyone who asked that *you* were the author of some of this work, would you?"

"To tell *you* the truth, Uncle Luther, sometimes I almost wish you had. Sometimes I wish *everyone* knew about it."

"Don't be foolish. You would be an absolute pariah. Your husband would abandon you. Your daughter would turn her back on you. You don't know what you're saying."

"I'm sure you're right," said Lorna. "Still, I wish I knew what had happened to him—the man who——"

"I can tell you what probably happened to him. What probably happened to him is what will happen to all of us in God's own time. He probably died."

Lorna was heartbroken.

Herb sold what he had on hand, but he had no way at all to sell any new designs. His uncle Ben had been dead for eleven years. Since Herb wasn't about to risk trying to make a coarse-goods connection of his own in Chacallit, his new designs never went any further than sketches, and the sketches never went any farther than the bottom of the metal box that he kept under his workbench.

It took a couple of months of coarse-goods work for Herb and Lorna to accumulate enough for a down payment on a small house for Bert and Ella. Lorna prepared the full Sunday-dinner spread for the occasion of their presenting the money: carrot and celery sticks, olives, sweet gherkins, Waldorf salad, fricasseed chicken, dumplings, peas, chocolate cake.

Herb paced the kitchen floor while Lorna got things ready to go out to the table. "Come on, Lorna," he said. "Tell me what you're going to tell them."

"Don't you have any confidence in me?" she asked.

"Of course I do. I just—are you sure Bert will believe it?"

"Well, no."

"No?"

"No, I'm not *sure,* but I think so. Here, take this chicken out to the table and have them come and sit down."

When Ella and Bert came to the table, Herb began pouring beer for everyone. There wasn't quite enough left in the bottle to fill his own glass. He started for the kitchen.

"Oh, Herrrrb," said Lorna. "Forget about it, can't you? I want them to see what we have for them."

"Now, be patient, Lorna," said Herb. "They've been waiting for five years. They can wait a minute longer."

"But *I* can't," said Lorna.

Herb went into the kitchen, got another quart bottle of beer from the refrigerator, opened it, brought it into the dining room, filled his glass, and started for the kitchen again.

"Herrrb!" said Lorna. Herb chuckled. He set the bottle on the sideboard and sat down at the head of the table.

"We have something to give to you," said Herb. He turned toward Lorna, and she lifted a napkin to unveil, on the table between them, a small box, wrapped in white paper and tied with a white ribbon.

"This is for you," said Lorna.

"Shall I open it?" asked Ella.

"Sure," said Herb. "Go ahead."

Ella untied the ribbon, tore the paper away, and opened the box.

"I—I—oh—" was all she could say. She pushed the box toward Bert, who looked into it and frowned. He took a stack of bills from the box.

"Now, Herb," he said. "What is this all about? You know how I—"

Herb just smiled. He had no idea what story Lorna had invented, but he said, with every confidence that what he said was true, "Lorna can tell you all about it."

"Herb's too modest to tell you himself," she said. Herb coughed and looked into his plate. "All these years, he's been investing the rent money you've been paying us."

"You have?" said Bert.

"I should say so," said Herb.

"He's been investing it in the Studebaker company," said Lorna. "And he's done very well. This is the profit."

"Well, that's nice," said Bert, "but we can't——"

"You didn't listen to what I said," said Lorna. "This is the *profit*. It's not the money you paid us, just the money Herb made from the money you gave us."

Bert shook his head. "I'm still not sure about——"

Lorna looked hard into his eyes. "Of course, we kept out an amount equal to the interest we would have made if we had put the money in the bank," she said.

"Well," said Bert, "in that case——"

When Bert and Ella and I were settled in a little house of our own, Herb and Lorna were alone at last, truly private for the first time ever. On their first night alone, Herb began bustling around as soon as he got home from work, laying a fire in the fireplace, plumping the pillows on the sofa, humming "Lake Serenity Serenade" while he worked. As soon as he and Lorna had finished dinner, Herb lit the fire and began fussing at it with the bellows. When he had it going to his satisfaction, he went into the kitchen and tugged Lorna away from the sink, tugged her, against her coy objections, into the living room, to the sofa, where he sat her down and sat himself beside her and put his arm around her.

"I've been waiting years for this," he said.

They kissed.

"Mrs. Stolz," called Herb, "can you hear me?"

They listened to the silence.

"Elllllla!" he called. "Are you listening? Your mother and I are spooning!"

Lorna giggled.

"I'm unbuttoning her dress!" called Herb.

They brushed cheeks.

"She's squeezing my——"

Lorna put her hand over his mouth. "Shhhh," she said. "We do have—"

A loud and urgent banging at the front door.

"—neighbors."

"Oh, no," said Herb. He hopped up and ran to the door. "Who is it?" he called.

"It's Dudley!" cried Dudley. "I was walking by and I heard shouting. Is there some trouble?"

"No," said Herb. "No trouble."

"You're quite certain, Herb?" asked Dudley.

"Dudley," said Herb. "Go home. I'm making love to my wife."

Silence. A muffled laugh, from the sofa. Another muffled laugh, from outside, on the porch.

"Good night, Herb," said Dudley. Footsteps down the front steps. A pause. Footsteps back up the front steps. "Have fun."

Herb returned to the sofa, where he and Lorna allowed themselves to carry on like a couple of passionate youngsters, the passionate youngsters who had made love in that rowboat on Lake Serenity, whose sexual inventiveness had created the animated coarse-goods business. In a while they moved to the floor, in front of the fire. The importance of that fire, what it meant to them, was another thing that I couldn't have known then.

Every fall, during those years when Bert and Ella and I had lived with Herb and Lorna, all five of us would drive upstate to buy firewood. Herb had constructed a small trailer just for hauling wood, and he and Bert, with the help and advice of Lorna and Ella, would get this hitched to the car the night before, so that we could leave before dawn the next day. We would get up and dress in the dark, and we would slip out of the house in silence, so that we wouldn't disturb the neighbors, but also because all of us enjoyed the unusual nature of what we were doing, I think. We would eat our breakfast on the road, in the car, while Herb drove. There were always hard-boiled eggs, baking-powder biscuits, fruit, coffee, and milk. The coffee was kept in a tall Thermos bottle protected by a cylindrical sleeve of leather. The milk and cream were in mayonnaise or jelly jars. The butter was packed into a crockery bowl. Salt and pepper were folded into tiny envelopes of waxed paper.

Lorna sat in the front, beside Herb, and she handed him his egg, his biscuits, and his coffee when he asked for them, so that he could keep driving. When he finished eating, he would say, "Would you ignite me—"

He would pause, turn toward Lorna, and wink. She would smile—sometimes even giggle—and redden—sometimes even poke Herb—as if it were possible for us to understand his reference to the night the ballroom burned.

"—a nicotine, please?" he would finish at last. Lorna would light him a cigarette, a Kool.

Before noon, we would reach the place where we bought the wood. I remember it as a farm, with chickens in the yard outside the house. All of us would work to load the trailer. I carried the kindling. Herb and Bert would concern themselves for some time with making the load stable and tight and safe, and there were likely to be disagreements between them about the best way to accomplish this. Lorna and Ella were vigilant, concerned, compassionate peacekeepers, but I think that it may have been on these wood-buying trips, more than at any time during the routines of daily life in close quarters at home, that the strain of living together showed most clearly. At the time, I couldn't have understood why.

We would eat a picnic lunch, and then we would drive back to Babbington. "It will be dusk by the time we get back," Lorna would say. "We'll all have to work like the dickens to get the wood stacked under the porch before it's too dark to see what we're doing."

It *would* be dusk by the time we got back, and we would all work like the dickens to get the wood stacked under the porch before it was too dark to see, but we never quite made it. The last bit of stacking was always done by the light of a kerosene lantern, assisted by flashlights that grew dimmer by the minute. When at last the wood was all stacked, Herb and Bert would carry some in for the first fire of the new season, and we would all sit in the living room and drink cocoa and watch the flames. We would eat dinner in the living room that night, something that Lorna and Ella had made the day before and just had to heat up, like chowder or stew. After a while, Lorna would begin to yawn, elaborately. Soon, she would insist that Herb come to bed.

"But I'm enjoying the fire, Lorna," he might say.

"Herb," she would say, "let's go to bed. Let Ella and Bert enjoy the fire by themselves. Come on, Peter, you come to bed, too. It's time for you to get to bed."

Bert and Ella and I couldn't have known that for all the years they had lived in that house they had wanted to make love in front of the first fire of the season.

17

In Which
Herb 'n' Lorna Come
to the Brink
of Despair

After a postwar slump, the demand for slide rules began to pick up, and Edwin Berwick asked Lorna to return to work. At about the time when she began her new duties as supervisor of the cursor department at Hargrove Slide Rules, technology took another step toward the slide rule's eventual obsolescence when the first programmable computer—that is, the first computer that could store a program in its memory—became operational: UNIVAC 1.

Herb never did become the top Studebaker salesman in the country, but he was the top salesman at Babbington Studebaker year after year, and that distinction won for him and Lorna several trips to South Bend, Indiana, home of the Studebaker company. During the dozen years or so after Bert and Ella and I left, Herb and Lorna had a new car nearly every year. They owned a 1949 Land Cruiser, a bullet-nosed 1950 Commander Regal DeLuxe convertible, a 1952 Commander State Starliner hardtop, a beautiful white 1953 Commander Starliner hardtop, a 1955 President State hardtop, a 1956 Golden Hawk, a 1958 Commander Provincial station wagon, and a 1960 Lark VIII DeLuxe convertible.

For some time, Herb had been developing a vague desire to do some camping. This desire was the child of another, stronger desire, the desire to make some of the dozens of useful campsite gadgets he had seen plans for in the handyman magazines he subscribed to. He was itching to get started on some of these.

One evening Lorna said, "Herb, you remember when we drew those arcs on the map and chose Babbington as a place to live."

"Mm," said Herb.

"Have you ever wondered what it would have been like if we had moved to West Burke, Vermont, instead?"

It was all the opening Herb needed. In the months that followed, he bought basic camping gear and built a wind-powered generator, a miniature refrigerator, an inflatable sofa, a campfire oven, collapsible cots, cotside reading lamps, and a Geiger counter hidden in a picnic basket, since it *was* possible to strike it rich with a uranium find, and if he was going to be tramping around in the mountains, he might as well be doing something useful. The following summer they made a camping visit to West Burke. They returned every summer for the next fifteen years.

I remember those trips well. Bert and Ella and I went along on many of them. I remember a campground at the edge of a lake, surrounded by mountains. I wonder what I failed to notice, though. Did Herb and Lorna slip out of their tent on moonlit nights, row to the middle of the lake, and make love there? I don't know. I used to sleep right through the night.

Piper Poker survived the war, at least in the Spotters Club. The Spotters continued to meet weekly, at the home of a different member each week. Sometimes, on evenings when the club gathered at Herb and Lorna's, Lorna would baby-sit for Bert and Ella so that they could go out to see a movie. At other times she would go to visit one of her friends from work, or she would go to Whitey's and spend the evening with May. Piper Poker was the only game the Spotters played— until they began playing the stock market.

On one of those evenings, divorced from Lorna's cautious skepticism, Herb succumbed to the Piper failing. He let himself be convinced that the Spotters' buying a few shares of stock was an undertaking free of risk, since they would only invest money that they had already lost. That was the essence of the argument advanced by Bob Schoop, who proposed the venture.

"Look," Bob said, "it'll be fun, we might make some money, and it's a nothing-to-lose deal. Here's what I say we do: we skim something off the top of the winnings every week and put it aside. We use that as a fund to buy some stock. What have we got to lose? The winners still win—not quite as much, but they still win—and the losers would have lost anyway, so what's to lose?"

Poor Herb. He should have known better. He should have realized that this would lead to trouble. I think it may have been Lorna's ruse, the story she used to convince Bert to accept the money for the house, that made Herb think that perhaps, just possibly, the Piper curse had been lifted from him, that maybe he really could make some money by investing. Since there did seem to be nothing to lose, Herb and the others agreed to the plan.

From the start, the Spotters bought cautiously, and they made such small investments that they had, if not nothing to lose, next to nothing to lose. An aspect of their caution was their insistence on buying stock only if they had "inside information" about the company's condition and its future. The folly of trusting inside information is discussed in Lucille Prang's amusing little "nonbook" *A Thousand and One Wrong-Headed Notions* (great bathroom reading), under number 842, "They know more than you do":

> *Why do we think this? You've heard the argument: "The poop that you and I and the other schmoes can get our hands on isn't the real poop. Only they have access to the real poop, so they know what's what." They have inside information. They know the business. They must know what they're talking about. Well, let me tell you something: don't bet on it.*

The Spotters began following the stock quotations in the paper, and they pumped friends, family, and casual acquaintances for any bit of information that would give them the inside track on a good thing. When the first photographs and descriptions of the forthcoming Lark arrived at Babbington Studebaker, Herb decided at once that he had something important to pass along to the Spotters. He knew that the Lark was a car he could sell to people who had been turning him down for years. It was small but solid looking, inexpensive and economical, and, as Lorna had said at once when Herb showed her the first pictures of it, it was cute.

At the next gathering of the club, Herb could hardly contain himself. He delivered a thorough presentation. He passed the photos around. He displayed charts that compared the Lark and the Rambler, the only other small American car available at that time. He read a list of Babbingtonians whom he considered prime prospects for each Lark model, and he was able to explain exactly why a Lark was just the car for each person on the list. These were persuasive arguments for buying Studebaker stock, but more persuasive than any of those was the argument of Herb's own conviction. That was what impressed the Spotters most. Herb had inside information. Herb knew the automobile business. He must know what he was talking about. He certainly seemed convinced. This was their chance. Not only did the Spotters Club decide, unanimously, to buy stock in Studebaker, but two of the members ordered Larks.

When the Spotters bought, the price of Studebaker stock was low, Studebaker sales were low, and the company had debts of more than fifty million dollars. When the Lark was released, the picture began to change. Larks sold. Studebaker stock rose. The company moved into the black. The Spotters did well. They did so well that, secretly, each began buying more stock on his own. The fact that they were investing individually came out when Simon Misch mentioned that he expected to be able to send his son to college by selling "some of his Studebaker stock."

Herb was surprised. "I hadn't really thought of it as being divided up that way," he said. "But it does make sense. And it's a good cause. I guess if we all agree to sell some, we could—"

"Oh, I didn't mean the club's stock," said Simon. "I—uh—I've been buying a little on my own—now and then—whenever I've got some spare cash."

Others began admitting it, too. It was soon clear that all of them had been buying, and that they had been buying more and more heavily, using not merely spare cash, but money wrung from household budgets, withdrawn from savings, earned in overtime hours, even money from their children's paper routes. They had all come to think that this was the chance of a lifetime, that they were never likely to run on the inside track again.

Then the "big three"—General Motors, Ford, and Chrysler—brought out their compact cars—the Corvair, the Falcon, and the Valiant. Studebaker's advantage was lost. Sales began to fall. The company began an accelerating downward slide, like a runaway croquet ball in Chacallit, on its way down Ackerman Hill, headed for the chilly waters of the Whatsit.

Herb read the sales reports. He read the stock quotations. He read the company announcements. He listened to the rumors. He passed every scrap of information on to the Spotters, but he simply couldn't believe the clear, solid evidence he found, because he had so thoroughly convinced himself that Studebaker was on the right track. He preferred to believe the most unlikely of the encouraging rumors, the wildest of the optimistic forecasts. So fervent was he in his convictions that, as the price of Studebaker stock fell, he persuaded the Spotters to buy more. Herb was convinced, and he convinced the others, that with a full range of cars to sell, from the sporty Hawks and rumored Avanti to the practical little Lark, the company was in a perfect position to appeal to the entire vast and various stewpot of potential car buyers. The company would succeed. The stock would rise. All the Spotters believed him, and Herb believed himself. He also invested more and more heavily.

Slowly, as time passed and the fortunes of the company grew worse and worse, Herb came to see that he had finally done the foolish Piper thing. The Avanti would never have widespread appeal. The Lark would never outsell the other compacts. Studebaker would not recover. The stock would not rise. The Spotters would lose their money. So would he and Lorna. Herb was ashamed.

The essence of the Piper failing was a tendency to let the heart rule the mind. We all suffer from this disease at some times, to some degree. It has consequences other than bad investments. It makes some of us write books and compose music and paint pictures. It makes some of us try to restore two-hundred-year-old wooden houses or twenty-year-old British sports cars. It makes some us fall in love. It makes some of us insist that, of all the people who have collaborated on an error, we are supremely blameworthy. That is how Herb felt. He couldn't escape the feeling that all the blame for the losses the Spotters were going to suffer was his. He could think of only one way out, one way to make things right and relieve his conscience, and the key to the door that led to that way out was coarse-goods work. Herb hoped that he could earn enough money to buy the

Spotters' stock for what they had originally paid for it. (He expected, by the way, that they would refuse to sell. He thought they wouldn't want to let him increase his suffering to relieve theirs. He expected that he would have to persuade them that he was buying the stock because he still believed that he would make a profit on it. He was wrong. These feelings were merely further symptoms of the essential Piper failing.)

Fundamentally, the plan made sense. Herb had, however, no goods left to sell. The last of them had gone toward raising money for Bert and Ella's house. Uncle Ben was long dead, and Herb had no idea who Ben's contact in Chacallit had been. Throughout Herb's years in the business, he had never wanted to know, had never wanted to become so involved that he needed to know, so he had made it a point of honor to know nothing about aspects of the business that didn't concern him. Now, Herb couldn't imagine himself going to Chacallit and trying to make contact on his own. He thought, instead, that he would try to do all the work himself.

He could certainly design new pieces. He could certainly sell new pieces if he had some. If he could make them, he'd be set. He certainly tried.

He spent night after night in the cellar, pretending to work on one project or another—new camping gear, household gadgets, a shortwave radio for me—but actually he was trying to carve little men and women who could perform the ingenious, intriguing, and complex acts he had devised for them. He had no talent for it, and every figure was a failure. If he managed a leg that pleased him, it was likely to be attached to a trunk that seemed to belong to another figure altogether, someone much smaller, whose other leg was turned to the first at an angle that is never achieved by pairs of actual human legs. On the face of this poor figure appeared, in place of the desired expression of preorgasmic glee, a twisted grimace, as if his lover had, at what ought to have been the height of his pleasure, stabbed him in the back. Still, he thought of selling them, until the thought struck him that the figures were so grotesquely malformed that it would take a client of grotesquely malformed desires to be interested in them. They weren't beautiful. He would have been ashamed to sell them. He knew who could carve beautiful, elegant little figures, knew that she was sitting right upstairs, working at her puzzles and problems, but he couldn't bring himself to ask her.

Lorna couldn't do it all by herself, either, though she tried. She wanted desperately to help Herb out of his financial problems, and coarse goods were, she knew, her best hope for helping him.

"I tried," she told May, "but I can't do it. I wanted to make some of those animated figures, but it was ridiculous. Whenever Herb was down in the cellar, puttering away at his projects— I shouldn't say it that way. 'Puttering' makes it sound as if I'm belittling him. I'm glad he has those projects of his. They give him something to do. They keep his mind off his troubles. I was happy for him, really, when I thought of him down there puttering while I was giving myself a headache trying to figure out how to make those figures move their parts—"

"Yes, indeed!" said May. She raised her glass. "I'll drink to that. Here's to the dignity of labor and the pleasures of moving parts."

Lorna chuckled despite herself. "Anyway," she said, "whenever he was working in the cellar and I felt that he wasn't likely to catch me, I tried to figure out how to make the men and women move, even in just some simple way, but I couldn't. I would get such headaches— horrible headaches. Finally, I had to admit that it's just not the sort of thing I can do. I said to myself, *Lorna, give up. You've wasted a lot of time trying to make these little people move. Just make some that* don't *move, and get to work at it.* So I started in on that, and—oh, my heart just wasn't in it. I knew I was doing the right thing—but you know—" She stopped. Her head was down, as if she were looking at the tabletop, but her eyes were focused somewhere far away, on an old dream. When she spoke, her voice was husky. "It was those charms that I saw in *Life.* 'Moving parts.' I'll never forget those words. That was what appealed to me. That was what I wanted to make. I couldn't get that phrase out of my mind."

"Well, we *all* want moving parts, dear," said May, "and we all want another Manhattan." She raised her hand and wiggled her fingers at Whitey.

"None for me," said Lorna, "I couldn't."

"Well, I can," said May. "And I will. Just one, please, Mr. White."

"I finished some pieces anyway," said Lorna, "but they weren't very good, and while I was working I began to see that there was another problem. I wasn't going to be able to bring myself to sell them. My face would get flushed and my hands would start shaking whenever I even *imagined* selling them. Where on earth would I find people to buy them? Not 'people.' Women. It would have to be women. Can you imagine me showing them to men? What would I say? How would I bring it up? 'Excuse me, would you like to buy a charm that shows a man thrusting his penis into a woman's—'"

"Shhh!" said May. She looked around quickly. "My dear," she said, "it's good you didn't have another Manhattan."

Lorna giggled and colored. "I did have an idea, though. Suppose I made some other charms, simple things, horses or dogs. I could advertise those. Suppose someone called me and said, 'I'd like to see your charms—'"

May snorted.

"All right, all right. I might take a box full of charms to a woman's house. I'd begin taking them out of the box, putting each on a piece of velvet to display it. A couple of horses, a dog, and— 'Ooops! How did *that* get in there? Oh, no, no, you wouldn't be interested in that— that's something I did for—well—it's a special order. Well, I suppose there's no harm in letting you see it. I have to admit that the workmanship is really very good, if I do say so myself.'"

"Well done!" said May. She clapped her hands.

"Oh, but it seems so ridiculous to me. I can't imagine that it would ever work. It wouldn't work for me, anyway. I'd start blushing and trembling as soon as I thought of showing one of my couples, and I'd forget everything I meant to say."

"Why not just sell horses and dogs?"

"I'd never make enough money," said Lorna. "Herb doesn't know this, but I've kept track of every cent that he put into Studebaker stock, and I found out how much the others lost. May, we wouldn't have enough to buy them out even if we sold our house, and the house is all we've got. All our savings has gone into Studebaker, and Herb's salary and mine from Hargrove Slide Rules don't add up to much more than we need from week to week."

"Lorna, you have to let me—"

"Shhh. Don't say it. Not yet. It might come to that. It might. And if it does, I'll come to you. But I hope not. Herb would be sure to find out eventually, and it would humiliate him so. I just hope that something else comes along. You know the worst of it?"

"What?"

"I know who could give those figures moving parts. I know who could sell them, too. Herb could."

◆　　◆　　◆

In those difficult years, Studebaker's declining years, Herb and Lorna had much to worry about, and worrying changed them. I didn't notice the change; during those years I passed from childhood into adolescence, and I was far too interested in the ways that I was changing to notice what was happening to them. Oh, I noticed the details, but I didn't see the pattern. I was blinded by self-concern and also by the idea I had of them, an idea that I had already held for so long that it possessed the tempered strength and burnished gleam of immutable truth. Now, forced to reconsider them, I see what I never saw then.

Their characteristics became exaggerated. Herb's projects became less and less practical, more and more baroque. Now nearly all of them were undertaken more for the process than the product, as if, to apply perceptions years removed from the events, he worked at them only to be busy at something, only to be working, not to be useless or idle. They were rarely completed, or, if completed, they were rarely successful. In fact, more and more of the projects he chose to undertake were of the type that, he must have known from the very start, he was unlikely ever to complete: complex, interminable, tedious projects with countless opportunities for error, for failure. Was he punishing himself? Perhaps he was.

Lorna began concocting her own mathematics problems and logical puzzles, and these too were increasingly intricate and purposeless. Often they would involve long strings of operations on long strings of numbers. Lorna would peer at her slide rule through a magnifying glass, and even at the time I had some understanding of the fact that she was looking for an answer beyond what the slide rule could provide. Her logical puzzles became more confusing and exasperating, and they began to exhibit autobiographical elements. Here's an example. I think that Lorna based this one on a similar puzzle devised by Lewis Carroll.

Two homely sisters were on their way to school one day and suddenly realized that they had forgotten what day of the week it was.

"We'll be laughingstocks," wailed the younger of the homely sisters.

"Oh, be quiet," said the older of the homely sisters. "We can decide what day this is if we just stop and think." She sat down on a

stone wall and thought. "Let's see," she said, thinking aloud. "What day was yesterday? What day will tomorrow be?"

Just then, the homely sisters' quick-witted and pretty younger sister came skipping along, whistling a happy tune.

"Oh, help us, sister," wailed the younger of the homely sisters. "We've forgotten what day of the week this is, and when we get to school we're sure to be laughingstocks for having forgotten."

"Well," said the quick-witted and pretty sister with a twinkle in her eye, "when you can call the day after tomorrow 'yesterday,' then the day that you call 'today' will be as many days away from Wednesday as was the day that you called 'today' on the day when you called the day before yesterday 'tomorrow.'"

Off she skipped, trying very hard not to giggle, leaving her sisters with their mouths agape.

There is bitterness in that puzzle, bitterness and sorrow, the kind of sorrow that, Henri Bergson points out in *Time and Free Will*, begins as a facing toward the past. But, thank goodness, there is no sorrow that isn't sweetened by some joy, and there were some sources of joy in those years, some things that turned Herb and Lorna toward the future, toward hope. I think I was one. I *hope* I was one. Children often are a source of joy for their grandparents, so perhaps I was. Still, however happy they might have been at times, their worry was always there, cold and threatening, like the winter wind that blew through the Whatsit Valley.

18

In Which
Herb 'n' Lorna Are
Saved by the
Art of Love

Then I threw a party at Herb and Lorna's house, and at that party
Mark Dorset fell in love with the Glynn twins, and, therefore, everything turned out all right, eventually.

I had grown up while Studebaker had declined, and at about the
time when the Avanti and the first transistorized electronic calculators
appeared, I met the love of my life, a girl named Albertine, an exotic,
beautiful, intriguing girl, of whom I spoke to my friends so often and
in such tedious detail that they had begun to sidle off when they saw
me approaching, slinking off to the grease pit so that they wouldn't
have to hear about her again. None of my friends knew her, since she
went to a private school and lived on the east side of the Bolotomy
River, in a part of Babbington separate from the rest of the town, a
remote and unfamiliar region, a place unto itself. I wanted Albertine
to meet my friends, and I wanted them to meet her. So I decided to
throw a party. Like most people at sixteen, I was embarrassed by my
parents, so I didn't want to have the party at home. I wanted to have
it at Herb and Lorna's. They were delighted when I told them and
consented at once.

Among the people I invited was Mark Dorset, a new friend, a newcomer to Babbington. He accepted, but with mixed feelings, since he was one of those high school students for whom a party meant, primarily, the possibility of romance, a possibility sweet in anticipation, but which too often vanished as soon as the party began.

I knew how he felt. I had sometimes felt that way myself, before I met Albertine. In the hours before a party, while I was deciding what clothes, what look, what attitude to wear to this affair, the party as it *might* be would run through my mind again and again, a wonderful scampering thing, elusive and attractive, darting from possibility to possibility. With whom would I fall in love? Who would fall in love with me?

Ahhh, but the parties in fact never equaled the parties in anticipation. For a few early moments, really only the first few moments after I had walked through the door, the pleasure of possibility remained, but soon the possible began a slow dissolve into the actual, and toward the end of the evening the actual was likely to take a form something like this (and at one party it took a form exactly like this): the girl with whom I had fallen in love, to whom I had confided some of my most cherished hopes and dreams, who had listened so wide-eyed while I was confiding those hopes and dreams, whose wide eyes had inspired me to some quite spine-tingling turns of phrase, who had held my hand during the if-only-the-world-were-just part, who had kissed me quickly and shyly in the hall and again, slowly and thoroughly, while we sat on the porch, left suddenly (squeal of tires, smell of rubber, cloud of smoke) in a battered convertible driven by a guy who had quit school the year before and now installed linoleum flooring, left laughing, leaving me behind, grinning like an idiot to hide my disappointment that this girl for whom I had had such hopes, to whom I had said so much, could have fallen at the last minute for muscles and a ragtop.

Mark was often one of those people who were still hanging around after a party, when it was time to clean up, one of those who, having nothing better to do, would scramble around, trying to find all the bottles and glasses, trying to reconstruct vases, to wash beer stains from the rugs and upholstery, trying to hide from the parents any evidence that a party had been thrown in their house.

The party I threw for Albertine was different. Mark came with small hopes, but it turned out to be a wonderful evening. He fell in love, doubly in love, with the Glynn twins, Margot and Martha. By the time Herb and Lorna returned home in the small hours, Mark was euphoric, happily befuddled, drunk on love, adolescent love. He was learning how pleasant desire could be, how unlike the desperate longing he had known, when it wasn't hopeless, and he was experiencing a sweet torture from feeling that he was going to have to choose between those identical beauties, that he couldn't have them both. Better than all these feelings, though, was his feeling that Margot and Martha loved him. He could see in their eyes, in their grins ("You look like the Grin Twins," he said), that they weren't going to run off in a convertible with a linoleum installer, but would leave with him.

Mark was sitting on the living room sofa with his right arm around Margot and his left arm around Martha, when Herb and Lorna, who had come in through the kitchen, suddenly appeared in the archway between their dining room and their living room. His first impulse was to jump up and thank them, he felt such a rush of gratitude. He was grateful for their having brought all this about, for having provided the house, the fireplace, the sofa—that sofa upholstered in scratchy, rose-colored fabric that he knew he would never forget—on which he had become so happy. At the same time he was a little worried for them, worried that they'd feel they were in occupied territory. He thought they might be offended by the way he and the others had taken over their living toom, made themselves at home. We had built a fire (for its flickering, aphrodisiac light), and that seemed to Mark a violation. There was party clutter everywhere: bottles (beer in quarts and Haig & Haig Scotch in Pinch bottles, which were chic in my circle then), cigarette packs and butts and ashtrays and lighters (in memory, it seems as if all of us had Zippo lighters with totemic college emblems), snack packages and the remains of some onion dip. There were couples in various styles of embrace, and there were loud conversations. Lorna took all of this in, and she smiled. There was endorsement in her smile, not the condescending youth-must-be-served sort, but an elevating this-is-meet-and-right sort, as if the purpose behind Herb and Lorna's return was not to see what we might be doing wrong, but to see that we were doing it right. Lorna's smile seemed to give to everything we were up to in her living room the endorsement of an elder, a sage. This interpretation comes long after the fact, I admit, and I can't pretend that I read all of it in Lorna's smile that night.

Herb was right behind Lorna, wearing a similar smile. He was less forward, eager but hesitant, and he stood in what I thought of as his ready-when-you-are posture, bent slightly at the waist, as if he wanted to come right on in and start shaking hands but felt that he had to wait for an invitation—not an invitation into his own living room, certainly, but an invitation into our party, into our youth.

Lorna called out, "Hello!" in a tone she might have used to welcome guests to a party of her own. The sound of her voice occasioned some squeals in corners of the room and a crash in one of the bedrooms down the hall. There was much scrambling and tucking in of shirts and blouses. I hopped to my feet, greeted them, and began introducing them at once, sometimes to couples who were still buttoning themselves up.

They sat down. I made them drinks, and they began chatting. From them came the familiar cuddly, soothing, reassuring warmth, the active ingredient in the kind of hug mothers use as an analgesic for the pain of a scraped knee. Most of my friends, charmed by them, warmed by them, attracted to them, stayed around for another hour or so. We did a little cleaning up and put things in order a bit, but for most of the time we were just talking, sitting in front of the fire. Finally, everyone but Mark and the Glynns and Albertine and I had left. It was time for me to walk Albertine home. I urged Herb and Lorna to go to bed and leave the rest of the cleaning to me in the morning. They said they would, but I could tell that they didn't mean it. The five of us left.

It is possible that, without that quiet, domestic ending to the evening, the love that Margot and Martha felt for Mark would, when the three of them finally left, simply have evaporated in the outside air. Instead, as soon as Herb had closed the front door behind us, Margot linked her arm with Mark's, snuggled against him, and said, "Weren't they wonderful?"

"Oh, yes," said Martha. She snuggled against Mark from the other side. "They're so sweet. They're so *homey.*"

"You can just see them serving Thanksgiving dinner, can't you?" asked Margot.

"Right!" said Martha. "She'd be wearing a starched apron, with ruffles—"

"Oh, of course!" said Margot. "And she would have made about three pies—"

"And he would carve the turkey at the table," Mark said.

"That's just the way it is," I said.

We separated at the end of the street. Albertine and I took our time walking home. Warmed by Herb and Lorna's happy domesticity, we sketched something like it for ourselves. Mark and Margot and Martha, similarly warmed, were allowing themselves (but without admitting it) to hope that somehow they might, as a trio, achieve something like it, too.

Over the next few years, while Herb and Lorna's financial problems deepened, Mark saw them fairly often. Sometimes he would see them at my house when they were visiting. More often, though, Mark walked to their house specifically to visit them. The Glynns lived near Herb and Lorna, so Mark often headed for No Bridge Road after seeing Margot and Martha or after finding that the girls weren't at home when he called. Unfortunately, for quite a while, especially during summers when the three of them were home from college, Margot and Martha were frequently not at home when Mark called, because the three were trying to fall out of love. They weren't able to decide what to make of themselves, what to do with themselves, if they remained in love. When they were together in public as a trio, when they went to the beach, to the movies, to dinner, to someone's house, or to a dance, they were friends. They weren't pretending to be "just friends." They *were* just friends, friends of a romantic and flirtatious sort, but still just friends. That's how they felt. That's how they thought of themselves. When they were alone, when they sat up late together in the courtyard of the old carriage house where the Glynns lived, or when they walked through town and along the docks in the evening or at night, holding hands and talking, they were lovers, but they were lovers who didn't go to bed together. Oh, how they didn't go to bed together! The agonies they went through during that time may have acquired an amusing and poignant flavor as time has passed, and they have aged, and mores have changed, but what agonies they were then. For the average young couple in that place and time, however much groping they might do, actually achieving coitus was like breaking a tape at the end of a hundred yards of moral, emotional, cultural, psychological, and physical hurdles. Mark and Margot and Martha were neither average nor a couple. For them, there were extra hurdles to leap. Loyalty and jealousy wouldn't let Mark sleep with either Margot or Martha alone or let either of them sleep with him alone, and convention kept the three of them from trying to entangle themselves simultaneously (in some way that they could, to tell the truth, only begin to imagine). What they referred to as their "Situation" (and they talked and talked about their Situation on those nights, on those walks) made life confusing for all of them. Margot or Martha would date almost any other boy who asked her out alone, hoping that some night she'd fall in love with someone else, that she'd be able to leave Mark to her sister and go her separate way. That didn't happen, and as time passed it seemed less and less likely to happen. Mark even tried to make himself fall in love with other girls. It wouldn't work. The three were in love. They didn't know what to do.

There is a great need, when one is having trouble with love, for a confidant, but what they felt and what they wanted seemed so bizarre and impossible that they couldn't manage to talk about it. They wanted some kind of plan, something that would show that there was a future for them, but it was too soon for them to see it. You know how it is—when we're young we don't know how we want to live. We don't even know what there is to want. We only know conventional names. We only recognize commonplace models. It takes years for us to see how many ways there are to live.

In the back of Mark's mind, he knew—or at least he had some kind of hunch—that Herb and Lorna were the people he wanted to—needed to—talk to, so he visited them often. As Studebaker's fortunes fell, Herb spent less and less time at the showroom and more and more time at home, tinkering, so the chances were good that he would be at home whenever Mark dropped by. To alleviate his worries, Herb had thrown himself into building equipment for the tour of the United States that he and Lorna had always wanted to make. Mark would often find him working on the trailer he was building from pieces of old Studebakers. He might be cutting up a garden hose to make a speaking tube to run between the trailer and the car that would pull it. He might be building, from parts of a sewing machine and a vacuum cleaner, one compact device that would do the work of both and make toast to boot.

Lorna also spent more and more time at home, in part because the demand for slide rules was falling, but also because she wanted to keep an eye on Herb, to be sure that his enthusiasm wasn't a mask, that he wasn't falling into despair over the Studebaker decline. Most often when Mark dropped by he would find her cooking, or planning the route for their tour, or working at recreational mathematics and logic problems, sitting on the porch or on the sofa, that scratchy rose-colored sofa, with a Whitman's Sampler beside her.

One night at the very start of summer vacation, after Mark had finished his junior year in college, he was walking to the Glynns' along the dark and twisting road that had once been the driveway to the mansion, burned long ago, for which the Glynns' house had been the carriage house. A convertible passed him. In it, Margot was sitting beside a dark-haired young man who wore a blue blazer, a young man who seemed self-confident and rich. In a few minutes, a motorcycle passed. Martha was perched on the back of the seat, holding on to a sandy-haired guy with thick arms, a guy who looked self-confident and lusty. Mark had never actually seen Margot and Martha with other boys before. He realized that he had hoped their dates were straw men, intended only to show that they had *tried* to fall out of love with him but failed. He walked on to their house, and he stood outside for a few minutes, debating with himself whether he ought to go in and find out from their parents who these rivals were. He decided not to go in. He began walking. He was afraid that he might on this night lose not one but both, and that fear made him weak, empty, desperate. He walked into town and bought some beer, and then he walked back to the Glynns' and sat outside, drinking the beer and waiting. Mr. and Mrs. Glynn went to bed. The dark and the silence made Mark terribly miserable, and the beer made him a little dizzy. He began walking again.

He found himself, beery and blue, at Herb and Lorna's. It seemed as if one minute he was on their porch, and the next minute he was sitting on their sofa, saying, "It was right here on this sofa that I fell in love, and it was the most miserable thing that ever happened to me. The most wonderful thing and the most miserable thing. The most *miserable* thing. Let me explain why I say that. I say 'the most miserable thing' because it isn't going to work out. It just isn't going to work out, and it isn't going to work out because there isn't any way it *can* work out. I can't have two wives, it's as simple as that."

Somehow, he next found himself sitting between Herb and Lorna at the kitchen table. Herb was pushing a hamburger at him from one side, and Lorna was pushing a huge plate of something that he didn't recognize at him from the other.

"What is that?" he asked Lorna, trying to be very precise in his speech because he had begun to sense that he was a little drunk, and he didn't want it to show.

"This is potato salad," she said. "And Herb's got a hamburger for you." She dropped her voice. "You ought to eat something, Mark," she said.

Mark looked closely at the potato salad. "It looks as if it isn't finished," he said. "In other words, that is, it seems to me that some-one stopped making it in the middle. It looks like just potatoes." He chuckled.

"Oh," Lorna said, surprised, laughing. "It's German potato salad. It doesn't have any mayonnaise."

"And you'll never eat any that's better than Lorna's," said Herb.

"You know," Mark said, "I know why you're doing this. You're worried that I'm drunk and I won't be able to walk home if I don't eat something." He put his arms around them, and as soon as he had he felt that he had put the three of them into an awkward position. "You don't have to worry about me," he said. He gave them a squeeze that he would never have presumed to give them if he had been sober, and then he let go of them. "I'll be careful," he said.

"You have to at least try some of Lorna's potato salad," said Herb.

Mark laughed. He adored them. There was in Herb's voice such boundless pride in Lorna's potato salad that Mark gave in and began eating at once. He stayed for a couple of hours, eating a bite now and then, taking a swallow of coffee now and then, and talking, talking, talking. He told them all about Margot and Martha, how he felt about the girls, how the girls felt about him, how the three of them felt about each other, how hopeless their prospects seemed to be. They were wonderful listeners. They didn't offer a word of advice, but Mark left them feeling that things might work out. He still had no idea how *exactly* they might work out, but he had the general idea that everything might, somehow, be all right.

Only when Mark was about halfway home, when rain had begun to fall and his memory had begun to clear, did he realize that not only had he confessed to them, in a rambling, uncertain way, grinning, blushing, groping for a suitable vocabulary, that he wanted to go to bed with Margot and Martha, to make love to both of them, but he had also admitted that he had no specific idea how, gracefully, admirably, romantically, such a thing might be done. He remembered the looks they wore: looks of interest and curiosity but not a trace of embarrassment, and he even remembered telling them about the way his mother had blushed at the end of the evening when he had brought Margot and Martha home to dinner for the first time. A little tipsy, she had giggled and said to him before he went to bed, "Remember that you can't be in two places at once."

After Mark left, Lorna began moving around her kitchen, following her accustomed patterns, clearing the dishes, washing them. Herb went through the house in his accustomed pattern, turning lights off, turning the radio off, locking the doors. Everything they did was familiar, habitual. But tonight there was something odd about all this homely activity. They were making far too much of it, and the little sounds attendant to it, each click of a lock, each creak of a door when Herb tested it, each clink of a plate on the counter, the slosh of the water in the kitchen sink, the squeak of Lorna's towel when she polished a glass, echoed in the house like amplified recordings, hyperprecise, hyperaudible, because the only background for them was the echoing silence of people wholly preoccupied by their thoughts.

Lorna was recalling her mistake of so many years ago, when she had told Ella that she had to do the conventional thing, that she had to choose between Buster and Bert, but she was also imagining the pleasure of carving that handsome Mark, those beautiful Glynns. Though the mechanical question of their intricate entanglement aroused and intrigued her, it also made her head begin to ache, so she set it aside and concentrated instead on sculptural details: the girls' smooth necks, their plump lips, their breasts, ripe fruit from the land of youth (and four!—a bountiful harvest!), their bellies and thighs, where she would be able to show off her skill at suggesting the strength beneath the curves, an effect like rocks softened by snow, the smooth muscles along Mark's back, the lenticular concavities in his tense buttocks, the venous ridge along his erect penis, its jaunty cap— She caught herself breathing hard, clutching the edge of the sink. Her heart was all aflutter. In her belly she felt the old familiar ripples, and between her legs the eager wetness of—

"It's an interesting problem," said Herb.

Lorna flinched and cried out, "Oh!" She hadn't been aware that he was standing there, at the back door, looking out, into the dark. She blushed, as if somehow Herb might know what she'd been thinking, might know how elementally she had responded to what she'd been thinking.

"You scared me half to death," she said. "Don't sneak up on me like that."

"Sorry," said Herb. "I thought you heard me come in."

"That's all right. What did you say?"

"I said it's an interesting problem. Mechanically, I mean," said Herb. He coughed.

"What—um—? Oh, you mean Mark—and the girls?" She pulled the stopper in the sink, and the water swirled away.

Herb cleared his throat. "Yes." His ears reddened.

"He's a nice boy. Nice looking." Lorna looked at the dishcloth, lying in a wet lump in the sink. She rubbed her thumb along the porcelain.

"An interesting mechanical problem," said Herb. He looked at Lorna's reflection in the glass. He felt his ears and cheeks burn. He reached into his pocket and tugged at his shorts to make room for his erection. "Lots of moving parts," he said.

Lorna turned from the sink to look at Herb, and even in the rude light of the circular fluorescent fixture Herb could see that her elusive loveliness had returned. For some time fear and fretfulness had poisoned Lorna's system like allergens, had made the skin under her eyes puff and redden, had made her forehead break out, had made her cheeks pale and her jaw slack. Now, instantly, she seemed cleansed, cured. She had been revivified by what I think I'll call God's Own Wonder-Working Tonic, an invigorating compound of three potent ingredients: work to be done (keeps the eyes bright and focused on the future), self-respect (keeps the head up, also the corners of the mouth, and makes the past, on the whole, a pleasant place to visit), and lust (keeps important bodily fluids flowing and makes the present thrilling).

"Herb," she said. "I want to show you something." Her heart was racing. She dried her hands on her apron. She could feel them tremble. She took the flour canister from the shelf. She hesitated for the briefest of moments; then she pulled the lid off and turned the flour out on the counter.

"Lorna?" said Herb.

Lorna poked her fingers into the flour and pulled out what she wanted at once, her only souvenir of her coarse-goods work, one of the animated ones, one that she had modified to please herself. She wiped the case on her apron. Then she turned and held it out toward Herb in her trembling hands.

Herb's jaw fell. He brought his hand to his mouth. "Oh," he said. "Is that—? How did you—? So you know. I—"

Lorna pressed the stem, and the lid popped open. There was one of the little couples, but this pair had been carved with special care. They resembled, quite clearly, Herb and Lorna, and the arena for their enthusiastic performance was not a rumpled bed but a rowboat.

"Why, that's—"

"It's us," said Lorna. "I made it."

"You? I. I made it."

"What?"

"I made it. Isn't that what you meant? That you knew? You found out?"

"Herb, I made this. I carved the little rowboat. I carved these figures. I had to fit the little sections of their bodies onto fine wires and rods that fit onto—"

"Wires that run onto pulleys, rods that run to shafts that are turned by the gears in the bottom of the case."

"That make the man and woman perform—"

"The way I designed them."

"It can't be."

"Wait here." Herb dashed down the stairs to the cellar and, in a moment, dashed back up them, carrying the green metal box marked with a skull and crossbones. He set it on the kitchen table, opened it, lifted the tray from it, and pulled out a stack of papers. "Look," he said. "Look here. These are my designs. All of them." He was beaming. He spread the drawings out on the table and stood back with his arms crossed over his chest, proud, exhilarated.

"Herb—"

"Lorna—"

All these years?" she asked.

"I guess so," he said.

"Oh, Herb," she said, "ignite me, please, right this minute."

Later, in bed, in the pleasant lassitude after love, it all came out, slowly. If we had overheard, if we had been, say, Dudley, outside, beneath their windows, eavesdropping, we wouldn't have been able to catch it all, just a snatch of mumbled revelation, a bit of whispered confession, the occasional bold declaration, a giggle, a chuckle, with interstices of silence, of ignorance, where we would have been forced to imagine, to insert ourselves in their murmurings, using what we know to suppose what they said.

"That duck, that papier-mâché duck that Uncle Luther made for me—that was how it started. Uncle Luther. I still get a cold feeling in my stomach when I think of his hand, the missing fingers. But I loved to sit on his lap—and you know, *now* I think I can remember feeling his—his erection, under me. I wonder if I *really* remember that, or have I just imagined it? Well, he never touched me when I was little, but he—he did later."

"You don't have to tell me—"

"Oh, it was nothing, really. But Bertha and Clara, especially Bertha, were so jealous of me, because of him. Bertha was mad for him. His 'little lady.' That's what he called her. I had forgotten that. Anyway, it was Luther who taught me to model, and to carve, and it was Luther and Bertha who gave me my original inspiration. You know the story I've told you, about seeing them having—doing—making love once. The truth is that I saw them doing it many times—"

Herb thought she was confessing, using Bertha as her stand-in. He brushed his lips against her cheek.

"To tell you the truth—" she began. Herb pressed his finger to her lips. She kissed it. "Let me go on," she said. "The truth is that I spied on them, but always from a hiding place, and I never had a clear view. I'd see parts of them only—their heads or a leg, two legs, Uncle Luther's back, thighs, whatever—and I had seen animals do it, and birds, chickens, and so I put together what I knew and what I could see and I imagined some things that—some things that may not even be possible, things I've never even dared to suggest that we try. And then Uncle Luther taught me to carve, and when I was good enough he asked me to work on little naked people. He made models, papier-mâché models, but I used other models too, models in my mind—what I remembered of Uncle Luther's body, and Bertha's, and what I learned about my own, especially my own. I would stand in front of the mirror and study myself, run my hands over myself, check the modeling of my body, and there was always a lot of me in the women I carved, always. I was never just a *copyist*. I—*personalized* my work. I made the couples do what *I* wanted to do. And then Luther tried to make love to me—and he revolted me. And everything changed. I despised him, and I despised what he had taught me to do, or I thought that I *ought* to despise what he taught me to do, but, you know, I never did. I never despised it, not really. I loved it, but I was ashamed all the same."

"*I* got into it because it was a way to make money, that's all," said Herb. "You know how my family needed money in those days. I was just a boy really, and my father was a bankrupt. Uncle Ben got into the business somehow, God knows how. He was always onto one scheme or another, Uncle Ben. I remember when he showed me the first one—a shirt stud. I didn't even know what a shirt stud was. Carved on it was a woman, with her legs spread, and she was playing with herself. Did you—um—did you—did you make—"

"That one? I might have, I did lots like that, but so did the others, and there must have been places all over the country where—or maybe there weren't. Oh, but there must be now, don't you think?"

"I don't know. That's a good question. I know I wish I had that stud or one like it. I'd really like to know. It may be just my mind playing tricks on me, but she—"

"No, she wouldn't have looked like me. If I made it, she wouldn't have looked like me, not her face. Her body, but not her face. I used the faces of my friends. God, if any of them ever found out! But her body would have been mine. I don't think your memory is that good, though, Herb."

"Oh, I don't know. I studied her pretty closely. You know, Lorna, I used to—I used to—oh, hell, I used to masturbate when I was looking at her."

"Oh, I used to do it *all* the time, even in the workroom. We worked in a room at the mill, an unmarked room. There were only five of us, never more, and I was excited all day long. It was a constant thrill. My chest felt tight all the time, my fingers would tingle, and I'd shift on my seat, squeezing my legs together, for hours, *hours,* and sometimes I would just have to *run* to the ladies' room, and I would sit down on the toilet and just touch myself once, just *touch,* and *whooosh*—up in flames! I wonder if it got to the men the same way— the men who worked on coarse goods. They had their own work- room. My God, that's hilarious, isn't it? They had their own work- room. Good to keep everything proper, I suppose. I knew them, the men, knew them all, but we never talked about what we did, never compared notes. I knew their work, all of it, but we never spoke about it, just walked past each other with our eyes down, ashamed, and all the time we were igniting one another secretly."

"You know, that first time Uncle Ben showed me a piece of goods, he told me to look at the workmanship—he was always proud of the workmanship."

"So was I. So *am* I."

"So am I. But there's more, lots more. Lots more to tell. Did you know that was why I started selling books—Professor Clapp's? It was because of coarse goods. It was so I'd have a way to get into people's houses—a front, you could call it."

"So that *is* how—Herb, I thought of almost the same thing, when I was going to try to sell—oh, Herb! Herb. I thought you were dead. Uncle Luther said you were dead—you—the man who designed the routines. You know what?"

"What?"

"I think I was—infatuated—in love with you. Without knowing who you were."

"Really?"

"Really. Do you mind?"

"No. No, I don't mind. Now, where was I?"

"Oh, Herb, I just thought of something! We're saved! Do you realize that? I didn't think of it until now, just now! We can make the money back, all of it!"

"Shhh. I know. I know. But don't you want to hear the rest of the story?"

"Just the high points. I want to get to work."

"Well, let's see. I did pretty well for a while, and then I was drafted."

"Oh, Herrrrb."

"I've wanted to tell you all of this for more than forty years."

"Oh, I know. I know. Go ahead."

"Well, when I got called, I figured that if I sold some goods to the other boys while I was in France, I could keep sending money to my mother. I had to get some goods to sell, so Uncle Ben and I came to Chacallit, that time when you and I met."

"But, do you mean that when you came to our house selling books, you were going to try to sell some goods to my father?"

"No. Oh, no. Heck no, not right in the manufacturer's backyard. I just came to sell books—to earn some money for the trip back to Boston. Then, in the war, I sold a lot, and then, when it was all over and we were just waiting around to be shipped home, that's when Pershing gave me my medal."

"Medal?"

"You know the story about Pershing shaking my hand because I fixed those cup handles—well, it's not true. He never shook my hand. He gave me something, a coarse medal, you could say."

Herb hopped out of bed. For a moment he was a shadowy figure, barely visible, receding; then suddenly he was silhouetted in the bedroom doorway when he snapped on the hall light; then he was an illuminated figure, receding. Lorna noticed (she had a practiced eye) his thin legs, the prominent tendons behind his knees, his knotted calf muscles, his droopy buttocks, a bruise on his shoulder blade, and was astonished at how much she loved him. In a while he was back, and for just a moment in the light of the hall before he turned the light out she saw the grin on his face, the unruly strands of white hair falling over his forehead, his little old penis, and she was so pleased with him that she got the giggles for the first time in she didn't know how long. He had brought with him the metal box from under his workbench, the one with the skull and crossbones on it. From it he pulled a little leather pouch. He spread the top open and held it out toward her. Lorna cupped her hands under it. Into them Herb dropped the button Pershing had given him.

"Herb!" she said at once. "This is from Chacallit! I know it is! They made lots of these little buttons. Luther had the most ridiculous argument about how they would raise morale. But I didn't work on them. Luther and I quarreled, and—oh, but I made some little statues. I used to slip them into the Comfort Kits that I put together for the Red Cross. But—oh, that's beside the point. Do you think General Pershing bought this button? No, of course not. Someone must have given it to him. Maybe those buttons *did* raise morale. I suppose the men traded them, or sold them, used them to barter for whatever they needed, for soap or— Soap! I have to tell you about Baltimore. Oh, I'm sorry, I interrupted you. Go ahead."

"Lorna. Lorna. Do you know what they called those?"

"Called those?"

"Those carvings that came in the Comfort Kits. You were my competition, do you realize that? Do you know what they called those carvings?"

"My carvings?"

"Yes. You were famous. *They* were famous, anyway."

"Famous?"

"They called them Comfort Cuties."

"Comfort Cuties. I like it. It's cute."

"Cute. Well. Oh, God, cute reminds me of something ugly. And I mean ugly. You know, it was really my uncle Ben who invented moving goods?"

"Animated. We called them animated pieces. With moving parts. Oh, Herb—moving parts. May loved that, moving parts."

"You told May?"

"I had to tell *somebody*. But moving parts. Do you remember those charms? Those charms in *Life*? I wanted to make charms—I *still* want to make charms—with moving parts. You know, *parts.* Can we, Herb? Can you design them, and I'll carve them, and you sell them?"

"Sure. Of course. Why not?" He paused. "Lorna—"

"Mm?"

"I always thought you'd be ashamed."

"I *was* ashamed. I told you. I was terribly ashamed. But I *loved* it, too. I was just a girl. I didn't understand that there was nothing to be ashamed about."

"I didn't mean that. I mean ashamed of me."

"Ashamed of you? My God, I've admired your work for years. I think you're—a genius."

"A mechanical genius."

"A mechanical genius. That's right."

"And you. Those little people. They were beautiful. You're—an artist."

How the bedsprings sang that night!

"Careful, Herb," said Lorna, "we'll set the whole neighborhood on fire."

Perhaps they were no longer up to the vigorous, eager, reckless pleasures of youth, but those are rather conventional pleasures anyway, and Herb and Lorna were uniquely capable of something else, something richer, something skilled and clever, the considered, measured pleasures of a couple of master couplers, ready at last to reap the harvest of decades of imagination, to plant the seeds for the mature masterpieces of a pair of love artists.

19

In Which
Herb 'n' Lorna Retire
to Florida

They earned the money, and they had a great time doing it. More important than the money, and more satisfying, was the work they did during the intense months that they spent earning it, a time when the whole house seemed to sing, when, in fact, it did ring with music, the record player in the living room going all the time, playing their old favorite songs over and over and over again, turned up high to play over the sound of their work.

They cleared the living room, carrying all the furniture to the room behind the bookcase, the room that first Mrs. Stolz and later Ella and Bert had lived in. There they piled it higgledy-piggledy, facing any which way, chairs and tables and whatnots and lamps all in a huddle, done with, past use. In the living room they left only the piano, the console radio and record player that Herb had bought for Lorna, and the rose-colored sofa, pulled away from the wall, to the center of the room, closer to the fire. Herb brought his workbench and Lorna's and all his tools and all of Lorna's up from the cellar into the living room. There they worked, all day, every day. Herb hammered and welded, bent and cut and pounded on a tiny scale, fashioning the armatures and cams and gears and pulleys that made the couples move. Lorna bent over her enormous magnifying glass, carving the couples themselves, poking the tip of her tongue out between her lips when she made the finest, most exacting passes with her miniature files, grinning when she achieved a satisfactory likeness of a friend or neighbor.

For the first time, Herb could talk to the sculptor who would have to realize his designs, the woman who would have to create the little people who were going to have to perform as Herb had imagined they would. And for the first time, Lorna could sketch an idea of her own, model it roughly with her hands in the air, try to describe it in words, and have Herb make it work. Or, greatest pleasure of all, in the evenings, when they had finished their work and eaten dinner, they would sit side by side on the rose-colored sofa, in front of the fire, in the midst of their work, surrounded by their benches and tools and supplies and works in progress, and admire what they'd done. Often, one or the other would suggest something new.

"I've got a kind of complicated idea, Lorna," Herb might say.

Lorna might look up at Herb over the top of her glasses, run the tip of her tongue over her lips, and ask, "How complicated?"

"Pretty complicated."

"Well, then, I think we'd better try it out in the lab."

When they had bought all of the Spotters' stock, when every Spotter had been saved, they began working for themselves, first to make up what they had lost, then to make up what they had spent to buy the stock, and then to finance the circuit of the United States they had been looking forward to, and their retirement.

A station wagon would have been the practical choice, but Herb was no longer in a mood to be practical, so he ordered a gold metalflake Avanti for the grand tour. The day the Avanti arrived, Herb hustled it into the service department, which he persisted in calling the repair shop. Old Randolph was long gone, but his son, Randy, or, to Herb, Young Randolph, ran the service department now, and he was as fond of Herb and as indebted to him for technical advice as Old Randolph had been. Herb had been discussing his plans with Young Randolph for some time, so he knew just what was needed. He had already fabricated a heavy-duty trailer hitch, and he had heavy rear springs and shocks, enormous mirrors, fog lights, and other equipment on hand, all of it unusual gear for an Avanti. When the Avanti arrived in the shop, Young Randolph put his hand on Herb's shoulder, and said, "Herb, I'm going to build you the best trailer puller in these United States."

Herb left the repair shop and walked directly to the office of the current president of Babbington Studebaker, Wilbur Haggerty. The men had taken to calling him "Haggard Bill" because of the visible effects on him of Studebaker's going to the brink so many times and scrabbling back, but just barely, leaving Haggard Bill Haggerty limp and sweaty, his heart pounding. Herb gave notice of his intention to retire in two weeks. The next day, at Hargrove Slide Rules, Lorna simply quit, to the surprise and great relief of Edwin Berwick, now president, who had been wondering how to tell Lorna that in a month the name of the company would change to Hargrove Computational Devices and that within a year they would begin producing electronic calculators and stop producing slide rules.

They spent the next two weeks stocking the trailer. Herb had, of course, outfitted the trailer with gadgets of many sorts. Some were practical, like the two refrigerators. A larger one held their stores, and a smaller one held things needed every day, like cream for coffee and food for the day, transferred from the larger. With careful planning—and Lorna provided the careful planning—there would be no need to open the larger one more than once every other day. Others were romantic, like the record player. Herb bought and restored a portable wind-up record player, not just because it wouldn't require electricity, but because he and Lorna could carry it away from the trailer, to have "Lake Serenity Serenade" with them if they walked off into a grove of trees to find a pretty spot to eat lunch and field-test any animation ideas that might come to them on the road.

Toward the end of the two weeks, late enough so that people wouldn't be able to make a fuss over them, they said their good-byes. That was that. They put their furniture and furnishings in storage in the Hapgood Brothers' warehouse, left the selling of their house to Bert and Ella and told them to keep whatever money it brought them, and left. They got out of Babbington with shocking speed; at least, it shocked me. It seemed as if, once they had decided to go, none of what they would leave behind mattered to them any longer. I couldn't understand how they could sell that house; it was so full of Herb's gadgets—disappearing bookshelves, clattering dumbwaiters, the cooling system that pumped groundwater through salvaged Studebaker radiators, the weather station on the garage roof, the mailbox on a rope and pulley so that Herb could reel the mail in from the breakfast table. How could they let all of that go, how could they leave their friends, Ella, me? They did, and they made it look easy. Now I think that, subconsciously, they were in search of something that they knew they couldn't get in Babbington. They would never have put it this way—I doubt that they would ever have even thought to put it this way—but I think it was artistic freedom.

They followed a zigzag route that took them through a number of small towns that Lorna chose for their names: Candor, New York; Freedom, Independence, and Paradise, Pennsylvania; Leroy and Huber Heights, Ohio; Pershing, Indiana; Piper City and Lovejoy, Illinois; Baring, Amoret, and Peculiar, Missouri; Hope and Paradise, Kansas; Ovid, Loveland, and Model, Colorado; Story and Paradise Valley, Wyoming; Epiphany and Eureka, South Dakota; Twin Bridges and Paradise, Montana; Bliss and Deary, Idaho; Opportunity and Paradise Inn, Washington; Zigzag, Carver, and Sisters, Oregon; Fortuna, Enterprise, Commerce, and Paradise, California; Inspiration and Paradise Valley, Arizona; Loving, New Mexico; Happy and Goodnight, Texas; Plain Dealing, Eros, and Darlington, Louisiana; Castleberry, Alabama; Climax, Georgia; and, finally, Punta Cachazuda, Florida.

While they were traveling, they wrote little. All I got was a postcard now and then:

Breathtaking scenery. Weather VERY HOT. Yesterday
caught in blizzard of tumbleweed. Scratches all over Avanti.
                            "Guppa" and "Gumma"

The trip was, they told everyone, meant to be a long vacation. Their announced intention was to return, find a smaller house in Babbington, nearer the water, maybe even a litle place at the beach, near May's. I was impatient for their return. I wanted them to return so that things would be restored to their most stable state: the state at which I had perceived them to be when I was a child, the steady state. (How upsetting it is when people demonstrate their independence of our steady-state notion of them: when people go away, when friends we'd thought of as a happy couple surprise us with a divorce, when our parents call one evening and tell us that they've put up for sale the house we think of as home, even if we haven't visited it in a couple of years and haven't slept in it in a decade.) Shortly after Herb and Lorna reached Punta Cachazuda, the Hapgood Brothers' warehouse burned to the ground, and nothing of theirs was saved. When they heard the news, they felt that they'd been released by the fire from any obligation to return. Said Lorna, in a postcard from Punta Cachazuda, "It may not be paradise, but I think we'll stay."

Punta Cachazuda lies on the west coast of Florida, the Gulf Coast, where the beach sand is as white and fine as confectioner's sugar, and the sunsets make a person pause and muse. There would have been no Punta Cachazuda at all had it not been for the effect of one of those thought-provoking sunsets on Humboldt Bagnell. One evening, years before Herb and Lorna arrived, Humboldt and his wife, Bitsy, nearing the end of *their* trailer tour of the United States, had found themselves between towns at the hour when they were accustomed to drink a couple of Manhattans and chat, so they decided to stop, pull off the road, have their Manhattans, and spend the evening where they were. They carried their second Manhattans to the water's edge and watched the sun redden and slip into the Gulf.

Humboldt found that the sunset inspired him to muse. He looked around him and mused on what was left of his future. He contemplated the prospect of living the rest of his life right where he was, and he found that he liked it. He bought a tract of land and built a modest house. Subsequently, in the evenings, when he sat on his patio and watched the sun go down, he began imagining a town around him, dreamed of wandering streets that didn't exist, pictured himself greeting people who hadn't even seen the place yet. He began buying more land, and he began tinkering with it, improving it, sharpening the distinction between land and water by eliminating the ambiguous marshes, filling here and dredging there, until every bit of Punta Cachazuda was a well-formed island, peninsula, or waterway. Then, house by house, Humboldt and Bitsy began building the town, extending the roads and sidewalks as they went along, all according to a plan pinned to the wall of their garage.

The streets of Punta Cachazuda wandered through the town as if they'd been laid out whimsically, but in fact there was a purpose behind their intriguing sinuosity: they divagated to skirt boredom. The canals and creeks and artificial peninsulas and islands, the twisting streets, the bridges, and the tiny parks made Punta Cachazuda look, especially from the air, like the sort of omnium-gatherum land-scape that model railroaders build from papier-mâché. Indeed, the town had the ragged edge of an unfinished work in papier-mâché: at the limit of development the road and sidewalk petered out, and the wind blew miniature dunes of sugary sand onto the lawn of the last-built house.

Humboldt relied on word of mouth to sell his town to potential residents, so he and Bitsy died before they saw much of it populated, but his children, who embraced his vision religiously, eventually saw Punta Cachazuda become what Humboldt and Bitsy had hoped it would be, a small town filled entirely with old people with time on their hands. The houses were similar but not identical. They were small cement-block houses, each with a tiny cement patio on its west-ern side, where at sunset Punta Cachazudans sat and watched the maraschino sunsets. Each house also had something that most Punta Cachazudans had never heard of before they arrived there—a "Flor-ida room," an incursion of the outdoors into the envelope of the house. (Imagine that you were to sneak up behind a house with a conventional screened porch and yell, "Boo!" Startled, the house would draw a sudden breath and inhale its porch. Now the porch would be inside the house. It would be a Florida room.) The Bagnell-built house that Herb and Lorna chose was a significant one in the history of Punta Cachazuda. It was the first one built beyond the limit of the plan that Humboldt Bagnell himself had drawn on a roll of shelf paper and pinned to the wall of his garage. It was the first house in a new territory, a new beginning in a literal as well as a figurative sense, since the sons and daughters of Humboldt and Bitsy, unable to agree on a layout for the extension of the town, had resorted to tracing the original and taping it to the shelf paper at a point where they could effect an easy anastomosis of the streets, sidewalks, and canals of the old with the replica streets, sidewalks, and canals of the new.

Because it was the first house of a new era and the first house on a new street, the Bagnells made an event of Herb and Lorna's purchase, throwing in a set of patio furniture with the house and (since they were also having a difficult time agreeing on street names) offering Lorna the chance to name the street on which the house stood. She thought of dozens of possibilities, including Whatsit Way, Piper Pass, Lovers' Lane, Animation Avenue, and Studebaker Street, but then she had an inspired thought. "Mr. Bagnell," she asked Bobo, the oldest of the offspring of Humboldt and Bitsy, "will there ever be a bridge at the end of this street?"

"No," said Bobo with inherited authority. "Oh, no. Definitely not. We Bagnells have everything planned out. We have drawn the plans for the new section of Punta Cachazuda in the same spirit as our father drew the plans for the original section, and I guarantee you that we're not going to change them, not a bit. There will be no bridge at the end of this street."

And so, once again, Herb and Lorna were at home on No Bridge Road. Their house was like the others. In truth, since it was the first house in the replication of the original section of town, it was exactly like the house that Humboldt Bagnell had built for himself and Bitsy. From their patio, Herb and Lorna could see, for several days out of most months, through gaps between the other houses, the notable sunsets.

In Punta Cachazuda, Herb and Lorna wore shorts most of the time. All of their exposed skin browned. Lorna began a shell collection. Herb began buying tools again and built a folding workbench in the garage. They allowed themselves, gladly, to be drawn into the social life of Punta Cachazuda, and soon their calendar was full of potluck suppers, card parties, shuffleboard and croquet tournaments, surprise birthday celebrations, and galas for each of the traditional holidays of the United States, Canada, Mexico, and most of the European countries. They fit right in. You would scarcely have found a reason to distinguish them from the average Punta Cachazudan unless, some night, you had peeked through a gap between the curtains that hung inside the window of their garage, while the average Punta Cachazudan was watching the eleven o'clock news, and had seen them at work on animated erotic sculpture. They never sold any of their work. They never even showed it to anyone. It was their secret hobby. Lorna found shell an intriguing and demanding medium, and she enjoyed combining bits of many types of shell to produce subtle shadings and textures. Herb found that, freed from the confinements of jewelry, his mechanical imagination was positively rejuvenated, and he whistled while he worked.

The primary pursuit of most Punta Cachazudans was to discover and employ new methods of killing time. They passed the hours with games of cards and shuffleboard, shell gathering and fishing, gossiping and arguing, but the most popular way to keep busy was to learn something new. Punta Cachazudans loved to attend classes and workshops. A few were taught by instructors from local schools and colleges, but most were taught by other Punta Cachazudans. Some of the instructors were retired practitioners of the arts they taught. Others were lifelong amateurs. A few were just eager, well-meaning frauds. Because the classes reflected their instructors' vocations and avocations, they ranged all over the vast savannah of human interest, from celestial navigation to astrology, from watercolor painting to plumbing. Language classes, of the type geared to teaching foreign clichés and phrases useful for a traveler, were especially popular, and Punta Cachazudans who had taken these classes loved to season their speech with the exotic phrases they had learned, with the result that many a conversation in Punta Cachazuda had a Babelic flavor:

"Hey, *guten tag*, Ray. *Comment ça va?*"

"Oh, not too bad. *Pas mal.* Can't complain. *Es muy caliente,* though, *nein?*"

"*Bozhe moy,* you said it! *Sehr warm, sehr warm.*"

"*Buòn giorno,* Ray, George. *Wie geht es Ihnen?*"

"Oh, *pas mal,* Harry. *Pas mal, gracias a Dios.*"

"Can't complain, Harry. And how about you? *Kak vy pozhyvaete?*"

"Well—"

"You keeping busy? *Fuyez-vous les dangers de loisir?*"

"Pretty much. Thought I might do some fishing this afternoon. Want to come along?"

"I don't know. I'm kind of pooped."

"Oh-ho, out with the *lustige Witwe* again, Harry?"

"Well, heh-heh."

"You know whay they say—*a buen bocado, buen grito.*"

"Ha, ha, ha."

"*Cela va sans dire, nein?*"

"*Mais oui. Das versteht sic von selbst* all right."

Herb took Spanish and Predicting the Weather, and he joined the Green Thumbs and the Poker Hands. He taught the Hands to play Piper Poker, but none of them cared for it much, and they only agreed to play a few hands of it whenever the club met at Herb's because they thought he was a nice guy. Lorna took Backyard Botany and Small-Boat Handling and joined the Shell Gatherers and the Never-a-Cross-

Word Puzzlers and organized a group that assembled Comfort Kits for patients in nursing homes and hospitals and for children in foreign lands.

After a while, Herb posted a notice on the recreation hall bulletin board for a class that he proposed to teach: Repairing Things Around the Home. He had only a few students, most of them women, perhaps because the men felt that they didn't need to be taught how to repair things around their homes, or perhaps because the men didn't care to repair things around their homes. Lorna offered a class on devising and solving logical puzzles. At the first class quite a few people showed up just to be polite to Lorna, and even more people showed up to find out what the heck this was all about. Attendance fell off considerably at the second class, many of the students pleading headaches that had set in after the first class. At the third class, Lorna was left with just one student, Andrea Cogliano, who had developed a genuine passion for brain-racking puzzlers. Herb tried offering a course in salesmanship, but no one showed up at all, since no one in Punta Cachazuda had anything to sell or any desire to sell anything. He was more successful with a class called Making Useful Gadgets. In the second year he deleted "Useful" from the title, and the course became one of the most popular among male Punta Cachazudans, who took to whistling while they worked and—later, of course— formed a number of whistling quartets on the barbershop model, organized concerts, staged whistle-offs, and so on.

Lorna offered to teach soap carving and at first attracted only a small number of students, since so many were still wary of Lorna-induced headaches. Attendance grew and grew, however, when the word got around about Lorna's talent as a sculptor and teacher and because rumors began to circulate, whispered on the shuffleboard court or at the market, that if the students progressed acceptably Lorna might bring in live models.

Life in Punta Cachazuda wasn't bad. May visited them each year for a couple of weeks, and even she agreed that it was not bad.

It really wasn't bad, you know. I had been going to Florida in the winter for—oh, I don't know how long, but I had always gone to Miami Beach. It was just where everyone went then. It was where you had fun. In the sun. I never dreamed of going anywhere else, and I certainly didn't like the sound of this Montezuma place when they first wrote to me about it. It sounded just deadly. *Well, it* was *deadly in a way, of course. There wasn't anything like a nightclub, or even a bar. There was a* recreation hall. *Really. But on the other hand, there was all that gorgeous sand and those* transfixing *sunsets. I couldn't have lived there, of course, but still it* wasn't bad.

Life was pleasant, their time was filled, and they were doing some of the best work of their lives, but sometimes, watching the sun set into the Gulf, they had the thought that something was missing. They had no audience.

20

In Which
Herb 'n' Lorna's Secret
Is Revealed and
They Are Enshrined

Mark and Margot and Martha were again the catalytic agents. When Mark graduated from college, Herb and Lorna sent him a congratulatory card, inside which Lorna had written the following note:

Dear Mark,

"Congraduations" and all our best wishes. It's hard to believe that you've already graduated from college. I guess you know that all our things burned in the Hapgood Brothers' warehouse fire and that we're going to stay here. Herb and I would love to have you and the "Grin Twins" come to visit us here in Punta Cachazuda. All the oldsters will make a fuss over you, but I think you'd enjoy yourselves anyway. What do you say?

Love,
Lorna and Herb

The situation for the trio had not improved. Separately, they had come to the conclusion that there was no future for them as a trio, that some kind of choice must be made, some choice that would leave a pair and a singleton. They said yes to Herb and Lorna's invitation, thinking that a vacation might help, might move them to a resolution. They drove down to Punta Cachazuda and spent a wonderful week there. They saw all of Herb and Lorna's slides of their trip, played countless games of cards—canasta with the women for Margot and Martha, poker with the men for Mark—swam in the Gulf of Mexico, collected shells, sat in the sun, listened to stories about the trip, praised Herb's watercolor portraits of Punta Cachazudans, and puzzled through some logic problems with Lorna. On the night before they were to leave, Margot and Mark became engaged.

It was a perfect night—a clear sky, a bright half-moon, brilliant white sand, a soft breeze. M & M and Mark were walking along the beach, hand in hand in hand, carefree. "Mark," said Martha suddenly, with a playful tone in her voice that disarmed him, "you've been cheating on us." She looked straight into his eyes. His heart began to pound, and his palms began to sweat. He opened his mouth to protest, but she laughed and said, "Don't say that you haven't. We know you have. We know you've been cheating on us because we've been cheating on you. We have to—the only way we can get laid is to go to bed with somebody else." There was a silence, and then they all burst out laughing. It was real hysteria; they fell against each other and stood in a huddle, laughing at the ridiculousness of their Situation. Finally Martha said, "Mark, ask Margot to marry you and end this." She was serious.

"But—" Mark began.

"She's the older one," said Martha. She turned and walked away. When Margot and Mark caught up to her, they had become an engaged couple, and Martha had become Mark's fiancée's twin sister.

The next day, Lorna planned the full Sunday-dinner spread for their last meal together: carrot and celery sticks, olives, sweet gherkins, Waldorf salad, fricasseed chicken, dumplings, peas, chocolate cake. Margot and Mark and Martha had decided to save the announcement until they were all at the table together, and they must have looked like impatient children while they waited for Herb to pour beer for all of them.

"We have something to give to you," said Herb when he had finished pouring. He turned toward Lorna, and she lifted a napkin to unveil, on the table between them, a tiny box, wrapped in white paper and tied with a white ribbon.

"And we have something exciting to tell you," Mark said. He looked in turn at Margot and Martha. All three of them were grinning, pleased, excited.

"Well," said Herb, "since I'm the oldest—"

Margot and Martha and Mark snickered. Herb gave them a quizzical look. "It's nothing," Mark said. "It just has to do with our announcement. I'll explain in a minute."

"Well," said Herb again, "since I'm the oldest, I'm going to go first."

"Oh, Herb," said Lorna, "can't you see they're bursting to tell us? The three of them look like the cat that swallowed the canary. Let them tell us their announcement first, Herb."

"Oh, no, no," said Martha. "That's all right. Herb *should* go first. Age does have its privileges." The three of them snickered again. "You'll find out why we're laughing," said Martha.

"Well," said Herb, "now you've got me so curious that I want to hear what you've got to say."

"Please, Herb," Mark said, "you go first."

"Nope," said Herb. "I've made up my mind. I'm the oldest—" He paused, waiting for a laugh and getting one from Margot, who just couldn't hold it in—"and I say I want to hear the announcement."

"Good for you, Herb," said Lorna.

"All right," said Margot. "I'll make it." She sat up straight, folded her hands in her lap, and said, "Mark and I are going to get married."

Silence. Mark and Margot and Martha sat there smiling, saying nothing, and Herb and Lorna sat there with their mouths hanging open, saying nothing. After what seemed like quite a while, Lorna looked at Herb and then looked at the little box on the table. It seemed to startle her. "Oh," she said. She reached out impulsively and covered the box with the napkin again. "Oh, my," she said.

"Well," said Herb. "That's a surprise."

"It's wonderful," said Lorna, as if she had just recalled that that was what one said in such a situation.

"I'm very happy for them," said Martha, beaming and nodding her head. She seemed to want to convince them that she was. "Really," she said. "Margot's older; that's why she got him."

"Oh, yes," said Lorna, smiling, but smiling in an abstract, theoretical way, as if she were testing the theory that a smile might be the appropriate response.

"You're the first to know," Mark said.

"Well, it's lucky that we have a present for you," said Herb. He seemed to have recovered his exuberance all at once. "It's something we're really proud of, and there's quite a story behind it. Wait until you hear—"

"Herb," said Lorna. She was shaking her head rapidly, her brow was wrinkled, and she was looking down at her plate.

Herb went on, but he faltered. "Wait until you hear how we worked it out. See, I—um—it turns out that Lorna and I both, for years—that is, we never knew that we both were in—um—we got to thinking about what you said, Mark, after that night—"

"Herb," said Lorna again.

"Well," Herb went on, "it took a lot of thought, a lot of thought, but we came up with—and then Lorna carved it out of ivory, a very good piece of ivory, and just wait till you see the workmanship on this—"

He reached for the box, but Lorna had her hand clamped firmly over the napkin that hid it. "No, Herb," she said. "We can't give it to them now."

Herb turned toward the trio, confused and, more than that, disappointed. "But—" he said.

Lorna raised her glass and said, "To Mark and Margot: every happiness for now and ever more. And to Martha: may you find someone just as nice as Mark."

They all drank, but the atmosphere in which they drank was certainly strange. The next day, during the good-byes, Herb apologized for "all that gift business," and Lorna said that they'd send Margot and Mark something "more appropriate." When they asked what the gift was, Herb was all set to get it and show it to them, but Lorna wouldn't let him, and she said that the best thing would be "for all of us to just forget all about it." Then she looked at Mark and Margot and Martha for a moment and added, "At least for now."

All the way home Mark and Margot and Martha wondered what the heck was in that box.

The next evening was one of those when the sunset would be visible between the other houses, and Herb and Lorna were sitting on their patio, waiting for Frank and Andrea Cogliano to come over to watch the sun set and drink some Old Fashioneds. The Coglianos were late, and the sky began to redden without them. Herb was reading the paper, but Lorna was admiring the gold-leaf effect on the rippling surface of the Gulf. It reminded her of the flaming wavelets on the surface of Lake Serenity the night the ballroom burned, and, of course, it put her in a reflective mood. "Herb," she said after a while, "I wish we could tell *somebody*. What do you suppose people here would say if we told them about—our work?"

Herb didn't say anything.

"I mean—our work, Herb. The jewelry. Coarse goods. The charms. The moving parts. The sculptures. Everything."

Herb spoke from behind the paper. "Oh, I don't know," he said.

"Even more than that," said Lorna, dreaming. "Suppose we taught them. Suppose we gave a class."

Herb let his paper fall. He was wearing the look of a boy who has just been asked, "Do you suppose I can trust you to go into town and sell the cow on your own?"

"I think everybody would love it," he said. "If you want to know the truth, I've wanted to tell people ever since we got here. Every time I meet someone new, it's always the same thing. Everybody introduces himself by telling you what he used to do. 'I'm a postal clerk,' he'll say, 'retired, of course.' Or, 'I'm a tugboat captain—retired, of course.' And I say, 'I'm a Studebaker salesman—retired, of course.' Well, what the hell, I've got nothing against being a Studebaker salesman, but I was just itching to say, 'I'm a coarse-goods designer and salesman—retired, of course.'"

Lorna had been grinning. She stopped. "I didn't mean to have them make things to sell," she said.

"Oh," said Herb. "Why not?"

"Well, that would—" She caught herself.

"Cheapen it?"

"I—"

"I'm surprised at you, Lorna."

"So am I. I'm sorry, Herb."

"Is that what you've thought—all along?"

"I'm—not sure."

"Damn."

"Oh, Herb. It's just that it seems to me—I suppose it *always* seemed to me—that the bad part of what I was doing—the ugly part—"

"Was the part I was involved in."

"No."

"Yes."

"Not the mechanical part."

"But the selling part."

"You said yourself that you only got involved in it because you needed the money, your family needed the money."

"Yes. Yes. But—I liked it. I *loved* it. That was the best stuff I ever had to sell—better than the fifty-five Starliner. Much better."

"But wouldn't it be even better, wouldn't it *have been* even better if you hadn't had to sell them?"

"That's not what you mean. I know what you mean. You mean, 'Wouldn't *they* have been better if they hadn't been made to sell?'"

"I suppose I do."

"I don't think so. Would the Starliner have been better if it hadn't been made to sell? There's no telling what kind of strange ideas Loewy would have come up with if he hadn't had to make a car that *somebody* would buy. You know, all you have to do to see what I mean is to look at the gadgets I started making back there when I was spending all that time in the cellar, worrying. And the gadgets that the fellows in my class like to make. They're things to kill time. They're—"

"Herb."

"Well, you know what I mean, Lorna. They're—silly."

"Many of the things you've made were very clever."

"Oh, they were *all* clever, but some of them were silly."

Lorna laughed and put her arms around Herb. "I think I understand what you mean," she said.

"So you wouldn't mind if we sold what they make—the *best* of what they make?"

"No, I wouldn't mind."

"Everybody could use the extra money. Besides, if they've got something to sell, I can get them to show up for my salesmanship classes."

"Hello-wo-wo!" It was Andrea Cogliano. She was tapping at the front door. Lorna went to let her and Frank in, and Herb folded the paper and put it aside. Andrea came onto the patio in the middle of an explanation for their being late. "—and would you believe we left the house twenty minutes ago?" she was saying. She bent over to give Herb a kiss on the cheek and squeeze his knee.

"*Guten Abend,* Herb," said Frank. "*Das ist ein schön Sonnenuntergang, n'est-ce pas?*"

"Sun-in—?" asked Herb. Frank pointed at the sanguine pellet dropping Gulfward. "Ah!" said Herb. "*La puesta de sol.*"

"Yeah. 'Sol's pot,'" said Frank.

"Heh-heh," said Herb.

Andrea told a complex and not uninteresting story of glasses forgotten, mislaid, discovered, dropped, stepped on, and broken beyond repair. Herb served drinks, and Lorna put out an oval platter of celery and carrots and green olives stuffed with pimiento. When Frank, at the end of Andrea's story, pulled the twisted glasses from his jacket pocket and put them on, Herb and Lorna laughed heartily, but you and I would have been able to hear their nervousness, I think, if we'd been there. Slowly, cautiously, tentatively, made apprehensive by the fact, which they both understand so clearly, that they were about to put at risk their continued residence in Punta Cachazuda, they turned the chat from glasses to classes. Lorna expressed a desire for something new. Herb concurred. The Coglianos concurred too, and Herb got up to make another round of drinks. Lorna hopped up to get some more carrot sticks.

In the kitchen she asked Herb, "Are they just being polite?"

"Hard to tell," he said. "Go easy for a while. See if they've got anything to say."

Herb passed the drinks around. The sun dropped below the horizon; a plum glow remained. No one said anything for a while. Then Frank, as if from depths of thought, offered the observation that "It *would* be nice to have something new."

"Maybe *Japanese,*" said Andrea.

"That's a good idea," said Lorna.

"How about investing," said Frank. "Understanding the stock market and that sort of thing? There are some smart cookies here, you know."

"Well, I—that's a good idea," said Herb.

"Or—say!" said Frank. "How about handicapping?"

"What?" asked Lorna.

"Betting on racehorses," said Herb. "Not a bad idea, Frank—"

"You know, *I've* had an idea," said Lorna. She could feel her nervousness in her neck and across her shoulders, where the muscles tensed in an unfamiliar way. "I—uh—" They were looking at her.

Under the table, she clenched her fists. "Make us another Old Fashioned, will you, Herb?" she said.

"I just did."

"Oh. So you did. Well, drink up, everybody, and Herb will make another round." She drained her glass.

"My goodness, Lorna," said Andrea, "you don't usually——"

"Oh, I just feel frisky tonight. Drink up." They did. "Make another round, Herb. Before the last of the light is gone. I'll tell everybody my idea when you get back."

Herb dashed into the house, whipped up more Old Fashioneds haphazardly, slopping whiskey, spilling sugar, hacking chunks from an orange and tossing them in, and, as soon as the drinks were ready, dashed out to the garage. From under the folding workbench, he dragged the footlocker in which he kept his tools. He tossed the tools onto the floor, whistling while he worked. From the very bottom he took a metal box with a skull and crossbones on it, one of the few things he had brought from the old stucco house in Babbington. From the very bottom of this box he took a leather pouch, and from that he took one of the two Watchcase Wonders that he and Lorna had. He dashed to the living room, where he pried Lorna's papier-mâché duck apart and took from it the other Watchcase Wonder, the one that they had made for Mark and Margot and Martha. It was still wrapped. He thought better of unwrapping it, put it back in the duck, and reassembled the halves. The he ran back into the kitchen, grabbed the flour canister, and, with both thumbs, popped the lid from it. He poured the flour onto the counter and began poking through it to find a couple of the tiny sculptures he and Lorna had hidden there. Shortly he came back onto the patio, grinning like the cat that swallowed the canary, whistling happily, with flour all over his hands and forearms, carrying a tray with the drinks.

Lorna held her drink in both hands and said, "Well. Here's my idea. I——" She looked at Herb. He was beaming. He was impatient. She winked at him. She said, "You know Herb is a Studebaker salesman—retired, of course." The Coglianos nodded. "I wondered if you knew that he also used to design, and sell, jewelry and—art objects?" The Coglianos shook their heads. "Well, he did," said Lorna. "He designed it, and I made it, and he sold it."

"C'est bien vrai?" asked Frank.

Herb thrust his floured hands forward and spread them open. In them he held a silver watchcase, which the Coglianos regarded with patient interest. Herb pressed the stem, the lid opened, and the Coglianos leaned toward the center of the table for a closer look. Herb began twisting the knob. Lorna allowed herself to breathe when she saw the fascination on the Coglianos' faces.

"You made this?" asked Andrea, looking first at Lorna, who smiled discreetly, lips together, and then at Herb, who nodded vigorously and fairly shouted, "*Mira esa hechura,* will you!"

The classes were a success from the start, though Herb and Lorna tried to keep them from growing too quickly by swearing the students to secrecy. The secret was a hard one to keep, as hard as the original secret discovery of one's own sexuality, that secret we're immediately eager to spill, the biggest and best secret that we ever have held in common, the secret that joins us. How rare it was and how delightful it must have been for the wrinkled citizens of Punta Cachazuda to get, late in life, a chance to wear again the self-satisfied smirks they had last worn when, as adolescents, they each had first discovered whatever bit of the great mystery of human sexual pleasure each had first discovered. Rarer still, and quite possibly more delightful still, was the unexpected return of the opportunity to reveal the discovery to a friend, or, if one's friends already knew (and how disappointingly often they did or pretended to), to an acquaintance, anyone who would admit ignorance and listen. Many a student of Herb and Lorna's rediscovered giggling. Every one of them was bursting to tell someone else, and most of them had a specific someone in mind. I wish I could say that they wanted to tell out of a spirit of generosity, an elevated desire to enlighten other Punta Cachazudans, but in most cases, it was a desire to show, even though it would be only for the brief moment of the telling of the secret, that they knew more than their fellows. It's a baser desire, but it may underlie more didactic efforts than the nobler one.

Since every student wanted to enlist someone else, and neither Herb nor Lorna could resist for long the pleading of one student to bring in another, the classes grew and grew. Not every student arrived in a state of ignorance. A few brought with them treasured, and long-hidden, examples of coarse goods. Two of these were products of Herb and Lorna's unwitting collaboration. One, they discovered to their great surprise, was an item they had sold to a lanky, dark-haired, gum-chewing gas-station attendant in Sundown, Texas, not very long before their arrival in Punta Cachazuda.

The first classes, hardly classes at all, were held in Herb and Lorna's garage. When the enrollment exceeded the capacity of the garage, they expanded into the living room, and when the combined garage and living room became too crowded, they began meeting twice a week, then three times a week, and eventually they were meeting six days a week and still were unable to accommodate everyone. Clearly, the thing to do was to crawl out from underground and move the classes to the recreation hall. By this time, the secret was hardly secret within the town: nearly every Punta Cachazudan with any mechanical or modeling ability at all was enrolled in one of the classes and had set up a little clandestine workshop at home, usually in the garage, most of them built according to plans Herb furnished, so that the whole operation could be folded against a wall and concealed behind what appeared to be a handy swing-away ironing-and-mending center. Those who couldn't make erotic jewelry or sculpture sold it, and those who couldn't sculpt or sell modeled. To get the use of the recreation hall, the Punta Cachazudans were going to have to speak to the only people in town who weren't yet in the know: the Bagnells. It dawned on Herb and Lorna and their students, when they found themselves giggling and blushing while discussing the need to approach the Bagnells, that the timidity they felt, the fear they felt, the embarrassment they felt, were nearly identical to the feelings they would have felt, or had felt, in admitting—confessing—to their parents, however indirectly, that they had experienced some of the secret pleasures that separate adults from children.

A delegation was chosen. They marched, giggling in spite of themselves, to the home of Bobo Bagnell and demanded, biting their tongues to keep their faces straight, that they be given permission to use the recreation hall for classes in the design and manufacture of erotic jewelry and objets d'art. Bobo, baffled, consented, in the belief that the bizarre request was just part of a scheme to get him to come to the recreation hall the following evening, where, he supposed, the Punta Cachazudans intended to throw a surprise party to celebrate his eightieth birthday. The next evening, he dressed in his white linen suit and walked to the recreation hall, which, he could see, was filled nearly to capacity. When he entered, a moment passed before anyone noticed him, but when people did, they began to applaud him, and their applause made more notice him, and *they* began to applaud him. When they began singing "For He's a Jolly Good Fellow," Bobo's eyes misted over. The cupcakes and coffee they served him were not, he admitted to himself, a *lavish* spread for an eightieth birthday celebration, but it was the thought that counted, and he thought that the decorations on the cupcakes, little amorous couples intimately entwined, were clever, amusing, and flattering.

In the years that followed, the Punta Cachazudans tried to confine their secret to the town, to protect their art and industry from an uncertain reception outside, but there was in them that urge to tell, and now and then one or another gave in to it, and the secret spread somewhat, underground, whispered or mumbled. The farther it spread from Punta Cachazuda, the more preposterous it seemed, so there were no southward swarms of the curious and salacious except for a small flock of young people inspired by a mention in the second edition of *The Whole Earth Catalog:*

> *If you're going to be in the area, you might want to check out a neo-Transcendentalist erotico-artistic community in west coastal Florida called Punta Cachazuda. I didn't have a lot of time to really get to know the place, but I got a lot of good feelings about it when I was there. These people are old, but a lot of them are into some interesting ideas in collaborative art and city planning, and I think there's some kind of pan-linguistic movement going on here, too, like home-grown Esperanto or something. Check it out. —Allspice*

That, however, was a passing curiosity, and the widespread recognition that Punta Cachazudans simultaneously feared and desired didn't come until recently. We'll get to that in a moment, but to be faithful to chronology I have to tell you what happened next.

Herb had never really been healthy after he and Lorna reached Punta Cachazuda. He was bothered by a flurry of minor ailments, and they left him weakened and wary. Then one evening, after he had finished teaching a class in the articulation of hip joints, he had a heart attack. It struck him while he was sitting quietly in his easy chair, reading the latest issue of *Amateur Mechanical Engineer.* The attack scared the hell out of Herb and made Lorna so solicitous of him that he couldn't help laughing at the way she bustled about, doing for him. Her own heart ached with concern for him. She couldn't stand being out of reach of him, and the possiblity of losing him seemed to be dwelling in their little cement-block house like an unwelcome guest. At night she often found herself awake, murmuring a plea to this presence, this possibility of death, to get out of her house, to go visit someone else for a while, to go, go away. After a while Herb's fear began to wane, and he began to make light of the first attack, calling it, as many of his Punta Cachazudan cronies did, "his warning." Lorna began letting him out of her sight again, and she began to feel that the possibility of death had moved on, was visiting elsewhere for a while. When she returned from a shopping trip one morning, Herb was dead, in his easy chair.

One glorious fall day, years later, I gained, accidentally, an understanding of how Lorna must have felt then. I was driving alone along a country road, feeling an exhilaration that sometimes comes to me on a fine fall day and at no other time. It is due, I think, partly to the vestigial rhythm of the academic calendar, which makes spring a time of anxiety and fall a time of rebirth, new opportunities, a clean slate; it is also due in part to the crisp weather, of course, and the autumn colors in the countryside. In the road ahead of me was a dead male pheasant. He was lying on his side, with his neck extended and one wing in the air. At the side of the road was a female pheasant, his mate. She approached him, calling, not keening, but calling out. Then she turned away, began to walk away, turned back and called out again, turned away, turned back, and so on, as if confused and almost annoyed, as if she were saying, "Come on now, get up. Quit fooling around. We still have a long way to go, a lot to do. Don't lie down now—we have a long way to go together." I stopped the car and watched her in painful fascination. I couldn't have driven on anyway; my eyes were full of tears.

Lorna stayed on in Punta Cachazuda for a couple of lonely years, but then the house where she and Herb had lived together in Babbington came back on the market, and Lorna bought it, for cash, and returned to Babbington. Everything that she and Herb had had in the house had been lost in the warehouse fire, so Lorna lived with secondhand furniture that she and Ella picked up in a week of rapid shopping, which Ella enjoyed enormously but Lorna thought of as something she wanted to get through as quickly as she could. Ella had been attracted to new Colonial-style things, but Lorna had wanted to duplicate as closely as she could the feeling the house had had when she and Herb had lived there, when it had been furnished with things that Herb had made and things they'd picked up here and there over the years, so she avoided stores that sold new furniture and steered Ella toward secondhand shops. The house was furnished and looked cozily cluttered, but there was a hollow in it, a rarefied pocket where Herb should have been.

Of Lorna then, May said:

Well, after he died, I mean, after Herb died— Well. Oh, Lorna and I still had some grand times— No. No, we didn't. Not really. I tried to play Lorna to her May—cheer her up, make her look forward to something—but she was just coasting after Herb died, you know. Just coasting.

When her cancer was diagnosed, Lorna told no one, but something about her manner, a finality in the way she began to handle her affairs, in her visits to old friends, convinced Ella that something was fatally wrong, and because cancer was what Ella feared most, she guessed, correctly, that that was it.

Mark and Margot and Martha visited her. Ella had told them what she feared and made them promise not to betray to Lorna in any way what she had told them. They found themselves, against their will, looking for and finding signs that Lorna was weakening. Was she thinner? Was she fragile? Was she too tired? Was she having trouble breathing? Yes, she was. She was eager to hear their news, but it seemed that they didn't have enough news to fill the time they spent with her, certainly not enough to fill the hollow in the house. The news they had brought was gone too soon, like firewood that's too dry. After an hour or so, Lorna began to drift into reminiscence. The three M's loved hearing her stories, and they would have listened contentedly for hours, would have asked for more, would have asked the questions they were curious about, if they hadn't worried that the reminiscences were painful for her, that perhaps it hurt her to have Herb come to mind. The truth was that Herb was always on her mind, and reminiscing about him was more pleasant than painful. Not having him with her was what hurt her; remembering him didn't hurt her at all.

Mark drove to the Gilded Peacock and brought back cartons of chicken chow mein. While they ate, Lorna recalled their visit to Punta Cachazuda and the fricasseed-chicken dinner at which Margot had announced their engagement. When Lorna began talking about that dinner, she sat up straighter, and her spirit seemed to return to her. Soon she was even laughing. This wasn't just the feeble laughter she'd managed earlier in the evening, but real laughter, laughter that betrayed her illness when it made her breathless, but a joy to hear despite that.

"Poor Herb," she said. "I remember the way he tried to go on with the speech he'd practiced and give you the gift I'd made." She laughed again and ran out of breath again. "You can't imagine what we went through to make that."

Her expression became serious. She put her fork down. She put her elbows on the table and laced her fingers together. "Tell me something," she said. "Tell me how it's working out. Are you happy?"

"Are we happy?" Mark asked.

"Are—all three of you happy? Martha, you haven't married. I wonder—I wonder if I know why. What—how—how do the three of you—get along?"

"Oh, very well," said Martha. "We get along beautifully together."

"But—how?" asked Lorna. "I want to hear all about it."

"Well—" Mark said sheepishly, looking into his plate.

"You remember the night when you told Herb and me that you three were in love, don't you?"

"Of course," said Mark.

"You told us everything then."

"I was a little drunk."

"You're a little drunk now, aren't you?"

"Just a little."

"I'll tell," said Margot.

"Me too," said Martha.

Together, the three of them managed to tell Lorna what sort of life had evolved for them. Shyness, coupled with the youthful assumption that the experiences of the old have been too limited for them to understand young lust, kept them from telling her quite everything, but they told her most of it.

♦   ♦   ♦

With the marriage of Mark and Margot, the trio seemed to have found a solution to their Situation, a conventional, traditional solution. Martha was maid of honor at the wedding, and after Margot and Mark left the reception, they didn't see Martha for months. Naïvely, simple-mindedly, all three imagined that their Situation had been left behind in their crazy past, part of a complicated courtship that they would recall with laughter in the years to come. None of them knew how much more complicated their Situation would grow.

Margot and Mark had been married for a little more than a year when Mark had to travel to Washington for a conference. He didn't *have* to go; going was supposed to be good for his career. For several reasons, he didn't want to go. For one thing, he was afraid to fly. For another, he was afraid of making a fool of himself at the conference. In the end, he decided that he ought to go. The night before he was to leave, while he and Margot were packing his things, he was nervous, as one might expect. He would be the most junior person attending, and he knew that this was his big chance to improve his standing among his colleagues and, of course, his big chance to make an ass of himself. He was also feeling sentimental; he and Margot would be apart for a week, and they hadn't spent a single night apart since they had been married. Margot seemed a little "on edge," and Mark was touched by what he took to be a reaction to the thought of their being apart, concern for his safety, for his chances, for them, their chances. When Margot got into bed, she turned onto her side, away from Mark. He turned the light off, reached out for her, and stroked her hip.

She said, "I'm sorry. I'm just too tense."

Mark told her that he understood, and he rolled onto his side, facing away from her, facing the wall, in fact, for at that time they were sleeping on a ridiculous and uncomfortable bed that Mark had built from two-by-fours, a bed that was shoved into a corner of the bedroom, so that Mark slept nearly surrounded, with a wall at his head, a wall on one side, and Margot on the other. The truth was that Mark didn't understand at all; he was hurt and annoyed. He felt that Margot owed him something, a demonstration of her love for him, her confidence in him, her pride in him, since he would be taking a real risk by getting into an airplane and flying to a distant city for the sake of improving his position among people whom he regarded as a bunch of pompous, egotistical, capable, urbane, and frightening bastards, all for the sake of making life better for him and Margot in the future, a little more luxurious, a little more exciting. He had expected to get from her a token, something to carry with him through his ordeal: he had expected not just that they would make love on the night before he left—their marriage was only a year old, after all—but even more, that there would be in Margot's lovemaking new heights of passion and abandon that he would remember with a smile during the days in Washington, drawing from the memory new strength and wit when he was doing verbal battle with some hoary luminary in one of the symposia. Instead, he got nothing.

In the morning, before Mark left for the airport, Margot was up early, and she made him an elaborate breakfast. While he was eating his waffles and sausage and drinking his orange blossom, outwardly composed, inwardly contending with a clamorous mob of emotions, she sat across from him and simply watched him. She was happy. She was experiencing, Mark could see, genuine pleasure; it manifested itself in a Grin-Twin grin, a luxurious stretching, an unfamiliar way of savoring her coffee. Mark finished eating. He went to the bathroom and urinated and washed his hands and brushed his teeth. When he came out, Margot was waiting in the hall with his coat, scarf, gloves, and suitcase. When they kissed good-bye, she kissed him with a tenderness that made him feel absolutely wonderful.

"Mark," she said, pulling away, taking his hands in hers, and looking him in the eyes, "when you get back, I won't be here."

"Oh, my God," Mark said. The effect her words had on him, dropping him in an instant from wonderful to miserable, was to return, an hour and a half later, when the plane to Washington hit an air pocket.

"Oh, I'm sorry," she said at once. "I didn't mean it that way. I'm not leaving you. I love you, Mark." This had the effect that the plane's leveling off had later. Mark was relieved, but his confidence had been shaken; he had been reminded how little holds us up. "I just need a vacation from you," Margot said. And then it all came rushing out of her. "You worry too much, Mark, and you try too hard to plan ways to be content and happy, and worst of all you worry about being happy or not being happy, and you're always worrying about the future, about whether you'll amount to anything, whether we'll be comfortable, and your worrying's wearing me out. Besides—" She turned away from him and looked out the door. "—it isn't fair. It isn't fair to

Martha. I think about her, alone, and I can't—enjoy myself with you. I need a vacation, and she needs a turn with you. She'll be here when you get back. She's going to take my place for a while."

Martha was waiting for Mark when he returned. She met him at the door, looking impish. She gave him a hug and the quickest of kisses. She had a Scotch and soda ready for him, she made poached salmon for dinner, and after dinner she made love to him with the reckless passion he had expected from Margot a week earlier. In time, a little more than six months' time, Martha had had enough. She came out of the bathroom after her shower one Saturday morning, still working at her hair with a towel, and stopped in her tracks when she saw Mark sitting at the kitchen table, drinking coffee, smoking a cigarette, worrying, and making a list of topics that he thought required Martha's worrying as well as his own. Martha watched him add items to the list for a couple of moments and then went on into the bedroom and in a very short time came back out, dressed, striding toward the door.

"Where are you going?" Mark asked.

"Shopping!" she shouted.

"With your hair wet?" he asked. She slammed the door on his question.

A couple of hours later Mark was sitting on the kitchen floor, painting a metal cabinet that he had picked up at a used-furniture store. He heard the door open. He heard footsteps. He made a point of not turning from his work. If Martha was not going to share his depression, well, then he had nothing else to share with her for the time being. He heard the usual sounds of unpacking groceries, and then he heard an unaccustomed one: the pop of a champagne cork. He couldn't have hidden his surprise if he had tried. He laid his brush across the paint can, stood, and said, before he even turned to look at her, "Welcome back, Margot."

A pattern was established that was, probably, beneficial for all of them during a difficult time. They discovered, in a roundabout and difficult way, a means to two qualities that most marriages need to be successful: stability and change. Because Margot and Martha had since childhood called each other "Mar," a change from Margot to Martha or from Martha to Margot was known among the trio as a changing of the Mars. Like a change in the weather, a change of Mars had its front, and the front brought confusion, unsettled emotional weather. When the Mars changed, the returning one was refreshed, a little coy, and had a voracious sexual appetite and a conversational urge that filled the house with ardor and chatter for a week or more. Then a new front would arrive, and all of them were buffeted again by shifting gusts. They longed for gentler weather.

"Well," said Lorna when they had finished. "Well, well, well." There was a twinkle in her eye, and she hopped up from the table with all of her old energy. On the sideboard was her old papier-mâché duck. She pried the duck apart, and from it she produced the very box that Mark and Margot and Martha had seen in Punta Cachazuda. Clearly enjoying herself very much, she said, "I kept it for you because I had a hunch that the marriage idea wasn't going to work out. I don't mean that I thought you would break up; I mean that I thought you'd get back together. Here," she said. She handed the box to Mark. "I hope you all—" She paused and gave them a mischievous grin, and her cheeks colored "—enjoy it."

Mark started to untie the ribbon, but Lorna stopped him. "Oh, no," she said. "I'd be much too embarrassed. If Herb were here, it would be different, but I'd be much too embarrassed alone. Open it when you get home, when you're alone, just the three of you."

They were staying with Margot and Martha's parents, as they usually did when they visited Babbington. The house was dark when they returned. They crept inside, fixed themselves drinks, and settled onto the living room sofa. Mark put the little box on the coffee table in front of them.

"All right," said Martha. "I claim the right to open it, since I'm the youngest, and the youngest usually gets the short end of things."

"Do you really feel that way?" Mark asked.

"Maaark," said Margot, "she's only kidding. Go ahead, Mar, I want to see it."

It looked like a pocket watch. Martha opened the case. Inside was a bed, no larger than a commemorative stamp, carved from ivory, with rumpled sheets and, on the rumpled sheets, entangled, three ivory figures, two women and a man.

"Oh, my God," said Margot. Her mouth dropped open, and she covered it with her hand.

"I'm going to get Daddy's magnifying glass," said Martha.

With the aid of the glass, they could see that the women were good likenesses of Margot and Martha, though not so good that they could decide which was which.

"That's deliberate," said Martha with respect and admiration.

The man was just as certainly Mark. He said so.

"I'm not sure, Mark," said Martha, giggling. "This guy is really, um, large."

On the side of the case was a tiny knurled knob. Slowly, gently, Mark turned it.

"Oh, that's wonderful!" said Margot.

"*That's* me," said Martha. "I'm on top."

"Look at that!" said Margot. "Mark's actually—oops—now he's out again."

"Ooooh!" squealed Martha. "What a quick switch!"

"Will you look at that!" said Margot. "What workmanship!"

"Back it up, Mark," said Martha. "Can you make it go backwards? I want to see how we did that, or how we're *supposed* to do that."

"No, let them keep going," said Margot. "Oh, look! I knew it! I knew we could work something like that."

"If I can just raise my hips that way—" said Martha.

"Slide my left leg under—" said Margot.

"Rhythm. Rhythm is important," Mark said.

"Can your back take that, Mark?" asked Margot.

"I can build up to it," Mark said, hoping he was right.

"If we miss a beat," said Martha, "we'll be permanently entangled."

It was a long and sweaty night. They did not achieve the impossible, but they discovered a taste that they had been suppressing, one they have indulged ever since.

And then, well, I'll let May say it:

> And then, well, Lorna died, too. At least neither of them had to go through that dreadful Alzheimer's business. I mean, what a damned injustice it is for someone who's been an absolute delight to have to become all sort of baffled. But—they didn't, thank God. They even became famous—quite famous. They're the only famous people I know, really. The only famous people I've had dinner with. I

wish they were around to enjoy it. I'm sure they would *enjoy it. I know* I *would enjoy it.*

Today, in Punta Cachazuda, clusters of multistory condominium buildings occupy most of the section nearest the Gulf, where Humboldt and Bitsy Bagnell built the first of the original cement-block houses. Each of the apartments boasts a balcony that faces Gulfward, and on these balconies the residents sit at sunset and think. The town has reproduced itself many times, spreading farther and farther inland. Its plan of meandering roads, sidewalks, and canals has become the model for many other communities along the Florida coast. The town's population is many times what it was when Herb and Lorna lived there, and fully ninety-six percent of the residents are engaged in some aspect of erotic sculpture.

Notoriety came, when it came, first through admiration, not condemnation. The revival of interest in crafts and folk art led to the "discovery" of erotic jewelry and the other erotic crafts and arts, to the revelation of the "colony" in Punta Cachazuda, and to the Smithsonian's mounting of the erotic-jewelry exhibit. In the current cultural climate, the Punta Cachazudans prosper, and their art prospers, despite the occasional outraged yowl. Since it is in the nature of humankind to diversify in matters of taste, it shouldn't be surprising that today's Punta Cachazudans work in a bewildering variety of media and styles. There are traditionalists who insist on ivory, who make nothing larger than a Watchcase Wonder. There are ultraminiaturists, some of whom "carve" with laser light and observe their work under electronic magnification with the aid of computer-enhanced imaging made possible in part by a grant from ChacalliTech. There are "charmers," who produce coy, vulgar, cheap cast-metal and plastic charms with elementary moving parts. Apparently enough people consider these trinkets amusing "gag gifts" with which to mark birthdays, engagements, and wedding anniversaries to make manufacturing the things a profitable business. The charmers are to be distinguished from the "charm*ists,*" say the charmists, whose work is equally vulgar, but, because they work in precious metals, not cheap. There are some who work life-size, in the pliable flesh-emulating plastics used for bouncing baby dolls. Their work may be obscene; I haven't made up my mind. There are also, I hasten to say, many Punta Cachazudans who have no collective name for themselves, who make intricately animated, individualized, affectionate, delightfully lusty charms and men's jewelry in the Lorna-and-Herb tradition.

The Punta Cachazuda recreation center today is much more than the single cement-block building it was in Herb and Lorna's time. It is a cluster of buildings, situated in the empty place left between four replications of the original plan for the town, like one of the four-cusped bits of dough left after cutting cookies. Its handsome buildings and broad lawns make it look much like a college campus. The largest and most impressive of the buildings are the sculpture studio and the hangarlike mechanical shop, in either of which, at any time of day, you will find men and women whistling, and sometimes giggling, while they work on erotic sculpture and the mechanisms to make them move.

At the center of this recreation campus is a huge wind-driven erotic mobile. It is a smooth, idealized work. It depicts a copulating couple, a dozen times life-size. When the wind passes over the arched and rounded surfaces of their bodies, they rise and fall, embrace and draw apart, tumble and turn, kiss, caress, and couple, in ways designed by the artist but powered, prompted, and provoked by nature. In a zephyr, their movements are gentle and tender. In hurricanes, their antics are the stuff of legends, of giants in the earth, whose couplings make the ground beneath us tremble. The figures are intended, I'm sure, to represent Everyman and Everywoman, but in a certain gesture, a little eccentricity, a moment in which they pause and he brushes her cheek with his lips, from certain angles, in a certain slant of light, I seem to see my grandparents, Gumma and Guppa, Herb and Lorna.